ALL THE QUEEN'S MEN.

'What is this . . . operation of yours which needs my help so badly?'

'You need my operation as much as I need your help, friend,' O'Neil shot back at him.

Kassim inclined his dark, scarred head.

'That may be so, Connor O'Neil. I cannot judge until you tell me.'

O'Neil grinned fleetingly, although the world-wide consequences of his gamble were far from funny. He got out of his chair, staring at the man whose fellow Arabs had named 'Hassan the Hawk'.

'I am going to hijack the Queen of England's royal yacht.'

D0892656

Cover design by Lyndon Loder

ALL THE
QUEEN'S MEN...

Guiy de Montfort

Hamlyn Paperbacks

ALL THE QUEEN'S MEN . . .
ISBN 0 600 20338 7

First published in Great Britain 1980
by Hamlyn Paperbacks
Copyright © 1980 by Guiy de Montfort

Hamlyn Paperbacks are published by
The Hamlyn Publishing Group Ltd,
Astronaut House, Feltham,
Middlesex, England
(Paperback Division: Hamlyn Paperbacks,
Banda House, Cambridge Grove,
Hammersmith, London W6 0LE)

Made and printed in Great Britain by
Hunt Barnard Printing Ltd., Aylesbury, Bucks.

ALL THE QUEEN'S MEN ...

This book is respectfully dedicated to the Memory of Lord Mountbatten, the Rt Hon. Airey Neave, MP and all those who have died for the love and honour of their country ...

And for the children of Cambodia, in whose suffering innocence is reflected the cracked mirror of our time. This is for you, that you might forgive us ...

For my lady, with love and gratitude.

For my father, who never understood it all.

My grateful thanks are formally recorded to those who helped me research this novel, believing it should be written, and who cannot be named.

A special thank you to Michael Klinger, Jeffrey Archer and Bob Peart, who first encouraged me to write what the camera cannot always say.

Thanks, too, to Susie and Lyndon Loder, Cynthia Moody, Jan Dugdale-Moore, Brian Bissell and Tony Townsend for their special assistance.

Finally, I would like to be able to thank the various Armed Services and other official bodies for their advice and assistance, but such co-operations were withdrawn or withheld once the novel's subject matter became known.

AUTHOR'S FOREWORD

Should I be asked whether this story is based on true facts –
and how I came by them – a prudence learned in the hard
school of life would cause me to turn the question in the
manner of Sir Thomas More when confronted by the angry
demands of Henry VIII.

He said: 'If you believe it to be true, then it is true – according
to each man's conscience.'

I say: 'Look at the world around you today and judge for
yourself . . . according to your conscience.'

If my story entertains you, then I have succeeded in my job
as a writer. If it also makes you think more clearly about the
deeper issues of our human existence, then I have succeeded
as a human being.

The rest is up to you.

Guiy de Montfort
November 1980

'Terrorism is the first resort of the coward – and the last resort of the man whose beliefs cannot stand the light of reasoned examination.'

– George Alfred Burroughs, DSO, DCM
  March 1979

'If a man has a political belief, he has the right to defend or expound it – by whatever means he can – if its liberty is forcefully opposed by the State.'

– 'Captain' James Connor O'Neil,
  Madigan's Brigade
  December 1978

PROLOGUE

5 February 1979

Her Majesty the Queen was nearly ready to go. And a lot of people within Buckingham Palace's gilded maze of reception rooms, offices and private apartments would be very relieved.

Relieved that the preparations had been concluded smoothly, because this particular royal tour had neither precedent nor comparison for the Queen or her husband in half a century of fulfilling their individual and joint roles as Britain's best known ambassadors. And it was a task which became more and more difficult to carry out as the problems of international security rose and the country's international standing fell.

But this tour was different. Or so everyone in the Foreign Office believed. Except George Burroughs, that is. He didn't give a damn about increased trade orders nor for the fact that this was the first time a female head of state had been so honoured.

To him, the whole idea was a ghastly mistake and he could only hope his would not be the only head to roll when it turned into a diplomatic nightmare. Apart from cursing Holman's stupidity, there was nothing left he *could* do but wait it out. And pray to a God he hadn't bothered with for years . . .

The figure with the scar tissue puckering his dark features brush some sand off his ordnance-survey map and stared back into the desert scrub once again to make sure they were entirely alone before concentrating that flat gaze of his towards the huge stretch of water he had selected as their killing ground.

Although dexterous in most things, he still found it difficult to write and muttered his calculations with a hint of shrillness in his voice to the silent man by his side. His companion wrote without complaint, understanding his leader's tension. It had not been easy to come here and they were still faced with the nerve-stretching business of getting out of the country again. Nevertheless, he comforted himself with the thought of what all this careful planning would bring them in wealth and reputation amongst the international terrorist fraternity they courted for their group's proper recognition . . .

5 April 1979

The big ship steamed carefully through the mist, slipping into her designated berth in Portsmouth harbour like a wraith. There was no ceremony accorded to her. She seemed almost ashamed to be back, so quiet was her late arrival.

The small group of high-ranking officers from Naval Intelligence and the Home Office stood by their Ministry cars, waiting patiently on the deserted dockside, and said nothing. There was nothing left to be said. The decisions taken were final.

They sipped at their warming brandy flasks in the cold dawn light and noted that none of her usual flags or bunting were flying. All but her mast-head lights were out. Only the steady navigational red, white and green glowed eerily in the haze. It was that kind of homecoming.

She showed herself briefly behind her misty curtain, nudging slowly alongside. It was not her normal berth – nor the customary civilian docking crew. Naval ratings secured her hawsers, working silently and hoary-breathed in the subdued greyness.

A single gangway was run out from the ship. Armed Royal Navy sentries quickly stationed themselves at each end of it and unslung their automatic weapons. They were cocked and ready for instant use.

The party on the isolated dockyard went aboard immediately with their bulging briefcases, perfunctorily returning the stiff salutes. A bosun's pipe, ear-splitting on the stillness, screeched over the humming tannoys.

'All hands muster on Number One Mess Deck! All hands muster on Number One Mess Deck! Duty men stand fast! Duty men stand fast!' Then the grim silence locked round the ship once more, blanketed by the lingering mist.

Fifteen minutes later, the officials from their respective Ministries began to inspect the ship for damage and take statements from all the officers and crew. It was a long, serious business and nearly 08.30 before they left for London again in their Ministry vehicles.

One hour after their departure, the officers and ratings not part of the watch-on-board began to descend the gangway on extended home leave. There were none of the usual wisecracks, and the numbers coming off seemed curiously depleted.

But at least she had come home . . .

5 September 1979

The man stood hidden inside the huge sadness of the crowd, just one more watcher amongst the thousands as Earl Mountbatten's funeral cortège slow-marched towards Westminster Abbey. 'Lord Louis' was hideously dead. A stunned British people had come to mourn his murder, standing in motionless wedges of silence on London's packed pavements.

It was a beautiful day. It should have pleased the old sailor. He would never have wished on any of his mourners the discomfort of seeing out his end in the perennial English rain.

Now he was gone. A mood of sorrowful gloom lay over the country. The last of the Heroes was being put to his rest. There was no one left to comfort Britain as she faced a tarnished future on the uncertain edge of the 1980s . . .

It was no different from Parliament Square anywhere else along the ceremonial route, lined throughout by servicemen with heads bowed and rifles reversed, guarding his final way. Even the tourists were quiet, mingling with a grieving nation and the armed Special Branch officers patrolling a crowd that was ten deep in places.

The man noticed how the sailors pulling the gun-carriage were visibly sweating in the heat, and felt for them. He felt sorrier still for the bandsmen in their thick tunics and bearskins, recalling his own time in Her Majesty's Brigade of Foot Guards.

He also realised that not one of them would have missed the historic privilege of escorting this sailor-statesman to his memorial service, and bitterly regretted that the men who called themselves his brothers, on the edge of Irish extremism, had used his mission earlier in the year as part of their mad reasoning for such a heinous murder – and the massacre at Warrenpoint.

The man sighed deeply, scratching at the matt of dyed beard essential to the disguise he had affected in order to be here, and thought some more about the men killed in that cruel ambush.

'Men' the press had called them. But the soldiers from the Second Btn of the Parachute Regiment blown to bits at Warrenpoint had been little more than boys, straight out to the hit-and-run savagery of Ulster from basic training. 'Discounting' the colonel from the Queen's Own Highlanders, a major and the NCOs with them, their average age had been nineteen. And those kids on Mountbatten's boat . . .

Although the mourning public would never know the full story, this man did. And he thanked God that the expected arrival of the other target had been delayed by toothache, sparing the Queen a mother's grief to add to the stunning death of her favourite uncle.

The man turned his bereted head, feeling the tears hot in his eyes. Christ, this wouldn't do! Maybe he'd been more shaken up than he realised by that business in the spring.

Perhaps it was down to his injuries . . . or something. God knows they still hurt.

He smiled. Why the hell should *he* care about the English or for some ageing earl who'd pushed his luck by taking a holiday in the very cradle of Irish Republicanism? But he did. And it annoyed him as deeply.

Tears of anger welled on his cheeks again. Sure, he knew the Provos, and the INLA, had plenty more tricks up their sleeves. He'd even heard talk of the Ulster Freedom Fighters avenging Mountbatten by having a go at the Pope when he visited Ireland. They were all the same. Would they never learn, 'reprisals' changed nothing? They only clamped the lid tighter on a boiling pot.

The British would weep for a week now and then forget, hoping the 'problem' would go away. Their military leaders didn't stand a chance while the bloody politicians talked action and stood still. So people's frustration would escalate – along with the needless killings.

He let the tears roll freely. He was not alone in the crowd. Many were moved to crying by a sense of personal loss beyond immediate understanding.

But a small boy, held high on his father's shoulders to see history in the unmaking, stared at the man's face for a distracted moment and nudged his parent.

'Why's that man crying, daddy?'

'That man' shook his head and began to push his way out of the crowd as the father tried to hush the child with an embarrassed, apologetic grin.

It was too late. The man had already disappeared.

As the massed bands reached the great open doors of the waiting Abbey, accompanied by an almost obscene whirr of cine-cameras and clicking shutters gathered at the end of this long march of national sorrow, the man limped painfully away.

A policeman on duty at the foot of Westminster Bridge glanced at him with momentary suspicion, noted the General Service Medal on his military-style raincoat – and let him pass. Probably sickened by what those Mick bastards had done to old Lord Louis.

The Royal Navy ratings chosen to bear Mountbatten of Burma's heavy coffin into the Abbey took up their positions again for the fourth time that morning, waiting the quiet order to lift their precious burden into the massively-vaulted church which entombed kings of lesser stature than this good man.

Trumpets echoed through the Abbey, traditional homage to a fallen warrior. The notable and the famous stood side by side with his sad Queen, searching their own lives for something of his departed spirit, and listened to the silver notes dying against the glorious stained glass of a forgotten history.

The figure in the belted raincoat heard none of it as he limped for the 'safe house' in Willesden that was his temporary lair until he knew he could leave the country again.

For him, there was only the remembered horror of the spring. And the man limped on towards his haven, with his lonely pain the constant reminder to events he could never forget . . .

CHAPTER ONE

Christmas Day 1978. It was not a good time of year.

Callaghan knew he would have to shoot him. The court martial evidence left no other choice. The Captain would have insisted on it anyway.

With the present state of morale in both the Provisional IRA and the Irish National Liberation Army, strict discipline was vital within this elite breakaway unit. Rape was a capital offence in Madigan's Brigade – so named after one of Ireland's obscurer heroes of the Easter Rising in 1916.

It was up to the Adjutant now. O'Rourke looked slowly round the faces trying him in the lamplight. Your man's as guilty as hell, sure he was. But Jesus, they'd show some mercy – considering the time of year? He could see from their expressions he was out of luck this time.

He was still shouting obscenities when they frogmarched him into the big field. She was only an RUC's whore of a wife, for Mary's sake! He was still a good Catholic!

It made no difference. There were no words of comfort for him. Not even a blindfold. Christ it was cold. He could see the rifles coming up with the sun. O'Rourke had heard somewhere that a man got an automatic erection when he was hung. Pity to be shot. Captain Bloody O'Neil and his sodding Brigade could go to the devil . . .

Soft pink light flooded into the little village just south of the border from County Armagh, It yawned awake to the faint sounds of gunfire crackling across the frozen snow.

It was unusually cold in Damascus, despite being December. O'Neil wished to God he could have a decent drink instead of this filthy Arab coffee. He thought back to the last time he'd been in Syria, years before. It had been so hot then that even the flies had given up fighting the heat, settling like sweat on the clayed walls in dark, buzzing patches.

The big house on Mohammed Zaid Street in the 'Malki Quarter' of this walled city had been crowded out for nearly a week. The long, narrow room at the rear of the house stank of body odour – unaided by the coolness. Banks of low cushioned benches ran right round the large room, breaking only for the double doors leading out to the gated court-yard.

The small groups of men, sitting uneasily in each other's dangerous company at the low brass tables, argued in harsh, voluble whispers – and completely ignored 'Captain' James Connor O'Neil and his burly giant of a lieutenant from the breakaway off-shoot of the Irish National Liberation Army.

Most of the international terrorists, at this 'conference' to co-ordinate the KGB's political subversion around the world, wore the standard green denim or jeans and T-shirts of their deadly trade. Only the delegates from the Middle East, with their colourful burnouses topping flowing white robes, stood out in sharp contrast and aloof watchfulness.

Many races were represented at the tables. And many causes. Dark-skinned Arabs rubbed necessary shoulders with darker-skinned Africans, slant-eyed Orientals and the olive tones of the Latin contingent.

The groupings, all Marxist in origin or outlook, ranged from Japan's Red Army, GRAPPO, the Italian Red Brigade and Basque separatists to the military wing of the PLO, Black September, Iraq's Fedhayeen and the loud-voiced SWAPO men from Namibia.

Even the shattered remnants of the Baader Meinhof gang were there – and the deathly independence of Carlos, 'the Jackal'. Violent death in many forms and convictions sat round this room, talking merciless retribution on the innocent and guilty alike.

At a larger table in the centre of the big room, two men in dark Savile Row business suits sat by themselves. One, the personal representative of the host country's Deputy Foreign Minister, Abdel Khaddam, said very little. The other held the rank of major in the Subversion Directorate of Syrian Intelligence.

It was he who would occasionally call over a delegate from one of the other tables. After talking with him for a few minutes, he would then address the room on a particular point. It was clear that he fronted the conference for his Soviet masters.

Ironically, the common language in use was English, but its sole native speakers continued to be studiously ignored. O'Neil had been down in Tripoli trying to buy arms for the cause in Ulster when he was tersely summoned to Damascus.

During the four days he'd been hanging round the edges of the conference, waiting to find out what they wanted, he had been made very aware that his presence was only 'accepted' at this secret rendezvous under wary sufferance. Most of the other terrorist groups in attendance looked on the IRA and its quarrelsome offspring as amateurish and undisciplined.

O'Neil turned to 'Big Pat' Docherty towering over him. What a wonder it would be if these chattering Arabs ever got round to them! The wry grin lopsiding his piratical features took the bite out of his growing impatience.

Docherty shrugged massive shoulders and scratched his itching crotch. He said nothing, pushed open the double doors with a huge fist, and climbed the narrow steps leading up to the flat roof.

Nobody tried to stop him. Few would have dared. The guard already stationed on the roof nodded distantly at the giant. As he sat down heavily, Docherty wondered at their ideas of secrecy and security.

He could hear one of the 'souks' in the distance, its sounds reaching up to him faintly on the chill air. Down in the bazaar itself, traders shouted their doubtful bargains and ragged Arab kids pestered passersby with noisy pleas.

Docherty stared moodily at the surrounding villas behind

their silent walls, hating it all. Sweet Mother of Christ, he hoped they'd get out of this flea-hole soon. He longed for Ireland's green hills and the fight against the bastard 'Brits'. There was a certain SAS sergeant down in Fermanagh – he'd done for Danny Flynn in a snatch raid over the border – who was just aching to get the wrong end of Docherty's special talents in killing.

Pat Docherty was a big man. Big in size and bigger in heart for those he loved. But in his hates, 'Big Pat' was very small and very mean.

O'Neil understood him better than most. He used the giant's strengths as other men might use a shovel.

Nobody moved to help Hamad Jabal. The whole Syrian village had been made to witness his sentence. Even the children stood silently inside the dusty circle, staring at the man with dark liquid eyes, indifferent to his suffering.

The one they called 'El-Nesr' kicked the man in the groin, punishing him with pain. The man did not cry out nor beg for mercy. He knew that Allah would not forgive him. Neither would these villagers he had stolen from.

The man's wife watched her husband's seed being cruelly destroyed and felt nothing. In her eyes, he was already dead.

Trust was the key to the Palestine Action Commando's continuing survival among their Syrian 'friends'. That and an absolute faith in the next man's courage and total loyalty to the group. This he had broken.

Another child had died in one of the Palestinian camps that morning, starved of healing drugs in a family sick with the hopelessness of it all. When the Hawk heard about it, as he always did, it had made him even angrier at having to waste any of his men's lives. But discipline was the only way they would ever gain a homeland.

The penalty for theft in many Moslem countries is still to cut off the thief's right hand. Thereby, the hand with which he performs his toilet must also become the hand with which he eats. In this man's case, he would have his stump

18

sealed in hot tar and then be driven far out into the desert. It was unlikely he would survive either the shock and loss of blood from his wound – or the long trek without food and water.

The man knelt for the last real moments of his life, gripping the desert between the fingers of his free hand. He hardly felt the clawed blade slice through his wrist before he fainted. He certainly did not see his severed hand drop in a red mess at the Hawk's booted feet.

President Jimmy Carter attended church service in the White House with his wife and Amy. He prayed with Baptist earnestness for a lasting peace in the Mideast.

He also wondered through his fingers at his own political future if he didn't close his Camp David initiative with Anwar Sadat and that damned redneck, Begin.

The senior Secret Service agent guarding the President over Christmas stood respectfully aside as America's chief executive came back up the aisle. He thought the President looked played out, and he wouldn't have taken bets on the man lasting through to run for a second term.

In London people excused themselves and ate with polite gluttony, opened their presents, got drunk, saw family relatives with warm affection or resigned the day to aunts and uncles who seemed unable to accept that anyone ever grew up.

Others wandered about in aimless loneliness, wishing the 'celebrations' were over and done with. Then the ache of having nothing to do and nobody to do it with might not seem so bad.

Bedsitters sat in a freezing no-man's-land of city back-streets, metering out their tenants' empty Christmas by the shilling. The cooing army of London's pigeons and quarrelling sparrows made up the nearest thing to a festive choir any of them would hear.

A little girl, skidding across an icy Lambeth street to show her best friend a new doll, was hit by a seasonally early drunken-driver. Her short life stained the road. So did the bottle dropped by the man in the car as he stumbled out, horrified at what he had done.

The Foreign Office intelligence officer in Room 504, Century House, sighed and turned off the lights as the evening brought in fresh gusts of snow. He had been quite willing to stand in as duty officer. Now the pain in his legs told him the Middle East Desk had seen enough of him for that particular day. There'd been nothing else he'd wanted to do. Christmas had become just a word for him. He hadn't bothered with the bitch for fifteen years – nor she with him.

George Burroughs felt so bloody tired these days. The kind of tiredness that made your lungs ache. He'd be glad when his retirement came up at last.

Perhaps the Department would appreciate him when it was too late. He was sure something big was on the move in Syria. If it blew up in the West's face, he prayed some of the muck would fall smack in the middle of his vacated Desk.

Especially over Holman.

Burroughs loved his job and hated his boss. A common enough complaint. But co-operation of the closest kind was vital in an SIS Department (MI6) concerned with monitoring and evaluating the West's interests in an unstable Arab world.

The relationship between Burroughs and his chief had done nothing to help him do his work. Thank Christ the bastard was stuck two floors above him at 'The House' – the modern office block which contained the Foreign Office's Intelligence/Radio Traffic HQ – and its MI6, MI9 Secret Service counterparts, all tucked away on Lambeth's famous Walk.

The cold which had clothed the English countryside in an overcoat of glistening frost, disturbing even nature's wiser animals curled into hibernation until the spring, bit into him sharply as he turned slowly into Westminster Bridge Road.

It nagged at the scars he carried with uncomfortable persistence. They reminded him of his age.

He heard a siren echoing over the bridge and wondered where the speeding ambulance was going as it tore past him, narrowly missing his inclusion in its mercy dash.

It took George Alfred Burroughs, DSO, DCM, a good twenty minutes to find a taxi back to his silent flat in Cheyne Walk.

A child was born on this Christmas Day. One of several in the capital city of the Irish Republic. It wailed into the world with a healthy gusto. A Dublin priest, in sympathy with the absent father away over the water, blessed the easy birth in a raised glass of the household's 'best'.

The father wondered about his pregnant wife – and hoped for a boy to perpetuate the endless struggle for a united, independent Ireland.

Council workmen, on double time, helped the police clear up the wreckage from the IRA bombs which had gone off during the Christmas week in selected English cities, causing no deaths this time but frightening the hell out of everybody yet again.

It was Christmas Day, 1978. Not a very happy ending to the year. But life – and death – went on in their various guises, mindless of the season.

CHAPTER TWO

O'Neil was glad of the half-day break in the long conference. He was just as thankful to be away from Big Pat's moaning as to when they'd be going home to Ireland.

The big Irishman had been very suspicious when they had received the 'request' to come down from Tripoli into this vipers' nest of so-called hard men. The only one who had impressed O'Neil was Carlos, mainly because he looked so inoffensive.

What the hell, O'Neil thought as he walked alone through the bazaar. He should have brought Tim O'Rourke along on a trip like this. He smiled to himself. Poor old Pat. All he knew, or cared about, was fighting the British. O'Rourke was near uncontrollable at times but O'Neil appreciated the wry sense of humour that went with the man. Good comrade to have at your back in a scrap.

He walked on for a while, deep in thought, ignoring the curious stares of the Arab stall-holders. Men of his colouring were seldom seen – or welcome – in Syria these days.

Someone tugged persistently at his sleeve. He clipped the street urchin lightly round his ear, digging out some change.

'Sod off, you little hound,' he grinned, holding out the money.

The ragged child beamed up at the lanky figure and ran for it with his prize. O'Neil shook his red head, picking up his train of thought again.

So . . . these Arabs wanted him to organise a huge bombing and terror campaign across the whole of Britain and Ulster for the summer of '79, did they? And they'd supply all the arms he could handle, with which to kill off old enemies – and some new ones on their behalf.

When the conference had at last got round to the INLA, that fancy major had called out to him stiffly. The 'Englishman' would come to his table. *Now*.

O'Neil had countered him quietly in the hard accent of Northern Ireland. ' "English" is it? We're all Irishmen in our army, mister. You might as well get it right if we're going to do business together.'

He'd sat down at the table, a whimsical smile on his face. Big Pat thumped into the chair next to him, staring at the Syrian major with unfriendly black eyes.

The intelligence officer had flushed visibly under his dark skin. He was further irked by the loud snigger from Joshua Nkomo's Patriotic Front delegate. A sharp look from the Deputy Foreign Minister's man told him to get on with it.

The major had explained things carefully to O'Neil in stilted English, resentment hidden behind his sunglasses. The conference had many causes to discuss – all involved with the establishment of international Marxism. The IRA and INLA were considered part of that struggle, the major had added, his face betraying nothing.

Only just, you fly little man, O'Neil had thought as the Syrian continued. First the line and here comes the baited hook. It looked as if the traitor Sadat was going to sign a peace treaty with the hated Israelis. And one which excluded any homeland for their Palestinian brothers. The Syrians and their Iraqi comrades planned to mount a big push against Kuwait some time in August as a first retaliatory step towards wrecking Carter's imperialistic dreams for the Middle East.

It was important, so the major had maintained, that the British weren't in a position to send troops to help that dog, Sheikh Jabir al Ahmed somebody or other. Could their revolutionary brothers in the IRA and INLA tie up the British forces in their own lands and distract attention away from the Middle East?

The more damage to Britain's industrial and essential installations they could effect into the bargain, so much the better. Anything that hurt the Western dogs of capitalism . . .

O'Neil sniffed as he walked on. Brothers indeed! It amused him how they all suddenly became 'brothers' when the dirty work had to be done. They made him laugh. Didn't they know that the Brits were already overstretched in NATO and crippled by defence cuts?

Personally, he doubted if the British Army could successfully mount a display team in Aldershot's backyard! Still, if this was what these Arabs wanted, he would make damn sure he got what he wanted out of them in return.

Out of idle curiosity, O'Neil paused at a newsstand and was surprised to see a copy of the *Morning Star* on the untidy stall. In English too. He fished into his pocket for some more change.

The paper was nearly two weeks out of date. Typical. What the hell. It would provide an amusing read later. He needed a drink. Black syrup, he supposed, and strolled over to one of the street cafés.

The liquid in the small brass cup was scented, sickly and bitter-sweet. He hated the stuff. He went out again into the crisp sunshine, casually leafing through the pages of dead news – and suddenly stood stock still.

A small article had caught his eye. O'Neil began to read intently, quite oblivious of the crowd banging into him.

The *Morning Star* was criticising the forthcoming royal tour of the oil-rich Gulf States by Queen Elizabeth II and the Duke of Edinburgh. Any Communist journal worthy of the name would of course disapprove of this monarchical exchange of wealth and privilege. But what really worried the *Star* was the unifying effect such a royal visit might have on the solidly pro-western sheikhdoms of eastern Arabia against their Marxist neighbours, particularly with the real possibility in the air of a lasting treaty between Egypt and the Israelis. It neglected to mention that even the moderate Arab nations were deeply unhappy with the proposed settlement's total exclusion of any solution to the Palestinian problem.

It also failed to inform its readers that much of the Arab world's 'concern' over the Palestinians had little to do with either historical justice or political ethics. Rather, they wanted an end to the guerillas' embarrassing and stateless presence in their own lands.

The internal politics of it did not really interest Connor O'Neil that afternoon. He scanned the article again. When was it? February. Just two months before Mr and Mrs Queen would be swanning around the Middle East in their damned royal yacht.

He tossed the offending newspaper into the overflowing gutter and walked on. Minutes later, he stopped dead in his tracks again and ran back to retrieve it.

It was sopping wet. Water dripped off the newsprint like tears as O'Neil gripped the paper with quiet excitement.

'Holy Mother of God,' he whispered to himself. 'I wonder if it could be done?'

O'Neil stretched his arms, trying to work some air into his clammy armpits. The Syrian major stared at him sourly, impatience working a muscle in his jaw.

'Well, Captain?' he demanded in his stilted English. 'Can you help us, or can you not?'

O'Neil grimaced inwardly. He would have to be careful just how he answered. His own forces were thin on the ground and the IRA had been having a bad time of it lately from the security clamp-downs on their arms caches and street warfare tactics, especially in Belfast. But he needed that promise of arms – and the money which would go with it. He was also stuck in Syria until – and if – they decided to grant him an exit visa. So was Docherty.

'I think we can,' he replied cautiously. 'But I'll need to dream up some kind of a stunt if I'm to recruit the amount of men necessary for a large-scale operation the likes of which you're after. That'll take time, don't you know?'

The major looked puzzled.

' "Stunt"? What does this word mean. You will explain.'

'I'll explain all right, you unlovely abortion, thought O'Neil and smiled the smile that had charmed a host of women into his bed and a dozen or more British soldiers to sudden, unexpected deaths.

'It means, Major, I will need a propaganda coup. Something big enough to get my people flocking into our army.'

The major smiled back thinly, removing his sunglasses. Two dead brown eyes stared flatly at O'Neil, without humour.

'Then you will think, Captain. Your . . . people will come if you call loud enough, I am sure.' He replaced his glasses slowly.

'Meanwhile our hospitality is yours. And the lieutenant's. I want a plan from you by this time tomorrow.'

He glanced at his gold Omega chronometer.

'You may go.'

O'Neil nodded, still smiling. A plan was already forming in his agile mind – one so daring and unbelievable that he doubted if even this bunch of fanatics would have the nerve to join in. Behind his teeth, he wished the gallant major the health of a dead camel and any ball-aching disease which went with it.

George Burroughs was bloody furious. He ripped the grading slip off the 'Classified' file in front of him, stuffed it in his pocket, rocketed up from his desk and out of his office, slamming the door behind him.

'Right, Sir High and Mighty Holman! This is it!' he snarled.

He strode down the shiny, Ministry of Works (tiles: plastic, green) corridor in Century House as fast as his limp would allow in a bizarre imitation of one of those jerky clockwork dancers on a mirrored musical box, stopping only to thrust his large frame round the last of the office doors on his floor.

'Mac!' he yelled unnecessarily. 'I'm going to see Holman! Pass me out!'

The Assistant Head of Section looked up briefly from his papers and removed his tortoiseshell spectacles carefully. 'Teddy' MacAllister, MC and Bar, was a tall, thin West Highland Scot with impeccable manners and grey wavy hair.

He favoured check country shirts and tweed slacks and wore a British Field Sports Society club tie with everything. He liked and respected George Burroughs.

'Trouble again, old boy?' he enquired gently in his soft burr. He knew what George was like when he got a bee in his bonnet.

'Trouble?' Burroughs ground back. 'Not for me there bloody isn't!'

When he arrived at the Foreign Office in Whitehall, he was kept waiting to see his chief. For nearly an hour. It was quite deliberate. Sir David Holman believed in such things, especially since his subordinate did not have an official appointment with him. It did nothing to improve Burroughs' mood.

A Corps of Commissionaires messenger came softly across the highly polished parquet flooring. Burroughs glared up at him from his chair in the reception area. The sergeant saluted him smartly.

'Sir David will see you now, sir.'

Burroughs looked the man up and down. He had the Military Medal for gallantry among the World War II campaign ribbons on his uniform. It saved him from the worst of Burroughs' tongue.

'Right,' was all Burroughs said as he headed for the old-fashioned lift. Sir David was in his own chief's office, completing a briefing session with Lord Pennington's deputy. The Minister was away in Bahrain and his deputy had requested Holman's intelligence assessment on a pressing Middle East security problem. Although the SIS echelon was seldom officially acknowledged in the hallowed rooms of the Foreign Office, and worked 'independently' of the Diplomatic Service, it was often called in for such meetings to give advice or expedite situations outside the gentler finesse of diplomacy.

For all that, the Foreign Office neither wanted nor dared to enquire too closely into the workings of its grubbier counterpart. Burroughs knew this, of course. It only served

27

to increase his resentment for both career diplomats and career Civil Servants, like Holman, who didn't really want to know what it was all about when the chips were down and the talking had to stop.

Lord Pennington's assistant secretary met Burroughs as he came out of the ancient lift on the third floor.

'Good morning. Sir David is waiting.' The tone was reproachful.

Burroughs stared at the sleek young man in his Marlborough College tie and inwardly sighed. Where did they get them from? Christ, no wonder Britain hadn't any teeth nowadays and the whole bloody world could pull the old lion's tail as it pleased.

'Is he?' he grunted. 'So have I, lad. For the last bloody hour.'

'Sir David is very busy, Mr Burroughs,' the assistant defended coldly.

Burroughs did not reply. The assistant took his grim silence as having scored a point against the lower orders and took a stab at adding another one for the Establishment.

'None of us like having to work on Boxing Day, you know,' he continued tartly. 'If it wasn't for these Middle East peace talks, I would be spending Christmas with my parents in Worcestershire.'

Burroughs could not bring himself to bleed for this prissy little sod but he grinned suddenly, becoming almost boyish.

'Missed your hols, have you? That's what I like to see, boy. A bit of loyalty to the old firm. Pity it's not a two-way street around here.'

He paused, staring even harder at the nonplussed young man. They did not teach junior officials how to deal with men like George Burroughs. That only came from years of experience and well-earned battle scars of their own.

'Your family tied up in this game, are they?' he asked, suddenly all friendliness.

The assistant shook his neat head haughtily, refusing to be mollified.

'No. My father farms six thousand acres near Tewkesbury, actually.'

Burroughs patted him paternally on his tailored shoulder.

'Never mind, son. They'll be able to save you some turkey, eh?'

He pushed past the offended junior and went into his chief's temporary office without knocking.

It was all one might expect for a very senior Minister of the Crown. Walnut panelling faced the high walls. They were hung with non-Ministry of Works original flat-racing prints by Stubbs and Frith. Lord Pennington liked to remind his many visitors that he currently owned a string of very successful racehorses. His devotion to them was said in some quarters to be higher than his commitment to his work, but that might have been spite.

The absent Minister's deputy had already completed his session with Holman and had left for the country again – after graciously suggesting, with a hint of dry malice, that Sir David might care to use his Minister's office for his unscheduled meeting with the 'fellow' from his Department. He was perhaps fortunate to have missed the intelligence officer's tight-lipped invasion of his master's territory.

In the short time the deputy had been gone, the big leather-topped desk had had Holman's unnatural neatness imposed upon it, despite his limited tenure.

The 'In', 'Out' and 'Pending' trays now stood in an exact line. Two signed photographs of Her Majesty the Queen and the Duke of Edinburgh were angled perfectly to a solid silver Georgian inkwell stand. Even the three 'Highly Classified' SIS files lying in front of him had been similarly dressed-off with parade-ground precision. The superficialities of order were important bolsters to failed ambition.

Sir David Jervais Holman, KCMG, was staring blankly into space when his 'fellow' walked in. Perhaps he was dreaming of former days, when he might have been a serious contender for permanent occupation of this Minister's office and title. Or at least as the Permanent Secretary.

He looked up keenly at Burroughs from beneath neat

grey eyebrows as he sat down uninvited in one of the leather armchairs usually reserved for the important callers, ignoring a much humbler upright chair placed precisely in front of the desk.

Sir David's small, compact figure looked rather lost behind the desk's imposing largeness. He ran a manicured hand across traditionally silvered diplomat's hair, careful not to disturb the parting split in a white slash on the left side of his tidy head, and glanced meaningfully at a gold Hunter fob-watch.

'Well, Burroughs. This is rather . . . irregular. I shall be leaving in fifteen minutes. It is my wife's birthday.'

The voice was as cold as the man. He was not easy to get along with, for an ex-diplomat. Especially if you had to work under him.

Burroughs came straight to the point, unimpressed by his chief's personal schedule, and dug the grading slip out of his crumpled suit pocket. Holman always made him feel like a tramp – and about as welcome.

He tossed the slip on to the desk and returned to 'his' armchair.

'I want to know why such a low priority's been placed on that file I sent up to you last week . . . sir.'

Sir David flushed at Burroughs' thinly-disguised insolence. It only served to emphasise the high colour already in his cheeks from years of combining his wife's passion for spectator field sports with the endless drinks circuit considered necessary between the higher ranks of passing governments and the Whitehall mandarins who remained quite immovable and unmoved by the fortunes of the day-to-day politicians they could always circumvent.

Burroughs' chief sat with the dying flush of his anger and steepled his fingers.

'File? There are "files" coming up to me all the time, as you are well aware.'

He stared at his subordinate, a rapidly icing neutrality adding coldness to grey eyes that were always coldly neutral, even when looking inwards. Or nearly always so.

Burroughs shifted irritably in his chair. His legs were really hurting today. Trust the bloody man to make sure the chairs were virtually below the level of his desk, he thought irrationally. It was not his chief's office.

'The Appreciation File on the Syrian situation. I included a press-clip sent on to us by the BOTB. I'm sure those bastards are up to something.'

'I take it you are referring to the Syrians, Burroughs,' Holman rejoined coldly. He did not take kindly to swearing.

Burroughs shifted in his chair again. Could hardly see the little runt smirk from here. He had a dislike of small people, unusual in a big man. It tended to be the other way round but, coupled with his long opposition to Holman's appointment as an Intelligence Director, it had festered into a positive hatred.

'Yes, I mean the Syrians.' He leaned forward urgently. 'Look, sir, our man in Damascus has reported a big conference going on out there. All the major terrorist groups appear to have sent delegates. Add that to this newspaper report of a Somerset factory having just received a damned great order for medical sutures from the Syrian Ministry of Health, and the thing looks nasty. I've been working on this region's scenario for months.'

Holman stared at him.

'Medical sutures? I don't see the connection, Burroughs. And these, ah, "conferences" have happened before, have they not?'

Christ, the man was exasperating. Burroughs tried again.

'An order like that can only mean one thing, sir. They're preparing for war. The last time anything of that size was put in, it was by Cuba – just before the Angolan business blew up. The BOTB's enquiries found out the factory had been expecting an order for, say £50,000. Instead, they got one for nearly £250,000. That works out at around *fifteen* metres of sutures for every man, woman and child in Syria! What the hell for? They've got a closed economy, so their Ministry of Health would have to front the order for the army.'

He straightened up and pulled out his cigarettes. Holman did not like people smoking in his presence either, and Burroughs knew it.

'If this peace initiative of Carter's with Israel and the Egyptians goes through,' he went on, 'the Syrians and the Iraqis aren't going to sit on their backsides doing nothing about it. Nor are the Libyans – or the PLO.'

He stared back hard at his chief.

'And this terrorist conflab is not the usual run of things. I've heard rumours that Colonel Solenov is in Damascus . . . and Carlos/Sanchez, call him what you will. "The Jackal" himself.'

Sir David brought himself upright behind his borrowed desk.

'I really feel you are over-dramatising the situation, Burroughs.' He paused, unlacing his fingers. 'You retire shortly, I believe? I would suggest you leave your, ah . . . concern with your successor.'

Burroughs stood up angrily. He leant across the desk, menacing Holman with his bulk, anger rippling through his frame.

It was men like himself and the men he had to send out who risked their lives and their sanity, while Civil Service crap like this little bastard suffered at most a missed promotion if they ever got it wrong. And Holman had got it wrong all right – right out of the Diplomatic Corps. Yet his fellow dips and the bloody Establishment had covered for him all the way into his present job!

He banged a fist down on the desk, making Holman jump.

'No! Of course it bloody well "concerns" me! It's *still* my job – and yours!'

Holman did not like being interrupted, nor in such a manner. He coughed and straightened the photograph Burroughs had knocked out of line.

'You forget yourself, Burroughs,' he reprimanded, even colder. 'I will look into this matter further. If I feel it warrants any action at this time, I will advise my Minister on his return. That is all.'

I bet you will, Burroughs seethed as he left the office. All Holman could do was pass his recommendations up to the Service's Director-General, who might pass them on to the Permanent Secretary, who would decide if he wanted to bother his Minister with it, especially considering the Minister did not officially recognise the existence of people like himself or the Department he worked for.

Would Holman *never* learn? So bloody concerned about his screwed-up career, he wouldn't go for a pee without first clearing it with the bloody Foreign Secretary!

He passed Lord Pennington's assistant secretary as he reached the lifts.

'It's not so cold today is it, sir?' the young man remarked, trying to be a good trainee diplomat and attempting to patch up his earlier encounter with this frightfully aggressive fellow from Century House.

'Go to hell!' Burroughs snarled and slammed the lift door in his face.

Perhaps, over the years, Burroughs should have come to accept that the Civil Service machine in Britain was literally frightening in its complexity and check-against-check systems.

At the lowest end of the scale are mere Clerical Officers – the paper-pushers and minor minions who make the public's life a misery, from the VAT office to car tax.

Above them sit the Executive Grades, where real ability is often killed by the strata above them. Their ranks or military equivalents, depending on the Ministry, run from Executive Officer up to Principal Officer, which senior executive status Burroughs had achieved – and stuck at – some years before.

The problems can really start at the top of the tree. This is where the policy-makers sit, as opposed to the servants of policy. These are the men who can break a government-of-the-day Minister or run rings round him, if they so choose.

They range from Assistant Secretary and Under Secretary to the man at the helm – the Permanent Secretary – although he again is often a political appointment and subject to the whims of government change.

The real power lies just underneath him with the Deputy Secretary or his immediate subordinate, the Under Secretary. These gentlemen are always career Civil Servants; part of a faceless elite who control and decide what their political 'bosses' can or cannot do, will or won't know about.

They carry enormous power inside a system and protocol procedure that is so all-embracing of Mr Average's life that he, let alone those following a political life, would never get to the bottom of it.

A man of Burroughs' Civil Service rank did not stand a chance. It did not matter how right he was about something, if he offended the system then he would never get the matter past his immediate superior. Holman, as just that, deluded himself with talk of 'his' Minister but was just as handcuffed by the men above him. Frustration wasn't in it.

George Burroughs sat up very late that night in his flat. The midnight movie played itself out softly in the background. He sighed and got up to pour himself just one more whisky, knocking over a photograph on the small Jacobean sideboard.

The flat was well-appointed, with wall-to-wall carpeting in every room. He had collected some nice pieces over the years, especially his early English porcelain.

His small circle of friends, most of them ex-Army or in his present line of work, were surprised at this gentler side to his nature. His cat was grateful for it too. The friends also wondered, on their infrequent invitations into his home, how he could afford a place on one of the Thames's most desirable of waterfronts.

Although he was reasonably well-paid and his Army disability pension helped, he could not have either acquired the flat, nor kept it going, without the bequest and its interest left to him by an old Army colleague, whose life he had saved in Malaya. But George Burroughs never discussed his personal affairs. It was a good six months after the event before even his closest associates discovered his wife had left him, and even longer before they knew for certain he'd got his divorce.

He picked up the photograph and stood staring at it, slightly drunk and on the edge of alcoholic depression. Christ, those *were* the days! The picture showed him in major's uniform on receiving his DSO from the Palace.

Burroughs had gone into the Glosters, after service as a boy soldier straight from the orphanage in Teddington. By sheer aptitude and a great deal of determination, he had worked – and fought – his way up through the ranks to become the battalion's intelligence officer. By the time he was captured during the Korean War, he had seen active service in the deserts of Palestine and the steamy treachery of Malaya, winning the Distinguished Conduct Medal whilst still a sergeant.

The wounds he received trying to escape from the North Koreans had ended his active service career in the only thing he really knew or loved – soldiering. The mind-bending 're-education' torture he endured during that terrible winter in the bitter cold of captivity had not helped heal him. Although brave, intelligent and highly disciplined with anything analytic, he was lonely. Lonely in a softening Western world – and perhaps indelibly scarred in more ways than one.

By dint of his rank and service record, if not his social background, he had got into the SIS with the substantive rank of Major. Using the same ability and determination he'd applied in the Army, he put his analytical brain to work, becoming one of the Foreign Office's leading specialists on terrorism. Particularly in the Middle East.

He had done well enough, he supposed. But he knew his maverick ways and abrasive manner had not gone down easily with his superiors. Half of them were fools in his opinion. Strangely, for a man used to being analytical, he refused to recognise that the open expression of his opinions on that score had ensured he would go no higher in the Service. Or he wouldn't admit it.

Burroughs did not really care any more. He'd been

reasonably happy, despite his disastrous marriage to a woman ten years his junior. With his heavy build, everyone said he looked more like a policeman than an ex-soldier. He was just that in a way: one of the world's peace officers in the real sense of the word, wasn't he?

He grunted. Perhaps he should have gone into the CID and joined all the other rip-off merchants . . .

Burroughs finished his drink and went to bed. Lying in the darkness, he wondered what the hell Carlos was up to with that crowd in Damascus? Helped by two sleeping tablets, unconsciousness finally overtook his tired speculations.

O'Neil spent the evening in his room on Mohammed Zaid Street. They'd only be rabbiting on about Sadat down there.

He had a large ordnance map of the Middle East spread out in front of him on the floor and had covered the Suez Canal Zone with pencilled calculations.

Docherty came in and thumped his giant frame down on the bed. The whole room shook in protest.

'You any idea when we're going home now, Captain?' Docherty's voice rumbled up from his barrel chest in a deep growl of thunder.

O'Neil did not look up, studying his map with intense concentration.

'We won't be, Pat. Not yet awhile anyhow.'

The big Irishman's black eyes went dead. He scratched his curly black hair with fingers as thick as pipes.

'Sweet Mary, why's that?'

O'Neil looked up and regarded his disappointed lieutenant with a mad twinkle in his blue eyes. Big Pat cheered up a little. That look usually meant something was on.

James Connor O'Neil, late of the Irish Guards, slowly tapped the map with his pencil. Docherty's gaze followed his captain's finger to the *Morning Star* article beside the map.

He picked it up and read with slow deliberation. His astonished eyes travelled back to the map and then on to

O'Neil's smiling features, disbelief widening the black pupils.

'Jesus, Captain. You're kiddin . . . are you not?'

O'Neil shook his red head with slow emphasis.

'No. I am not. We, my bucko, are going to pull it off. And the whole world will tremble with the shock.'

CHAPTER THREE

Burroughs slid quietly into the adjacent chair and sat for a full ten minutes watching his friend at work before interrupting him. Sammy Cook exacted that kind of respect from people in the know. His hands flew over the complex mass of dials and keys in front of him, playing the bank of high-frequency radio equipment with all the artistry of a virtuoso concert pianist.

'Piano Sam', as he had been dubbed around the Foreign Office's HQ Communications Centre in Century House, had come up the hard way like George Burroughs. It had a lot to do with the kinship existing between the two men. He had lost his left leg to a landmine in Aden during his National Service in the Signals. Two years of trying to run a small electrical repair shop in North London on his disablement pension had convinced him there had to be a better way of using his extraordinary talents with the air-waves.

Having completed a series of exhaustive interviews for a research job with Cable and Wireless, he had suddenly found the Foreign Office quietly stepping in and was discreetly whisked off – at twice the starting salary offered by C & W – into the secret world of diplomatic ciphers and SIS listening watches. He had been with the FO ever since, and loved every intriguing minute he could devote to his increasingly sophisticated devices, fed from the forest of receiving masts at Cheltenham.

Sammy Cook removed his combined headphones and throat mike with a mock sigh, neatly lifting the piece of paper out of Burroughs' large fist.

'You'll get me shot one of these days, George,' he jibed quietly, running his eye over the transmission form. 'Same as before, is it?'

Burroughs nodded, lowering his voice as the other operators around them bent to their equipment like worshippers at a religious ceremony.

'Yes. Damascus. 18.30 local time. Danvers will be ready to receive. This one's urgent.'

Cook grinned at him and Burroughs could not help grinning back.

'They always are with you, George my old mate.'

Burroughs gripped his arm, suddenly serious. Cook sat very still. He knew Burroughs would not take this unauthorised risk for the hell of it – nor ask him to do so. There was no clearance signature on the form.

'Listen, Sam. It's different this time. The feel of the thing. I've been sitting on top of this thing for six months now and I *know* something is on out there. Just can't put my finger on it yet, but I will.'

'As the actress said to the bishop, eh!' Cook quipped at him, trying to lighten the tense atmosphere. He became very businesslike.

'All right, George. I'll transmit in two series, your personal code. Any reply will come round to your flat by special messenger or me personally. OK?'

Burroughs squeezed his arm. 'Thanks, Sammy. Bloody Holman will screw the whole thing up if it's left to him. Had the cheek to tell me to think about my retirement instead of "over-dramatising" this business.'

Cook's face showed surprise. 'Blimey! I'd forgotten about that. Not long now, is it? What'll you do with yourself?'

'Couldn't tell you right now,' Burroughs shrugged. 'Open a night school for spies maybe.'

'Yeah . . . Trade could be a bit slim. It's a dying business,' Cook cracked the old joke lightly.

'Hmm.'

The grimness had not left Burroughs completely. He got up, punching his friend gently on the shoulder.

'Be hearing from you then . . .'

Cook did not look up: his attention was back on his receivers. He stuck a thumb in the air and concentrated on the fast-coder transmission coming in from Prague.

Burroughs stood in front of his own desk at Century House and surveyed the four rows of telexes and cables laid out across it. They were reports from 'friendly' intelligence agencies around the world on the terrorist groups from their regions who were known to have sent someone to the gathering in Damascus.

He turned to his Assistant Head of Section almost angrily.

'Look at it, Teddy. Every major terrorist in the book has arrived in Syria, and all Holman can do is say it's nothing unusual! I tell you – something bloody big is brewing.'

'Teddy' MacAllister tried to interrupt as Burroughs' hand swept down and chopped through the tension, cutting him off.

'You remember that press pick-up we got from the British Overseas Trade Board on those medical sutures for Syria? I'm convinced there's a tie-up between that and this little lot in Damascus.'

He scratched his fist.

'But what the hell can it be? The Syrians wouldn't need a bunch of outside terrorists to fight any war they're planning. Maybe there isn't any connection and this conference has a separate purpose . . .' he mused.

The Assistant Head of Section shuffled through the cables lying on the desk.

'I tend to agree with you, George,' he said. 'There's something going on. Didn't Clive Danvers say Solenov was in on it, too?'

Burroughs coughed on his cigarette, nodding his head. Should give the bloody things up.

'Right. That bastard, Major Konstantin Vinogradov is

hovering about in the background, as well. You know him. He covers for the KGB as First Secretary at the Soviet embassy in Baghdad. I know Syrian Intelligence is doing the fronting but you can bet your boots Solenov is pulling all the strings.' He grunted. 'And from the political leanings of that lot in Damascus. I'd say the KGB was setting up an international subversion campaign using all these terrorist organisations somehow.'

He stabbed a blunt finger at the cables.

'Look at the spread. Italy, Spain, Germany, Holland and France as one arm of the pincer. Rhodesia, Zambia, Tanzania, Zaire and those clowns from Namibia through to Japan and the Philippines as the other – with the Middle East situation as the hinge, so to speak.'

He lit another cigarette, forgetting his own counsel in his preoccupation with this proven pattern of sinister death.

'All the regions involved are highly sensitive, with major elections, electoral reforms or bloody great political changes in the offing for '79.'

'It certainly seems that way,' MacAllister concurred cautiously.

'Too bloody right it does,' Burroughs countered. 'What I can't understand is why neither we nor the United States appear to be on the direct target list. It doesn't make any sense.'

MacAllister shook his head sympathetically. 'No it doesn't, George. All you can do is keep working at it. You've got my support, you know that.'

Burroughs smiled thinly, hunching his powerful shoulders.

'Thanks. Holman's the problem, not you. How do I get round that bloody idiot?'

His hand flashed across the desk, spilling the cables on to the floor in a cascade of frustration.

'There's *got* to be an answer, for Christ's sake!' he shouted at the room.

MacAllister wasn't sure if he was referring to their chief or the Syrian thing. He thought about picking up the papers, hesitated behind his spectacles and left Burroughs to it. He knew he would pace for hours, trying to find his way through the questions that needed answering.

Burroughs did exactly that. Up and down, up and down. Right through till lunchtime, refusing to take any calls or speak to anyone. Then he gave it up in disgust, angry with himself for letting Holman rattle him, and decided to get out of town for the rest of the day. He was bloody well owed some time off.

He'd drive down to the coast, if he could get through, and drop in for a Christmas noggin with the commandant of the Small Arms School at Hythe, who was an old friend. If there was time afterwards, he could battle on to Folkestone proper and pay a surprise visit on old Mr Betts. It was long everdue. Maybe he'd stay overnight – and sod the bloody Department.

On the way down, Burroughs pulled his old Jaguar saloon off the 'one-lane-open-only' motorway, glad for a respite from the crawling pace of the traffic. A bit of bloody snow and the whole country came to a halt. Same every year.

He thought about the assistant secretary at the FO. With luck, when he went home, the little wet would get snowed up on daddy's farm for a long stretch and have to eat turkey until it came out of his silly cloth ears.

He took another look at the coded instruction he had sent to the SIS's man in Damascus. At least the lucky devil was in the warm.

Red Priority One. Flatfoot to Doormouse. All you have on old boys attending Big Bear's reunion. Need to know what celebrated and why Desert Dog running with the pack? Can you connect band-aids with the Chocolate Soldiers? Piano Player will try your tune at evening concert for seven nights.

Burroughs grinned to himself. He found a certain amount of relaxation in dreaming up these riddles for the coding clerks. It wouldn't fool the Syrian Intelligence boys for long, if they picked up the high-speed send, but it would make them work for it.

Translated, the bizarre message meant he wanted to know the exact purpose of the Damascus conference, if Danvers could find that out from his Arab contact; also, who was actually there, and why; what a loner like 'the Jackal' was doing at the gathering; and if there was any connection between the mysterious order for medical sutures and Syrian military moves in the Middle East.

Sam Cook would be ready to receive and decode all and any of his agent's answers each evening for seven nights between 8 and 9 p.m. GMT.

A motorway police Range Rover drew up in front of him on the hard shoulder. The driver got out, turning up the collar of his dark blue topcoat against the bitter cold. He shook his head as he walked back to Burroughs' car. Probably another engine failure, he thought. It looked clapped out.

'Afternoon, sir. You in difficulties? If not, best keep moving. It's going to freeze up again later.'

The officer peered through the slightly open window. Burroughs sighed audibly, wound down the window, held out his MI6 warrant card and wished the man would bugger off. He got a salute for his trouble.

'I see, sir,' the officer shivered. 'Not going to be many spies about on a day like this – unless you're looking for the one who came in from the cold!'

The police officer's joke froze on the sour stare he received in return. Burroughs stuffed the coded cable back in the glove compartment, set his radio-telephone to 'Hold' and started up his car again.

He tunelessly hummed the Glorious Glosters' regimental march as he snailed down the motorway. He always hummed it when spoiling for a fight.

The motorway policeman watched him move off. Stuck-up, that one. Looked as if he could handle himself, though.

Connor O'Neil was having his problems as well. He felt very frustrated. His plan was coming together in his head all right, so fast and audacious it made his brain sing with the sheer devilry of it.

The only trouble was he'd need help; on the spot back-up from these Syrian heathens or certainly from a crack guerilla unit operating within the Middle East itself. And he'd sooner trust the devil than this bunch attending that glorified talking-shop downstairs.

He prowled round his small room at the top of the house in the Malki Quarter. The dusk was giving way to real evening, drawing an indigo veil across the sparkling pink stone of the minarets towering distantly above the surrounding villas.

O'Neil did not notice the subtle changes in hue and colour, too busy with his own thoughts. What was that name he'd heard mentioned the day before? Some rebellious fellow who was upsetting the line-toers in the PLO. Kassad? Kassan? No . . . Kassim. Hassan Kassim it was. 'Hassan the Hawk' they called him.

He stopped prowling and stood still for a long moment, trying to recall exactly what he'd overheard one of the PLO delegates explaining to a member of the Italian Red Brigade.

It seemed this Kassim was a bit of a wild boyo – all fire and plenty of nerve but not much of a track record. He'd wanted the PLO to become even more active in international reprisals against the Israelis and their supporters, reckoning that Yasser Arafat was going soft since he'd been invited to speak at the UN.

Apparently, Kassim had become so disillusioned he'd joined up with George Habash. O'Neil smiled to himself. Now there was a man after his own heart. Habash was considered so extreme, even by the PLO, that they had kicked him out, forcing him to go solo.

Since then, Habash had been responsible for many of the more daring and spectacular terrorist raids into Europe, including backing Carlos in the Athens airport shoot-up, killing twelve people and wounding dozens more.

He began to prowl again. Habash might prove a little too difficult to handle on a jaunt like this. He'd want to take over and O'Neil wasn't having that! But this Kassim laddie could be just what he was after: Young, bold and as ambitious as he himself for a major success.

How the devil to get to him, though? He knew he was not coming to the conference but somebody down there should know where he operated from. It was time to go and find out.

O'Neil strolled casually into the smoke and chatter of the big room below. Docherty looked up from the magazine he was slowly reading and O'Neil shook his head imperceptibly.

The giant subsided back on to his couch again like a submerging whale, remaining watchful and ready for trouble as his captain headed circumspectly for the PLO man he had seen talking about Kassim. O'Neil knew he was taking a big risk. The PLO were dependent enough on Syrian good-will to report any untoward enquiries by an outsider like himself.

The PLO delegate was dozing on one of the couches near the double doors, an ear cocked to the desultory conversation going on around him. O'Neil sat down beside him with a friendly nod. He was conscious of the room watching him as the man lifted an eyelid. The man held the burnt-out stub of a small cheroot between his fingers. O'Neil fished out his own cigarettes.

'Can I trouble you for a light?' he asked politely.

The man looked puzzled. O'Neil made the motion of striking a match, hoping he would open up – and offered him a cigarette for good measure. Unexpectedly, the man smiled, nodded and produced a battered Zippo he had taken off a dead Israeli soldier. With relief O'Neil drew deeply on the flame. He was getting somewhere.

'You're with the PLO, are you not . . . comrade?' he ventured. 'You lads do a fine job for the cause.'

The PLO man eyed him gravely, decided the compliment

was sincere and took one of O'Neil's cigarettes with strong brown fingers.

'That is so,' he replied slowly. His voice was low and husky.

'We must do what we must do, and well – as you.'

The gravely returned compliment was acknowledged with one of O'Neil's 'charmer' smiles. He could see the man was warming to him.

'Sure we do our best. But I've few men like yours – or Hassan Kassim's.'

Silence hung in the air between the two men. Sudden suspicion had almost closed the Arab's dark eyes. He leaned closer to O'Neil.

'You know of . . . El-Nesr?' he probed, coldly alert.

O'Neil shrugged casually. 'Not really, friend. I've heard people speak about him here. Seems quite a fighter . . . '

He paused, letting the silence fill the moment, sizing his man up, and took the plunge.

'I was just thinking he might be a natural for one hell of an operation I'm planning.'

The PLO man sat up, his face betraying nothing.

'He is not . . . approved of. But he may like you, Irishman,' was all he would say and got up, straightening his burnouse.

O'Neil smiled at him crookedly and the wicked blue eyes flashed. He lifted a hand slightly.

'You never know, my friend. You never know.'

At that, Khalil al-Wazir, destined to become the PLO security adviser to the Ayatollah Khomeini's own secret police, who would take over from the Shah of Iran's dreaded Savak during the grim summer of 1979, turned on his heel and walked away.

O'Neil sat very still for a long time. He could feel the sweat, tension and fear trickling out of him down his legs. Jesus Christ, these Arabs were a difficult lot.

He lit another cigarette, trying to steady his hand, then got up and strolled over to where Docherty was sitting.

'My room. Now,' he said softly.

Docherty closed the door behind him quietly and sat down on the bed without a word. O'Neil was sitting in the only chair, tapping a pencil against his teeth. It meant he was worried. Big Pat maintained his silence, waiting.

'We're on to something, Pat,' O'Neil said eventually, excitement and concern mingling with the smoke from his cigarette.

'That laddie from the PLO knows more than he's letting on.'

He drew heavily on his cigarette.

'Perhaps he's in with this Kassim fellow. These heathens are forever sticking knives up each other. I've a feeling we'll be hearing from someone soon.'

Docherty grunted, shifting his bulk on the creaking bed.

'That's as maybe, Captain,' he growled. 'You think we can trust your man?'

O'Neil raised his eyebrows questioningly. 'Who? Kassim?'

The giant nodded. O'Neil smiled tightly and stubbed out his cigarette.

'I don't think we can afford to trust any of this lot, Pat. But we're stuck here until they decide to let us out of the country – and we'll need their help.'

He unfolded his map, spreading it across the floor.

'So, let's get on with it. I've been putting this idea together all day and that darling major'll want some answers out of me before he tucks us up in bed tonight.'

Burroughs felt pleasantly mellow. It had been good to see Bob again and talk over old times. Colonel Fullerton now. Kept a decent spot of brandy. He wondered fleetingly if he'd have made the pips to his crown under different circumstances and dismissed it from his mind.

This weather was piss-awful. He peered intently through the slapping wipers and tried to make out the diversion signs for Folkestone. It was quite dark now. The combination of rain and snow slush had turned the roads into skating rinks in the freezing cold.

He hoped Mr B wouldn't mind him dropping in out of the blue. It was beyond him why the old man didn't get himself a telephone. Maybe he'd had enough of the things in the Department.

Burroughs swung his rust-bitten Jaguar carefully into the neat street of semi-detached houses and pondered on how they'd cope with all the snow.

He grimaced. Personally he wouldn't want to live here amongst a load of retired vicars, old ladies and the 'nouveau-poor', trying to keep up appearances and waiting for loud-mouthed holidaymakers from the North to invade the place every summer.

The front doorbell chimed gently as Burroughs shivered in his thick British Warm. A small man with a shock of white hair and a goatee beard answered it, surprise and pleasure cracking his seamed face.

'Good Lord! Come in, George. Come in! What on earth brings you down here on a night like this?'

Burroughs stepped inside the tiny hallway, shook his coat on the porch mat and handed the old man the bottle of brandy Fullerton had given him.

'Hullo, Mr B. That's for you. Thought I'd get out of London for a bit. Chose a bloody nice day for it, didn't I?'

The old man laughed, examining the label on the second-hand gift.

'Thank you, George. Very thoughtful. You always were a rebel, son. Taken on Mother Nature as well, have you?'

They went through to the lounge. It was full of mementos from the Far East and what had been true Arabia. A framed photograph of Norman Betts on a camel stood atop the G-plan sideboard with a tray of drinks. The furniture was modern and plain. 'Mr B' was a man of noticeably spartan habits.

He poured his visitor a large whisky, however, and sat him down, looking at him quizzically.

'Well now, George. I wasn't expecting you.'

Burroughs rubbed his chin, trying to fight off his tiredness and the effect of the brandy. The warmth from the coal fire burning brightly in the grate didn't help.

'No,' he said. 'I hope you don't mind.'

Mr Betts smiled, lighting up his pipe.

'Of course not. Delighted to see you. It's not often enough. Keeping you at it, are they?'

Burroughs sniffed, tasting his drink.

'If you mean Sir David bloody Holman, it doesn't get any better.'

Mr Betts smiled knowingly. 'Still bucking the system if I know you, son. What's on your mind? There's usually something when you come all this way to see me.'

It was said without rancour and Burroughs grinned at him.

'Really, Mr B. You know I'd come a million miles for one of your smiles.'

The old man laughed. 'Con me not, George. You've got a problem. I can tell. Remember when I was teaching you the ropes in the Department? You'd wander into my office like a lost soul, talking about nothing and everything until I prised it out of you.'

Burroughs smiled gently. Christ, he loved the old boy. If only there were some like him now . . .

'You're right – as usual. Do you mind if I go over it with you? It could take a while. Can I stay overnight in the spare room?'

His mentor shook his white head. 'No, I don't mind. It'll do this senile brain of mine some good. Of course you can stay. Tell me what it's all about, George.'

Burroughs sat back in his Parker Knoll armchair and explained the whole Syrian thing in detail, adding a colourful description of his confrontation with Holman. The old man listened without interruption whilst his protégé of all those years before worked over his thoughts out loud.

Norman Healey-Betts had been a foreign correspondent between the world wars when the words still meant something, working exclusively for *The Times* newspaper.

He had been inveigled into Churchill's wartime Middle

East intelligence network and somehow elected to stay on in that kind of work after World War II, finally running the Department's intelligence assessment team on the Middle East Desk.

Ten years of retirement with an OBE and a Civil Service pension on which to eke out his memories had not seemed much of a reward. He was the nearest thing to a father George Burroughs knew.

When Burroughs finished, it was nearly 3 a.m. The old man relit his pipe and puffed on it thoughtfully.

'It's certainly a puzzle, George, and no mistake. Hard to know what to think. You say Colonel Solenov is in Damascus? And Carlos? Is that hard intelligence and from whom?'

Burroughs nodded, tiredness creasing his face. 'Pretty certain. My man has got himself a tame Arab inside the PLO.'

Mr Betts shook his head doubtfully. 'Hmm. Tame Arabs are usually owned by other Arabs in my experience, George. But my personal interpretation is a major terrorist offensive encompassing just about all the danger-spots for Western interests in which the Soviets want a toehold. That is to be expected. It's the Islamic bit that worries me.'

He noted Burroughs' surprise and went over to his bookcase, pulling out a large atlas. He opened it at the lead-in map of the world.

'Your job doesn't stop at the Suez Canal, George. In this world of ours today, all these regions are interrelated by economic necessities, military strategy and political expendability – or experiencies. Have it as you will. I think "expediencies" are our key.'

He began tracing a line with his pipe across the restless face of Africa and the Middle East. His line took in the Ivory Coast, Nigeria, Morocco, Algeria, Libya, the Sudan, all of the Middle East through to Turkey and Iran. It continued through Pakistan and Afghanistan, paused over the USSR's huge and uneasy satellites of Moslem extraction, and

4   49

completed its journey on the cold wastes of Mongolia and northern China.

'These are the real problem today, my boy. All those regions have a large and devout Moslem community – and I haven't included Somalia, Bangladesh or Malaysia.'

He struck another match to his pipe.

'Islam, George. Islam . . . Did you know there was once a Moslem empire which made the Union of Soviet Socialist Republics look like something from the Home Counties? The resurgence of a holy war for Islam is the gravest possibility facing the Russian leadership – not China on its back door nor the West at its front.'

Mr Betts smiled almost wistfully and struck yet another match, holding it up against the light. The smoke from his pipe curled round its flame like a living thing. There was something sinister about the gesture.

'Don't forget I lived amongst the Arabs for years. They have talked around it for generations – the Peoples of the Desert rising in a pure fire of religious zeal against the corrupt infidel to the west and the evil granite bear to the north . . . '

He sighed. 'It is quite a concept. But that is what is beginning to happen again, this time fired by petrodollars and strategic importance. Look at Iran. The Shah's doomed and he knows it. That is just the start. Fanatics like Gaddafi of Libya will lead the military and economic revolution, with the mullahs and ayatollahs stoking the religious coals. It will fan like a great flame across the whole of Africa and Asia, right into the heart of Mother Russia herself. The Soviets won't stop it. Nor will we.'

Burroughs frowned and added his cigarette smoke to the pall hanging over the room.

'I don't see the tie-in with this business going on in Syria. That's down to Marxism controlled by the KGB, surely?'

His mentor gestured at him reprovingly with his pipe.

'You should, George. You should. At the moment you are right but who's using who? The Soviets have pursued a policy of stirring up discontent in all the regions I showed you that had pro-West leaders or strong Western interests. Now those factions are beginning to turn the tables on them. Instead of facing into the Russian bear's Marxist hug, they are looking towards Islam for their true deliverance.'

He chuckled drily, tapping the atlas.

'Call it rebellion. Rebellion *against* being sucked into the faceless mass of the USSR's satellite system and *for* a mass identity of their own within the fervid pull of Islam.'

He pointed to a copy of the Prophet's writings on his bookshelf.

'The aspirations of the Koran, their Holy Book, are very similar to those of Marxism. But Islam provides a spiritual drive above and beyond cold political doctrine, George. And a feeling of belonging individually.'

His pipe had gone out again. He fussed at it with a touch of annoyance.

'Wretched thing. Do you know the tenets of the Koran? "A religious striving for the happiness of all society, the establishment of truth, knowledge, freedom, justice and well-being."'

His pipe stabbed at Burroughs. 'In a word, Marxism without the godless, hidden motives of the State. Remember, Mother Russia heaved Catholicism and Greek Orthodoxy off her breasts in the bloody days of 1917.'

Burroughs started to interrupt. Mr Betts stopped him gently with his raised hand.

'George, you *must* get away from thinking in terms of power blocs and military might alone. Look to the deeper things in man's nature – things beyond materialism and national security. Man has always longed for a superior master, a divine direction to give meaning to his existence. Why do you think the ancient kings ruled with such power? Or even the tsars? Divine right to rule and decide. The opiate of the masses to do nothing for themselves. It still applies, George.'

He laughed briefly into the night.

'In the West, we might call it trade unionism now. Its power lies in having material clout over and for the workers.

Material life is valuable, the ideal cheap. In the East, the ideal is sacred and life a cheap sacrifice to it.'

He grunted in dry amusement. 'The Soviet Politburo can cope with the itsy-bitsy countries of East and Western Europe, and with the loose-limbed outlook of a historically naïve America. Divide and conquer works very well in nations that are essentially industrial, geared to an inflationary economic system at that!'

Burroughs' eyelids fluttered with tiredness. Mr Betts persisted in his exposition.

'Discontent, in terms of a lack of money and a living standard judged on the basis of what you've got rather than on what you think, is a very easy target for political agitators and subversion. Particularly if it is falling or standing still.'

He paused to kindle his pipe in a labour of unsuccessful habit.

'But in Africa and Asia you have societies far older than any Western monetary structure. Their outlook has grown suspicious of the white man's Christianity, brought by his missionaries and followed up by often rapacious trade exploitation.'

He laughed again. 'I know that makes me sound like a raving socialist, and we from our side would argue that we brought development and "civilisation" with us. Try telling them that! Seriously, to countries that were Moslem to start with, Islam must seem an attractive alternative to the hard political wooing of the Soviets or the West's somewhat hypocritical paternalism.'

He leaned forward in his chair.

'Don't you see, George? It's pure. The Koran is pure, like the land. These are peoples of the land above all else. And of the desert.'

Mr Betts tapped Burroughs on his knee. He came to again, having been lulled by the heat from the fire and the old man's quiet voice.

'Don't forget either that we are talking of peoples with tremendous population masses. A basic oneness of cultures, far easier to mould to such a religious zeal than our splintered ideology, most of which we abandon when it suits us – like our faith.'

He wagged a finger at his guest. '*That* is what the Soviets fear, George! A gathering tide of Islam turning into a kind of . . . of Islamic super-power. On her back door, China presents a similar sort of threat.'

His finger lectured the air and he crinkled his faded blue eyes, seeing many things beyond the confines of his small Kentish living-room.

'There is nothing more dangerous than a huge mass of humanity when it is propelled by a single vision. Why do you think the Russians want to patch up their Communist differences with the Chinese after nearly twenty years? Brotherly love?'

The old man's chuckle blended throatily with the fire's coal-hiss.

'No! They *need* that combined bulwark to survive in the Super Power Game! No good Russian ever forgets that long ago the dread Tamburlaine swept out of Central Asia and occupied Moscow for over a year . . .

'Did you know his body still lies in its black onyx tomb at Samarkand?' he asked Burroughs suddenly. 'The rebellious Uzbeks trapped inside the USSR still believe he will return one day to lead them against the infidel Russian bear!'

He tapped Burroughs on the knee again, determined to hold his weary attention. It had been many months since he'd had the chance to exercise his brain with someone who should understand.

'There's your "expediences" for you, my boy. Russia *has* to court the Moslem world, just as we will have to. But she also needs to further their revolutions in the hope they will turn from the Prophet's greater glory to the greater glory of Marxism – '

Burroughs eased his back as his friend knocked out the remnants of his pipe into the fire.

' – or at least thank Mother Russia for her "support" by

making trade and military alliances with the Communist bloc rather than the West.'

He laughed again. There was little humour in it.

'The Soviets' little game has backfired on them, George. Now they're stuck with it. You and I can sit back and watch the Russians compete with the Americans for Islam's favours. And the Chinese will probably watch all three of them from the safety of Peking's wall-posters!'

He changed the subject abruptly.

'Is your Damascus man's cover good, George? You'll need to get in very close if you're really going to crack this conference of theirs. The KGB's obviously looking to all its influences on the international terrorist circuit as insurance at the moment.'

Mr Betts began to refill his pipe as he talked.

'I would guess that is why Carlos and half these other characters are there. To keep up the good work for the Marxist cause – and perhaps to remind their Arab friends of their obligations to Russia in terms of arms, technical aid and ideology.'

Burroughs shrugged wearily. 'What's safe in this game? He's an Information Officer with our Embassy. I think he's known to Syrian Intelligence. It's hard to be sure but they're no fools. He can only do so much and of course our beloved Director doesn't want to know.'

'Ah, Holman,' the old man smiled knowingly. 'You still a thorn in his side? Well, you'll be like me soon. Retired and out of it all.'

Burroughs grinned ruefully.

'He's a bloody tree trunk in *my* side, you mean! As for being "out of it", with Holman around I never feel *in* it!'

The old man laughed affectionately. 'Never mind, my boy. You'll look back on it all soon and be able to watch the birds come home to roost from a safe distance – the vultures, too. I think it's time for bed, don't you?'

He stood up stiffly, gripping Burroughs' arm with surprising strength when he saw his expression.

'Look, son. You can't fight all the world's troubles. We

live in an age of little men with little dreams for the most part, where there are no statesmen – only politicians.'

Burroughs tried to pull away gently but the old man held on to him fiercely.

'You've always done your duty but there's no room for the likes of you and me any more. We're scrap on the world's dump of forgotten honour, boy. Let those holding the strings these days pull up the cans, as they say.'

Burroughs put his arm around the old man's shoulders, noting how frail he was becoming.

'Too bloody right!' he laughed bitterly. 'Let's hope the can on the end of this one's so damned big it'll knock Holman right off his perch!'

CHAPTER FOUR

O'Neil lay awake in the lightening darkness, going over his meeting with the Syrian major. He had not been too pleased when O'Neil had told him he needed more time. And wanted to go to bed. But he had acquiesced. One extra day. That was all.

He glanced at his watch. Almost dawn. He must get some sleep if he was going to keep on top of these jokers. O'Neil wondered about this 'Hawk' laddie again and told himself to give it a rest. The plan was a gem. He'd push these heathens into backing it, come what may . . .

Sleep finally overtook him as the sun forced the darkness out of its way in a red orb of renewed energy.

The two figures in green combat suits and woollen hoods quietly slung their Israeli-made Uzi machine-guns over their backs and began to scale the high wall surrounding the silent villa.

It did not take them long. It took them even less time to reach the flat roof of the large, guarded house on Mohammed Zaid Street.

The night-sentry on the roof was sound asleep under a blanket. One of the raiders tapped him behind the ear with just enough force to ensure he would stay that way for some time to come. He'd have quite a headache when he woke up. It would serve him right for failing to do his duty.

O'Neil's locked door presented no problem to these men. The sleepy Irishman found himself staring into a pair of cold, hooded eyes before he'd a chance to react. The knife probing the skin at his throat said it all anyway.

The taller of the two raiders motioned him to get dressed. Quickly! Nobody found it necessary to speak. O'Neil knew it was pointless asking any questions. Submachine-guns have their own language. He was in trouble. Nobody was going to come to his rescue. Not at this time of the morning. He was on his own, with only the good Lord and his wits to help him.

His first thought was for Pat Docherty down the corridor, his second that that bastard PLO fellow had set him up. His third decided the Major wanted him out of the way, his usefulness outweighed by what he had seen and heard at the conference.

O'Neil pulled on his clothes but was damned if he would hurry to his death. The taller one prodded him impatiently with his Uzi's deadly snout and O'Neil swore softly to himself.

'We got a train to catch or something?' he inquired mockingly.

The taller one replied by smashing him across the face with his gloved fist. O'Neil steadied himself, tasting blood in his mouth. This boyo was really pushing it.

There was a noise outside the door. Both the raiders froze, concern showing in their hooded eyes. O'Neil laughed at them quietly through his split lips.

'Afraid, are you? What kind of men is it the Hawk has

around him, that have to take a man like thieves in the night?' he probed, guessing.

The tall one responded by lifting his fist again. O'Neil backed off, a grin twisting the swelling at the corner of his mouth.

'All right, my buckos. There's no need for that.'

He was just buckling his belt when they grabbed him from behind, pinning his arms at his back. He felt the handcuffs click home, viciously pinching his wrists. A blindfold snapped across his eyes, cutting out the dawn, and a voice whispered in his ear. 'Do as you are told, English.'

They bundled him out into the corridor, first checking it was clear. A hurried, stumbling journey saw them across the roof and down the outer steps to the courtyard.

The guard still lay in his induced slumber. The taller one grinned to himself under his hood. He would not like to be in that one's boots when he woke up. The Syrians were known to be merciless to those who failed them, especially their own.

O'Neil heard a car door being opened. He groped his way inside with some painful help from his captors. If he ever got out of this . . .

The small white Peugeot started up, driven by the taller of the raiders. O'Neil began to breathe deeply and regularly, forcing the air down into his lungs. He must stay calm and try to work out where they were taking him.

The Peugeot picked up speed, tyres humming on the narrow streets. He could hear the early morning sounds of the city. Engine noise bounced off the walls, their closeness slapping warm air against his face through the open windows. Perhaps it was going to be a sunny day. Better to die in the sunshine . . .

The passing noises began to change, to lessen. The air had become cooler and the tyres drummed on the smooth road with a dull monotony. He was sure they were on the main military highway out of Damascus, heading into the desert.

They were travelling very fast now. O'Neil had difficulty in staying upright as the car slewed round a bend. He reckoned they'd been going for a good hour and off the main highway for the last fifteen, twenty minutes.

The ride was getting bumpy. Loose stones clattered under the wheels, whanging against the chassis. Jesus, he was thirsty. His mouth felt dry. Are you afraid, Connor O'Neil? Dear God he was, but with a fearful kind of anger, and he'd die laughing in their stupid, hooded faces if needs be! Heaven help that lot in Damascus when Big Pat found out. He'd fell them like empty Guinness bottles in a pub brawl before they put *him* down! The car stopped suddenly. One of them spoke in Arabic to somebody outside the Peugeot. The door was yanked open. O'Neil crashed out into the growing sunshine on all fours. He spat sand. Sweet Mary, the indignity of it all!

He was assisted to his feet none too gently and frog-marched through a doorway, banging his elbow painfully as they brought him up sharply. The blindfold was ripped away without warning.

O'Neil blinked his eyes and found himself staring at a lean young Arab of about thirty. The Arab was flanked by three unblinking compatriots, their submachine-guns aimed in an uncompromising stitch across his heaving chest.

O'Neil knew instinctively that this was Hassan the Hawk. He looked like one. The face was dark and thin, prominent nose curved in a cruel beak; the head small, alert and proud. He could imagine him sweeping down on his prey with all the self-indulgent glee of that hunting bird.

The man stared at O'Neil's cut features. His eyes did not blink. It was as if his eyelids had been pinned back permanently by the burn scar running in a livid rumple of grafted tissue across his forehead, just above what remained of his eyebrows.

Perhaps he sleeps with the damned things open, O'Neil thought as his own eyes were drawn to the man's hands – or at least where they should have been.

The shock hit him like a bucket of cold water. He felt it

flushing over him. Poor bastard. He hadn't *got* any hands. Instead, two stainless-steel, double-hooked appliances extended from his wrists. On this man, they were talons.

Hassan Kassim got up from behind his makeshift desk and walked round to O'Neil. He pointed at O'Neil's mouth, which had started to bleed again, and shot an angry question in Arabic at his raiders. The tall one shrugged, muttering something in reply.

O'Neil smiled disarmingly at Kassim, determined he wasn't going to be intimidated by him.

'Well, Mister Hawk,' he opened lightly. 'I'd be obliged if you'd take these irons off me. Then I can shake your . . . hand. I always like to be properly introduced, don't you know?'

Hassan Kassim said nothing. He clicked a hook at one of O'Neil's hooded snatch-squad. The taller of his captors turned the key in the cuffs, freeing him. They dropped to the earthen floor with a metallic thud.

O'Neil rubbed at his wrists, said 'Thanks' and swung a haymaker of a right cross into the man's hooded face. He went down like a felled tree under the chopping blow.

Everything froze for a split second, then the other raider brought up his Uzi. Here it comes, thought O'Neil. It had been worth it.

Kassim raised a hook commandingly, knots of hard muscle rippling in his bared forearm.

'No!' He wanted this intriguing foreigner alive for the moment.

O'Neil stood dusting himself off and grinned brilliantly at him. Nobody took any notice of the prostrate guard.

'The fellow was a wee bit rough with me. And I don't take kindly to being called an Englishman. I had all that out at the conference, as no doubt you've heard.'

He wanted Kassim to know that he realised the PLO man he'd spoken with was the guerilla leader's inside man.

Kassim nodded and smiled back. It changed his whole face. He dipped a hook into one of the pockets of his short-sleeved military shirt and pulled out a packet of American cigarettes. O'Neil watched, quietly fascinated, as he adroitly hooked out a cigarette and lit it with a match on the heel of his boot.

'Yes, I have heard . . . Captain O'Neil,' he replied softly. 'It gave me pleasure that someone stood up to Major Khalid.'

His voice was surprisingly light, like the swish of a fast wing on still air, the English well-modulated. He noted the surprise on his captive's face and laughed out loud. It was a peculiar sound.

The men with him looked uncertainly at one another. They began to laugh as well. O'Neil joined in, not quite sure what it was all about but knowing the ice had been broken. He'd found his man.

When the laughter had died down, Kassim thrust out his right claw.

'You see, Irishman? We are not all camel-scratching savages. I was educated in England – at the London School of Economics.'

O'Neil smiled. He could imagine. The LSE had been a real hotbed of revolution in its time. He took the hook rather gingerly. Kassim laughed again and the claws closed on his fingers, vicing pain through his hand. He does like his little displays, thought O'Neil, determined not to show any discomfort.

The men around them grinned widely until Kassim released the claws with a click. O'Neil felt the blood rushing back to his fingers – it hurt almost as much as that damned hook. The guerilla leader nodded his head. O'Neil supposed he'd passed some kind of test. He found it all rather juvenile.

The man on the ground started to get up groggily, nursing his aching jaw. Kassim moved very fast, slashing him across the face with one of his hooks. It ripped through the woollen hood, drawing a crimson gout from the man's torn cheek.

Kassim said something to him harshly in Arabic and turned back to O'Neil as the man stumbled from the tiny house.

'I told him never to take anything for granted if he wished

to see his children grow into men. The scar will help to remind him.'

It was said carelessly, as if O'Neil's understanding of his actions did not matter to him. He smiled again. It was not returned this time.

'The Indians of Bengal have a saying about tigers, Connor O'Neil,' he remarked, regrouping his justification of such viciousness. 'If you see a pair of eyes blazing in the night, beware. It may be *two* one-eyed tigers!'

He threw back his small head and laughed again – a high, keening sound. O'Neil went cold inside. It reminded him of the noise a hawk made on its killing dive. He thought the man a little mad. He would need to be for what O'Neil had in mind.

The guerilla leader calmed suddenly, becoming very still. He stared at the lanky Irishman for a long time, an unwinking bird of prey on the desert lands he loved so much.

At last he spoke. 'You have something for me.' It was a statement, not a question. 'We will talk of it,' he added. 'Come!'

He scooped up a long white 'djellaba' cloak, flung it round his wiry shoulders and swept out of the house. O'Neil grinned to himself. Some character! It got more like *The Desert Song* every minute, he thought as he followed him out into the sunshine. Nevertheless, O'Neil accepted that the man's fanaticism, displayed in these little extremes of his, made him very dangerous. He would have to play this one carefully.

Kassim moved swiftly across the small village towards a white, clay-walled house, slightly larger than its neighbours. Villagers and his own men alike moved unquestioningly out of his path. The sun was well up now, the promise of a fine day in the offing. O'Neil hoped it was a good omen for the audacious proposals he was about to put in front of this strange young man with hooks for hands . . .

The house was cool inside. Kassim motioned him through into a large, sparsely furnished room. Its single, brass-bound table was piled high with maps, arms, boxes of ammunition – and carton upon carton of export American cigarettes.

Kassim indicated one of the canvas-backed chairs and sat himself down in another. Two of his men were already in the room, weapons slung over their shoulders with casual arrogance.

Hassan Kassim clicked a hook at them and said something softly in Arabic. The men grinned, threw amused glances in O'Neil's direction and closed the heavy door behind them as they went out.

This lot seemed very sure of themselves for a bunch of so-called freedom fighters who'd not done too much as yet, O'Neil thought. If this boyo reckoned he'd got himself some kind of an Irish clown to play with, he was just about to get the shock of his life.

He leaned forward, set on taking back the initiative he had originated in Damascus. Besides, lack of sleep was really getting to him now and he was in no mood to join in games of Eastern promise with this reject from a scrap-metal yard.

He picked up one of the Czech-made hand-grenades lying on the table, casually weighing it in his hand. He saw Kassim tense and was childishly pleased.

'Look, Kassim,' he came out bluntly. 'You might think you're the greatest thing on two hooks around this patch of sand but the real boyos in the PLO don't want to know you. I'm not sure I do either.'

He sat back, still holding the grenade. Kassim's face had gone very white under its dark skin. O'Neil guessed he had hit the right spot in the man's ego, and pressed home his attack. He'd only one chance to close a deal with this character. And he would do it his way.

'I've got an operation planned that'll need more balls than I fancy I'm going to find around here,' he jabbed again. 'But since you dragged me out of my bed without so much as a by-your-leave, you can damn well drop the games and listen.'

He paused, awaiting the guerilla leader's reaction. He was pushing his luck and he knew it. His thumb moved towards the grenade's flick-catch. If he had to fight his way out of here, he'd take this laddie with him.

Hassan El-Nesr Kassim did nothing, eyeing him coldly. One hook tapped a remorseless tattoo on the arm of his chair. O'Neil thought briefly that maybe he'd pushed him too hard.

Then Kassim laughed his shrill noise again and banged his steel hook against his chair in undisguised delight. O'Neil did not relax his grip on the grenade. Kassim clicked a hook at it, breathless from his madman's glee.

'It is not primed, my brave Captain!' he gasped. 'One thing they *did* teach me at the LSE was never to leave blank cheques lying around!'

O'Neil threw the thing back on the table. He couldn't help smiling.

'I didn't think it would be,' he countered lightly. 'But I could have beaten your brains out with it.'

Kassim roared. He liked this red-headed gambler. His hook beat another wild rhythm against the chair, and suddenly he reverted to that disconcerting stillness.

'Very well. What is this . . . operation of yours which needs my help so badly?'

'You need my operation as much as I need your help, friend,' O'Neil shot back at him.

Kassim inclined his dark, scarred head.

'That may be so, Connor O'Neil. I cannot judge until you tell me.'

He knew just how limited his successes had been so far, but it would take more than this amusing foreigner to make him admit to it. Yet.

O'Neil grinned fleetingly to himself, although the world-wide consequences of his gamble were far from funny. Bluff given and bluff called, my bucko. He got out of his chair, paced the length of the long, white room and turned abruptly on his heel, staring at the man whose fellow Arabs had romantically named 'Hassan the Hawk'.

'I am going to hijack the Queen of England's royal yacht.'

CHAPTER FIVE

George Burroughs did not enjoy his drive back to London. He felt dog-tired, like a spent fart in a North Sea gale. The weather was terrible, the journey tedious, and he always felt sad when he left old Mr Betts. He was never quite sure if he would see him again. Although his former mentor was unaware of it, Burroughs knew full well that his old friend was slowly dying of stomach cancer.

When he got back to Century House late that afternoon, there was a cryptic message waiting for him on his desk from Holman.

Report to me immediately you check in. DJH.

He screwed up the message slip and tossed it into his metal Ministry of Works wastepaper-bin.

'Oh Christ!' he muttered to himself. 'What's wrong with the little sod now?'

Sir David's own secretary was her usual coldly efficient self, so he got no joy from her as he sat outside his chief's office two floors above his own. He lit another cigarette and stared stolidly through the hard frown instantly creasing Miss Pymm's severity.

'Miss Prim', as the lower and more irreverent orders in Century House called her, was in her mid-fifties, tall, angular and dried up from years of looking after a querulous invalid sister and equally demanding senior Civil Servants. Such maternal instincts as had managed to survive now protected her present master with all the formidability of a dread-nought.

A green light winked impatiently on her desk intercom. She adjusted her glasses, pearl-rimmed, and arched her neck at him.

'You may go in now.' Her tone could have split an iceberg.

Burroughs was tempted to offer her some of the Arctic back but smiled nicely instead with exaggerated politeness.

'Thank you very much, Miss Pymm.'

The look she gave him bounced off Sir David's office door as he closed it behind him with a bang. Holman was standing by the window, his back to him. Burroughs wondered about sitting down because his legs were hurting, thought *To hell with it*, and sat.

His chief turned round, mouth tightening at the impertinence. The hand holding a clutch of decoded transmissions shook slightly. He was very angry.

Burroughs silently hummed his regimental march in his head and waited. The explosion, when it came, was rigidly controlled.

'You had no right, Burroughs. No right at all. You should have cleared any transmission with me. I instructed you quite clearly that this matter was in abeyance until and if I decided otherwise.'

Burroughs stood up, buttoning his jacket.

'I've been with the Department a damn sight longer than you have, with all respect . . . sir. If I can't get you to listen to years of bloody hard-won experience in this game, then what the hell *am* I supposed to do? Worry about upsetting some puffed-up Under Secretary in Whitehall while the Middle East blows up in all our faces?' Burroughs retaliated.

Holman had gone a very peculiar colour. Burroughs thought he was about to have a seizure and tried to remember the medical officer's extension number. No, better to let the little prig peg out. Then he might get something done around here.

Holman's fist cracked down on his desk. A silver-framed photograph of his county-bred wife, who spent most of her bored time in charity work avoiding the realities of an unsatisfactory marriage, stared disapprovingly at this unseemly

5

display of temper from a small mahogany table in the far corner. There was blood on Holman's fingers where he had skinned his hand on the edge of the desk. He ruined a spotless white handkerchief as he glared at his subordinate.

'How dare you! Retire shortly you may, but any further such . . . such arrant insubordination and I will have you suspended! Is that clear to you, Major Burroughs?' he demanded.

Burroughs stared back at him with open contempt.

'Yes, Sir David. It is clear. I just hope it is clear to you that I will continue to do my job as I believe it should be done right up to the day I retire from here.'

He paused to light a cigarette and blew a cloud of smoke in Holman's direction. If he was going to challenge him, he might as well go the whole hog.

'I think any Enquiry,' he went on, past caring, 'would back me up for the right reasons – even if yours didn't.'

Holman's face paled with fury at the embarrassing reminder, hands gripping the edge of his desk, white-knuckled. Burroughs hit at him again where he knew it would hurt.

'However, sir, if you wish I will tender my formal resignation from the Service right now. The Minister can decide whose experience is the more valuable.'

'I'm not interested in your resignation,' Holman struck back. 'Only that you observe the correct procedures. I have to answer to the Minister, not you. You may have felt your theories justified such a cavalier piece of action, Burroughs, but rules are rules.'

The yellow bastard's backing down, Burroughs thought. His small victory was taken away by his chief's next remark.

'Be that as it may, you will not send any transmission to a foreign station again without my personal signatured authority.'

Holman drew himself erect.

'I have reported Cook to his Departmental Head. I suggest you might learn something from the disciplinary action he is likely to receive.'

Burroughs' mouth set like a trap. He silently apologised to

his old friend for dropping him in it, vowed he would do something for Sammy Cook, and thrust his chin forward.

'Have you? Perhaps you'd be good enough to let me know what my Damascus man had to say?'

'Your man, Burroughs?' Holman queried coldly. 'Danvers works for this Department, not for you personally. Nor is the Communications Centre in existence for your personal radio traffic.'

Burroughs bunched his fists. Christ, he'd like to chin him. Much more of this crap and he would! Holman recognised he had gone far enough and stepped back from his desk slightly, holding out the yellow decoded sheets.

Burroughs literally grabbed them from him and began reading through Danvers' replies without a word.

When he had finished, he handed them back grim-faced, his annoyance forgotten among the implications of his operative's findings. He sighed, feeling curiously deflated. The anticlimax of being proved right?

'It's worse than I thought,' he commented grimly. 'They've got every political lunatic in the book there. Bloody Carlos *is* in on it, damn him. And Danvers confirms it was Colonel Solenov he spotted leaving a small hotel in the Malki Quarter.'

He sat down again, staring at his chief.

'There's a big one on all right. You saw that bit about the other man with Solenov? Danvers thinks it was General Zharkevsky himself. He's number two now to the KGB's big chief, Andropev.'

Holman nodded stiffly. 'I did. And I do not require a Who's Who in the KGB from you!' he snapped back. 'However, I am not prepared to sanction Danvers' request for a back-up operative at this time.'

He rapped his desk imperiously when Burroughs tried to interrupt.

'We have no hard facts that this conference is other than the usual Soviet intelligence-gathering from its Marxist sources.'

Burroughs felt the pressure building up in his chest again. God, the man was such a bloody fool!

'You can't be serious?' Disbelief pushed the anger off his tongue.

Holman eyed him coolly. 'I am perfectly serious, Burroughs. Danvers has only been working on your, ah, theories for little over twenty-four hours. When and if he produces something more substantial, then I might act on it.'

'Substantial!' Burroughs could not resist snorting. 'You don't call Zharkevsky's presence all the way from Moscow substantial?'

He leaned forward, intensity in his big hands.

'Look. I've been working on this thing for weeks now. Bloody months in fact. So's Danvers. I don't think there *is* any link between those medical sutures and this lot in Damascus, other than the obvious.'

'Obvious? I fail to see anything obvious so far,' Holman retorted.

The little prig would fail to see his own navel unless it was shoved under his nose. He would dearly love to achieve that physical impossibility for him, Burroughs thought and pressed on.

'The Syrians and Iraqis are bound to make some kind of move against this Sadat–Begin treaty, if it comes off,' he explained impatiently. 'So will the Libyans. That move will have to be a military one and I don't think against Egypt directly – she's too strong. They can hurt her a lot more by getting the Arab League to apply economic sanctions, like we are in Rhodesia. No, they'll pick on one of the weaker pro-Western states because, in their eyes, anyone with Western leanings is automatically a supporter of Israel against Arab interests.'

He snorted derisively, warming to his theme. Holman wished he'd hurry up and get it over with. He never kept his wife waiting. She wanted to go shopping, or something.

'The fact that a lot of the moderate sheikhdoms are unhappy with the way this Carter treaty is shaping up won't make any difference to the real fanatics like Gaddafi and his friends in the PLO.' His tone was impatient.

Holman glanced with equal impatience at his pocket-watch. 'Yes, yes. I understand all that but what has it got to do with Danvers or this conference, as you call it?'

Burroughs let out his breath in a hiss of exasperation. Why the hell should he hold this little dummy's penis for him?

'Surely you can see it?' he demanded. 'The Sadat–Begin treaty will go against everything the Marxists are trying to do. It will tread all over Arab unity and the PLO's cause and send the Syrians, Iraqis and Libyans round the twist.' He coughed on his cigarette.

'Their Soviet backers have already got themselves kicked out by the Egyptians. They can't afford to lose any more influence in the region. If the Gyppos gang up with Israel, bang goes a major toe in their plans for a real foothold out there – apart from the problem Russia's got with a switch-over to Islam.'

'Islam?' Holman frowned. 'I don't – '

'I'll explain that some other time,' Burroughs cut across him, snapping off points on his fingers like a man hewing wood. 'The Soviets would have to do something and they can only risk doing it through their Arab pals in the anti-West countries. With the SALT II talks on the stocks, they've got to get someone else to front any dirty work for them in the Mideast.'

He lit another cigarette without even bothering to stub out his last one in Holman's virginal ashtray. Holman fussily ground it out with a look of disgust. Burroughs ignored the silent reprimand as he turned over his thoughts.

'This little lot in Damascus cover the whole span of Soviet mischief-making in just about every trouble-spot you care to name, including the Middle East. The link is disruption of Western interests and better co-ordination with the Marxist factions they can call upon in any sensitive area they want to lock Islam out of by getting in first.'

He drew heavily on his cigarette.

'The Russians are playing for time. I'm sure of it. These

SALT II talks are pure bullshit and Carter's desperate enough politically to fall for it.'

He shook his head, swivelling in his chair to stare out of the window. He did not register Holman's look of distaste at his language and would not have cared anyway. He turned back to the desk.

'It's Chamberlain and Munich all over again. They'll smile at the West in one breath and use any terrorist cause going with the other to keep up the pressure anywhere they want control. And we're going to get shafted by our own stupidity.'

He banged his fist into his hand. 'That's what this conference in Damascus is all about!'

He sat back, feeling tired and drained. Holman was relieved.

'I think Danvers' cover is blown. He's clearly under surveillance and it'll tie his hands,' Burroughs continued. 'If you won't put in a legitimate field operative to help him, let me go out there and have a sniff around.'

Holman shook his head decisively and rose from his chair.

'Out of the question. We will wait and see what develops. Danvers may come through with something more positive for me to justify your . . . suppositions to my Minister.'

His face said the meeting was over. Burroughs shrugged and got up. He knew Holman would do nothing rather than ruffle any feathers in the high places he relied on to keep his tarnished career going.

'Very well, sir,' he replied tersely. 'But I intend to make out a full situation report and I want it sent up to "your" Minister.'

Holman flushed and sat down behind his desk again, the official barrier against all challenges to his authority. Burroughs thought rude things about him and waited for the blast.

'I am not concerned with what you want, Burroughs!' he snapped. 'It would be wholly pointless at this juncture. I have the facts, such as they are. You will clear any further intelligence you may glean on this matter through Mac-Allister. Is that understood?'

Burroughs nodded, saying nothing. He understood the gutless wonder all right but he was buggered if Holman was going to muzzle him on this one.

He left the office to his chief's cautious machinations, feeling angry and frustrated. Miss Pymm looked up from her advance post, machine-gun eyes trained on his passing.

Burroughs suddenly felt light-headed. He knew what he was going to do. Holman could scream the place down afterwards. It wouldn't matter a sod then. As for that virgin bitch he called a secretary . . .

He stopped and walked back to Miss Pymm's desk, giving her a broad, conspiratorial wink. She recoiled, horrified.

'Look,' he suggested quietly. 'Why don't you come round to my place after work tonight, get your knickers off and I'll give you a good time, eh?'

He was halfway down the corridor before Miss Pymm could even begin to unlock her face. The shock of his words shivered down her thin frame to regions untouched by human hand.

She was still trying to marshal her bodily functions, outrage and trembling limbs when Sir David swept by with a curt nod. Miss Victoria Pymm clung to her electric typewriter as if her life depended on it.

'That man. That awful man . . . ' she whispered to herself.

To a casual eavesdropper, it would not have been clear whether she meant George Burroughs or Sir David Jervais Holman, KCMG.

CHAPTER SIX

When O'Neil reappeared at the big house on Mohammed Zaid Street with Hassan El-Nesr Kassim, it was early evening. The silence in the conference room was total.

O'Neil walked straight up to Major Khalid at his solitary table and sat down, with Kassim. The major did not move a muscle but several of the guards on the fringes of the room had closed in, their guns very much in evidence. For all the complexities of his highly intelligent mind, O'Neil favoured simplicity in his dealings with others. His first question was therefore blunt and to the point.

'Where's Pat Docherty?'

Major Khalid removed his sunglasses and stared at him flatly. He had a large bruise on his cheek. Although his face showed little else, the lanky Irishman would have sworn Khalid was relieved to see him.

'Your lieutenant is . . . well,' the major answered slowly. 'Three of my men are in hospital. The man is an animal.'

'Cut up rough, did he?' O'Neil smiled back without sympathy. 'I thought he might. I asked you where he was.'

'In his room. Under guard,' Khalid shrugged stiffly. 'For his own safety.'

O'Neil shot him an enquiring grin and glanced at Kassim, who was sitting very still. The rest of the room remained equally silent.

'There are those here, Captain,' Khalid explained with quiet menace, 'who do not like the presence of . . . strangers.'

If Khalid's remark was aimed at Hassan the Hawk, he showed no reaction. His hooks lay quite still on his lap, like dead things. O'Neil filled the silence by pulling out his maps and notes on the spectacular plan he'd arrived at with the motionless guerilla leader.

'My friend and I have drawn up the "plan" you were wanting, though it might be a wee bit out of your league.'

He grinned at the major again and acknowledged Kassim's fleeting smile of thanks for his inclusion with a slight flick of his hand.

'I'm sure you'll accept my apologies for the delay in coming back to you, Major. I had some pressing business to attend to on behalf of this little caper.'

He paused, eyeing the grim intelligence officer with wry amusement.

'It was one of those offers you cannot refuse, don't you know?'

Kassim gave a shrill bark of laughter and O'Neil widened his smile into an unapologetic grin.

'How's the laddie who was guarding my beauty sleep?' he enquired innocently.

The major flushed. He knew these two were mocking him. They would pay for it later, as the guard had done. With their lives.

'I asked *you* for a plan,' he snapped back. 'Why have you brought this . . . man here?'

The words seemed to stick in his throat. O'Neil's grin widened until it threatened to split his face.

'Now now, Major,' he admonished. 'I thought we were all brothers for the cause?'

Khalid did not reply. O'Neil's blood sang. Squirm, you nasty little man, or go for your guns. He would ram his own right up the piddling major's nose if he didn't. Khalid remained silent.

'Mr Hawk and I have formed an association, my dear Major,' O'Neil challenged lightly. 'One of necessity I'd call it, since I'm not going to get what I need from the likes of you.'

He knew he was clowning it up a bit. He always did when he had a real fight on his hands. And this one he had to win.

'You're looking at Havoc Incorporated,' he went on in his

bantering tone. 'Of course, we might be willing to consider a bid from you to take a shareholding in our enterprise – at the right price.'

Khalid worked his jaw muscles, conscious of the whole room looking in on this trial of strength.

'You would do well to remember that I too can call the price – on your leaving my country alive or dead, Captain O'Neil,' he countered coldly in his stilted English.

O'Neil shrugged with exaggerated unconcern. 'Suit yourself, Major. You'd pay a higher price for my funeral than you might imagine.' His words were lined with steel.

He started to get up.

'Sit down!' Khalid's voice hissed across the silence.

'What do you want?' The major's question disappeared into the hatred icing his dead eyes.

O'Neil smiled his most charming of smiles and shifted on his chair.

'That's better, Major.' He pointed to the notes and maps lying between them on the table.

'It's all in there. I shall want an accurate, detailed breakdown of Her Majesty's itinerary in the Gulf from you – and all the arms on my list to do it with.'

Khalid frowned. 'Majesty? Who is this person?'

'Patience, little soldier,' O'Neil reprimanded gently.

He ignored the major's answering glare and indicated Kassim with a jerk of his red head.

'We've written you a bedtime story of kings and queens and handsome princes – and how even fairy tales can be made to go wrong. I'm sure you'll find it all quite fascinating ... and a darling idea.'

He smiled piratically and got to his feet again.

'Well now, Major. I'm getting awful weary. It's bed for me soon. No doubt you'll extend your hospitality to my fine new friend here. We're hungry, dirty and in need of a bath.'

O'Neil made it sound like an order. He stretched elaborately for his silent audience.

'I'm off to visit the animal Docherty, if it's all the same to you. I hope you've been nice to him. He's a holy terror when he's upset.'

He smiled brilliantly. 'Of course, you've found that out already.'

Khalid continued to stare at him coldly. O'Neil reached over the table and patted the startled Syrian's hand.

'You run along now like the good fellow you are and show our pretty plan to that other fancy gentleman of yours, eh?'

He glanced casually round the listening room, smiling softly. His blue eyes sparkled mischievously as he noted the intense interest of the watching delegates.

'Where is he, I wonder?' he mused and turned his gaze back to Major Khalid. The intelligence officer visibly gritted his teeth.

'My superiors will be informed of your return, Captain. You will not leave the house again. There will be guards on your door to see you obey me.'

He rapped the pile of papers separating them like a frontier.

'I will send for you if I consider there is anything of value to us in here, Englishman.'

O'Neil's smile tightened at the deliberate insult.

'At your service, I'm sure . . . tin soldier,' O'Neil muttered under his breath. He nodded cheerfully to Hassan Kassim and walked steadily out of the big room.

For a long moment there was nothing but the silence. Then a wave of loud chatter surged over the surrounding tables. Khalid rose coldly from his seat and curtly motioned the maverick guerilla leader to follow him.

They passed the PLO's resident liaison officer lounging on one of the cushioned benches. Kassim did not acknowledge him but Khalil al-Wazir smiled contentedly and took another long pull at his favourite brand of American cigarette.

'Big Pat' Docherty scowled blackly at the Syrian guard as he came into his small room. Although he was armed, the young soldier was careful not to come too close to his massive charge.

Docherty's fist still hurt like the devil but he was quite willing to add another of these heathen pigs to his current score. His scowl broke into a wide smile when he saw his Captain follow the guard through the door.

O'Neil took in his lieutenant's swollen hand and the vicious weal above his left eye. He smiled wryly at Docherty.

'I hear you've been running amok, my lad,' he greeted him quietly.

The giant shrugged his mountainous shoulders.

'They kept on asking me what'd become of you,' he rumbled. 'I got bored with it. You all right, Captain?'

O'Neil nodded. He could imagine Big Pat flicking his tormentors off his back like flies. He also knew from harsh experience that the giant would readily kill anyone who tried to harm his beloved Captain. O'Neil sometimes found such doglike devotion difficult to cope with. He grinned affectionately at his lieutenant.

'Sure I am. You mustn't go upsetting the natives. It's all a wee bit primitive in these dark outposts, don't you know.'

He laughed shortly, his tiredness showing.

'They still cut off your balls out here, Pat. Then what would that pretty colleen of yours do?'

Docherty grinned back at him, scratched his crotch and got off the bed. He had to stoop to avoid the ceiling. The guard took a step backwards towards the safety of the door.

'Is that a fact, Captain?' Docherty sniffed and then grinned again. 'I should think my wife'd be glad of the rest. It's four kids we've got already.'

He stared out of the small, iron-grilled window, thinking about that other son of his from way back.

'I suppose she's given birth by now. I wanted a boy.'

O'Neil patted the giant's shoulder. It was like touching rock. In the confusion and pace of the last few days, he'd quite forgotten that Docherty's wife was expecting any day now. So far, she had borne the man nothing but daughters. No wonder he wanted to get home.

'She'll be fine,' he assured him. 'Father Rattigan promised he'd keep an eye on things. I'll try and find out what you've got yourself when I next make contact with the Brigade.'

Docherty nodded glumly. He hated it here and it all seemed to no good. Maybe the Captain would change all that. He needed to.

O'Neil fished out one of the packs of American cigarettes Kassim had given him, offered it to his lieutenant and then to the guard. The soldier shook his head and took a firmer grip on his automatic rifle, staring at O'Neil. These foreigners were very strange. You locked them up and they showed you friendship.

'We're getting somewhere, Pat,' O'Neil continued quietly. 'I've found just the laddie for our operation. Rather, he found me.'

He laughed softly, rubbing at the tiredness in his eyes.

'You'll meet him later, no doubt. A couple of his side-kicks snatched me very neatly from my bed. Left the guard with a thumping headache! I ended up in some village way out in the desert. It seems to be his base at the moment. Fell out with the PLO and then Habash. Couldn't get them to do anything, so he tells it.'

He shook his head, reliving his dramatic introduction to Hassan Kassim.

'Bit of a wild stallion, more like. Wants to run his own herd but he'll do for what we've in mind.'

Docherty frowned, grinding his cigarette out on the stone floor.

'You're meaning this Kassim? I don't like the feel of him at all,' he growled.

O'Neil grinned at him wryly. 'Come on, Pat! There's not a man born you like who's not a Catholic or in the Brigade!'

The giant shrugged again. 'Nothing wrong in that, Captain. You know where you are with your own. I'm thinking of those National Front mules last year . . . and that business with the American,' he reminded him gruffly.

He would follow the Captain through hell itself if necessary, but thought some of the outcasts O'Neil had chosen to run with in the past both outside the high standards exacted within the Brigade – and less than useless.

Because he was always slow to say much, Docherty was aware that even the Captain thought him dull in the head. But he'd been taught as a child to keep his own counsel. Until he'd grown big enough to break his brutal father's drunken neck with a single blow.

The five hard, long years he spent in prison had reinforced that principle. From the day he came out, on his twenty-third birthday, and through all the intervening twenty-one years of a turbulent life, he had preferred to express his opinions in actions. There were enough jabberers in the Movement as it was.

O'Neil well understood the reasons for his lieutenant's suspicions. The joint operation proposed by the National Front, and to be funded by them, had turned out to be a disastrous comedy. The same had been true of his brief flirtation with NORAID's people in the States, there was no denying that. Only his last three independent operations had been really good and hard-hitting, apart from the bank raids around Ulster.

Nevertheless, a maverick unit the likes of which he was running had to consider every opportunity which came up. And he believed he'd struck oil this time with Hassan Kassim.

'I think you'll take to the laddie,' he reassured Docherty. 'He's quite a card for a man with no hands.'

Docherty looked puzzled but O'Neil declined any further explanation. He stretched, cracking aching muscles.

'I'm away to my bed, Pat. That fancy Syrian major's got our proposition on paper now. It makes for a pretty story.' He smiled piratically. 'I'm betting the gallant major'll bite on it. If he doesn't, we'll be hard put to get out of here alive, my bucko.'

Docherty grunted and held up a huge fist, staring darkly at the guard. The young soldier hefted his rifle at him, puny in defence, and took a step nearer to the doorway.

'Let them try an' stop us,' he rumbled ominously.

'Oh, they'd try all right,' O'Neil chuckled. 'But I fancy we'd take a few of theirs with us!'

He punched the giant lightly in the chest.

'It'll not come to that, I'm thinking. You get some sleep now. I'll see you in the morning.'

O'Neil turned on his heel, nodded pleasantly to the guard and made his way through the door. It slammed behind the soldier, finality on the night.

Docherty heard the key turn in the lock and went back to his bed. He sat down heavily, frowning to himself. He would trust the Captain with his life but he still didn't like the smell of this thing at all, Arabs were Arabs and not to be trusted. No doubt about that.

Suddenly he laughed, thinking about the devilish twinkle in his Captain's eye when he'd first put up this madcap scheme. If anyone could pull it off, your man was James Connor O'Neil. He remembered what a top Provo back home had once said about O'Neil: when he wasn't working with Connor O'Neil and his Madigan's Brigade, he wondered what the devil found to do in the afternoons?

Maybe it'd work out after all. And the giant laughed again as he got ready for his bed.

The young soldier guarding Docherty's locked door heard him laughing and shook his head. Truly, all these foreigners were a little crazy . . .

Burroughs telephoned Sammy Cook's home from his flat that evening. Cook's wife was not very receptive. No, she didn't know when he was coming home, Mr Burroughs. He would have to ring back later – if he wanted to.

Burroughs said he did and would. He put the receiver down with a grimace. He'd had Sam and Mary Cook round to his place for dinner a few times over the years and been to their home in Chiswick. It had never been with any great frequency, admittedly. He'd not got to know Mary well but things had always been friendly and she seemed a nice if somewhat dull woman.

He supposed Sam had really got a fly up his nose over this business with Holman and his DH. Christ, what a miserable little tyke Holman was!

He got up from his small antique bureau and went over to the drinks cupboard. Maybe a whisky would ease his headache. Must be tension. Burroughs downed it in one and poured himself another. It didn't seem to help.

Cigarette smoke joined the whisky warming his throat. What a lousy way to make a living. The friends you didn't send to their deaths – or worse – on field operations, you put at risk without even knowing it in a minefield of petty-fogging bureaucrats who ran all their lives. And with a twisted bastard like Holman helping to pull the strings, nobody was safe!

He splashed some more whisky into his glass. Perhaps Mr Betts was right. He'd be a darned sight better off out of the whole rotten, rule-ridden business. Patriotism seemed to be a dirty word around Whitehall these days. Breaking people who broke the bloody 'rules' appeared to have more importance than either the jobs they were trying to do or the beliefs they were meant to represent.

Burroughs looked at his watch. Nearly 9 p.m. Might as well watch the Nine o'clock News and then try Sammy again.

He turned on the set, pushing the button for BBC 1 – he distrusted the commercial interests that governed ATV. It took a few minutes for the sound and picture to find each other on the old EKCO television. It really was time he got the bloody thing replaced.

When the image appeared, Burroughs wondered why he'd bothered. A television journalist – one of an ever-growing army of media super-sleuths – was expounding his latest, on-the-spot situation report from the Lebanon. He snipped away at that unfortunate country's torn history, using an armoury of clever phrases and very little real understanding.

Burroughs sighed and thought about turning the thing off again. It made him want to throw up. Another long-haired know-it-all thinking he'd got all the answers off pat, just because he'd been shot at. Should try swapping jobs with him for a week and see how it really was!

He knew he was being unfair. The immediacy of television reportage demanded instant solutions to the news and the journalist was probably working under pressure from an impatient editor in London.

Burroughs looked at his watch again. Ten more minutes of this crap before the News. He could get his typewriter set up for his report in that time.

He grinned to himself. Holman would go spare. It could cost him his own job. Never mind. Better to go out with a bang than a whimper – not as T. S. Eliot would have it. He was due to step down soon, as Holman kept reminding him, so what did it matter?

He took his ancient portable typewriter out of its case and placed it on the dining-room table, hoping it still worked all right. Having sorted the copious notes he had already made, he wound a sheet of Her Majesty's Stationery Office foolscap into the machine and stepped back. Right. Ready to go, Sir bloody Holman.

He turned to go into his lounge again and stopped dead. Good God! What if Miss Pymm was really to turn up?

The idea amused him greatly. He was still laughing about it as he went back into his sitting-room to hear the first of the seemingly endless crises which made up the BBC's Nine o'clock News.

Sir David Holman undressed with clockwork precision, neatly placing his clothes in their various designated resting places. His light grey suit, properly zippered into its plastic cover, hung back in the wardrobe among the numbered row of suits he always wore in strict rotation.

Today's socks, collar-detached shirt, vest and underpants were carefully dropped into their individual wicker laundry baskets for the maid in a routine that was rigidly adhered to, whatever kind of a day it had been. Tomorrow's suit and its accoutrements were already laid out on a long wooden clothes frame, awaiting his 7 a.m. pleasure.

Holman got into a pair of dark blue silk pyjamas and dutifully walked through the communicating door to his wife's bedroom. She was sitting up in bed reading a detective thriller. If his wife was also awaiting his pleasure, she did not get much of a reward from the brief peck on the cheek he gave her before returning to his own bedroom.

Lady Holman put down her book with a sigh as he quietly closed the door, and wondered what was eating at him this time. She switched off the bedside lamp, turned on to her side and directed her thoughts to the next day's three charity committee meetings.

Sir David climbed into his single bed with equal neutrality and lay on his back for a while, thinking about his latest confrontation with George Burroughs. How he detested the man! There were days, more frequent of late, when he cursed ever having accepted his face-saving post with the Department.

The big town apartment house just off Westminster's Smith Square stood silently under a snow-greyed moon. Ice and snow combined to wink coldly on the surrounding streets.

An old stray dog limped across the deserted square, growled briefly at the down-and-out huddled in a side entrance of Transport House, and quickened its pace as hunger gnawed a reminder to its empty belly.

A patrolling police car stopped to move on the wino. It took two of them to drag him to his feet. His language echoed in a loud slur of abuse against the unsympathetic buildings as he shambled away.

The junior of the three officers in the vehicle, not yet hardened to the realities of his job, was moved to comment on the irony of the derelict choosing the Labour Party's headquarters as a place to seek shelter.

The two older officers showing him the ropes laughed at his sensitivity and the young policeman's soft shell unconsciously began to grow its first layer of hardness.

London settled into sleep. Her citizens dreamed their dreams – or lay awake with Sir David Holman, waiting for the dawn to still their fears.

CHAPTER SEVEN

Clive Danvers pulled his battered Mercedes quietly into the far end of Mohammed Zaid Street and settled down to wait. Fortunately it was his day off from his job at the British Embassy as an Information Officer in the Commercial Section.

He enjoyed his work and was thought to be rather good at it. Only the Ambassador and Head of Chancery knew of his duality as an SIS agent. He was never sure if the Ambassador approved or not. Her Britannic Majesty's representative was a courteous man by nature and would not have openly showed his disapproval of such necessary bulwarks to the gentler machinations of diplomacy.

Danvers had been in Damascus for nearly two years. In that time, he had built up a useful if small network of 'friendly' contacts within the dangerous world of Arab politics and intrigue. The limited funds allotted to him by Whitehall doubtless helped in a country where the wealth was typically in the hands of the few and poverty still dragged itself through the noisy streets on deformed limbs and swollen bellies.

He had joined the Diplomatic Service after a stint as a short service commission officer in the Light Infantry. He liked soldiering but found the life rather too narrow for his tastes. A career on the fringes of diplomacy had seemed to offer a wider scope and he could put his post-Army business degree to good use.

When he'd first been approached by the SIS during his annual furlough from his initial embassy post in Cairo, he was both flattered and intrigued. It had not taken him long to make up his mind. Five years serving with the SIS had taught him that most of the work in any kind of espionage consisted of painstaking research, patient enquiry and the routine sifting of seemingly unrelated information into credible patterns for counter-intelligence action.

In the real world of spies and spying, James Bond would have proved a massive embarrassment to all concerned.

Danvers wound down his window. It was going to be another hot day. He thought about the letter he'd just received from his mother in England. Her graphic description of the weather conditions back home made him glad to be out of it.

Danvers liked George Burroughs. They had only met infrequently in all the time he had worked for the Department and all but one occasion had been at the London headquarters during leave periods. The exception was a memorable night on the town together which had turned a working relationship into friendship, bound by a common dislike of their recently appointed chief, Sir David Holman. That was nearly two years ago.

He shared Burroughs' present concern over this terrorist meeting on his patch. It didn't look too healthy. Although a lot of questions still had to be answered, he was sure the conference at the house down the street was something out of the ordinary. It was risky for him to mount such an open piece of surveillance, but time was not on his side. The last message from London had made the urgency quite clear. His own contact within the conference had fed him some useful titbits but the man was frightened and wary of discovery. Danvers was not too sure when he'd hear from him next.

His own position was far from secure, come to that. Instinct rather than hard proof told him that Syrian Intelligence were on to his activities – or at the very least suspected him. He would have to be careful.

O'Neil had not slept well, despite being so tired. There was too much on his mind for that. He was still feeling somewhat jaded when the guard slammed in with his breakfast and banged it down on the small mosaic table without a word. His minders had obviously changed shifts. This one was big, ugly and surly.

He picked at the plate of sweetbreads without enthusiasm, decided he really couldn't face them and sipped his way through the sickly Arab coffee he disliked so intensely.

Docherty was having much the same sort of problem with his food. It was an insult to a man of his size and appetite. Sweet Jesus, what he wouldn't give for a double helping of bacon and eggs, lashings of Gallagher's sauce and a smooth glass of Guinness! He wondered if the Captain was getting the same treatment as he tried to make the best of the meagre offering.

O'Neil was just finishing his coffee when the door crashed open again. His guard jerked a thumb at him. 'You! Come!'

O'Neil did not get up off his bed. He gazed quizzically at the soldier.

'You're an uncouth fellow, are you not?' he smiled quietly. It did not reach his blue eyes.

The guard brought up his rifle and stepped further into the room. Foreign pig. The message was clear enough. O'Neil stood up. He pushed the gun to one side.

'Have a care, soldier boy. I'd hate that thing to go off in here. I've got a murderous head this morning.'

He walked out into the corridor nonchalantly. If his guard understood, it made no difference. He fell in behind his charge and prodded him in the back with his rifle. O'Neil stopped and turned round, waving a finger slowly under the man's nose.

'Do that again,' he said conversationally, 'and I'll ram it right down your miserable throat.'

The guard blinked. O'Neil's tone would have been difficult to misinterpret. He wiped a hand across his nose and motioned his prisoner on with a surly wave. The rifle did not touch O'Neil again.

O'Neil naturally made for the conference room. The guard stepped in front of him, shaking his head angrily.

'No!'

He pointed to another door impatiently. It was closed. O'Neil shrugged, opened it and walked in.

Major Khalid was seated behind a more conventional desk. He had O'Neil's notes and map spread out in front of him. The room was devoid of any character. Just four walls, the desk with two telephones on it, and a small square of woven carpet on the stone-flagged floor.

Kassim and Docherty had already been brought to the room and stood silently flanked by their guards. The Deputy Foreign Minister's man was again absent. Khalid was in uniform. The row of medal ribbons on his tunic surprised O'Neil. Perhaps there was more to the man than met the eye.

'I have read your suggestions, Captain,' Khalid said coldly in his stilted accent. 'We will discuss it in detail. Now.'

O'Neil's expression did not change. If this piece of camel dung thought he was going to drop on his knees in gratitude, he could think again.

'Have you now?' He jerked his head at the soldiers. 'We'll discuss it all right but I want these goons of yours out of here – and something for me and my friends to sit on.'

There were no chairs in evidence other than the major's. Khalid's mouth tightened and his eyes narrowed behind his sunglasses. Never would he take to this impudent foreigner but the man's plan was both exciting and excellent. Its success could alter the whole balance of power in the Middle East. His own success would be assured as well. Beyond that, he was now under strict orders from his superiors to co-operate with these men and make a deeper assessment before the plan was put up to their Soviet comrades.

He spoke in his own tongue to the guards. They were to wait outside. One of them could bring three more chairs – and some coffee.

The guards filed out. A few moments later, three upright chairs were introduced into the meeting. The door closed again. No one had moved. Khalid gestured at the chairs and forced his face into the semblance of a smile.

'Please sit down . . . gentlemen. I have told them to bring coffee.'

O'Neil exchanged glances with Kassim. Things were looking up.

'Thank you, Major,' he responded. 'I was sure we could do business together.'

One smile was all Khalid could bring himself to manage. He nodded stiffly. 'We may, Captain. Your plan has caused . . . interest. We are pleased with it,' he conceded. Graciousness was not one of his fortes.

'Not my plan, Major – ours,' O'Neil corrected him gently. 'My associates here had a lot to do with it.'

Khalid acknowledged O'Neil's observation with another stiff nod.

'That is so. But you will be – how do you say it? – the whipping boy if your plan fails. We will go through it and see.'

He removed his sunglasses and bent to O'Neil's notes. O'Neil settled himself more comfortably on his chair and handed round his cigarettes to Kassim and Docherty. It looked like being a long meeting. He just hoped his cigarettes and his thirst would last out. The thought of having to drink any more of that coffee . . .

Danvers stared at his watch again. He'd been there for nearly three hours and seen nothing of interest. Nobody had entered the gated courtyard, or come out. It was stifling in the car. He couldn't risk hanging about much longer.

Suddenly he stiffened. There was movement at the far end of the long, narrow street. Although he was a good three hundred yards from the house, Mohammed Zaid Street ran in an unimpeded straight line and his excellent sight was prudently aided by the macro-zoom lens on his new OM2 Olympus camera.

The gates were swinging open. A Syrian military jeep

nosed its way into the street. Danvers brought up his camera and adjusted the focus. He instantly recognised Major Khalid of Syrian Intelligence as he worked the camera's automatic repeater-shutter, but who were the three men with him? Should have got some good shots anyway.

He started up his car. He'd have to follow them. Two of the men were Europeans, he was sure of that. He could feel he was on to something important.

The jeep pulled away rapidly, turning into the maze of walled streets at speed. Danvers hung back as far as he dared. He must not lose them. They were bound to come out on to one of the main squares in the end. Then he could chance passing them for a better look.

Khalid continued to drive fast. It was unfortunate that he had to take these men to his Ministry in broad daylight, but certain things could be arranged more efficiently from there.

O'Neil was sitting next to him. Docherty had managed to wedge his giant's bulk into the back of the jeep with Kassim. If the hood had been up, it would have proved impossible. He was trying to give the little Arab as much room as he could. Docherty still didn't trust him and even more didn't fancy coming into contact with those evil hooks of his. They looked as if they could tear a man's heart out. But it was good to be away from that stinking house.

They swung out of the labyrinth of bumpy sidestreets into one of the large squares. O'Neil glanced into the wing-mirror again. Still there. He tapped the Syrian on his shoulder.

'I think we're being followed. He's been on our tail ever since we left the house.'

Khalid glanced at him, puzzled. 'Who?'

'The grey Mercedes!'

O'Neil had to shout above the increased traffic noise in the square. Khalid's eyes flicked up to his driver's mirror, suddenly alarmed. The car seemed familiar. It was difficult to tell who was driving. There were other vehicles between them and it. He had to concentrate on the road in any case.

The standard of driving in Syria was suicidal at the best of times.

The khaki jeep travelled right round the big public square, forced to a slower pace by the volume of traffic. The grey Mercedes stayed with it, although well back.

Khalid made a decision. He abruptly swung the jeep across the flow of cars and pulled up sharply on the edge of the square. Hooted protests followed his reckless manoeuvre.

Danvers cursed. There was no way he could stop too. He was right on top of them. He turned his head slightly as he drove past. Didn't know the red-headed chap. The big one in the back was a real giant – and the thin Arab with the hook . . .

Good Christ! Danvers nearly hit another car. Hassan Kassim! What was *he* doing with Khalid of all people? It didn't make sense. Kassim was *persona non grata* with just about everybody who counted in the PLO and their supporters. He *had* to get back to the Embassy. The sooner he got his pictures developed and off to London the better . . .

Khalid stared hard at the Mercedes as it shot past him and picked up speed. He knew that face, surely? Of course! The young Information Officer from the Commercial Attaché's office at the British Embassy. Captain Assad had been keeping an eye on him for suspected intelligence activities. Now they had something. He must deal with him, and quickly.

Although he did not fully realise it, Khalid had made a bad mistake. In braking so hard, he had forced Kassim to cling to the side of the jeep, exposing one of his hooks. The guerilla leader's face was not well known, even inside the Marxist Arab states, but – since blowing off his hands with a faulty timing device on a raid into Israel – the steel hooks he carried as his most visible scar had become legendary amongst the Middle East terrorist organisations. It was rumoured that Kassim had killed with the things, literally decapitating his victims.

By stopping the jeep at all, the Syrian intelligence officer had made another grave error of judgement. It had enabled

Danvers to get a good look at the other two men with Kassim – good enough to clarify for him any blurring there might be on his hastily taken photographs.

Khalid shook his head and started up the jeep again. O'Neil leaned towards him, equally grim-faced.

'Who was he, Major?'

'He will be dealt with.'

'I'm sure he will, Khalid,' O'Neil persisted, steely-toned, as they continued their interrupted journey. 'But I want to know exactly what you know about him. Right now.'

Khalid's narrow mouth tightened further. 'He is nothing. A minor official at the British Embassy here.'

He decided against adding that his people had been watching Danvers for some time. O'Neil was not satisfied. Nor was Kassim.

'Why should a minor official be so interested in us? You know the answer, I think.' Kassim spoke in English for O'Neil's benefit.

Khalid's back stiffened. To be interrogated in this manner by these criminals. 'There is nothing more,' he replied shortly.

Kassim leaned forward and gripped the major's shoulder with one of his hooks, squeezing.

'Major,' he hissed softly in his ear. 'I can break your bones so very easily. That would be a pity. There *is* more you can tell us.'

He increased the pressure. The Syrian winced with a combination of pain and embarrassment. This was intolerable. He would lose control of the jeep.

He swore at Kassim in Arabic. It only encouraged the guerilla to tighten his grip. Khalid thought about trying to get his revolver out of its buttoned holster. He knew he'd never manage it without running the very real risk of having his neck severed by those murderous hooks. Kassim was known to be quite capable of it. It was said he was close to madness. In any case, Khalid had his orders and could not trigger off a shooting in public. None of them needed that kind of publicity or attention. The business with this Danvers was bad enough.

Khalid swore at Kassim again. It was really hurting now. He could feel the vicious double claw cutting through his tunic.

'Very well, dog of dogs!' he spat out.

Kassim smiled faintly and released his hook with a click. It left a jagged rent in the major's tailored uniform.

'I am pleased. We should all be friends,' Kassim mocked him.

Khalid eased his bruised shoulder, a deep flush of anger staining his features.

'You will go too far, little sparrow,' he ground back. 'I can have your wings clipped so you drop to the earth and stay there! All of you – I hold your lives! Remember that!'

He slammed his foot down on the accelerator. The jeep leapt forward. Kassim lifted his hook again with a sudden anger equalling the major's. Docherty's huge paw shot out and caught the guerilla's arm in its massive strength. The giant rumbled into a deep belly-laugh.

'What a nonsense of man you are, Khalid!' Docherty ribbed him. 'You'll do no such thing to a comrade of mine, whoreson. There are those above you who want us now, so you've said yourself. I'd snap your spine if ever you tried.'

The giant was surprised to find himself defending Kassim. O'Neil grinned gently. Maybe he'd make a team of them yet.

'You have something to tell us, Syrian,' Kassim reminded the major and gave Docherty a friendly nod of thanks.

Khalid scowled. They would all answer to him when he was ready. 'The man is named Danvers,' he replied with sullen reluctance. 'We suspect him of working for British Intelligence. He is being watched. Now I will deal with him.'

'You better had, Major,' O'Neil sniffed. He sounded unconvinced, his eyes glinting dangerously in the bright sunlight. He sniffed again. 'Or the operation's off and you can explain *that* to your Moscow pals. I fancy they'd clip your wings before they got round to ours, laddie.'

'I have said it will be done,' Khalid retorted tightly. He

turned the jeep into another narrow street and drew up outside a faceless modern building. There were armed soldiers guarding it from behind a fence of heavy-duty wiremesh. The building's opaqued windows were all barred. Grimness seemed to be the watchword. It was not a place to enter lightly or get out of again easily.

'We are here,' Khalid announced coldly.

They climbed out of the jeep and followed him in silence into the stark Military Intelligence headquarters. The guards stared at the sheer size of Pat Docherty but the armoured main door was opened instantly to the major and his party.

They disappeared from sight for their meeting with destiny as the door promptly closed behind them again with an ominous clang.

CHAPTER EIGHT

Two hours and several phonecalls later, they emerged from the joyless building and were driven back to the house on Mohammed Zaid Street by a Syrian military policeman. Major Khalid remained at his office – to arrange the next meeting in a chain of command that stretched all the way to the Kremlin.

The journey back was made in complete silence. There had been enough talking for one day and each man stayed with his own thoughts on the amazing undertaking now becoming a reality.

O'Neil felt quietly elated. The whole shebang was really getting off the ground. The Deputy Foreign Minister's representative had set the tone of the meeting in Khalid's office with his soft-spoken presence.

Yes, the plan had been approved in principle. It would,

however, still require the final sanction of their Russian 'advisors'. Captain O'Neil and El-Nesr Kassim could expect to be summoned to meet with them shortly. The Minister's man was confident of the outcome.

O'Neil went over the details of the astonishing operation, checking off the logistics of it all in his head as the jeep sped back across the city.

The British Queen and her husband were due to commence their royal tour of eastern Arabia on 12 February 1979. Their historic visit to the pro-Western Gulf States was known to include Saudi Arabia, Kuwait, Oman and Bahrain. They would be arriving in Kuwait by Concorde for the first leg of their tour, and then sailing on to Bahrain in the royal yacht.

That much was certain at this stage. Their exact itinerary would have to be obtained through Syrian Intelligence and diplomatic sources and by O'Neil's people back home. Apart from the itinerary, they must get hold of a detailed plan of the royal yacht's layout. That was one of his designated tasks. They'd also need to know what arms were kept on board, and roughly the number of officers and men making up her complement, including their varied functions.

Another essential was a breakdown of the security arrangements on board, the security personnel involved, and so forth, who would be travelling with the royal couple.

It could even take longer than estimated to gather all the information required, but training for the daring mission had to begin at once – if they were to be ready in time. The tour was now less than two months away. It was not very long for O'Neil and Kassim to mould their force into a deadly and effective fighting machine, capable of pulling off the hijack of the century.

Whenever the tour officially ended, it was assumed the Queen and Prince Philip would return home on the royal vessel, taking the opportunity for a leisurely recovery from what was undoubtedly going to be an arduous if unique visit.

Since Syrian Intelligence already knew that the royal tour had been scheduled to terminate in the Oman, *Britannia*

93

would inevitably sail for home by the shortest route available to her – via the Suez Canal. The British Royal Family were known to be anxious to set an example in these energy-conscious times.

O'Neil rubbed at his eyes, tiredness still with him, forcing his brain to grapple with the operation's ramifications.

From the point of view of controlling the royal yacht's seizure, the isolated and well-named Bitter Lakes in the middle of the Canal's long, narrow waterway provided an ideal striking-ground. That too would need to be carefully surveyed – a task assigned to Hassan Kassim and his unit.

Any attempt to grab the *Britannia* during the actual tour itself had to be foolishly suicidal. The security precautions surrounding the Queen were likely to be unprecedented. It was better to wait until it was all over and a more relaxed atmosphere prevailed aboard the royal yacht as she steamed for home.

It was also already common knowledge, and the talk of the souks, that the fabulously oil-rich chieftains of the Gulf sheikhdoms planned to vie with each other in presenting Her Majesty with priceless gifts with which to demonstrate their vast wealth. Thus it had been agreed at the meeting that the killing of two birds with one stone made the plan doubly attractive to all concerned. Not only would their world-shaking hijack cause major political repercussions but net them a fortune in gold, silver and precious gems, worth millions.

Add to that all the personal treasures belonging to the Royal Family already on board the royal yacht, and the *Britannia* would be turned into a floating mint – and a 'royal mint' at that.

O'Neil chuckled softly to himself. Hassan Kassim stared at him and wondered what fresh piece of devilry was passing through the lanky Irishman's fertile mind. If O'Neil had known what else the guerilla leader was thinking, he might not have been quite so amused.

The jeep was nearing the end of its return journey. O'Neil

turned in his seat and gave his lieutenant a reassuring wink. 'I've a fancy we're going to pull this thing off, Pat.'

It was the first time anyone had spoken since they had left Khalid's office. The giant nodded, saying nothing. The little Arab still worried him for some reason he couldn't fathom. He'd bear watching.

Kassim stared blankly at the walls as the jeep roared on through the claustrophobic sidestreets. His hawkish face gave nothing away.

O'Neil returned to his own thoughts. The whole idea was a real dandy. Dear Christ, the repercussions hardly bore thinking about.

He'd never been genuinely interested in the Middle East's complex problems – who the hell could ever understand these Arabs? But he recognised the immense kudos both Madigan's Brigade and Kassim's outfit would command from the 'international terrorist fraternity', as they were described by the media.

'Fraternity'? He smiled to himself at the description. It was more a brotherhood of necessity than anything else, most of them at the beck and call of Moscow's faceless manipulators and all of them really only interested in the fight as it related to their own political backyard. Nevertheless, it was a 'brotherhood' he would be able to call upon without question – *if* this operation was the stunning success he intended it to be.

Both he and Kassim needed a major coup. O'Neil knew that only too well. But the wider implications of the raid were not lost on him. He had pointed most of them up, admittedly at first as window-dressing in order to get the help he needed out here, but now they truly excited and almost appalled him in their consequences.

With the Queen and Prince Philip held at gunpoint alongside the yacht's crew, there was not a government on earth who'd dare to stop them getting away again after the raid. Of course, no real harm must come to either the Queen or her immensely popular consort. Their deaths or serious injury would lose the raiders any sympathy they had gained, and the whole world would turn to hunting them down without mercy.

And therein was O'Neil's greatest problem, personally and professionally. He was not interested in holding heads of state for ransom nor in the murderous tactics of the Provos in killing prominent figures to make their point. He had heard many such ideas put up in the past, from commando-type raids on Buckingham Palace to poisoning the water supply on the British mainland. To him, such schemes belonged firmly between the pages of the surfeit of highly implausible espionage novels appearing almost daily on the bookstalls.

O'Neil regarded himself as a soldier, not a terrorist. He had a soldier's proper cause in fighting to free his homeland of a foreign Government and its Army of Occupation. Soldiers fought soldiers, not the civilian population. He would gladly take on any government, or its military forces, which denied a people their rightful freedoms. But there he drew the line.

He recalled a furious row he'd had with Gerry Adams, bespectacled and Marxist-trained leader of the Provisional IRA. In O'Neil's book, the Provisionals had become 'murderholics', drunk with killing for killing's sake. And the INLA were little better. That was why he had broken away from both organisations and formed his own elite Brigade.

The men under his command were hand-picked, tested and subject to a soldier's discipline and a soldier's code – and God help any who broke it. If these Arabs chose to think of him as part of the IRA or its INLA counterpart, let them. He would get the promised arms and money he wanted from them first and worry about how he'd fulfil the obligations which went with them later.

The Provisionals had accused him of being a romantic, better suited to buccaneering on the Spanish Main than modern guerilla warfare. Theirs was a war of attrition and political ideology, with no quarter given and none expected in return.

And that was why *they* would win in the end. Because

the British still conducted their military business like a game of cricket, with rubber bullets instead of a bat and ball.

That didn't wash with O'Neil and it had nothing to do with sentiment or romanticism. He was shrewd enough to realise the dangers inherent in the Provos' policies and that, where they hurt the very populace they were trying to 'free', they ran the risk of their tactics eventually souring all but the real fanatics against them. True, they might gain that 'freedom', but to what end if every face was then turned from them in disgust and sorrow?

Having acknowledged that in his own mind, why then did he admire men like George Habash and 'the Jackal'? Perhaps it was for their tactical brilliance and nerve. Or was it because O'Neil wished he possessed their simplistic and dedicated ruthlessness?

An outsider looking into O'Neil's motivations might have suggested he was trying to have the best of both worlds in wanting political change to be hastened at the point of a gun, but balking at the ultimate reality of such an outlook: Becoming an international terrorist.

Either way, O'Neil accepted that he was something of an anachronism. A psychiatrist would have probably defined him more bluntly as a man with an identity crisis, which he had elected to solve outside of the law.

Be that as it may, having captured the *Britannia*, his demands would be simple enough: An aircraft to fly the raiders to Libya with their glittering booty – and for that safe conduct he *would* break his own rules and take along hostages from the crew, if necessary, to be released on touch-down. He knew the cynical practicality of politicians, even those who supported terrorism like Gaddafi, and accepted that the Libyans would be happy to involve themselves indirectly as a place of refuge but not openly supply him with an aircraft. Even Gaddafi would not stick his neck that far into the noose of international disapproval.

He'd also use the full brunt of the media to impact his deed on the world's gasping nations – the same media that had misreported his personal aims as a soldier of freedom in the past. At least that was something he and Kassim would have no difficulty in agreeing about. Maximum publicity for maximum effect.

He realised this was going to be tricky. The guaranteed publication and broadcasting of the raiders' reasons for hijacking the royal yacht was not something the governments involved would do lightly. But they had one of two choices: his way or no way. Needing the exposure, on that he would be as ruthless as the little Arab who had clicked his way into his plans.

Those reasons were: to demand that the political machinery be put in motion for a Palestinian homeland on the territory stolen by the Jews of Israel, assisted by the British Government of the day – an issue tacitly ignored in the present negotiations between Sadat and Begin; the setting up of an internationally-recognised commission from the United Nations to settle the basis of a politically and economically viable unified Catholic Ireland and the withdrawal of Britain's military presence; and a worldwide amnesty for the men who had taken part in the unbelievable hijack of the century.

Irrespective of the outcome of their demands, it was planned to scuttle *Britannia* smack in the middle of the Canal's narrowest section, so in no way could the raid be hushed up. The entire world would know about it, and the men who had achieved this incredible thing. *And* it would be executed with a style and verve that would give the media something to gloat over for months afterwards.

At the very least, it would dislocate the oil supplies to the West coming via Suez. Sadat's role in the hated Middle East peace talks between Egypt and the Israelis would be damaged, if not wholly discredited, since the stark hijack would occur on Egyptian territory. It would certainly sour relations with the Western powers and might even go as far as wrecking the peace initiative completely. And that would be one in the eye for 'Peanuts' Carter and his do-gooder administration.

O'Neil chuckled to himself again. The audacity of it all was enough to make the devil himself quit hell for a safer place! In his heart, O'Neil doubted if the outraged governments involved would or could accede to the issues they'd want settled. But anything was possible.

The jingoistic 'Send a gunboat!' days of Queen Victoria, and splendid characters like 'Pip' Palmerston, had disappeared from the international negotiating scene generations ago. A certain style that appealed to O'Neil's buccaneering instincts had gone with them. More's the pity, he thought. At least then one could fight for a cause cleanly and clearly. Who could really cope with the double-talk that was today's 'diplomacy'?

He sniffed wryly. It made little difference to the fact that they would walk out of the raid a good few million pounds the richer, with which to carry on the struggle for political justice.

It would be one hell of a gesture if nothing else. The British would know they had a new force to reckon with in Eire and it might well rally true Irishmen to the Madigan Brigade's flag. The Palestinians and their Marxist 'comrades' would have shoved a fistful of fingers up the noses of those oil-fat traitors in the Gulf.

He smiled, sourness twisting his features. It'd serve the devils right for slavering all over that German woman, who called herself the head of the heretic Church of England. Maybe the Pope would make him a saint!

Most of all, it would tell the world that international socialism was here to stay and was going to strike again and again until the bloated pigs who ran the capitalist societies of the West collapsed in their own exploiting filth under the heel of the rebelling masses!

O'Neil felt quite breathless at the vision he had conjured up for himself. Calm it, Captain, he cautioned. Perhaps he really did subscribe to the ringing phraseology of the Far Left. Perhaps not. He was a socialist, hating inherited privilege and wealth with a cramping passion in his guts. But it was difficult to align the sentiments of Marxism with his

Catholic upbringing, and therein was another problem for O'Neil's contradictory outlook.

Whatever, there were a mass of difficulties with this present thing before glory fell upon any of them. For a start, Colonel Gaddafi of Libya still had to be officially approached for his co-operation. There was little doubt they'd get it, based on what the Syrians understood the venture to be. But getting out of Libya again could prove a hazard to say the least – when Gaddafi and his Syrian allies found they had been conned. The Russians would not take kindly to it either.

In their exploratory talks with Khalid, O'Neil and his guerilla friend had neglected to tell him or his superiors the whole gamut of their plan. O'Neil grinned, imagining the outrage all round. The Syrians thought they were 'merely' going to scuttle the famous vessel in the Canal and make off with all the booty they could lay their hands on, leaving Mister and Missus Queen paddling around up to their over-privileged knees in water. And the British and Egyptian governments with very red faces.

But once the raid was under way, neither the Syrians, Libyans nor their Moscow masters would be able to stop them carrying out the most daring part of their plan without revealing an 'interested' involvement. O'Neil would see to that.

If the Syrians and Libyans thought O'Neil's raiders were meekly going to sit around in Libya waiting to hand over several million pounds' worth of loot for an 'official' share-out, they'd got another think coming.

He and Kassim had already privately agreed that they would split it down the middle. Gold, silver and jewels were easily broken up, and not too hard to dispose of through the international fences O'Neil could get to, and had used before on fund-raising bank raids back in Ulster.

From then on, neither of their organisations would ever have to toady to the likes of these clowns or their Russian puppeteers again.

The first thing he'd do was lie low for a while; take a holiday as far away from the Middle East as possible. He wouldn't touch his end of the booty. He had some money put away. It would be wiser to feed the stuff on to the crooks' market a little at a time over a year or so, moving from place to place and never dealing with the same fence twice.

O'Neil wiped a hand across his mouth. It shook slightly and he was sweating. If they got away with it, he wondered if he'd really ever be able to go home again?

He couldn't see Kassim surviving in the Middle East either, with half the PLO, Syrians and Libyans after his blood. What the hell, there were plenty of hide-outs in South America they could operate from with that kind of money behind them.

He didn't understand these heathens anyway. They thought differently to anybody he'd ever known. He suddenly recalled an incident involving an Irish merchant skipper he knew, and laughed out loud.

His freighter had docked in Syria at Christmas-time a couple of years before. They'd been there right through to the New Year. The ship's decorations had been taken down on Twelfth Night, as was the Western tradition, but somebody had left one of the Nativity stars hanging over the wardroom door. A Syrian customs official had seen it, accused the master of supporting the Israelis – because the star looked vaguely like a Jewish emblem – and impounded the ship! It had taken the Irish Government three weeks of hard negotiation before they managed to get the entire crew released from jail.

He couldn't understand the Syrian thinking on this operation either. In one statement, they were dead against having anything to do with the West, and in the next Syria's President Assad was talking about some Arab union to open up trade with the Western nations. Libya, of course, was a law unto itself – with a messianic madman like Gaddafi at the helm. Nobody knew what he was believing in from one week to the next. Still, if he could be used to help this little adventure along, all well and good.

O'Neil shook his red head with a sardonic smile. Of a certainty, the can would rest firmly atop him and Kassim –

and the disclaimers would fly about like angels on a picnic! The Russians would covertly co-ordinate the whole shoot and then throw up their whiter-than-white hands in the direction of the SALT II talks. That other 'Red' herring, 'peaceful coexistence', would get slapped on to the counter as well!

It was ironic, O'Neil mused, that every time you thought you'd found an answer, all you had discovered was another question. No doubt the gods looked down on this comical globe and split their sides laughing.

The jeep pulled up in the courtyard on Mohammed Zaid Street. O'Neil was feeling a strange combination of exhaustion and elation. Dear God, if they pulled it off . . .

He walked back into the house with Docherty and Kassim. There was nothing left for it now but to wait on the next meeting with Khalid and his distant masters.

Clive Danvers worked late into the afternoon on his negatives. He stared at the luminous clock on the wall of his small darkroom and smiled with relief. Ten minutes should do it. Luckily he lived in an HMG apartment within the Embassy compound, away from prying eyes.

The first four-by-eights were already hung up to dry. He unpegged the prints carefully. Not bad. Not bad at all. The definitions were rather good. George Burroughs should be pleased with them. Maybe *he* could supply the identities of the two Europeans captured by Danvers' new Olympus.

He had to get back to his office if he was going to catch Walker-Smith. Thank God he'd already written a summary for London. It could go out with the photographs.

He turned off the infra-red equipment and put on his jacket. Couldn't let the Ambassador see him walking around half naked. The Old Man was hot on that sort of thing.

Danvers hurried from his apartment, making sure the double security locks were firmly home. He was cutting it fine. Walker-Smith flew back that evening.

The tall, lean man in the lightweight Gieves suit had just collected the last of the Embassy papers due to go back with him to London. He was tanned from constant travelling, a touch of greying hair spelling out his forty-three years.

His dark tie had a distinctive motif recurring on its silk weave. The running greyhound was surmounted by a small Victorian crown. It was the very special symbol of a very special job. Alan Walker-Smith was a very special kind of man.

He spoke seven languages, several of them Arabic dialects, and had topped his formal knowledge of other peoples with a degree in Oriental Studies after leaving the Army. He was also an expert in small arms and unarmed combat.

His service in the Parachute Regiment around some of the world's most vicious trouble-spots had been severed by the infamous Geddes' Axe, which had seen so many good men out of the armed forces in the name of progressive defence cuts.

His wife and small son, both of whom he adored, had been killed by an EOKA bomb outrage during his service in Cyprus. Walker-Smith had not even bothered to consider remarrying. Love and memories die hard in some men.

It took Walker-Smith a long time to adjust to the reverberating shocks of civilian life. Britain appeared to him to have swopped national pride and identity, which binds any nation, for the crippling national mistrust and discontent now diffusing it.

Because the shocks, when they hit him, were small but frequent ones, they hurt far more. A man could brace himself for the big punch. A constant jabbing simply wore him out. And he was without the protection service life had given him against the petty tyrannies of a country which had lost its way.

In his private opinion, the social order had not so much broken down as disintegrated into three divisions, all of them equally devisive for his country. 'Upper', 'middle' and 'working' class had nothing to do with it any more.

The Radical Left controlled the unions, whose enormously

rich pension funds were quietly buying up vast chunks of shares in private enterprise, whilst behaving with a greater dictatorialism than the 'capitalists' they were always at pains to condemn.

The Reactionary Right sat behind their faceless masks at the controls of Whitehall, breaking the policies of elected governments at will – and the backs of individual politicians who displeased them.

The Silent Majority sat in a silence he would have called apathy. Their number went across the board of class distinction, powerless to fight the few at both ends of the scale who ruined it for the many.

Of course, he accepted there were plenty of good men in the unions, just as there were others in Whitehall honestly dedicated to the welfare of the country as a whole. But it made him sad nevertheless to see such open disaffection on the streets. It all seemed so dull and without challenge, at least for him.

When he had been offered his present calling, he had accepted it with alacrity. He could never believe in the role Britain had adopted on the world stage nowadays, but his new job was one way of oiling a small cog in the machinery which might change all that in the 1980s.

Major A. M .Walker-Smith, DSO, retd., was a Queen's Messenger. One of that special breed of silent and resourceful men who carry State papers, and other highly classified material considered too sensitive for normal dispatch, to and from Her Britannic Majesty's embassies, consulates and residencies around the world.

They are often put at risk on their lonely journeys, and sometimes even murdered for the secrets they carry with such quiet courage, although no official figures are ever published or admitted to by Whitehall.

Clive Danvers caught up with Walker-Smith as he chained and locked a black dispatch case to his left wrist. They knew each other vaguely from the Messenger's previous trips on this particular 'rabbit run', as this elite body's slang termed an assignment.

The Queen's Messenger liked the look of him. He reminded him of how his son might have turned out. Danvers smiled warmly at him. Had to get this right.

'Hullo, Major. Could you take something to London for me?' he asked deferentially.

Walker-Smith glanced at the sealed package in his hand.

'Oh? Bit unusual for you Commercial boys, isn't it? Has H. E. or Chancery cleared it?'

He looked keenly at Danvers, his light brown eyes summing him up. Danvers coloured. He hadn't had time to put it in front of His Excellency the Ambassador, and the Head of Chancery was a fussy devil. He would waste valuable time cajoling Patterson into signing a clearance docket.

'Er, no. But it's top priority. I'm sure it'll be all right,' he added lamely.

Walker-Smith shook his head firmly. 'Sorry, old son. No can do without the proper authorisations. You should know that.'

Danvers' back went cold. He *had* to get this stuff off. He decided on a gamble. If he got a bollocking from the Department, it was too damned bad. They could do with backing up their field agents more positively at times.

He took Walker-Smith by his arm and guided him out of the mainstream of Embassy staff in the wide, cool corridor.

'You've got at least Class III security clearance, haven't you?' he probed quietly. The Messenger nodded, watching him carefully.

'Good. So have I. A good deal higher in fact. I cover for the SIS out here, Major. This packet *must* get to London quickly. If you're prepared to miss your plane, check me out with Patterson or Sir Giles.'

Walker-Smith thought about it, appraising Danvers coolly. It was hardly likely the man was bluffing, and he had to get that plane. The next one was in three days' time. As for the

Head of Chancery, he knew what Patterson was like. He'd never get away.

The Messenger made up his mind. Decisiveness was a necessary part of his survival kit in this business.

'All right. Clive, isn't it? Who's it to go to?'

Danvers' face broke into a relieved grin.

'Thanks a lot, sir. Get it to Major George Burroughs at Century House, could you? He's on the Middle East Desk. No one else, please. It's brewing up for a real storm out here. This information is vital.'

He hesitated.

'I'd phone in first and arrange an outside meeting. He's in the "Bible". Our chief's . . . well, difficult.'

Walker-Smith smiled. He could imagine. Some of these senior Civil Servants were real bureaucratic martinets. He nodded at Danvers.

'One of those, is he? Fair enough. I just hope the flak doesn't fly over this. I like my job.'

He took the packet and placed it inside the black dispatch case with its distinctive Royal Cipher on the flap. Walker-Smith smiled briefly at the Information Officer. It was time to go. The Embassy's Land-Rover was waiting for him.

'Don't sweat. I'll see to it,' the Messenger assured him and turned to go.

Clive Danvers watched him stride swiftly down the corridor. What a brick the man was. Thank God he'd agreed to do it. He could feel his shirt sticking to his back and glanced at his watch.

He had time for a quick shower before that blasted tennis match with the Commercial Attaché and his over-talkative wife. Still, that rather pretty new brunette from Secretariat was meant to be coming too . . .

Danvers stood for a moment in the corridor regaining his composure and then hurried off to change.

CHAPTER NINE

George Burroughs thought the boy looked soft, which he was not. He also thought him unintelligent, which he was not. The young man sitting opposite him thought Burroughs crude, which he was. And about as gracious as a walrus on heat, which he certainly was.

Chambers hardly knew the brusque, big-boned man seated across the none-too-clean table from him. Had he done so, he would have come to realise that Burroughs hid great kindness, integrity and deep patriotism under a rude exterior. And that he was trying to protect him in his own strange way.

Burroughs had long discarded most of life's niceties as meaningless, except towards the few friends he valued – as with his collection of china. He left the pretty talk to those who wished to indulge in it, speaking his mind as he and the circumstances found fit. It had landed him in a lot of trouble on occasions, and made enemies of men like Sir David Holman, but the nature of his work caused many kinds of casualties amongst its servants.

Nevertheless, he usually fitted his tongue and 'the circumstances' to his personal point of view, particularly when his sense of justice had been outraged. He had just finished stirring such a fuss over Sammy Cook's threatened disciplinary action that Cook's departmental head had decided to drop the action in favour of a stiff ticking-off. The radio operator's value was not underestimated by his superiors. Nor were the services George Burroughs' kind rendered to national security.

Burroughs' outspoken personal views were not a desirable

trait in an intelligence officer concerned with analytical judgements, where a cool objectivity was both the rule and the safeguard. However, as a colleague had once acidly remarked on his forthright ways, 'the trouble is our Maverick of the Middle East Desk is nearly always right, damn him.'

But in any organisation involving a civil service, and therefore a career-minded hierarchy, a man who relied so heavily on instinctive flair was regarded with suspicion and not a little jealousy. The more so if that flair invariably proved correct and underlined a professional knowledge and experience difficult to fault.

Burroughs was giving Chambers a piece of that experience there and then, if only to wise up this 'innocent' to the sinister, shabby and inevitably double-faced secret underworld of legitimate government he had entered.

They were in a small, rather seedy nightclub Burroughs occasionally patronised for its lax licensing hours. It stood slumped at the grubbier end of a Soho which had never been anything but doubtful. Now it grew steadily worse as the last of its real character surrendered to an ever-mushrooming trade in blatant pornography, seemingly beyond either the powers of its undermanned police force or an ineffectual City Council to control. Even the tourists were beginning to complain about it.

The Church Commissioners, that august body of Christian intention and the largest single owners of property in the West End and W2 after the Duke of Westminster, controlled and rented out many of the tatty buildings housing establishments given over to a filth that no other animal than the human being would have wanted any part of.

It made a man of Burroughs' outlook sick to his bowels. But it was a sad reflection of the age and he had compelled Chambers to walk through its rotten heart with him, hoping some of its grimy lessons would rub off on his young companion.

If any of it had disturbed Chambers, he did not choose to show his reactions to Burroughs, preferring to discuss political theories and their motivations with his sour escort in a slow but curiously high-pitched monotone.

Now it was half past two in the morning on New Year's Eve. Rather it had been up to midnight. Then 1979 had shivered in on a fresh loan of a twelve-month for the world to play with, cherish or ruin. Even the most determined of revellers had finally succumbed to the bitter cold – and gone staggering noisily home.

Only a few diehards, assorted lonely souls and men like Burroughs still gripped a glass between fumbling fingers, afraid of the night and fearful for what this new book-entry of a year might do to them.

The nightclub's tired and ageing female singer personified the strange mood of forlorn optimism which steals into the limbo hours before dawn, her sad little song wandering uncertainly over the deserted cube the club dared to call a dance floor.

Hopes and fears got heightened and distorted by the 'wee small hours'. Daylight brought forgetfulness, or new problems with which to make the next night a bad one too . . .

Burroughs was well on the way to being drunk those first hesitant hours of 1979. He liked a drink now and again but would have railed at any suggestion that he drank too much, too often. If asked, he would have blamed his present state on the tensions and frustrations of having to work under a pernickity bastard like Holman.

Up to a point, such a statement would have been fair comment from a man whose boss was driven by tense frustrations of his own. But Burroughs' long years of discipline and courage were beginning to slip away, along with his surviving illusions over his work and the faceless world he lived in now.

George Burroughs cared. And the caring had grown too much for him to uphold against the debilitating disappointment of his country's fallen standards and his own inability to do a damned thing about it.

Burroughs gazed at Chambers from his whiskied haze.

What the hell did a mere kid like this know? He'd not been through any of it. Come to that, would a spotty-faced youth reared at the gentle breast of a cushy Welfare State even care? He'd not been in on the last of the good times, nor witnessed the bad ones coming to haunt them all.

He sniffed derisively into his whisky, saddened beyond telling. In his increasingly disillusioned opinion, the whole business stank. It stank of a moral, political and military treachery that made a bitter nonsense of everything both his and the cruelly depleted generations of World War I had been taught was the unique, golden essence of 'their' sceptred British Isles.

He banged the table at Chambers.

' "This England"? Balls! Since the end of th-the follow-on bloody scrap, w-which became our Second World War in just one lifetime, m-men like *me* from those generations ha-have stood in helpless bloody anger, d'y-do you know that . . . eh?'

Helpless they had been as the 'Great' was gradually removed from its war-weakened Britain with remorseless governmental surgery by a tawdry succession of cynical and mindless political butchers – Tory and Labour – who appeared to share a collective and manic compulsion to endlessly seek apology for her once magnificent Empire.

Burroughs slopped more whisky into his glass. Useless talking about it to this four-eyed schoolboy.

'Y-Your generation's been brought up 'n-on empty rubbish like "You've Never Had It So Good" an-and you've never *known* anything else against which to check s-such lousy c-complacency, have you?'

Vandalising the things they'd never had to fight for was a savage mirror of their all too easy times.

The club's jaded singer finished her spot and wandered off the tiny stage, unoffended by the silence applauding her exit. It was just one more night to her these days and she ignored any special significance it might have held for the few remaining customers as she herself had been significantly ignored.

Burroughs swept another empty bottle out of his way and leant over the table unsteadily. The food had been almost as bad as the prices charged for the drinks and he was determined to get some value back on both.

'L-Listen,' he slurred. 'I-I didn't go to a bloody university but I-I can tell you this, boy. You won't last f-five minutes in this game 'less you listen to me. H-Holman never listens, damn him.'

Chambers sighed inwardly. He knew his appearance tended to make people either be over-protective towards him or dismiss his existence out of hand, but he really didn't need this run-down, boozy old has-been to hold his hand.

It was a cruel and unjustified assessment of Burroughs, although an understandable one. He had only seen the man's off-putting, maverick side at work, fighting Holman, and now another side of a man supposedly excellent in his field bolstered up by this aggressive drunkenness.

Burroughs was talking at him again.

' – an' that's the whole trouble nowadays, lad. W-We used to be the centre of 'n Empire an-an' it all depended 'n us. Now s'all gone . . . '

He took a long, shaky pull at his drink. Some of it dribbled down his chin, reminding Chambers of a senile old soldier he'd watched out of the corner of his eye on a childhood visit to an ex-servicemen's home with his father, who was on the board of trustees.

'All gone,' Burroughs meandered on. 'We're not wanted in Europe, no use to t-the Americans, at odds with most of our ex-colonies an' despised by the un'er . . . under-developed countries. Bloody Britain!'

Chambers tried to keep his eyes open as Burroughs thrust another drink at him before returning to his jaundiced attack on the 'men' he believed had sold out his country's past. And her future.

If the little fool couldn't understand, or keep awake, he was only being typical of the Britain he'd been unfortunate enough to inherit. And what a Britain that was!

As far as Burroughs was concerned, her post-war leaders'

equally lunatic need to hawk about a self-effacing, cut-price contrition to friends, enemies and former colonies alike, with a crawling 'humility' that would have shamed the bargain basement of a bankrupt religious bookshop, was another act of crazed self-destruction quite beyond his comprehension or forgiveness.

He gripped Chambers' hand across the table, forcing his tired attention back to what he was saying.

'Christ, boy! How I hate all the political b-bullshit . . . w-what they've done to us . . .'

He jerked upright, startling Chambers.

'D-Didn't know I like to read poetry, did you, b-boy?' he jabbed at him. 'Read a poem once 'bout the First World War . . . 'bout the Empire . . . men w-who "shaped that precious jewel of India an' . . . left countless of her sons 'pon the m-malarial plains of Africa. A-an' – " '

He struggled to remember the rest of it.

' " – so many, many more along Verdun's ripping wire . . . t-their blood mingling with the . . . poppies on Flanders' angry fields, broken dolls for 'n ideal . . . pleading remembrance." There!'

Chambers hated maudlin sentiment and regarded this as such. But Burroughs hadn't finished with him yet.

'D-Do we have to excuse all that excellence jus' because the British took as well as gave? Not in *my* book we don't! Haven't we given so much to the very countries who now s-sneer at us from the "independence" we first made possible, eh? Right! But the buggers still want th-the Foreign Aid we can ill afford to give 'em!'

Burroughs' fist slammed down on the table. Chambers nearly jumped out of his skin.

'Should give t-them a bloody hard, soldier's clip round their cheeky black ears instead!'

He had often been accused of being a racist, although he'd served with many coloured nations in the army and got on well with them all. But he was fond of making the pun, whenever challenged, that he liked to call 'a spade a spade'.

In his mind, enough of Britain's manhood had died with

smoke in their eyes, and the sound of the guns the last thing they'd ever heard, in other people's causes to justify some pride of place in the democracy of free speech. To him, the politicos at Westminster and the Civil Service mandarins in Whitehall behaved like a man who had just castrated himself for the hell of it and then ran round the conference tables of the world, shouting with hysterical glee. 'Look at me, everyone! I've got no balls!'

For Burroughs, there was neither sense in it nor justification for it. He cared and had cared long. Perhaps too long and far too much. An orphan child, his country had become his family as well as his hope.

He was, in short, a faithful servant betrayed and the grief of it was destroying him.

The victim of his aggressive sorrow was well on the way to being bored with Burroughs' inebriated tirade and simply wanted to sleep off the hot, alcoholic queasiness roaming his stomach.

Couldn't the wretched man talk about something else? Chambers felt ill enough as it was. Perhaps a few hours' decent rest might quell the bile threatening to erupt from his drink-drowned insides.

Peter Chambers was only twenty-seven, recently come to the Department from the Ministry of Defence after two and a half years as a junior political intelligence analyst.

The Chambers family's long and illustrious military background had bred in him an abiding interest in military history, which he'd coupled with his growing talent for strategic studies and their interrelationships with both political and economic forces.

Contrary to Burroughs' soured beliefs, his own researches had in fact demonstrated that nearly all wars were caused by economics – with the 'politics' dressed up accordingly. He'd come to believe that a balanced marriage of international trading requirements, 'complemented' by their strategic military capabilities, was the surest way of keeping the peace the world so badly needed.

He had entered the somewhat rarified atmosphere of the

8

War Office's 'backroom boys' on a powerful combination of family influence and a brilliant double first at Cambridge in the Political Sciences.

His famous father had wanted his only son to follow him into the Army proper, despite his sickly childhood, and had never quite recovered from the boy's quiet determination to seek a more intellectual involvement in the grim machinery of war. However, he had only achieved his aim at further cost to the strained communications already existing between them.

Major General Sir Arthur de Vere-Chambers, VC, KCVO, DSO, TD, had imposed his iron will on everything he touched, including the boy's ailing mother. She had died when her son was seven, worn out by three miscarriages and his father's strictured and demanding ways.

The General had always been a fine soldier; a man's man, respected by his troops. Indeed, a national hero of sorts, but no kind of a husband to the delicate and sensitive 'gal' he had married as a relatively young brigadier at the end of World War II.

The Hon. Lucy Elizabeth de Vere was emotionally unable to cope with her husband's driving energy nor his strangely Victorian view of marriage, and she feared the Army life which dominated all else in his mind.

Upon her untimely and frankly inconvenient death in the early 1950s, Sir Arthur had found his one surviving child a suitable nanny, then sent him off to the family's traditional public school, and gone about his career again with relieved gusto. He now paced out the autumnal years of his distinguished militarism on NATO's General Staff Co-ordinating Committee in Whitehall, content with frightening the life out of the minions who served his able but tetchy personality.

Thus, while other more naturally reared children played at soldiers, his son did not. With such an overweighted, paternalistic terrorism hanging over him, a boy of Peter Chambers' shy and lonely disposition had occupied his solitary childhood finding out the whys and wherefores of men at war. And about men like his father in peacetime.

Burroughs knew none of this, chiefly because he'd not yet found time to read the background security clearance reports in Chambers' personnel file. It would have made little difference to the instant dislike he felt when first introduced to him at the Department.

The fact that, since joining the Ministry of Defence, the General's son had already written a major and highly commended paper on his subject for the Joint Chiefs of Staff's Office was similarly discounted by him.

Chambers had further consolidated his reputation, with his Director's permission, by submitting two other related studies to the Foreign Office's own Political Intelligence Unit. He was now regarded as one of the rising stars in his field and the FO was still delighting at having poached him from the 'War House'. And poached he had been, with softly-spoken offers of monetary and status improvements baiting the juicy hook to rapid advancement.

Neither wars nor peace, or the changing years, diminish the internecine rivalry which exists between all government institutions everywhere. Co-operation was one thing. End-of-the-day kudos quite another.

The General had not approved of his son's sudden defection to 'that high-talking crowd of wine-sipping mamby pambies', the FO being a legitimate non-military target. But the latter years had mellowed him, if only to the extent of gruffly wishing the boy well. In truth, he was rather pleased by his progeny's success. That, like sex in his pre-Edwardian outlook, was outside any open expression verging on pleasure – including congratulating his own flesh and blood.

Although he would have to go through a formal acclimatisation in the various branches of his new service, Peter de Vere-Chambers was undoubtedly being groomed with almost indecent haste for a key staff position within MI6. Like most of his colleagues in the Department, his companion for the evening was aware of this. It had done nothing to help Burroughs' attitude.

They had placed Chambers on the Middle East Desk as part of this induction process and to teach him, with typical Civil Service subtlety, how things were 'done' in their section of Military Intelligence. Or rather *not done*, Burroughs suspected, since they'd put himself in charge of showing their blue-eyed prize the ropes.

Burroughs wished 'they' hadn't. He had enough on his plate without wet-nursing this cold little genius. He recalled his own on-site training with Mr Betts but refused to feel any kinship for Chambers. His strong antipathy had not only been fuelled by the lecture he received from Holman on looking after this apparently remarkable young man.

Unfortunately for him, the young man in question was short, thin and bespectacled – a red rag to Burroughs' odd fixation against small men. That had not helped his attitude to change either.

Chambers' face, scarred like a mining disaster by the ravages of acne, was sheened in an alcoholic sweat from all the unwanted drink he'd been pressed into consuming at the embarrassing, often shouted insistence of his drunken 'tutor'.

He was trapped in his seat by Burroughs' seniority and knew he would be forced to go on listening to this bitter-loud man with the striding limp until his lecturer had had enough or fell asleep across the littered meal.

For his part, Burroughs didn't give a damn what Chambers felt one way or the other. He firmly believed in the old adage that you could get the true measure of any man when he was in his cups. He would bloody well make this horrible little squirt open up, even if it meant Chambers puking all over his lap!

He laughed bitterly, spilling his drink on the table.

'What a joke! D-Don't know where the hell we are! N-No purpose, no drive an-an' no bloody brains left, have we, son?'

He stared owlishly at Chambers, getting no response and past caring. He took another slopping spill from his glass. Even the desire to get his 'pupil' going was fading as the second bottle of whisky took hold of his senses.

'Bloody country's finished . . . H-Holman rules . . . ' he

muttered into his drink. 'No more Mister Betts an' no more me . . .'

Chambers shook the sweat from his eyes, trying to concentrate on what Burroughs was saying, determined to outlast him. Talking back seemed the only way he'd keep down the bile.

'Oh, I don't know, Major,' he replied in his slow monotone. 'We are a trading nation after all, and we have to trade in order to live. Part of our Imperialist past you were talking about.'

Burroughs' head came up sharply at Chambers' use of his rank, unsure if he was being mocked. It made his head swim. What the hell. Let him yatter, he thought dizzily. He was getting too damned drunk to want to go on with it anyhow.

Chambers took his silence as a cue to develop his argument, adjusting his spectacles with schoolmasterly care. They remained slightly askew.

'Taking attitudes about other people's political systems, whether fascist, racist or communist, is none of our concern,' he pontificated with alcoholic assurance. It was that time of the morning when setting the world to rights seemed easy.

'The students can demonstrate all they want but governments should not take any notice, you know,' he declared.

Burroughs interrupted him with a burped grunt. For once, the boy was saying something he agreed with – at least about students. As for Western governments ignoring the political oppression of others, that was cold and unfeeling even though he'd be the first to admit Britain was in no state to do much about it.

His head dropped momentarily and Chambers sensed victory. It had become very important to beat this man at something.

'Personally,' Chambers strove on, 'I think that successive Labour governments have propelled us into economic disaster with their rigid stances against arms for South Africa, no warships to Spain and Chile, trade sanctions on Rhodesia, and their imbalanced favouritism towards the Middle East.'

He removed his spectacles, blinking blearily at Burroughs

through the pall of cigarette smoke hanging on the air. His glasses had left a savage imprint on the bridge of his nose, like a nip from some giant insect.

'No, we have lost huge amounts of revenue and contracts from such a rigidity,' he went on. 'I am in favour of trading with everybody, whatever their politics – unless they're directly at war with us. The Swiss do it, and very successfully. How else do we survive?'

Burroughs hiccupped loudly. 'S'all very well, lad. But n-nobody wants to work here any-more . . . 'trouble these days. 'Course, they *can* but everyone's screwing too much off the Welfare bloody State . . . ' He lapsed back into silence, staring at his glass.

The few remaining stalwarts in the little nightclub sucked on the stale air and continued to watch them with herdlike interest, wondering what this incongruous pair had in common.

Burroughs could have told them but it would not have been terribly flattering.

Their ponderous discussion was perhaps mercifully terminated by the arrival of Walker-Smith, back from Damascus. He had telephoned the duty officer at Century House earlier that evening only to be informed his unofficial assignment was not on call until the next day. But they had a number Major Burroughs could be reached at.

The Queen's Messenger rang Burroughs' home, where he was greeted by an answering-machine telling him of another number at which he'd be available until the early hours.

With understandable irritation after a tiring flight, the Messenger's third call was to the club, giving a description of his quarry over the telephone based on what he had gleaned from the duty desk at M16. His own security rating had been sufficient for him to obtain the information he'd needed.

The bouncer answering him at the 'Green Frog Club' had recognised his verbal sketch of Burroughs, suggesting with festive jocularity that the, er, 'gen'elman' in question was too far gawn to come to the blower, guv.

The Messenger thanked him shortly. No, there wasn't any message. He'd come on over. Yes, he did realise he'd have to part with a fiver to get in – New Year's Eve reduction like, on accahnt of goodwill an' all that.

Walker-Smith now stared distastefully through the smoky gloom and spotted his man at a table in the far corner. And hesitated.

He'd not been briefed that Burroughs was with someone, but he was due out on another 'run' later in the day and couldn't afford the time hanging about with Danvers' packet until and if Burroughs decided to make his way home.

Burroughs looked up without interest, expecting the bill, when the Messenger tapped him on the shoulder.

'Major Burroughs? George Alfred Burroughs?' he inquired coldly. He stared at Burroughs' face, creased by life and drink like a burst paper bag. Walker-Smith drank infrequently and disliked those who could not hold theirs.

Burroughs nodded cautiously, hazily recognising that the man looked official. Maybe that bastard Holman was keeping tabs on him.

'I am,' he answered carefully, trying to wind the words around his furred tongue. His mouth tasted like something long dead. 'An' w-who're you?' he managed to get out.

'That is not important,' Walker-Smith countered. 'I have something for you. It's urgent, Major,' he added meaningfully. The man seemed completely blotto.

Burroughs leaned forward aggressively, bunching his big fists as the Messenger wearily pulled up a spare chair. Everybody was suddenly calling him 'Major'. What the hell was going on?

'I-I do-don't know you, do I?' he queried loudly, sliding the question off his tongue with difficulty. He vaguely identified the motif on Walker-Smith's tie. Bit out of place in this dump. 'Whadayou want?' he demanded truculently.

Walker-Smith looked at him, considering the problem. He slid his ID card across the table to Burroughs, together with the big buff envelope, and flicked his finger at Chambers. He was in no mood for politeness. They both looked as if they'd been drowning in the stuff.

Burroughs focused on the ID's Royal Cipher, suddenly growing very attentive and trying to shake the muzziness from his eyes.

'H-He's with my Department,' he said, waving an explanatory hand over his bilious junior with all the fumbling authority of a second-rate magician, and passed his own ID card to the Messenger in a confusion of fingers. He indicated the envelope, forcing his tongue to work.

'F-For me?'

Walker-Smith nodded, relieved that he was getting some kind of sense out of the man.

'Yes. From Clive Danvers in Damascus. I've just got back.'

Burroughs grunted and slit the heavy seals with his discarded dinner knife. It left a smear across the envelope like dried blood.

He went through the photographs and summary slowly, trying to stop his hand shaking. It could have been the drink, shock or excitement.

'Good Christ!' was all he said, getting up unsteadily and heading for the club's main exit.

He stopped and weaved his way back to the table.

'Pay the bill, Chambers. I'll settle with you later. I want you in my office by 09.30 this morning. Understood?'

He held up Danvers' explosive packet, smiling grimly at the tired QM.

'Thanks for this, Walker-Smith. It'll help.'

It was something of an understatement. Burroughs signed the blue receipt docket still lying on the table and yelled at one of the club staff clearing up the long night's debris to find him a taxi – fast!

At that moment, Peter de Vere-Chambers elected to be sick, heaving uncontrollably over the drink-stained tablecloth.

But George Burroughs had already gone.

O'Neil, Docherty and Hassan Kassim found themselves woken up in the middle of the night by their guards. They were taken down to Major Khalid's temporary office on the ground floor of the sprawling villa in a gaggle of bleary-eyed wakefulness. O'Neil wondered what the devil was up now?

Khalid was in a fresh uniform. The extra chairs had been removed and he did not look in the mood to care about their comfort. He stared at them for a long moment, his stilted voice finally wedging into the deep silence.

'You will attend Colonel Solenov of Soviet Counter-Intelligence at three o'clock this afternoon. See you are ready. That is all.'

Back in their rooms, the three men took stock in their separate ways. Connor O'Neil was quietly jubilant; Docherty pensive and still unsure the business smelt right. Hassan the Hawk stared at where his hands used to be and felt fear for the first time in many moons. He thought back to that fateful raid into the Israelis' territory, when a faulty fuse had heralded the beginnings of so much pain, and fought to keep down the sickness rising in his throat.

They all knew the operation was on.

CHAPTER TEN

'Don't talk bloody rubbish!' Burroughs had snapped at him. 'The man's a criminal and a killer – like the rest of his kind!'

Chambers wished he hadn't opened his mouth. His head still hurt from the long night's excesses and he was sure he'd yet to really empty his stomach of all the drink forced down it. The light-hearted comment he'd made about O'Neil in an enfeebled attempt to ease the atmosphere between his grim colleagues had only aggravated Burroughs' foul mood.

They were all crowded into his tutor's cramped little

office at Century House. MacAllister had been called in, along with himself and Jim Nye of Special Branch Liaison.

It was New Year's Day 1979. By rights, none of them should have had to work on this public holiday, except for the duty officers in each section and the round-the-clock communications operators and their station controllers. Now the four of them stood in a sombre group, staring over each other's shoulders at the blow-ups on Burroughs' untidy desk.

Being a thorough young man, Peter Chambers had made it his business to read through all the files he was allowed access to in the Department's guarded 'reading room', housed deep inside the building's reinforced basement.

He had already covered several aspects of his new job, realising the task he had set himself would take months to complete. Nevertheless, although he'd only been with MI6 for five weeks, he had quickly accepted that he would need to master all the information he could command, *if* he was going to learn from or, indeed, even work with George Burroughs.

The background material on international espionage had fascinated him, opening up a hidden world of intrigue and astonishing happenings more incredible than any work of fiction.

Chambers learned about 'live drops', 'sneakies', 'dead letter-boxes', double-ended pay-offs, agencies within agencies and of the agents who sometimes worked both sides of opposing lines. And of Government-sponsored killings, known as 'wet jobs', beyond his wildest imaginings.

The stark revelation that one of MI6's sister services, MI5, probably 'wet-jobbed' Dr Stephen Ward during the height of the Profumo scandal, making it look like suicide, and that the KGB had milked valuable official information, via one of its Russian 'diplomats' involved, from many of the public figures attending the infamous Christine Keeler sex parties, had him riveted to his chair in dumbfounded disbelief.

The names of those inside both the Government of the day

and the upper circles of the Civil Service who were inferred to have left themselves open to blackmail, with all the consequences to national security, was a mindblower outside his limited experience.

That at least one Law Lord was similarly implicated and had used his unquestionable power and position to abet the huge cover-up following the public arraignment of that tragic scapegoat, John Profumo, was something he found difficult to grasp.

Even more astounding was the fact that the same Establishment, which had stood by whilst his career was destroyed in an understandable lie before the House of Commons, saw fit to assuage its own guilt by awarding Profumo a well-earnt CBE – for his quietly dignified service to charity – after many years of being shunted into a social and political wilderness.

There was even the hint that Dr Ward had been a KGB-recruited agent, paid off in the drugs and money he so desperately needed for his personal gratifications and his clients' habits, and his confession in or out of court would have brought the Government's downfall and the unavoidable disgrace of many Establishment notables.

Eye-opener enough, but there was more to come as he burrowed on through the files.

That any British government could have been party to such a hush-up saw Chambers a wiser if somewhat chastened young man, especially if it was really true.

The 'if' existed, since the various departments of British Intelligence are known to be notoriously partisan, exchanging information on a Needs Must basis rather than in willing co-operation.

Sir Alec Douglas-Home, Edward Heath and Sir Harold Wilson had all been at various times in their premierships victims of the Intelligence services' departmental obstructiveness, learning to their cost that their permanent opposites in Whitehall were a law unto themselves, governed by the protective tenets of the old school tie. Indeed, having displayed great patience with their obsessive secrecy, Sir Harold's temper finally got the better of him and he publicly denounced their cavalier behaviour, justifiable or otherwise.

Supposition was thus the best Chambers could hope to elicit from the fragmented MI6 files accessible to him. The very suggestion that their claims might be wholly accurate was shaker enough for someone of his isolated upbringing. Even his work as a political intelligence analyst had not really prepared his innocent outlook for all of this, being largely in the enclosed world of dry theories and 'hypothetics'.

But his shock did not end there, nor would ever end there again. He found it nigh impossible to shrug his shoulders and accept that this was how life in high – and low – places operated.

Further visits to the 'Registry' became close to a compulsion, the desire just to *know* superseding any of the sensibilities he'd possessed on first joining the Department.

Patient cross-referencing of the disturbing material in every minute he could spare turned up so many stunning facts, personal 'indiscretions' by men he'd always thought the backbone of the nation, as well as brazen professional hypocrisy, that he felt almost claustrophobic in the presence of it all.

He discovered more than mere hints that one very senior official and two not so senior civilians at what was then the Admiralty, before it became the Ministry of Defence (Navy) under Mountbatten's sweeping reforms, had allowed their own sexual tendencies to facilitate the enormous – but publicly played down – damage wrought to British Naval Intelligence by the homosexual spy, Vassall. None of them was ever brought to trial and all of them were 'retired' early. For the sake of Governmental and Establishment proprieties.

Although he could not know it then, even a book scheduled to come out in the autumn of 1979, and revealing that there was both a Fourth and a Fifth Man in the Philby spy debacle, fell far short of the mark.

Two more names, apart from theirs, and of far greater standing, lay in front of him, the result of an increasingly skilful guesswork as he sifted through the mass of documentation – their connections with 'Kim' Philby and his long-departed conspirators again only hinted at in the carefully worded reports.

Like Anthony Blunt, one had been 'turned', continuing to hold a top post in counter-intelligence but set to working out his final years by feeding his former Russian masters suitably doctored material under the watchful eye of MI6.

For a while, even the KGB's brilliant Colonel Philby, now safely back in Moscow, had been fooled. At least it had helped redress some of the grim havoc to British and American agents resulting from the betrayals put out by Messrs Philby, Burgess and Maclean.

The Sixth Man's ended usefulness in the late '60s, to both American and British counter-espionage, was rewarded with a fatal heart attack only days after his official retirement – which Chambers guessed had to be more than a timely convenience. And certainly no more than the man deserved.

The Seventh Man remained, and remains, a nebulous suspicion 'on the books', but Chambers grew sure he was Philby's true Control for those long years of suave treachery. This particular 'mole' had never been identified convincingly. Or if he was, it had never been acted upon. Staying a free and outwardly respected citizen, he supposedly met his death whilst 'holidaying' in Hungary some ten years later.

For all the public and Parliamentary furore that would break over the Establishment in November 1979, the cries for an Official Enquiry after the Blunt–Philby revelations would be met with official evasion and peek-a-boo statements designed to smokescreen the real truth. A few minor guilties, both Russian and British, would be offered up for ritual sacrifice. But the ultimately answerable would go, perhaps with greater caution, on their chosen way.

Apart from the very real consideration that Blunt was directly related to the Royal Family, and had disgraced that connection to the point where his prosecution at the time would have seriously and unfairly embarrassed Her Majesty,

125

Chambers discovered from his file that it was not his 'usefulness' as turned agent against the KGB which had so far given him immunity.

In 1946, Blunt had gone on a highly secret mission to Germany with Owen Morshead, then Librarian at Windsor Castle, on direct behalf of George VI. According to his file, the purpose of that delicate mission had been to snatch, if necessary, certain papers lodged at the Hesse family's castle near Frankfurt, then under American control.

It was not the letters of Queen Victoria to her eldest daughter, the wife of Frederick of Prussia, nor the letters of the late Queen Mary, wife of George V, to her German relations which in themselves caused Britain's war-weary King to worry about them falling into American hands. It was their relevance to other papers also held in the Hesse family's archives.

Although still shrouded in official secrecy to this day, those papers gave credence to the deeper discussions held between Hitler and Britain's Prime Minister at Munich in 1938; discussions which have never been made known to their two peoples. Along with the secret proposals put to another member of the royal Windsors before Nazi Germany's long slide towards defeat that he should become King again by a Hitler who had always believed that Britain would be his ally, their publication would have probably caused yet another Abdication.

As it was, Blunt succeeded in his mission by tricking the WAC officer in charge at Schloss Kronberg. And those papers were couriered safely to Windsor Castle's inaccessible vaults, thereby saving the so-called Anglo-American Alliance from any further strains, after enduring five long years of fighting the same war for civilisation.

It was also the last that would be seen of papers whose very existence had had much to do with destroying the reputation of an honest and honourable man called Neville Chamberlain, who came back from seeing 'Herr Hitler' convinced that their two nations would never go to war against each other again – and whose belief was founded on the highest authorities in his own land, substantiated by those damning papers.

Chambers was beginning to realise that perhaps such things as this had a lot to do with Burroughs' aggressive bitterness.

The goings-on between another duly-elected British Government in the '70s and the security services of various African states, along with some of the ugly facts he unearthed around the CIA's links with organised crime throughout the '60s and early '70s. had continued the erosion of his naïve beliefs in the sanctity of Western democracy.

It struck him that such a proclaimed sanctity had been severely tarnished by the murder, ruination and blackmail of prominent American politicians, showbusiness personalities and the like, including yet another revelation that the far from stupid Marilyn Monroe's potentially embarrassing affair with the fabled JFK had not ended in her suicide but at the paranoiac hand of Edgar Hoover's FBI – without the President's knowledge.

He knew about the persistent rumours over the murders of the Kennedy brothers, of course, but he was shaken to find that MI6 thought that Oswald was not Oswald at all, nor had the Teamsters' Union been solely responsible for Robert's death. Apparently, the autopsy conducted on Oswald after he was conveniently shot by Jack Ruby had revealed that three scars listed on the former Marine's medical check sheet were missing.

Linked with the highly secret evidence on hand that Ruby had been Oswald's (or whoever he was) local Controller and that Ruby himself was eliminated by forces other than 'cancer', it seemed likely that both of them had been KGB agents and 'Oswald' a Russian substitute. That amongst the complex skein of intrigue the CIA itself seemed inextricably linked with the Mafia-backed Cuba Plot, left Chambers surmising that all these parties had joined hands to put the Kennedys out of business for their own various ends. What else could anyone think?

Another report on the CIA, suggesting that Nixon had been victimised over the Watergate Scandal and that the Democratic Party break-in was designed to be discovered, thus embarrassing Nixon out of office and giving back to the CIA and FBI many of their powers then in the hands of the Oval Office's inner coven, was substantiated by further highly secret evidence that 'Deep Throat' had in fact been a senior CIA departmental chief. And the witnesses later to die (as in the Warren Committee's investigation of JFK's death) had met their end as part of a cover-up greater than Watergate itself, whatever one thought of Nixon's Administration.

Again, Chambers could only suppose that the ends justified the means, when an ideology's image and security were at stake. But it also made him wonder if any Government anywhere elected by the people could (or ever would) control the destinies of nations so at the mercy of their albeit necessary Secret Services?

But he was quickly becoming wise enough to accept that any democracy must sometimes fight fire with fire – and thereby carry its own quota of self-interested men as well as the truly good.

He also acknowledged, however, that the public denigration of British politicians was counterproductive and agreed with Dr David Owen that it was becoming a secondary disease to the country's unhealthy deprecation of itself.

The background intelligence material on international terrorism had proved equally fascinating, demonstrating to Chambers just how much he still had to learn about the nether world he'd entered so blithely.

Consequently, he spent many hours heaving the individually locked files off their electro-alarmed shelves in those guarded, steel-lined vaults. It was a tiring business in many ways. He thought it time MI6 got its records on to microfilm and linked to the albeit highly controversial police computer banks on New Scotland Yard's upper floors, where admittance was restricted to officers above the rank of superintendent by special-issue keys to the sealed elevator system.

O'Neil had been one of those who had particularly interested him in the Northern Ireland section.

He was clearly something of a romantic, exhibiting a style – sense of humour even – rare amongst these humourless traders in political terror. That the man was something of an enigma in terrorist terms had not escaped him either.

To his mind, Connor O'Neil did not fit the usual depressing pattern of fanatical though often confused political activists staring out at him from the heavy galleries of mug shots in their thick red binders.

The report stated he was highly intelligent, almost an academic in his thinking. From a sixth-generation landed Ulster family, he had been educated at a leading Catholic public school. He had excelled both on and off the games field.

Head of his house, O'Neil had gone on to the Royal Military Academy at Sandhurst and then to a commission in the Irish Guards. His Army evaluation reports called him a first-class officer and a natural leader of men.

After a second tour of duty in Northern Ireland during the growing days of real strife again in the mid '60s, he suddenly resigned his commission for 'personal reasons' and disappeared from sight – even to his family.

He emerged nearly six years later on the planning committee of the Provisional IRA, the intervening years unaccounted for in his file except for several trips to the Middle East, a minor role in the Six-Day War – on the Arab side – and at least one lengthy stay in Russia.

His time in the IRA was chiefly noted for the dissertation he circulated throughout the Province entitled, *A Political Solution for a Divided Irish People*. It was studied by politicians, security chiefs and rebels alike. It also won him praise in some surprising quarters at a time when any political solution was still a distant concept in regard to Ireland's problems.

Thereafter, he had quarrelled with the Provos' Marxist

9

hierarchy over their policies and set up his own force. Madigan's Brigade had become his life and his means of expression. Chambers felt, strangely, that he would like the man.

Now O'Neil's face was staring at him again from Danvers' photographs, as O'Neil had glanced up Mohammed Zaid Street from Khalid's jeep.

Chambers dragged his mind back to the latest vitriolic lecture from Burroughs, occasioned by his chance remark.

' – and don't you forget it, boy! There's nothing "romantic" about this bastard. He's a terrorist and that's all he is. They blossom like bloody weeds in our soft Western garden because of all the publicity the blasted media gives to every act of political violence!'

He coughed on his cigarette, waving it under Chambers' wrinkling nose.

'Wouldn't happen in Russia. They've got more sense. It can't work over there because they'd never let it get into *their* news, boy!'

Perhaps unwisely, Chambers felt he had to defend himself. Although still new to the Department, he knew he would have to get out from under Burroughs' crushing enmity if he was ever to function properly. Respect from his colleagues was equally important. And the growing anger he felt, having read those damning files, would not allow him to hold quiet.

'I'm sorry, Major Burroughs. You are quite wrong,' he began with all the firmness a queasy stomach and aching head could muster.

Burroughs stared at him in mock amazement. Or perhaps he was only concerned with mocking him.

'Wrong? Me? Listen, boy. When you've been at this bloody game for as long as I have, then you can tell me I'm wrong! Meanwhile, shut up and you might learn something!' He loomed over his trainee.

Chambers adjusted his spectacles in a fiddle of nervousness.

'No. And please stop calling me "boy". I have a name, like everybody else.'

He was committed now and continued in a headlong rush of protest.

'I spent nearly three years on political intelligence work with the Ministry of Defence before coming here. A-Am I expected to sit at your feet with my brain switched off, just because you don't agree with anything but your own narrow opinions, and h-half of them thirty years behind the times?'

He marvelled at his own boldness, glancing at the others. They both looked uncomfortable. Given no verbal support by either of them, he launched into another attack, this time edged with desperation.

'O'Neil's not a cardboard cut-out. He's not *just* a terrorist. He is a person, a mind, character. T-There are reasons for why he's the way he is. Analyse them and you are far more likely to find out what he is doing in Damascus – rather than trying to analyse an uncertain situation.'

'Oh really? Do you fancy him or something?' Burroughs scoffed acidly. 'I *know* what he is and it doesn't take your Freudian crap to work it out! Leave the sorting of this bugger to the *men* – boy.'

MacAllister thought it time he stepped in.

'I think that's enough, George. Don't you?' he interrupted softly.

Burroughs laughed bitterly. 'Dear oh dear, holding hands time is it?' he snapped back, temporarily turning his worried venom on the Assistant Head of Section.

'No, George. And you know that,' MacAllister replied with quiet firmness. 'But Peter is here in his official capacity. As one of the team. And a valued one, too.'

His last remark was all it needed to really set Burroughs off.

'Valued, is he?' he barked, ignoring the subject of his sarcastic anger. 'Not to me. Not until "Peter" can prove he's got something of *value* to contribute on this Syrian business.'

He rounded on Chambers again – a big, bitterly angry bear of a man.

'When I've seen you stuff the guts back into one of our lads, or a shovel is the only thing you can use to clear up the customers after one of these bastards has bombed a pub, then talk to me about your theories!'

His finger stabbed at Chambers, who had reddened with embarrassment at this admonishment in front of the others.

'O'Neil's a master at the publicity game. He'll use charm, style – whatever you want to call it – to further his opinions. It doesn't change the *fact* that he's a criminal murderer of at least eight British soldiers trying to keep the peace in Northern Ireland, and one of those bastards who prefers to use the gun rather than the legal process for any political gains he wants. If *you* want to be any bloody use to this Department, boy, stop thinking like a thriller writer and start thinking about *why* he's in Damascus!'

Chambers opened his mouth to speak, only to have it shut again by the force of Burroughs' tired fury.

'The political impact of terrorism is egged on by the media stampeding fear into governments and the public. Understand that! Men like O'Neil know it! Use that brain of yours to work out what this lot in Syria can do for him and what he can do for them. O'Neil's got some kind of stunt planned and I want to know about it!'

He turned back to the others, leaving Chambers uncertain whether to go or stay.

'Jim, get on to Northern Ireland Special Branch and find out who else besides O'Neil and Docherty from this Madigan's Brigade are out of the Province. I want a report from the SAS's deep penetration boys down on the border, as well. The Provos or those INLA maniacs might be in on this thing – I don't know.'

He wheeled on Chambers, who had foolishly decided to stay.

'*You* can go through every internal and external circular on any Government or VIP visits to the Middle East scheduled for the next six months. See if there's any link with these jokers in Damascus. I want a breakdown summary out of you by the end of today. With any likely suggestions you can dredge up from that genius I'm told you've got!'

'Teddy' MacAllister was next on his list of angry demands.

'Mac, I want to send a priority-one signal to Danvers. We've *got* to have more information on this conference out there. Especially why the hell O'Neil is in on it.'

MacAllister looked slightly uncomfortable. Burroughs stared at him.

'Well?'

MacAllister glanced at Chambers and Nye.

'George, step outside for a minute, will you?' he requested in his soft brogue.

Burroughs shrugged and did as he was asked. When they were out in the corridor, with the door closed, MacAllister told him the worst.

'I'm sorry, old boy. Holman has ordered me to clear any transmission you want put out with him. You know how it is. I'll have to ask him –'

Burroughs was about to explode, MacAllister could see that. He placed a hand on the big man's shoulder, staying him.

' – before I can allow it. Perhaps if you baited him less, he wouldn't be so . . . difficult, George.'

Burroughs let out his breath in an exasperated wheeze. Dear Christ, he couldn't win round here!

'All right, Mac. But I'll not lick the little sod's arse. I've already sent my own report straight through to the Minister. I'm sick and tired of his carping. Christ, man, we've got a job to do!'

The Assistant Head of Section smiled sympathetically.

'I agree, but not at the expense of your own. He'll have you out if you go on pushing him, old boy. Think of your pension. It's not far off. Is it worth damaging that?'

'They can stuff their inflation-linked hush money! I'm still doing the job at the moment, and I'll do it properly or not at all. If my hunch is right, there's bigger things at stake than that little tyke!'

It was MacAllister's turn to stare.

'What are you driving at, George?'

Burroughs sniffed loudly.

'Just this. There are two biggies coming up in the Middle East over the next two months or so: Carter's peace treaty and Her Majesty's royal tour of the Gulf States. Knowing O'Neil, I'd say one of the two – or both – are the reason for his sudden appearance in Lawrence of Arabia land. I *have to* find out. And bloody quick! So either help me, Mac, or step out of my way!'

He slammed back into his tiny office, glaring at its occupants.

'What do you two want? Written invitations? Get on with it!'

'Teddy' MacAllister walked thoughtfully down the corridor as Chambers and Detective Inspector Nye retreated in his wake. He hoped to God that George was wrong this time. But he was probably bang on target. He'd have to persuade Holman to co-operate. They'd all be out on their ears if George had got it right and nobody did anything about it . . .

Despite their 3 a.m. summons to see Khalid, all three of them were up again in good time, as clear skies promised another fine day. Although still confined to their rooms, O'Neil was allowed to hold a brief meeting with Kassim and Docherty whilst the conference got under way again downstairs.

His message to them both was equally brief and to the point.

'We've got one chance to pull this thing through with these laddies and their Russian playmates. So our presentation has got to be watertight. And united.'

He paused, staring at them, his eyes like chips of blue stone.

'If there's anything, anything at all you don't like about the plan, you'd best say so now. It'll be too late once we're in there . . .'

Docherty shrugged his huge shoulders. There was nothing

he could say that the Captain would be wanting to listen to now. Not with that mad light in his eyes. Hassan Kassim thought about his own 'plan' and held his counsel.

O'Neil nodded, apparently satisfied.

'Good. I'll see the pair of you at three o'clock then.'

He laughed, tension showing in his sharpness.

'Do you suppose they'll give us chairs this time – or stakes?'

His lieutenant smiled back grimly. Kassim's face did not change its expression of watchful expectancy. Jesus, thought O'Neil, you'd think they were going to a wake, from all the joy these two were showing.

He got up off his bed, the humour dying in his eyes.

'All right. I've things to do yet.'

O'Neil turned his back on them in dismissal, determined they would not see his concern at their apparent lack of enthusiasm. What the hell . . . they'd perk up soon enough when the action hit them.

Docherty and Kassim filed out, leaving O'Neil to his thoughts. They did not speak to one another as they walked back to their own rooms with the now ever-present guards.

The telephone call Burroughs received from Sam Cook had lightened his mood a little. Cook's thanks for his efforts in getting him off the hook with his departmental head made up for the restless hours he had spent during the remainder of the night after leaving the Soho night club.

When the internal phone rang again, it was his own chief. It sent his mood unerringly back to the bottom of his shoes. He was to report to Holman immediately. At his town apartment. MacAllister was to attend as well.

Burroughs sighed as Holman rang off peremptorily. He sat for a moment before picking up the receiver again to dial the Assistant Head of Section's extension.

Chambers ploughed his way through the official memoranda piled around him in a furrow of finished investigation on the small desk he had been assigned in the main Duty Room.

So far, the only visit of note was the Queen's royal tour, and he didn't think that was a realistic possibility for one of O'Neil's 'demonstrations'. Security would be second to none. Anyway, he couldn't really see O'Neil being stupid enough to risk harming or compromising the Royal Family. Terrorist or not now, the man had once served as a lieutenant in the Irish Guards and such things die hard in a soldier's make-up. Still, he'd better put it forward or Burroughs would crucify him again.

He took off his glasses, rubbing at the bridge of his nose. Nearly four o'clock. Burroughs would be back soon from his meeting with Sir David. Chambers wondered what that meeting was about and returned wearily to the minutiae of official appointments throughout the Middle East.

Kassim glanced at the Seiko chronometer strapped to his left 'wrist'. His men would have received his message via Khalil al-Wazir. They would be ready. It was time for him to flight his own course.

He could hear the guard shuffling with boredom outside his door. It was only a question of getting past him.

The guard did not even hear him, let alone feel the swishing claw lightly clip consciousness from his brain. The Hawk was free.

Burroughs met up with MacAllister down in the basement motor pool. They didn't say much to each other as Burroughs gunned the Jaguar's engine against the freezing cold. It cut out three times before finally firing properly. Getting a new car was another New Year's resolution he was going to keep, he thought, and glanced at his silent colleague in the passenger seat.

'Don't suppose we're being invited for a New Year's drink, do you?' he ventured.

MacAllister did not turn his head. 'I hardly think so,' he replied shortly, returning to his own thoughts.

He'd had no choice but to let Holman know of Burroughs' unauthorised report to the Minister, and he didn't fancy having to cope with George when he found out – which would be in about twenty minutes' time.

Holman had raged at him for at least as long on the phone. MacAllister liked Burroughs, respected his work, and thought Sir David 'unsuitable' for his role as an Intelligence Director, but could see no point in deliberately antagonising the man in the way George appeared to enjoy doing.

Personally, he was surprised the Director had let so many incidents go during the two years he'd been in charge of the Department's vital Middle East Section. But he was sure George had gone too far this time.

On the drive to Holman's apartment, Burroughs kept the conversation going by relating his trip down to see old Mr Betts, choosing to ignore the AHS's monosyllabic contribution. If he wanted to sulk just because he'd had a go at him earlier, it was all right with him.

They drew up outside Holman's town residence, their journey eased by the snowploughs and grit lorries at last out on the streets.

'Right. Let's get this over with,' Burroughs sighed.

MacAllister gave him an old-fashioned look as Burroughs climbed from the car and rapped without hesitation on the ornate brass lion's-head door-knocker.

The saying 'like a lamb to the slaughter' occurred to him, and was rejected. Some lamb, thought MacAllister as he got out of the car. The Assistant Head of Section wasn't looking forward to this contest of egos, and would not have cared to place bets on who would win the encounter.

They were greeted with frosty politeness by the Holmans' very English maid. She ushered them through the house to a large, high-ceilinged drawing-room, and withdrew instantly. They were not offered a drink.

Left so abruptly to their own devices, there was nothing else for them to do but stare at their surroundings. There was plenty for the visitors to stare at.

Lady Holman's taste was very much in evidence. Rustic scenes by a variety of minor Victorian landscape painters abounded. There was one reasonably good Whistler original to balance the overdone pictorial profusion. Several highly stylised equestrian statues stood in prominent positions around the room on a series of period tables.

A virtual gallery of framed photographs hung in pride of place along one Wedgwood blue wall, all showing the lady of the house either shaking hands with celebrities at her various charity functions or judging equally prestigious field-sports events. There was not a single photograph of her husband, with or without appropriate personages in tow.

The furniture was entirely antique but dominated by Dutch marquetry to the point of fetishism. Combined with the proliferation of insignificant art, bronzes, Edwardian vases, potted plants and the heavy crimson drapes at the windows, MacAllister thought it all rather vulgar. Burroughs simply found it oppressive.

When their chief decided they had been kept waiting long enough, he entered the drawing-room via the communicating doors from his dining-room.

It was the first time either of them had seen him informally dressed. Holman was wearing a rather tightly cut pair of light blue slacks, a light blue cashmere turtleneck sweater, and white Gucci shoes.

Having only ever seen him in the senior civil servant's stock pinstripe, the effect was something of a shock. It also set Burroughs wondering. He'd heard a number of vague rumours since Holman had come to the Department, but had always discounted them as a product of the man's wide-ranging unpopularity. Now he was not so sure. It would certainly account for a lot of what Burroughs saw as his chief's spiteful unreasonableness.

Holman did not waste time on pleasantries, even to Mac-Allister.

'I understand from my Assistant Head that you have seen fit to break one of the Department's cardinal rules, Burroughs. You will withdraw your report to my Minister at once. Fortunately he is still away in Bahrain and the damage you could have caused can be rectified.'

Burroughs glared at MacAllister. This was a great start to the year! 'Teddy' MacAllister flushed and wished he'd never involved himself.

'Thanks a lot, Mac. Personal hatchet-jobs one of your resolutions for 1979?' Burroughs inquired bitingly and turned back to Holman.

'No, sir. I cannot do that. And you cannot force me to,' he stated flatly, determined to control his anger. 'Every other "rule" around here seems to be made to be broken. So I'm making a few of my own.'

Holman's face had gone white with matching anger.

'How dare you speak to me like this in my own home! You may have only a few more months with us, Burroughs, but by God you will *not* get away with this . . . this monstrous behaviour!'

He snapped his fingers at MacAllister.

'You will witness this instruction. And I want it entered in the DO log. Either you withdraw that report and submit any complaints you may have through your immediate superior here,' he spat at Burroughs, 'or I will place you on suspension pending a departmental inquiry! I warned you before, damn you! You have twenty-four hours to avoid the consequences. Now *get out*!'

Holman had lost control of himself, fuelled by the row he'd had earlier with his wife over his insistence on missing their local hunt's New Year luncheon in order to confront Burroughs during this rare holiday break. She had already left for their West Country home near Berkeley in high dudgeon, leaving him without personal transport (his official driver was off for the day) and only the maid as company for the next couple of days.

Burroughs watched Holman's mouth opening and closing with impotent fury, and stared at him flat-eyed.

'You've threatened me with that before and I told you then to look to your own record,' he answered coldly.

139

Holman's face became suffused with an apoplectic crimson as Burroughs continued remorselessly.

'Your inability to make or hold to the right decisions, and the panic you get yourself in trying to cover your own weakness, cost the lives of five innocent civilians, two British soldiers and a member of your embassy staff in Dubai. The worst of it was the whitewash job put up to protect the embassy's good name and your neck. I'm not going to let you drag *me* into a repeat performance.'

He lit a cigarette with deliberate provocation.

' – unless you *want* the possible murder of our Royal Family on your conscience as well . . . sir?'

Holman seemed stricken into silence by the reminder, statue-still. His antagonist glanced contemptuously at his other embarrassed colleague.

'As for you, MacAllister. Don't *ever* tell me again I've got your back-up. I'd prefer to rely on Mickey Mouse. He'd about suit the way this bloody section's run.'

With that, he headed for the front door, leaving his chief and the Assistant Head of Section to discuss whether or not to proceed against him.

CHAPTER ELEVEN

O'Neil was checking through his notes and maps when Major Khalid strode into his room, agitation showing clearly on his dark features.

'We have a problem,' he announced angrily. 'Kassim has disappeared.'

O'Neil smiled faintly. It was no more than he'd expected. You cannot cage a wild thing and then yell when it doesn't co-operate.

'You've got a problem, you mean,' he rejoined sardonically. 'I'd not want to be wearing your shoes when your Russian dandies find out.'

Khalid scowled at him. O'Neil chuckled briefly.

'I wouldn't take on so, Khalid. He'll be there. But in his own time and on his own terms. Now, are we going to this meeting or are we not?'

'My orders have not been changed,' Khalid replied stiffly, common adversity demanding his tolerance of this impudent foreigner.

O'Neil stretched, then examined his watch.

'Then I suggest we get on with it, Major. It'd be a powerful shame to keep such important gentlemen waiting.'

Khalid scowled at him again. Since the arrival of Hassan El-Nesr on the scene, he felt he was losing control of the situation. He would have to do something about it – and very soon.

The greetings between Kassim and his three compatriots were brief but quietly jubilant. Now they would show these Moscow puppeteers hiding in their anonymous hotels how the 'wings of the desert' moved.

The small Peugeot sped through the backstreets which mazed the Malki Quarter until it reached the southernmost weave of the labyrinth, stopping some fifty yards short of a modest three-storey hotel.

Despite the tourist expansion President Assad was trying to encourage for his country, the majority of visitors were still from fellow Arab states, and the hotel had conceded nothing to Western tastes. Its very drabness assisted its convenient unnoticeability.

Its anonymity proved ideal for the two important guests lodged in what was the hotel's nearest thing to a suite at the rear of the third floor.

Contrary to popular telling in espionage thrillers, visiting KGB and GPU intelligence officers do not use their local embassies when on assignments in foreign countries – except in dire emergency. Only their people actively employed on a Soviet embassy's listed strength – and usually accredited as trade or cultural attachés – operate from within that embassy's internal facilities.

The reason is a simple one. In many territories where they have diplomatic representation, an open use of an intelligence presence would both embarrass the host country and undermine the embassy's effectiveness, and the nature of Soviet political subversion requires its perpetrators to work through local Marxist sympathisers or guerilla groups.

Although such covert behaviour makes a mockery of any Soviet claims for 'peaceful coexistence' with the West, recent revelations about Western governments' similar operations, notably the United States' CIA, in Latin America and Europe respectively, have rather deflated the outraged protests fronted by the politicians of the day.

Kassim and his three comrades took only hand-guns with them as they slipped through the hotel's deserted backyard, avoiding the KGB security men posted at the front of the building and in the hotel reception area.

They moved quietly up the stairs from landing to landing (there was no lift and therefore no sudden discovery to worry about) until they reached the third floor. Kassim's information was good. He knew exactly in which rooms he would find his quarry.

Halting at the far end of the landing, they held a whispered discussion on how they would get rid of the agent standing on guard outside the vital door. It was quickly decided that Rashid Khadir would draw the man away whilst the others waited on the stairs.

They achieved their first objective with almost laughable ease. In itself, that should have alerted them. Posing as one of the hotel's staff, Khadir walked straight up to the guard and told him in halting English that he was wanted urgently by his comrades downstairs.

The guard, on secondment from the Soviet Embassy, made a business of eyeing him suspiciously before apparently deciding that the request was genuine and following Khadir towards the stairs.

142

His mistake was made painfully unclear to him as the butt of a Walther PK cracked across the back of his head. The four days he spent in the Embassy's sick bay, with mild concussion, caused him to wonder if his contrived 'careless-ness' had been worth it – except to the Colonel.

When the Hawk quietly entered the two-bedroomed suite, the Colonel was just pouring himself a drink.

He was humming an opera piece as he splashed some Perrier water into his glass. He always carried a supply of the purified water with him on his trips to the Middle East, and liked to watch the bubbles add sparkle to the Scotch whisky, of which he had been a devotee since his first assign-ment in Britain shortly after the end of World War II – in-volving his British counterpart Philby. In fact, it was Philby who had introduced him to the delights of the finest whisky blenders in the world.

The Colonel held the glass to the light before sampling the ten-year-old malt, then turned to face Kassim's concerted guns. There was neither fear nor surprise in his amused grey eyes. Since receiving Khalid's agitated telephone call, he had been expecting something like this.

Alexis Leonid Solenov, Hero of the Soviet Union, Order of the Red Banner, and holder of the Hammer and Sickle Gold Medal, threw back his fine head and laughed in a dazzling display of gold fillings.

'Come in, Comrade Hawk. Come in!' he chuckled in per-fect English. 'And save the melodramatics for the streets of Beirut!'

For a second, Hassan Kassim was disconcerted. He would have been surprised if this KGB colonel had not known something of his past doings, but he had not expected his own sudden appearance, fully armed, to be met with such a reaction. Anger, yes. Caution, certainly. But amusement?

Hassan Kassim was even more disconcerted when four of the Colonel's local agents stepped out from their hiding-places, their own guns drawn.

The Colonel chuckled again, enjoying himself. Four against four. He seldom carried such obvious weapons and was not armed now. A man of his position did not buy a dog and then bark himself.

'You see? You were anticipated, my friend. Perhaps you should learn to play chess. Part of the business of survival. I learnt it on the Russian Front in '44!'

He suddenly became very serious, menace replacing bonhomie on his mobile features.

'I suggest you surrender your weapons. I would regret my men having to take them from you by force. It would upset the balance of my plans . . . and yours.'

Kassim stared at the Russian, knowing he had been compromised in front of his own men.

He saw a tall, elegant figure in his late fifties. Solenov wore his tailored Western suit like a uniform. He was a strikingly goodlooking man by any standards, and his prematurely white hair added the finishing touches to an appearance which belied his grimly devious calling.

A graduate of Leningrad university, he spoke five European languages, had been an Olympic-grade fencer, had written three noted manuals on the art of subversive espionage, claimed one of the Bolshoi Ballet's principal dancers as his current mistress, and wore the blood of many men on the soul he did not accept he had.

Cultured, articulate and equipped with a ruthless intellect to manage his ruthless dedication to Marxism, the State and his own comfortable advancement within it, his wickedly subtle sense of humour was judged a contradiction that made his superiors wary of him and his subordinates often terrified.

He was also a Jew. An eventual protégé of the dreaded Beria, his father had been a noted physics professor, murdered during one of 'Jo' Stalin's paranoid purges against 'Jewish pseudo-intellectuals'. His only son had never responded to his father's religious devotion nor to his mother's sense of her race's history, finding it boring and over-emotional. Even in his teens, he had decided to erase all such risky traces from his background by whatever means he could.

The Second World War provided the young 'Solenov'

with the perfect opportunity. In a Russia of such vast size, where the advent of Lenin's Communism had not seen an appreciable end to the inefficiency and widespread corruption that had existed under the final tsar, war with Germany only added to the bureaucratic confusion.

His murder of a 'pure-bred' Russian soldier went undetected. The boy was a raw recruit around his own age, about to join a tank unit based near Stalingrad and hundreds of miles from his home town on the edge of the Black Sea.

Talking with his victim in the People's Cafeteria attached to the railway station, which he frequented in the hope of finding such a dupe, it was neither hard to get from him the information he needed on the recruit's family and the unit he was going to join, nor to persuade the youth to come back to his place for a meal whilst he waited out the long interval between connecting trains.

The youth never arrived anywhere with his new-found friend. Instead, he received six inches of cold steel as a gesture of friendship and the local disused well as his grave.

Darkness covered the callous deed and saved his murderer from serving out the war in a Jewish labour battalion, Russian or German.

Armed with his victim's identity papers, movement order and uniform, the new Solenov quickly adjusted to military life. Promoted twice in the field for outstanding bravery, he eventually came to the attention of perhaps the greatest general in Russia's bloody history: Zhukov.

By the end of the war, he had seen action throughout the Eastern Front, including the bitter battle for Stalingrad in temperatures so far below zero that a man's hand would freeze to his weapons in a matter of seconds.

Highly decorated, noted for his tactical cunning and leadership, he saw out the end of the war in Berlin itself. Far from hating the Germans for invading his country, he found himself admiring their efficiency and cold, intellectual approach to racial supremacy, feeling nothing for his fellow Jews gassed and starved into extinction. His own atheism was guard enough against anything so emotive.

But danger was not over for him even yet. Despite having used his one leave period in 1942 to trace Solenov's family and raze their house to the ground in a fire that wiped out the boy's widowed mother and two younger sisters – a case of arson never to be solved – there was still the question of his own kin.

Recruited into the State Security Service, the dashing young tank major swiftly moved up the rungs, surviving jealousy and competition until he came face to face with Beria. Beria liked the look of him, the way his mind worked, and sent him off to university and the KGB's training unit.

Emerging from both with flying colours, his final erasures became easy. Having engineered his father's murder as a 'traitor to the State', he sent his mother to the endless hell of Siberia, where she died of pneumonia. All close relatives of the real Solenov went to similar ends, never knowing what they had done to deserve such a terrible visitation of tragedy. He was safe.

If Beria ever suspected his origins, it was never stated and his access to his own personnel file made sure it never was. The years went by. He scored notable espionage successes, always dodging the purges by dint of his devoted record to the State.

Stalin's death brought him only further trust from the new masters and his loyalty was never questioned again. True, many in the KGB and the Kremlin's Politburo did not know quite what to make of his Westernised manners and tastes, but his efficiency and record spoke the loudest for his continuing favour in high places. He fully expected to become a general, even a marshal, by the time he retired.

'Alexis Leonid Solenov' was a very dangerous animal, a survivor, made the more so by his ability to adapt his camouflage at will. Wise men gave him a wide circle. The foolish lived, and died, to regret that they had not.

As he now lit a Sobranie 'Black Russian' with his milled-gold Dupont lighter, he was about to demonstrate a particular facet of his complex character.

'I think we'd best draw this hunting-bird's claws, don't you?' he asked the senior of his agents in Russian. The man looked puzzled and then grinned, appreciating the cruel humour behind the Colonel's 'question'.

Kassim and his men had already put up their weapons, accepting that a pitched battle was to nobody's advantage at this stage. One of the Soviet agents took charge of them, removing the butt-loaded magazines from three of the guns and ejecting the chambered Colt's bullets into his hand. Another frisked each man. Nothing else was found.

The Hawk continued to stare at Solenov, his face a dark, scarred mask of neutrality, torn inside between laughing at their predicament and raging at his humiliation. But Solenov had only just started with him. He nodded to his senior helper. The man advanced on Kassim, covered by his comrades' machine-pistols.

'You will remove your jacket and shirt. Now.'

His English had none of the Colonel's refinements. Kassim shot a hard stare at Solenov, who smiled back benignly.

'I am sure you will understand, Comrade Hawk.'

He flicked a manicured finger at the scar tissue running across the Hawk's brow. 'I like my face as it is.'

The agents moved in as Kassim slowly peeled off his jacket. Growing impatient, the one who had already spoken jabbed him in the ribs with his pistol, careful to avoid those hooks.

'The shirt.'

Kassim shrugged, his face still showing nothing.

'I will need help.'

'But of course,' the Colonel laughed humourlessly. 'It must be difficult . . . being a cripple.'

Kassim flushed angrily and clicked a hook at Khadir. The Palestinian stepped forward to unbutton his leader's shirt, with the nearest thing to an embarrassed apology he could muster on his face.

There were more scars on the guerilla leader's body, all relics of that terrifying mishap in Israel. Slabs of muscle sat against his chest and biceps; when clothed, his wiry build

147

was somewhat misleading as to the mucle power he wielded to operate his deadly hooks.

The hooks themselves were literally sheathed to his forearms by a series of spring-loaded metal rods, operated by muscle pressure. Each forearm was covered in a moulded leather 'skin' from wrist to elbow, rather like a long evening glove. Straps, crossed over his back and chest, running like twin bridles down his upper arms, gave the whole apparatus extra security and leverage. It must have taken a lot of getting used to.

Having removed Kassim's shirt, Khadir stepped back uncertainly as the Colonel's agents moved towards Kassim in a phalanx of guns. While two of them held his wrists, the senior man began to unbuckle the straps.

Moments later, it all lay in a heap on the floor. The Hawk's humiliation was complete. Standing there, clawless and with his stumps a pink shine of skin grafts, his vulnerability was cruelly obvious. The outrageousness of Solenov's action was something he would never forgive the Russian, but for now it had to be endured for the sake of wider aims.

Solenov nodded his silvery head again, apparently satisfied. 'You may put your comrade's shirt back on,' he instructed Khadir and smiled enigmatically at the guerilla leader. 'I think we can talk safely now, my friend.'

Kassim waited until his shirt had been buttoned for him, and then directed his hawklike stare at the Colonel. Solenov felt a brief flash of apprehension, which surprised him.

'We will talk,' Hassan Kassim replied softly. 'But you would be wise to understand that taking away my "claws" does not take away my Commando's talons. You should also know that I do play chess, "Comrade" Colonel . . . Be careful I do not upset the board over you. Checkmate is only victory if both players abide by the rules.'

Colonel Solenov raised his eyebrows. 'I see . . . Well, we will have to wait for that, shan't we? Meanwhile, Major Khalid and your partner in this venture will be arriving shortly. At this stage of the game, I suggest you put *your* proposition to me before any other moves are decided between us all.'

Kassim treated him to his unblinking stare again and kicked his hooks out of his way, pushing past the guards to one of the cushioned settles.

It took him less than ten minutes to outline his alternative proposals and Colonel Solenov's wary respect for the man had increased tenfold by the time Connor O'Neil arrived on the scene.

But he still did not choose to release the Hawk from his undignified nudeness in front of his other 'guests'. In Solenov's world, mastery took many forms and was not easily surrendered. If Hassan the Hawk wanted that, he would have to wrest it from him.

Kassim accepted this. He also thought that this KGB colonel might easily get blinded by his own confident arrogance.

When O'Neil arrived at the hotel with Docherty and a still agitated Major Khalid, his amusement at Kassim's upstaging turned to anger when he saw what the Russian had done to him, but he did not show it. Khalid was openly delighted and, although O'Neil could not understand what was said between them in Arabic, it was obvious that the enmity existing on their side of this operation was not going to be easily healed.

Nodding to Kassim in recognition, he strolled over to Solenov and stood looking at him, his hands in his pockets.

'So you're the laddie all the fuss is about, are you?' he inquired lightly. 'I'll not be offering you my hand, if you don't mind. I'd hate to finish up like my friend here.'

Solenov eyed the tall Irishman for a moment and then laughed.

'And you must be Captain O'Neil. I do not think I will offer you mine, either. From what I have read of you and your ideas, your wits are sharp enough for *me* to finish up like our wild young friend!'

O'Neil inclined his head at the Russian's rather tasteless

compliment. Privately, Solenov was thinking that he had got more than he'd bargained for with these two. The giant looked a troublesome third. But their plan was superb and the Palestinian's refinements to it much to his liking.

Solenov lit another Black Russian and motioned his guests to join Kassim on the cushioned settles placed round the suite, suddenly becoming coldly businesslike.

'Very well, gentlemen. We will begin. But first, you must meet my superior, who will decide whether or not this scheme of yours is to receive our blessing.' He turned to his senior agent, speaking in English. 'Ask the Comrade General if he is ready to join us.'

The man nodded and went through to a double bedroom beyond the sitting-room. He returned moments later with a figure far more in keeping with the popular conception of a Soviet spymaster.

General Grigori Zharevsky was a squat bear of a man, the muscles from his peasant beginnings still bulging under his ill-fitting Russian suit. Closely cropped iron-grey hair sat in a monk's ring around his almost neckless head, and his deep brown eyes were nearly hidden inside the rolls of fat creasing his typically Slavonic features. He was a movie-maker's dream come true.

As he marched across the threadbare carpet in a solid stomp of hard-won authority and girth, O'Neil noted that three fingers were missing from his right hand.

The General nodded curtly at the assembled plotters, his small, sharp eyes coming to rest on Kassim's pink stumps.

'So, you and I have something in common. That is good,' he began in English as badly cut as his suit. His voice was like unwashed gravel.

'I lost mine to the cold outside Stalingrad, fighting the Germans,' he went on, holding up his own souvenir. 'I am glad to learn that your disability was honourably earned fighting the wretched Jews.'

Kassim said nothing as the General turned to his subordinate, reverting to Russian.

'You are a fool, Solenov. You do not gain a man's loyalty

150

by humiliating him – only his treachery. Give him back his . . . hands. Now.'

Colonel Solenov stared at his General, along with the others. They were like chalk and cheese, the one sophisticated, amoral and self-interested, the other rough and crude but with a peasant's honest love of his country.

Alexis Solenov hated him and Zharevsky distrusted this man's smoothly accomplished climb to power with all the earthy instincts of his origins. But, inside the Union of Soviet Socialist Republics, powerful men learned to beware of the sudden changes that could place a lower enemy over their heads, and they sheathed their dealings with their minions in a guarded veneer of comrade-to-comrade vocabulary. The General sometimes forgot himself. Solenov never did.

'Immediately, Comrade General,' he replied in Russian. 'I only thought to protect your presence from any harm. These men are unknown to us.'

The General's brusque grunt said he was not appreciative of Solenov's consideration for his welfare.

'Get on with it. I want this meeting started,' Zharevsky growled.

Solenov gave his men the order in Russian, only to be interrupted by the General in English.

'I have told my Colonel that these games are unnecessary between us. We are all comrades, eh?' he chuckled with crude affability. 'And we will need all the weapons we have for this one, I think! You may use my bedroom, Comrade Kassim. Replace your – your hooks, if you wish.'

Kassim smiled tightly at the General. 'Thank you. I am ɓ . . . pleased that you at least seem to realise that this operation requires all of us to work together.'

If his barb hit home, neither Khalid nor Solenov showed it. O'Neil was quietly amused and admired Kassim's cheek, considering he had elected to break that 'unity' by pre-empting their collective arrival.

When Hassan the Hawk came back from the General's bedroom fully re-equipped, the meeting got under way.

It went on for several hours, the General content to allow

Solenov to conduct its business now he had been put in his place. Having accepted the basis of O'Neil and Kassim's joint plan, it was left to decide on the logistics and modus operandi of the astonishing proposals. Here, there was occasional disagreement, particularly from Major Khalid. He was overruled by the General, to the relief of O'Neil and his guerilla partner.

By the time they were all ready to leave, the operation had been hammered into a realistic and deadly shape, with each man assigned specific tasks for the operation's initial realisation.

Firstly, it was agreed that the plan was both viable and worthwhile. Her Majesty's royal yacht, *Britannia*, would be hijacked, robbed and scuttled in the Suez Canal – to coincide with the final phase of Carter's Middle East peace initiative.

Secondly, it was agreed that the attack should take place on the royal yacht's return passage from the Queen's tour of the Gulf States, rather than during it – when security would render the raid impossible.

It was also accepted, after some hard argument by O'Neil and General Zharevsky, and opposition from Kassim and Major Khalid, that no personal physical harm must come to either of the royal couple should they still be on board.

The object of the raid was to make a political statement and grab the political prize of ruining the Sadat–Begin talks – and of course all of the treasures which would be aboard *Britannia*, received as gifts from the Emirates.

No useful purpose would be served by turning half the world against the raiders, if the Queen or her husband was injured. Or worse.

A series of practical and logistical problems had to be sorted out – with the tour only weeks away.

Major Khalid would handle the procedures, vis-à-vis the senior Libyan delegate to the conference, which would be necessary for obtaining Colonel Gaddafi's vital co-operation over sanctuary for the raiders once the hijack was completed.

Kassim would conduct a careful survey of the Canal Zone for suitable sites at which to seize the *Britannia*. O'Neil was to organise, through his Brigade back in Ulster, a detailed breakdown of the yacht's layout, arms, complement and security arrangements.

O'Neil and Kassim were to have joint control of the training programme for their combined force, and Major Khalid would co-ordinate the whole affair with Colonel Solenov, as the KGB's link-man.

General Zharevsky would remain discreetly in the background, but everything appertaining to the operation was ultimately to be cleared with him.

Russia's KGB, Syria's PLO comrades and O'Neil's Brigade would supply the weapons, explosives and all other equipment required for the raid. Kassim's group would put up the majority of the men needed to pull off the propaganda coup of the decade and the greatest robbery-at-sea since the buccaneer days of the Spanish Main.

The exact details of the Queen's tour itinerary would be obtained via the various diplomatic and intelligence channels open to the KGB and the Syrian Intelligence Service.

A stern warning was issued by Solenov, and backed up by the General, not to underestimate the danger of their operation being discovered and foiled by Mossad, the Israeli secret service – perhaps the best of its kind in the world.

Neither Solenov nor Zharevsky had a very high opinion of either the British or Egyptian counter-espionage organisations, but caution on all fronts was essential.

As to the raid itself, the operation would have to be meticulously timed and executed. The raiders would expect to have completed their 'business' on board the royal yacht in six hours flat, before any chance of retaliation could be realistically mounted.

The whole operation, from its opening gambit of seizing the *Britannia* to the raiders' flight out again to Libya, with the royal yacht scuttled and all the booty they could viably transport taken with them, was calculated to take twelve hours at the most. It would be quite a day.

The meeting broke up as the evening light cast long

shadows over the city. It ended in harmony, with the help of one of Solenov's whisky bottles.

Raising his glass to the success of the incredible mission, the General let out a guttural chuckle.

'Well, my children,' he said jovially. 'We are comrades from many lands but one cause. International Marxism for the masses. You could call us a kind of United Nations . . . but with a difference, eh!'

The others joined in his laughter, wishing him a Happy New Year until they all met again one week away from this night that would change the face of world affairs.

When they got back to the big house on Mohammed Zaid Street, O'Neil caught Major Khalid by the elbow. The Major knitted his brows at this piece of undue familiarity as O'Neil spoke.

'Well now, Major. That was a grand little meeting. I take it you'll remove your guards from around our throats now? We're all in this together, didn't someone say?'

Khalid scowled at him for a moment and then forced a smile on to his dark face.

'That is in order, Captain. But I must have your word that none of you will attempt to leave this house without my knowledge and agreement. I am – ' he stumbled over the word in his stilted English, 'co-ordinating this operation. Remember that.'

O'Neil grinned at him cheerfully. 'Oh, you'll not have any trouble out of me or Docherty. It's your Mister Hawk you'll have to watch.'

Khalid scowled again. 'He is not *my* anything. Very well, the guards will be removed. You may inform the others.'

O'Neil watched the Syrian stalk off, amusement in his blue eyes. The gallant major seemed a wee bit put out that it was all going ahead. He'd have to live with it, like it or not.

His eyes clouded over when he thought about Hassan Kassim. That laddie needed sorting. Right now. There was too much at stake for anyone to start rocking the boat. Except Her Majesty's.

154

He found the guerilla leader in his room. Someone had just finished rubbing some surgical spirit into his stumps, so Kassim had his hooks off again. He did not look up when O'Neil entered.

'They giving you trouble, are they?' O'Neil inquired solicitously. He was genuinely concerned. They couldn't afford to have Kassim out of action at this stage. His liking for the man had been somewhat dampened by the guerilla leader's little display of ego back at the hotel.

Kassim stopped what he was doing with a shrug, staring at O'Neil.

'No. It is a regular thing. It keeps them from – how do you say? – chafing.'

O'Neil gave a noncommittal 'Ah'. He continued, 'That Solenov is quite a bastard to do that to you. But you did rather ask for it, did you not?'

Kassim's face darkened at the memory and then he smiled suddenly.

'That is true, my friend. He will live to regret it.'

It was O'Neil's turn to darken. He sat himself down in the only chair and leaned forward, his eyes cold.

'Now look, Hassan. Forget it. We've got an operation to carry out and that means working with Solenov. Sure, he'll bear watching. So will you, I'm thinking.'

Kassim gave another shrug. 'I do not think so. You and I have agreed that we will split the booty – all we can take between us. What is there for this Russian, except disgrace?'

O'Neil gave him a hard stare back. 'Just see you remember it, friend Hawk.'

Kassim stood up with a laugh, pointing at his hooks on the bed with one of his stumps. That shrill sound still disturbed O'Neil.

'All right, my Irish comrade. We will leave it! Come, friends should help each other. Put me together again, if you will . . .'

O'Neil could not help grinning. The fellow was impossible.

'You're welcome,' he smiled, picking up the paraphernalia which turned Hassan the Hawk into a deadly weapon.

As he strapped him up, O'Neil recalled a childhood nursery rhyme.

' "Humpty Dumpty sat on a wall, Humpty Dumpty had a great fall," ' he recited. ' "All the King's horses and all the King's men couldn't put Humpty together again . . . " '

The guerilla leader looked puzzled, then annoyed, thinking he was being mocked over his unfortunate incapacity. O'Neil quickly disabused him.

'It's an old kids' nursery song,' he explained. 'Only I'm thinking it's got itself a new twist. We'll take Her Majesty's royal yacht and Carter's little treaty apart at the seams. All the Queen's men won't get her back her pretty baubles nor Carter his place in history. This Humpty Dumpty was an egg, you see, and we'll scramble this one for sure!'

Kassim's shrill shriek of delight echoed round the stone-faced bedroom. He enjoyed O'Neil's company and liked his sense of humour. He could only hope the Irishman's sense of fun would hold up when it was all over and he found himself sharing an empty joke and emptier hands with that Russian pig.

George Burroughs got back to his office in Century House as Chambers was completing his notes in the deserted Duty Room. Burroughs felt a lot better for his confrontation with Sir David. It would teach the little sod where it was at. He didn't believe for a moment that Holman would take the matter further, whatever MacAllister might think.

Chambers stood up nervously as Burroughs flung his overcoat into the corner, expecting more trouble. His tutor's manner came as an agreeable surprise.

'Sit down, er, Peter. You got anywhere with all this crap?' he asked cheerfully, indicating the pile of papers in front of his assistant.

'I, um, well I think so,' Chambers stammered.

Burroughs hooked a small silver flask out of his back pocket, thumping it down on the desk.

'Take a pull on that, son. It's bloody cold in here.'

Chambers gulped, flushing. Oh Lord, not more drinking.

'Er, thank you.'

He gingerly took a drink from the flask, if only to keep Burroughs in this rare mood, feeling the scotch burn through his upset stomach. It made him slightly heady, since he hadn't dared to eat anything all day.

'Major Burroughs, I-I have put together some ideas,' he ventured. 'You may not think any of them relevant but – '

'Call me George, for Christ's sake!' Burroughs interjected convivially.

Chambers was not sure if he'd heard right.

'S-Sorry?'

'Call me George,' Burroughs repeated, on the edge of testiness. Try to be nice to the kid and he starts yelping. 'We're going to be working on this thing all hours God made, so we might as well learn to get on together.'

Chambers nodded, bemused by his change of fortune, hoping it would last.

'Yes . . . right, I, er, George. These are my notes.'

Burroughs pulled up a chair and took them from him. Ten minutes later, he had read through his assistant's careful, handwritten summary.

'Very good, Peter. I think you're on the right track,' he conceded. 'I reckon it's got to be something to do with either Carter's peace treaty or the Queen's visit. Don't know that I agree with you about the royal tour though. O'Neil and his little chums are quite capable of taking that on.'

He helped himself to the flask.

'I'm sending to Danvers for deeper information. With the stuff we'll get back from Northern Ireland SB and the SAS boys, I think we'll find some answers. Nothing else to do meanwhile but wait it out.'

Chambers agreed. Perhaps he'd be able to get a few more days down at the Registry. He pulled his thoughts back to what his companion was saying.

' – so you might as well get off home. I'll lock up here and take the keys back to the duty officer.'

Chambers smiled gratefully and got up to put on his coat.

As he was walking towards the door, Burroughs called him back.

'Look. About this morning. I'm sorry I had a go at you. Lot on my mind with this thing.'

Chambers started to protest that it didn't matter. The glare from his tutor shut him up. Couldn't the boy even accept an apology?

'I want you to understand about men like O'Neil. Know your enemy is the first rule in beating him. Sit down a moment, will you?'

He did as he was told, resigning himself to another long lecture. But, as Burroughs talked, his interest was gradually caught and he realised why the man's colleagues valued him, despite his difficult ways.

' – and in the old days of the IRA, they used to help the soldiers in the Bogside by patrolling the streets. Any trouble-makers were handed over without a fuss. Did you know that Finney Coyle, who was a giant of a man and leader of the IRA then, used to walk through Belfast on a Sunday with his brood of kids and chat with the British soldiers? And the women would bring them presents of sweets and biscuits in those days. It was never a game to the Irish, but there were rules and everyone observed them.'

He paused to light a cigarette.

'It all changed in the mid '60s, with the one-man-one-vote campaign. Instead of conceding politically, we British decided to chuck paraffin on a smouldering mattress. Bringing in the hated B Specials and the rigged elections soured the whole thing. Of course, the Marxists got their foot in the door with a vengeance.'

He sighed.

'The Provisional IRA was bred at their curdled breast, Peter, and turned it into an out-and-out war of bitterness and sectarian violence.'

Burroughs coughed on his cigarette.

'These jokers in the Provisional IRA and the Irish National Liberation Army don't give a damn about Ireland or the old Sinn Fein. All they want to see is Marxism as top dog and Ireland turned into the Cuba of Europe. The historical differences with the United Kingdom are being used as a platform for something far more sinister.'

His hand slammed down on the desk, making Chambers jump.

'They'll use any means to get it – and anybody. They fight amongst themselves with the same vicious treachery they use on our poor bloody soldiers! And the Americans who donate to their funds through NORAID and the Green Cross Society don't begin to realise that they're not giving to a cause for political freedom but to the nurturing of the same monster *they* tried to halt in Vietnam. *That's* what we're fighting, lad, and O'Neil is coloured as red as the rest of their kind!'

He stubbed out his cigarette and lit up another one.

'You know, history is seldom what it seems and even less likely to be written up as it was. Take this Palestinian business. They're being manipulated by the Soviets. Try reading a man called Walter Schwarz or the Irish writer, Gerry Hanley, who called Ulster "the kerbside of hell". I reckon the area surrounding modern Israel is its sister.'

Burroughs coughed again and took a long pull from the whisky flask on Chambers' littered desk.

'There was a lot of sympathy for the Palestinians at the end of the Second World War. The British troops sent in to clear them out didn't like the job one little bit. I know – I was there. The Palestinian refugees were ejected by the Jews with all the cruel violence they now exact on the Israelis. A quarter of a million of them!'

His hand thumped the desk again.

'You won't remember a sweet, white-haired old gentleman called Ben-Gurion. His followers originally treated the Palestinians worse than they ever treated the Israelis. The Jews have become what somebody, I forget who, once described as professional martyrs.'

Chambers risked a question.

'You're not condoning what happened in Nazi Germany, surely?'

'Of course not!' Burroughs snapped, forgetting his second New Year's resolution. 'I admire the Israelis – and what they've done to make their country into something. And most people are moved by the things that have happened to them throughout their history.'

Burroughs waved a finger at his assistant, who was part-Jewish.

'But I also remember what the Stern Gang did to our soldiers and the like. They were no better than the PLO today. That's how Begin got started in politics, for God's sake! They're a pushy lot, sorry for them or not, and, like the Provos in Ulster, they don't give a sod for anything but their own affairs – which makes them so bloody difficult to reason with.

'Look,' he leaned forward urgently. 'You're an intelligent young man but beset by kindness. Don't let your emotions get in the way of your judgement. No good in this game. What the PLO gets up to is inexcusable – of course it is – along with all the other political groups who try to make their point through terrorism. But there are always two sides to any quarrel – yes, I include mine with Holman!' he grinned wickedly.

'Just remember what I've told you, Peter. Nothing is ever as it seems at first. My old boss here, Norman Healey-Betts, taught me that. We all take stances to cover our own point of view. But until the world learns to temper national desires or political ideologies with the common things of common interest to us all – especially security of borders, energy, food and the ecology – it'll go on making the work of people like you and me necessary. And the secret service we work for.'

He glanced at his watch.

'Come on. Time we were gone. See you in the morning.'

Chambers nodded thoughtfully, wished him a Happy New Year, and left the Duty Room.

George Burroughs sat by the desk for a long time, listening to the evening sounds of London outside the snow-starred windows.

He knew he was a patriot of the old school, but there were moments when he wondered who *was* right these days, whatever he might feel constrained to say to a newcomer like Chambers.

He sighed and got up off his chair, peering through the windows at the snow falling steadily on Lambeth Walk. Bloody weather. Went with the times.

It took him twice as long to get his ancient Jaguar started this time and he swore at it most of the way back to his flat, soured by the loneliness he knew awaited him behind his own front door.

CHAPTER TWELVE

The following few days kept O'Neil and Kassim busy with the organisation of their operation. To everyone's relief, agreement came through from the unpredictable and messianic Libyan president that they could use his country as their initial sanctuary after the raid. He was also said to be delighted with the whole idea.

O'Neil had already raised his Brigade in South Armagh by radio, using the facilities now available from Syrian Military Intelligence and the code for the month pre-arranged with his adjutant. He did not forget to ask about Docherty's wife.

Now it was ten o'clock in the morning on a sunny day in Damascus and O'Neil had just returned from picking up the variety of answers he had required from his people scattered around faraway Ulster.

Docherty was in his room preparing a list of the weapons, explosives and various other equipment it had been decided they would need on this mission. So engrossed in his task was he that the giant did not hear his Captain enter the room.

'Pat. You're a father again, you old ram. It's a boy!' O'Neil grinned at him.

Docherty started, not quite taking it in. When he did, his face broke into a huge grin and he leapt up, sweeping his Captain into a massive hug.

'Put me down, you big oaf!' O'Neil managed to gasp. 'I want to see this operation away in one piece! Congratulations, anyway.'

'Jesus, Captain, that's grand news!' the giant boomed. He clapped the unfortunate messenger soundly on his back, nearly sending him flying, and then hesitated.

'I was wondering, now I've got a son again at last, if you'd be minding me calling him after yourself?' he rumbled diffidently, a small boy – in spite of his size – when asking favours. ' "Connor", that is.'

'I'd be honoured, Pat,' O'Neil smiled back. 'Give it a few weeks after the raid for things to blow over and you will be holding the wee fellow yourself.'

'Sure enough, Captain,' the giant beamed. 'How's Kathleen?' he asked, afterthoughts for his long-suffering wife.

'As right as rain. On Christmas Day, too. Father Rattigan says it went as smoothly as a pint of Guinness,' O'Neil assured him.

'I could do with one now, I'm thinking,' Docherty chuckled, religiously crossing himself.

'I'm afraid it'll have to wait, old friend,' O'Neil countered. 'But your split from this little adventure will buy you a pub of your own to –'

Their pleasantries were interrupted by Major Khalid barging through the door.

'We have a serious problem. Kassim is about to leave for Egypt, but we must discuss this first. Please come with me. Now.'

O'Neil exchanged glances with his lieutenant but said nothing, following the major out into the narrow corridor.

Kassim and his second-in-command, Rashid Khadir, were

already waiting in the Syrian's temporary office downstairs. They did not look happy.

'We will go into the conference room,' Khalid announced.

The terrorist groups had all left the previous day, armed with their regional plans for the new year's political mayhem. Somehow, the large house seemed even more sinister without their presence.

When everyone had sat down, the Syrian intelligence officer gave O'Neil and Docherty the bad news without preamble.

'We have a traitor among us. An informer to the British Intelligence man, Danvers.'

O'Neil's eyes narrowed dangerously, staring hard at Major Khalid.

'Danvers? Isn't that the laddie who was following us when we went to your Ministry? I thought you were going to do something about him,' he stated flatly.

Khalid flushed angrily. 'There has not been time, with all these meetings. But I am –'

'I don't give a damn for your excuses, Khalid!' O'Neil exploded. He could see the whole precious operation going up in smoke. 'Who the hell found this out?' he demanded.

Hassan Kassim pointed a hook at Rashid Khadir. 'My man. He has been shadowing this Englishman since that day. They have been meeting twice a week since the conference started.'

'Who has, for God's sake?' O'Neil snapped, his anger rising.

'Patience, my friend,' the guerilla leader snapped back. Tension sat on the room like static electricity.

'It was one of the servants put in here by our Major Khalid. The man had worked at the British Embassy at one time,' Kassim continued. 'I suppose that is where he was recruited.'

'Oh, bloody marvellous! Well done, Major!' O'Neil snarled at Khalid. 'Banjaxed by our own side!'

Kassim clicked a hook at him impatiently. 'Please, O'Neil. It is not so bad. None of the servants were allowed in this room while the conference was in progress. He cannot have learnt much for this Danvers.'

'Maybe not,' O'Neil snorted. 'But enough to report that we were all here – even *if* he didn't find out who we were!'

Kassim nodded, his own concern showing now on his scarred face.

'That is true. We have him at my camp. It will not be difficult to find out what he knows – and dispose of him.'

O'Neil nodded his agreement.

'That will not be necessary,' Major Khalid interjected. 'You will hand him over to me. My people will deal with him ... and with Danvers.'

'Great!' O'Neil scoffed. 'Do you think you can manage that, Major, without messing it up? And what about this operation now, may I ask? Has Solenov been told?'

O'Neil was furious. The Syrian nodded, coldly defensive.

'He has. The operation is to go ahead as planned. Neither he nor the General feel this . . . incident has affected its chances of success. This servant is of little consequence and could not have begun to guess at the true purpose of your presence here. He probably thinks it was to buy arms.'

O'Neil stared at him, his eyes blue with contempt. 'You'd better be right, Khalid. I don't suppose you've heard the story of the flea who brought down an elephant.'

Khalid looked puzzled as O'Neil turned to Kassim without bothering to explain himself.

'You ready to leave? Do you think there's any point still?'

The guerilla leader's eyes flashed darkly. 'You do not? Has your stomach gone for this thing just because a mouse has been found amongst the cats?'

He glanced at Docherty, who had started to rise from his creaking stool.

'Sit down!' he commanded.

'Yes, I am going. I will return in three days. Rashid, you will bring this . . . creature to the Major's headquarters. I hope your men are more efficient at their jobs than you,' he added, staring at the Syrian major with hawkish menace.

'It would not need a great effort for me to bring you down,

especially if you put my life at risk by your stupidity,' Kassim rounded off his insults.

Khalid flushed again, aching for the time when he could exact his own vengeance for the humiliations these foreign dogs had inflicted on him.

'It will be done. It is time for you to go . . . Palestinian. Or will you fly on your pretty name, if you miss the plane?' he jabbed sarcastically.

The guerilla leader threw back his head in a shrill shriek of black humour.

'Ah, my Syrian pig! Be careful I do not rip you into bacon with these!' he shouted, swishing his hooks under Khalid's alarmed nose, and swept off his stool towards the door, stopping to stare back at O'Neil. 'Will you not wave a comrade farewell, Captain? Three days is a long time in the life of a blossoming friendship.'

O'Neil unwound himself with a smile, feeling better.

'That I will. Be glad to get away from the smell of little men in here. Come on, Pat.'

As they saw Kassim off with one of his men, driven by a subordinate of Khalid's, the Syrian major moved quietly up beside O'Neil, intent on regaining some stature if only by divisive means.

'That man is a danger to us all, Captain O'Neil,' he commented softly, watching the military truck disappear down the narrow street. 'You would be wise to have a care and keep my side of the line,' Khalid went on. 'Such men look only to their own ends and have no loyalties.'

O'Neil turned his head and stared flatly at the dark figure beside him.

'You should know, Khalid. If I finished up with you on a desert island surrounded by sharks, I'd swim for it.'

With that, he made to leave. Khalid grabbed his wrist, coldly angry.

'I suggest you come with me to my headquarters. I will show you what a Syrian can do with traitors, let alone sharks,' he ground out.

O'Neil pulled his arm free with matching coldness.

'I wouldn't go with you to a graveyard, Major. You have the stench of death about you – and bad death at that. I can imagine what you'll do to that poor bastard and I don't want to see it. Just serve your purpose for this operation and keep your charnel-house games to yourself.'

Major Ahmad Khalid watched him walk back into the house. Although O'Neil did not know it, the Syrian's heightened frustrations would cost the informer dearly in unnecessary pain. A pain Khalid longed to place elsewhere.

Refused permission to accompany the daring mission by reason of the diplomatic consequences if the raiders were caught, Khalid was a man with a smart uniform, a soldier's experience and nowhere to play. It made him dangerous and bitter – and doubly unstable in a situation where the danger involved was as much an aphrodisiac as the prizes to be won.

Hell hath no fury, not even a woman's, to match that of a brave but unwanted bystander so tellingly spurned. And in their obsession with proving their own worth, such men can often undo the worth of those around them – and what value they have left in themselves.

When the informer was brought into Khalid's spartan office at the Syrian Military Intelligence headquarters, he was obviously terrified but as yet unmarked.

Khalid eyed the trembling Arab from behind his sunglasses, feeling the old excitement rising within himself. That he should have been so badly compromised by such a thing as this. Now the man would pay for it.

'Take him to the cellars,' he ordered the guards.

The man pulled away from them and fell on his knees in front of Khalid's desk, pleading with him. He knew what they would do.

Khalid hated displays of emotion, especially in others.

'Take him down!' he barked, embarrassed by the wretch's tears.

The military policemen heaved the informer to his feet,

166

dragging him out to the stairs leading down past the cells to the dreaded area beneath them.

Khalid could still hear the man's desperate cries, even though his office door was closed.

He reached for a pair of brown leather gloves on the desk and picked up a thin Malacca cane, caressing it between his trembling fingers. The rubber apron he took from behind the door completed his sinister equipment. It had been a long time – since the last one. Almost two months.

Khalid loved these moments, but he must be clean. No blood on him. To watch it spurt from his victims' bodies like sperm was thrill enough.

Although he did not understand it, the horrors he was able to inflict in those dreadful cellars, with their unshaded bulbs lighting his pleasure, was a sexual compensation for his lack of success with women. In their company he was awkward and ill at ease. This was so much easier. And just as satisfying.

The man was ready for him when Khalid felt calm enough to go down. His clothes had been removed by the guards and the doomed creature was frozen into unresistance by his own naked terror.

This particular cellar had no torturer's refinements. The bare brick walls had been tiled to facilitate the hosing away of blood and flesh after each session was over. Drain-aways in the stone floor carried off the last of the evidence – not that anyone would ever require it.

A single, bare light-bulb shone over the victim and his murderers and cast macabre shadows on the tiling, like something out of a Black Theatre.

Khalid's first stroke with the cane opened up the man's face from cheek to chin. His scream bubbled into a sobbing moan as Khalid spoke to him softly.

'You will tell me all I ask of you, filth.'

The informer nodded vigorously, still held firmly between his guards. At a signal from Khalid, they stepped aside, lounging against the walls, gazing with seeming indifference at it all.

Khalid smiled thinly at the terror-stricken informer, spittle dribbling from the corner of his mouth. The man's face was already covered in 'sperm'.

'Excellent . . . excellent,' Khalid whispered, almost to himself. 'Now we will begin, my pretty plaything.'

The guards were licking their lips, sweat standing out on their foreheads in spite of the clammy coldness, knowing what was coming as Khalid flexed his wrist with a deep sigh.

It went on for nearly two hours. After the first few strokes, Khalid had found out everything he needed to know. The rest was unabated sadism of the worst kind. Even the guards, hardened to it as they were, became nervous as Khalid went on and on. They had never seen the major like this.

The man's screams had long since ceased, his pitiful inert body huddled in a corner of this murderous nightmare. Blood and bits of his flesh were everywhere on the white-tiled walls, murals to his death.

Khalid's final act was to beat the man's genitals to pulp. Mercifully, he had been dead for some time. It seemed to make little difference to his executioner.

At last Khalid stopped, his heaving chest and the dark stain at his crotch the only signs of his satisfaction.

The thing the guards were ordered to remove was barely recognisable as a human being. It took one of them a good hour to wash away the last of his horrific passing.

The victim was just twenty-six years of age. He had paid dearly for his love of the money he got from the British, which allowed him to take part in the illegal gambling games to be found in the city – and chase pretty girls.

Meanwhile, Major Khalid had returned to his office, feeling deeply purged and at peace with himself. If there was a special place in hell for men like him, then Khalid was certain of an especial punishment for all eternity.

Whilst the Syrian indulged in his gruesome diversion, O'Neil was back with Docherty, going over their end of the logistics for the operation.

Having arrived at a satisfactory list of their requirements, Big Pat had asked his Captain about Major Khalid's role. It seemed strange to him that a man, admittedly of some importance within Syrian Intelligence but somewhat lowly in rank, should be in immediate charge of their various destinies.

O'Neil had laughed, his reply tinged with bitter realism. 'Oh, that is easy enough to work out, Pat! Sure, the Syrians and the PLO will back us up with all the equipment and information we'll be needing, just like those Russian chummies of theirs . . .'

He stopped to light a cigarette, grimacing at the harsh taste of Kassim's American brand.

'But we're on our own as far as the actual raid is concerned. They'll all duck out of sight if it goes wrong. Can't afford to get their hands dirty, now can they? So they will make damned sure that anyone they use up front is expendable – including us.'

Docherty nodded slowly, understanding. 'Then it seems to me, Captain,' he rumbled thoughtfully, 'that they'll not be complaining when we take all the loot for our services?'

'They'll complain all right!' O'Neil joshed. 'But at least they'll have their dirty work done for them – at their expense.'

The giant smiled. It would have frightened a tiger.

'I'm glad about that, Captain. I'd not want us to spoil all their fun.'

'Hmm,' O'Neil grunted. 'I am more concerned with whether or not we can trust our friendly guerilla leader. He'll bear some watching, Pat. So will that Syrian animal.'

Docherty grunted. 'I'll break both their necks if they try anything,' he growled.

O'Neil grinned, knowing he meant it.

'Enough of this. Now, which of our men are we going to

bring in from back home? I reckon MacLaughlin, Kennedy, Rooney, O'Rourke.

'O'Rourke'll be all right. He's the best we've got for a tight scrap like this one's going to be,' he added, seeing the giant's sudden frown. 'The adjutant can hold the fort until it's all over.'

Docherty shook his head doubtfully.

'The others are fine, Captain. I don't know about O'Rourke. To my way of thinking, he'll come up against Kassim as sure as eggs is eggs. The last thing we'll be wanting is trouble from our own, and you know what a wild one O'Rourke can be.'

'You leave him to me, Pat. It'll be just dandy,' O'Neil assured him. 'I'll get on the radio tonight and set it up.'

Khalid's reappearance in Docherty's room ended the discussion. He looked pleased with himself.

'I have dealt with the informer,' he announced in his difficult English.

'I bet you have,' O'Neil muttered. He didn't want to ask how.

'There is little to concern us,' Khalid went on, ignoring his remark. 'The dog knew only that there were two Europeans here not with the others. He knew about Kassim, of course, but assumed he was with the conference. Danvers would have already known it was happening,' he stated flatly, defying argument.

O'Neil was still not happy about it, but what could he do?

'All right, we'll have to take your word for it,' he conceded, handing over his equipment lists.

'Here's what I want. What are you going to do about this Danvers?'

Khalid frowned, tired of being questioned by these men in everything he did.

'My men will be watching for him, O'Neil. He will be dealt with the next time he makes an appearance.'

O'Neil nodded. 'See that he is, Khalid. Any more hitches in this thing and we go home,' he warned bluntly.

'Remember that is up to me, Captain,' Khalid retorted

coldly. 'You will not leave my country until I say so.'

O'Neil stared at him, saying nothing. If this miserable heap thought he'd keep them caged in this godforsaken place, he didn't know much.

'I've picked the men I'll be needing from my Brigade,' he said, changing the subject. 'I'll be wanting to use your radio tonight.'

'Very well,' Khalid agreed. 'I will arrange transport.'

O'Neil gave him a curt nod and received the same neutral gesture of dislike back from the Syrian.

As the door slammed behind Khalid's exit, O'Neil turned to Docherty, his expression grim.

'Pat, if there's half a chance we can get away with it, blow that bastard into the next world.'

Docherty raised a massive fist. 'It'd be a pleasure, Captain.'

Burroughs was back in his office next morning, before Peter Chambers had even thought about getting out of bed. Another transmission had come in during the night from Danvers via the SIS's main communications base at Cheltenham, from which it was cleared through to Century House.

Burroughs picked it up with a grunt of satisfaction. So, he *had* been right. It would be interesting to hear what bloody Holman had to say about this latest little snippet.

Danvers had confirmed that a large-scale terrorist operation *was* on the cards for February-March. How he had come by this was not stated but Burroughs assumed it was through his Arab servant contact – the man who had been infiltrated into the Damascus conference.

Unknown to either Burroughs, Danvers or Khalid, the soon to be murdered informer would manage to keep back one vital piece of information from his cruel torturer – if only because he would be beaten senseless before it could be extracted from him.

During one of the breaks in the conference, the servant had overheard two of the PLO's delegates discussing a rumour which was circulating at that Christmas meeting of political terror.

It seemed they had gleaned that these foreign strangers to their secret gathering had some kind of major scheme for consideration – something to do with the Gulf States and their treacherous pro-Western sheikhs.

In the way of the 'best-laid plans of mice and men', Khalid's mistake in employing Danvers' man had been of more consequence than he imagined. If his superiors had known this, Khalid would have undoubtedly joined his victim on the other side of the great divide. Or at the hands of O'Neil and his comrades.

Whatever, the informer had made this news his last delivery in exchange for the money which killed him. And perhaps did not die so nightmarishly in vain.

Danvers' message also stated that he was sure he was under suspicion from Syrian Intelligence, although again he gave no details. The report was more concerned with letting London know there was big trouble brewing somewhere around the Arabian Gulf.

Danvers' safety concerned Burroughs as much as his report. But he knew him to be a capable operative and would just have to hope he would be all right.

Burroughs sniffed and sat down behind his desk. Christ, the place was a mess! Didn't those bloody cleaners do anything? His office was like a blasted rabbit hutch as it was.

Then he remembered the New Year holiday, feeling foolish. He'd been so wrapped up in this business, time didn't mean much – except in the urgency to get to the bottom of his worrying puzzle.

When Chambers eventually showed up, expecting a telling-off for being late, Burroughs did not waste time on idle recriminations.

'Morning, Peter. Get hold of MacAllister, will you? Tell him I want an urgent meeting with Holman. Today.'

Chambers nodded, relieved. He'd been sick again and the last thing he needed was confrontation.

'Yes – um, is he in yet?'

Burroughs glanced up from the map he had spread out on his desk.

'Who?'

'Mr MacAllister, er, George.'

'He's "Mac" to you, like everyone else around here. Unless we're getting told off,' he grinned back.

Chambers smiled wanly. Burroughs seemed quite a nice chap really.

'He's in, son,' Burroughs confirmed. 'Go sort him out for me. I've got too much to do here.'

He meant he didn't feel like talking to the man. Not after he'd dropped him in it with Holman. Burroughs was not easily inclined to forgiveness.

Chambers was back in a few minutes, with the Assistant Head of Section in tow. The atmosphere in the office dropped several degrees, in keeping with the weather.

'What's this about?' MacAllister enquired neutrally.

'I want to see Holman. Today,' Burroughs replied in the same tone and lit a cigarette, knowing MacAllister hated cigarette smoke as much as their chief did.

'Danvers has come up with some fresh information.' Burroughs did not elucidate.

'I know,' the Assistant Head said simply.

Burroughs' features darkened. Were even his sources to be vetted now?

He was hardly being fair and knew it. As AHS, Mac-Allister had every right to see all traffic in and out of the section. And, after the blasting he'd received from Holman over Burroughs' unauthorised sendings, he was going to make sure there weren't any repeat performances. When and if Holman moved on, he intended to be sitting in his chair.

'All right, George,' MacAllister continued. 'I'll see what can be done. I happen to agree with you – this time. It doesn't look too good.'

Burroughs grunted but held his tongue. MacAllister's agreement was of supreme indifference to him. He would never trust the AHS again.

MacAllister stood for a moment in the awkward silence, then turned on his heel. If George wanted to play it this way from now on, so be it. But procedures were procedures, and that was that.

The meeting that afternoon with Sir David was not a pleasant one, nor had Burroughs expected it to be. The report from Danvers did nothing towards improving their relationship, since it went some way to proving Burroughs justified in his concern.

Nevertheless, Sir David agreed to a 'Most Urgent' going out to Danvers but not through the Embassy. This heralded the first disagreement of the afternoon.

'Come on, sir!' Burroughs protested rashly. 'Does it really matter? Surely an MU signal can be sent to the Head of Chancery – or even the Ambassador? They're both in the know about Danvers.'

Holman's face froze. So did MacAllister's. Here we go again.

'The Ambassador, Burroughs? Certainly not!' Holman snapped. 'H.E. has got far more important things to do than play errand boy for your inquiries. You are well aware that it is standard practice *not* to involve embassy staff in our Service's affairs.'

God almighty, thought Burroughs. You'd think he'd asked if the Queen could go shopping for him. 'H.E.' the Ambassador was there to assist Her Majesty's Government in any way required of him.

'We operate out of our embassies, for Christ's sake!' he retorted. 'It's two days before Danvers will be on a listening-watch again.'

'That is enough!' Holman almost screamed at him. 'You will transmit an MU priority signal on Danvers' frequency at the appointed time. Via Major MacAllister. Is that clear? And any reply will come to you via Major MacAllister. Is *that* clear? I will not have this insubordination from you!'

Burroughs glanced at the AHS. Keeping his head down as usual, was he?

'Fair enough, sir. Thank you for your time,' he replied with grim civility. 'I'll log Danvers' last report in the Daily Occurrence Book. Is that all?'

Holman's mouth tightened. 'No it is not. There is still the matter of your report to the Minister. I cannot force you to withdraw it and I take it you are still refusing to do so?'

'That's right, Sir David,' Burroughs nodded cheerfully.

'Very well. Then we will await my Minister's reaction, but I assure you that you have not heard the last of this matter, Burroughs.'

Nor have you, you little sod, Burroughs thought.

'Right, sir,' he verbalised. 'I will leave you to it. Must keep on top of the spies!'

When Burroughs had gone, Sir David turned to his Assistant Head with an exasperated sigh.

'The man's impossible!' he exploded. 'I can't go round sanctioning every Tom, Dick and Harry in the Department bothering Her Majesty's representatives, now can I?'

'Quite, sir,' the AHS murmured dutifully, gazing neutrally at Holman. It was like watching a slow puncture. Holman was unlikely to ever get an embassy posting again, so what did it matter?

'Do you think Burroughs is on to something important?' Holman asked suddenly.

'I think he may be, sir,' MacAllister replied carefully.

'Hmm. Well, we shall wait and see, MacAllister. Wait and see . . . Yes. Meanwhile, I want you to keep a tight rein on him. This report of his to Lord Pennington is going to cause enough trouble as it is.'

'Yes, sir. Is there anything else?' the AHS inquired in his soft burr.

Holman started out of his reverie of private worries.

'Er, no. I want to see what Danvers has to say before Burroughs does. Is that understood?'

'Of course, sir.'

As he left his chief's office, he could hear Sir David muttering to himself.

'Shocking : : : Quite shocking. The Ambassador indeed . . . '

It was to prove the most damaging mistake of Holman's already tarnished career.

CHAPTER THIRTEEN

Two days later, another report landed on Burroughs' desk. This time from Northern Ireland Special Branch. They had received an unusual account from the SAS down in Fermanagh, close to the border with the Irish Republic. It only served to increase Burroughs' own worries.

Men in the Special Air Service are seconded from other regiments of the British Army. There is no easy way in. Officer and ranker alike endure a long and arduous introduction and those who survive the severe training programme, which is not many, are perhaps more highly trained than any other member of Her Majesty's armed forces.

Apart from being quite deadly in all kinds of weaponry, unarmed combat, sabotage, in-depth surveillance, assassination and all things related, the SAS man is a specialist at the art of survival under the most appalling of conditions – physical and mental. The intelligence level is high but, above all, finely-honed.

Of a natural independence and self-sufficiency, he is also a super-cool killer when necessary. No man is indestructible, of course, but these men come close to it. Derived from Colonel Stirling's Long Range Desert Group during World War II, any man selected to wear the coveted blue beret of the SAS is a man to tread round carefully, if you can spot him.

The Service's motto, *Who Dares Wins*, is appropriate to the work they do in Northern Ireland. Going places in which no ordinary soldier would survive for five minutes, they specialise in long-term penetration of the terrorist groups that infest the 'bandit country' each side of Ulster's grim border.

Often as not, they work alone and out of uniform, infiltrating the heart of their quarries' habitats. It is lonely, nerve-racking and very dangerous. They will kill as the situation demands with few questions asked afterwards, and they expect as little mercy from the IRA as they are prepared to hand out. – If caught.

It was from a sergeant in one of these SAS teams that Burroughs got his next vital link in the chain stretching to O'Neil's plans for the British monarch and her gracious vessel, *Britannia*.

The SAS sergeant had learned that four top men from Madigan's Brigade were going down to Dublin, and thence flying to the Middle East. He had not been able to find out their exact destination, nor as yet the purpose of their trip. But all four were well-experienced in street warfare, sabotage, bombings and robbery. One of them had apparently been a merchant seaman before joining O'Neil's private army. Another a mercenary.

Also, although Northern Ireland SB didn't know if it was relevant, one of the Brigade's men had been found executed by some villagers after a summary court-martial on Christmas Day.

Burroughs mulled over the information. He knew where these characters were going, all right. They had to be joining O'Neil in Damascus. It all fitted.

He glanced at his watch. Time to get on to Danvers. Damn Holman's bloody restrictions! He supposed he'd better trot along like a good boy to MacAllister's office with the draft of his transmission.

Danvers was beginning to hate these treks out into the desert with his powerful SSHF transmitter in the boot of his old Mercedes. He was sure his luck wouldn't hold out much longer. The Syrian MI boys must be on to him by now, especially after that farce following Khalid's jeep.

At least it was dark and he'd managed to give the slip to that car he felt certain had been following him.

The report he'd received from his Arab contact's family that their son had disappeared still weighed on his mind as he set the single side-band, high-frequency sender-receiver to the required frequency that would bring Cheltenham on the air from halfway across the world. He hadn't felt able to tell Muhammed's family that their son was dead. As for the police . . .

The informer's lacerated corpse had been dumped outside the British Embassy in the early hours of that morning – on whose instructions and why, Danvers didn't know. But it seemed a somewhat unnecessary gesture, since the police would have interviewed somebody on the staff in the course of time and Danvers would have got to hear about it. The dead man had worked as a domestic in the Embassy for nearly two years before Danvers had recruited him, after all.

He couldn't, of course, approach the civilian police. That was too risky to his cover. Secretariat or Chancery would deal with that. But the story doing the rounds already was that Muhammed had been beaten to death – in direct contradiction of the 'hit-and-run accident' explanation put out by the police.

He supposed it had been done by Khalid's lot to warn him off. No, they wouldn't do that. More likely an attempt to flush him out, make him do something stupid – panic maybe?

Whatever the reason, it was a double-edged sword, since it told Danvers that somebody in the Syrian authorities was on to Muhammed's connection with the Embassy, and obviously for more reason than the fact that the poor devil had worked as a servant there. The gesture had to be meant for him. It was just the sort of twisted thing Khalid would do, trying to be cleverer than he really was.

Well, he was still ahead of them but he'd have to keep on his toes from now on in.

London came through bang on time. The instruction was a long one and only increased Danvers' anxiety as he waited for it to relay through to his specially adapted tape-recorder. He would decode it back at the Embassy.

The call signal preceding the transmission told him no 'Send' was required and he silently thanked Burroughs for realising that he needed to keep his air-time exposure to the minimum. Ten minutes saw the transmission finished and five more all his gear safely stowed in the car. He was back at his Embassy flat inside an hour.

Danvers was sweating by the time he had finished decoding Burroughs' transmission, despite the tropical cold which came in with the night.

The decoded instructions presented him with real problems. MI6's information identifying O'Neil and Docherty surprised him, but more so Burroughs' request that he look out for four Irish terrorists coming into his area over the next few days. It was just what he didn't need.

If Khalid was on to him, his latest assignment would be really risky. He poured himself a stiff drink and thought about it. Dammit, he'd *have* to radio back to London about Muhammed's murder. They would realise the implications for him, surely? He wasn't out here to get killed – or worse. Of course, he would follow his orders, but he'd heard the stories of how Khalid dealt with his suspects.

With a deep sigh, he got up off his bed and opened the monthly coding book. It meant another tense trip out into the desert. Why the hell the SIS departments didn't let their field operatives openly use Embassy facilities was a sore point with him at the best of times. They were all meant to be on the same side.

But he would have to go. Now.

Amazingly, Danvers got away with it again, although the fuse to his life's short ending had already been lit by Holman's intransigence.

Had Holman seen the need to involve the Damascus Embassy at Chancery – if not Ambassador – level, then his operative would have been able to use the internal facilities instead of these lunatic runs into the night.

His transmission was picked up by Cheltenham and passed on to Century House. Not only was Burroughs shaken by the news that Danvers' contact had been murdered, although again it confirmed his worst fears, he was also furious that his man had to be put at risk just because Holman was such a prig.

In the best tradition of his maverick temperament, Burroughs broke his chief's instructions and sent a direct Classified cable to Danvers at the Embassy – via Sam Cook.

His forgery of Holman's signature on the authorisation docket was little short of criminal, let alone the trouble he would inevitably let fall on his friend again. But Burroughs was past caring about the rules. To him, the need to know was paramount, and it was essential Danvers did what he was told. Whatever the risks. He *had* to find out what was going on out there.

On 5 and 6 January 1979, O'Neil's men left the Irish Republic for the Middle East via Dublin. They travelled on false passports and by different, individual air routes over a two-day period.

The replacement for Timothy O'Rourke was charged with the task of telling the Captain about the circumstances of O'Rourke's court-martial and summary execution. The adjutant had decided it was best left until O'Neil could hear it direct, rather than on the end of a radio receiver. They had had a close if somewhat fractious comradeship.

Liam MacFadden was not looking forward to it all.

Kassim meanwhile had arrived in Egypt without mishap, using false papers and with his easily identifiable hooks replaced by dummy hands. His 'assistant' from the Palestine Action Commando, Haffez Assad, similarly travelled in on forged documents and would make all the drawings necessary for their vital survey of the Suez Canal.

O'Neil and Docherty had a further brief meeting with Khalid, who questioned certain items on their equipment list – O'Neil suspecting it was mere cussedness for the sake of it.

In the end. O'Neil got his way with the Syrian but only at the expense of their love-mainly-hate relationship. It didn't bother the Irishman and Khalid had too much on his mind over Danvers to realise he was digging his own grave, one way and another.

Clive Danvers missed the first of O'Neil's men to arrive in Damascus. His official duties within the Embassy had kept him behind his desk for far longer than he had anticipated.

But at last he managed to clear his workload and take a couple of days off, on the excuse of wanting to perfect his handling of his new camera. He had deliberately built up a reputation amongst the Embassy staff of being keenly interested in photography. It helped explain away his absences and the sophisticated darkroom in his apartment. The endless friendly shots he had to take of his colleagues, especially the Commercial Attaché's overweight and over-talkative wife, was a price he wished he didn't have to pay. If it had been of that new brunette in Secretariat . . .

He had difficulty in deciding where exactly to watch for the Irishmen's covert arrival. How would they be coming in? Would they appear as a group or individually? In fact, would they come into Damascus at all, or assemble at Kassim's desert base – assuming O'Neil and Kassim were tied into something together, as poor old Muhammed had suspected?

In the end he plumped for the villa on Mohammed Zaid Street. He knew O'Neil, Docherty and Kassim were still there. Or at least, they had been. It seemed the logical place to start, since the Syrians' sense of security had already left much to be desired.

The only problem was Khalid's lot. They would be watching out for him, of that he *was* certain. And the villa would be the natural magnet they'd expect him to go for. Still, at least it was in the middle of the city. He doubted they would try anything on an accredited Embassy official with witnesses to hand.

His first morning back on surveillance netted him nothing but a sweat rash. The heat in the car was sticky-wet.

Halfway through the afternoon he was getting nervous of maintaining his vigil so close to the house when his luck gave him some short-lived generosity.

The second of the Madigan's Brigade men made his appearance.

To Danvers' astonishment, the man arrived by taxi with a member of the Hawk's Commando. Using his telephoto lens, he was able to get off several useful shots before they disappeared into the gated courtyard. He didn't recognise the Irishman of course, but he had to be one of O'Neil's group. The Palestinian was clearly remembered from the file he'd put together on the PAC. It was Rashid Khadir.

He couldn't believe the Hawk would have sanctioned such a flagrant piece of bad security. Danvers wasn't to know that Kassim was out of the country on his survey mission.

Wait a minute, he thought suddenly. What if they didn't care if he saw them? Why? *Why* wouldn't it matter to them?

Then it dawned on him and the world went cold. Dear God! They had no intention of letting him get back to the Embassy. He'd walked right into it. But . . . where were they?

He glanced up and down the long, narrow street. His was the only car in sight. The only people in the street were passers-by, weren't they? To hell with it! He'd seen one of Burroughs' suspects report in – and accompanied by Kassim's second-in-command. That was conclusive enough. The others would surely follow.

Danvers looked at his watch. Couldn't help the time difference. He'd better chance radioing London while his luck still held. They'd pick it up at Cheltenham. It was round-the-clock down there.

Danvers started up his old Mercedes, slamming the automatic gear into 'Drive'. Strangely enough, he felt he would be safer in daylight as he headed out of Damascus into the desert. Jesus, the games he had to play over communications!

He drove fast, keeping a constant eye in his driving mirror for any sign of followers. Until he got out of the city, it would be hard to sort out the innocents from someone on his tail.

Unbeknown to the British agent, Khalid had guessed correctly that his quarry would go for the villa and had placed two of his men on the roof of the house next door. From there, they had had a clear view of the whole street, maintaining contact with another three men across the road by short-wave hand-sets.

Danvers was observed from the moment he arrived and tailed from the minute he left.

Danvers did not spot his tail until he was on the military highway going north into the desert scrub. Even then he wasn't sure. There were three other cars behind him and another in front.

Three of them belonged to Khalid's men, although he was not with them for fear of being recognised by his prey. They were playing the standard trick of interchanging their positions so that the tailed never quite knew who were the tailers.

Once again, Clive Danvers was faced with making a decision, as when he was tailing Khalid's jeep. Did he make his move now or didn't he? He had to get a message off to London somehow.

He squinted through the windscreen in the bright sunlight. As is the way of the desert, the sun seemed brighter towards its waning but only because it sat nearer the horizon, dazzling oncomers.

Maybe he could use it to his advantage. He could see

through his mirror that the driver of the car only thirty yards behind him was not wearing sunglasses. His passenger was but that didn't matter.

Danvers braked suddenly and swung the car round in a screeching arc on the wide highway, the smell of burning rubber mixing with the acrid smell of his own sweat. Caught off-balance and dazzled by the sun, the man behind him was left standing. By the time the third car had realised it, being some way back, Danvers had shot past him in the opposite direction.

Now there was nothing for it. He zoomed off the road and careered across the slight banking into the desert scrubland, gunning the heavy car for all he was worth. He *must* put distance between himself and his pursuers.

But, as his tailers had made a mistake, so had Danvers. The clouds of sand dust spewing out from behind his Mercedes was like Moses's pillar of fire. There was no way he was going to lose them for long.

Fortunately for him, the scrubland began to turn into real desert. As long as he kept to the relative flats between the beginning dunes, the sand was baked hard by the unrelenting sun and he could keep going.

Danvers drove hell-for-leather, casting occasional glances in his mirror for sight of Khalid's men. It was hopeless. He couldn't see a thing out of the rear window for the clouds of sand he was churning up. He was committed now. The only thing was to go on.

The dunes were becoming more pronounced. If he could get this wreck up over one of the dunes, maybe he could buy enough time hidden in a dip and make his desperate transmission.

A likely chance came into view and Danvers heaved the car off the firm desert. The sweat was pouring off him now, soaking his shirt. Please God, let me make it. Please!

Danvers' fragile luck held out for a little longer. He made it to the top of the rise in a race of labouring engine and laboured swearing. Dropping down the other side of the sloping shift of sand, he lammed the car to a halt and leapt out. He ran round to the boot and heaved his transmitter from its rubberised padding, praying that it had survived the mad, bouncing retreat across the desert.

Grabbing the radio by its stainless-steel grips, Danvers struggled over the sand grained in a white sear of desert heat, along the shallow hollow. His legs felt like jelly and he fumbled with the dials, missing the fast-scrambler emergency frequency at first.

'Damn it, damn it . . . DAMN IT!' he cursed, desperately trying to stop his hands from shaking. Sweat fell on his fingers like rain, no comfort in the wicked heat. The aerial danced to his frustration.

At last he got it right, slamming down the 'Send' switch and activating the scrambler. He hadn't time to prepare a coded format anyway. The bloody thing would have to go out in plain language. He could only hope the world's unfriendly listening-stations would be defeated by the high-frequency fast send.

Danvers' pursuers had seen him gunning up the dunes, although the lead car was a good half mile behind him. One of the vehicles misjudged the deceptive surface, finishing up buried to its axles in the ever-shifting sands. The others did not wait. Like jackals scenting a kill, they came on. Remorseless. Certain of their victim.

Danvers' transmitter hummed with its urgent life as he spoke clearly and precisely into the microphone, steadied by the necessity of what he had to do.

'Doormouse to Flatfoot. Doormouse to Flatfoot. Confirm arrival of Madigan terrorists in Damascus. Repeat, confirm arrival of Madigan terrorists in Damascus. Located at conference rendezvous. Arrivals met by Palestine Action Commando, repeat Palestine Action Commando.'

He dashed the sweat from his eyes, trying to marshal his thoughts. He could hear Khalid's men grinding across the desert. Then it all went quiet.

Desperate to finish his message, Danvers did not have time to waste on speculating about their exact position. He bent back to the microphone. 'Link up suspected with Khalid and Solenov. Repeat KGB and Syrian Intelligence involved. Am being pursued by same . . . pursued by same. Cover blown . . . cover blown . . . Will attempt further transmi – '

Clive Danvers got no further. Nor had he expected to. The last sentence had been sheer defiance.

The first bullet caught him high in the shoulder, its report loud on the desert stillness. The jackals were not even bothering to use silencers.

The second bullet hit him in the left temple, taking away half of his head. Blood and bone rained over the transmitter, accompanied by a thunder of shots as Khalid's men pumped bullets into the radio.

It was all over in under half a minute. A twitching nerve in Danvers' hand caused it to close on the microphone with a violent jerk. Overreacting, one of the agents shot his dead fingers to pieces.

Well satisfied, they collected the remains of the transmitter for analysis and carried his body over to the Mercedes. It was thrown into the boot with careless triumph.

They trudged back to their own cars on the other side of the dune hollow, having stripped Danvers of his wallet and watch. There was nothing in the wallet to identify him, naturally. But the five hundred dollars of folded bills was swiftly split between them. The senior man kept his Yema *sous marine* chronometer.

The wallet would be handed over to Major Khalid, together with anything they found in the Englishman's car. There was no need to mention either the money or the watch. Spoils of the job, no?

About to leave, the agent elected to drive Danvers' car back to the city for disposal along with the body, suddenly called out. 'Hey, the head! Can't be too careful, even out here. Nothing must be left to chance, eh!'

The others were impatient. It had taken a lot of effort to get the old Mercedes back on to firm ground. Nevertheless, they waited for him.

The man made his way back to the grim hollow and scuffed sand over the remains of Danvers' brains and fragments of skull. They would probably get exposed again by the desert winds, but the sun would do the rest. He certainly wasn't going to pick them up.

The man grinned at his handiwork and wiped his shoe on his trouser leg. 'Go with Allah, English!'

The cynical salutation didn't matter to Danvers, of course. But at least his end had been quick. Unlike Muhammed's.

CHAPTER FOURTEEN

Liam MacFadden hadn't expected O'Neil's violent reaction to O'Rourke's death. And MacFadden's reaction to the Captain's explosion of anger was not expected by anyone.

When O'Neil grabbed him by his shirt-front, MacFadden lashed out, knocking him to the floor. MacFadden was no longer a young man either. Short of stature and nearer forty than thirty, his knowledge of ships and the sea was only exceeded by his ability with radio equipment. It had been the adjutant's decision to send him in place of the late Tim O'Rourke who, for all his wildness, was known as one of the best electronics men in Ulster.

Docherty sprang to his feet as O'Neil went down.

'Don't hit me!' MacFadden gasped. 'I've got asthma!'

'Leave him!' O'Neil shouted, picking himself up as the giant pulled back his huge fist. And then he started to laugh. And laugh. Tears rolled down O'Neil's cheeks.

'For Christ's sake! Asthma!' he choked. 'Dear God, you nearly brain me and then plead "asthma"! How the hell did you pass the Brigade medical, laddie?'

Docherty stood back, glowering at O'Neil's assailant, but left it at that. None of the others had moved, perhaps too astonished by the whole episode. MacFadden began to relax, catching air along with O'Neil.

'I – I held me breath,' he jerked out, grinning uncertainly.

O'Neil chuckled and stuck out his hand. MacFadden hadn't been with the Brigade long but any man who could put O'Neil down *and* get away with being a physical wreck had to have something going for him.

'Well enough, Liam MacFadden. Here's my hand on it. I'm sorry. You are not to blame for O'Rourke. Callaghan should have told me.'

It was one hell of a shock but the adjutant had been right. Rape was a dirty, evil thing to do to any woman. Discipline had to be maintained.

O'Neil surveyed the other men crowded into his bedroom.

'All right. Let what happened to O'Rourke be a lesson to you all. I won't have that kind of filth in my Brigade.'

Nobody spoke and O'Neil continued.

'Right. Now you're all here, it's time you knew what this is about.'

He paused. His recently arrived team from South Armagh waited expectantly.

'We're going on an operation the likes of which will make your hair curl. It'll be difficult, dangerous and profitable. I'll introduce you to our partner in this little jaunt when he gets back. Rashid Khadir and Yasser Rahman you've already met. They and Docherty here are under instructions to tell you nothing without my say-so. Rahman's in the dark anyway.'

He stopped to light a cigarette. He had their total attention now.

'For reasons of security, you'll be told what we're hitting once we're at sea. Yes,' he added, seeing their expressions, 'I hope you can all swim! Not that it matters,' he added further, leaving them even more puzzled.

'For the moment, all you need to know is this. The operation has the backing of some big brass – Syrian Military Intelligence, the PLO and the Russians. We will be working with an outfit called the Palestine Action Commando. They're a tough bunch of boyos, so we train up for the next three weeks – in the desert. Then we move on for more work-ups on the coast.'

He stared round his men, noting each one's reactions as he did so.

'I can tell you this at least. It's the biggest thing we've ever tackled and the cheekiest idea since Captain Blood pinched the Crown Jewels. If we pull it off – and we will – your names will be on the front page of every newspaper in the world.'

A ripple of quiet excitement travelled round the group, as their Captain's own excitement broke through the reserve inherent in men who lead their lives doing the sort of things they did.

'One last thing,' O'Neil cautioned. 'Until we leave here, no man is to go out of the house – not even for a breath of fresh air. And keep off the roof. We'll start briefing you tomorrow when Kassim checks in.'

The men spent the evening relaxing and swopping stories with Docherty. One of them had seen his new child and was quizzed exhaustively by the giant. Beer, fetched in especially by O'Neil, and some magazines, helped keep them amused as they acclimatised themselves to their new surroundings.

O'Neil himself had a coldly brief meeting with Khalid in his temporary office. Apparently, Danvers had been dealt with that afternoon and, even whilst they talked, two of Khalid's agents were 'arranging' a realistic motor accident out on the desert highway. Danvers and his car would become an unrecognisable tangle of charred bones and fire-twisted metal.

The Syrian police had instructions to be as obstructive as possible with the British Embassy when they asked for an independent autopsy, as they surely would. The police surgeon who would be dealing with the matter had already removed any bullets from the cadaver. Khalid did not anticipate any 'difficulties'. The British Embassy might be suspicious, but there was little they could do without implicating their own Intelligence services in the affair.

Khalid neglected to tell O'Neil about the radio transmission. After a brief discussion with Colonel Solenov at the hotel, it was considered best to leave the raiders in ignorance. They would have enough to worry about in readying themselves for their mission.

Although the transmission had been picked up by the Soviet Embassy's surveillance people, the fast-scrambler had so far defeated their efforts to break its sequences. From Khalid's report of his interrogation of the informer, it was doubted anyway that Danvers had much to tell.

O'Neil went to bed early that night, bored with hearing Docherty go on about his new son and restless for Kassim's return from Egypt.

He would be glad when they at last got into this thing. By God, his men would have to train with a vengeance. There was so little time.

Burroughs was summoned to Holman's office the following day by a grim-faced MacAllister.

Unable to do much more until he heard back from Danvers, and well aware that the lid would come off when he did, he was having a political discussion with young Chambers in the Duty Room.

' . . . You could be right, Peter,' he was saying. 'But give me a strong leader who is cruel rather than a weak one any day. Same applies to governments. In the long run, a weak administration is cruellest of all on the people. Especially economically.' They were talking about the strong line taken by the Shah of Iran.

Burroughs shut up as soon as he saw the AHS's expression. He didn't have to ask what it was about. They'd tumbled his forged transmission. Oh well . . .

'Sir David wants to see us both now,' MacAllister informed him grimly. 'Peter, you are not required.'

Chambers flushed. He always seemed to get left out when anything of importance came up – new boy or not.

Holman's face told its own story when Burroughs and MacAllister reached his office. But not the one Burroughs expected.

'Sit down, the pair of you. Burroughs, we have just received this in from Cheltenham.'

He handed the transmission transcript across his desk to Burroughs.

'It's from Danvers,' he added noncommittally.

Burroughs read it through twice and then the note from the Night Watch supervisor for Middle Eastern Section. They had had a lot of trouble with it. Bad static interference. Breaking up in places.

But the import of the message was there. Instinctively, Burroughs knew the sudden break in transmission had not been a technical fault. Danvers was in trouble, although he had confirmed the arrival of the men from Madigan's Brigade *and* linked them with Kassim and that bastard, Solenov.

He grunted and handed the transcript back to Holman, forgetting to be relieved that his own transmission had not been called into question. Holman's next statement knocked that right out of his head.

'Danvers was killed yesterday in a car accident outside Damascus. The Head of Chancery cabled this morning. Apparently, he was burned to death. Two, er, Arabs were killed in the other vehicle,' he added, as if it made things better.

Burroughs lit a cigarette, giving himself time to think. Poor little sod. Then he looked up, his eyes cold.

'I'm sorry, sir. It was no accident. I know Danvers. They were on to him. And I know why. It's all to do with O'Neil, Hassan Kassim and this bloody KGB colonel. I *told* you something was on, damn it! Now we've a man dead – and the only one covering the situation out there!'

'Sit down, Burroughs!' Holman snapped, as Burroughs got to his feet.

'I have asked the Embassy to look into it – thoroughly,' Holman went on. 'There is nothing we can do until we hear

191

from them. There are other matters I wish to discuss with you. I – '

'Wait a minute. You're not just leaving this, are you?' Burroughs asked incredulously. 'For God's sake, man, this confirms everything I've been trying to get through to you!'

Holman's hands crashed down on his desk, spilling coffee into his blue Wedgwood saucer.

'Silence! I am more concerned with your report to the Minister! I have heard from Lord Pennington this morning.'

Burroughs couldn't believe this conversation.

'Sod my report!' he retorted angrily. 'Danvers is dead. Doesn't that *mean* anything to you?'

Holman's mouth trapped his question, clamped shut, then: 'Of course. It is most . . . regrettable. I'm sure he was a good agent.'

'I'M NOT TALKING ABOUT DANVERS, FOR CHRIST'S SAKE! HE'S DEAD!' Burroughs yelled at him. 'Look at what's happening out there! There's a big one coming off. It all fits, you – you CRETIN!'

'Now look, George, you can't – ' MacAllister found his tongue.

Burroughs rounded on him, big hands bunched.

'Shut up, Mac, or I'll bust your jaw! O'Neil, Kassim, Khalid, Solenov, Zharevsky – a blind man could see it! They're planning a major operation. It's bloody obvious!'

He sat down in his chair with a crash. Holman wiped at his mouth with his handkerchief. He really couldn't cope with this madman.

'Lord Pennington says your report is interesting but in-conclusive. He . . . he has asked me – ' Holman started up, trying to draw strength from the Minister's sacred opinion.

Burroughs cut across him, whiplash quiet. 'Holman, I will say this once and once only. If you don't go back to your precious Minister and tell him that I seriously believe the Queen's life is at risk if she goes ahead with her tour of the Gulf, then by God I'll go see him myself and to hell with the consequences to your career. If that doesn't work, I'll go all the way to Buck House itself, with my cables, reports, transmission copies – the lot. *And* I will get on to Sir Timothy at MI9. Somebody's going to listen.'

Holman was stunned into silence. He sat very still for a long time, watching Burroughs' face, trying to make up his mind if the man would really do it. The repercussions were unthinkable.

'Very well, Burroughs,' he said at last. 'I will personally write to the Minister, with your views. It can go across by hand in the morning.' (As far as the Permanent Secretary, in actual fact.)

Burroughs nodded, calmer now. 'Thank you, sir. I suggest I go out to Damascus station meanwhile, to cover the ground until a replacement is put in.'

His chief shook his head emphatically. Couldn't have this boorish lunatic upsetting the Ambassador.

'That will not be necessary. The Head of Chancery and the Political Section can deal with the situation for the time being. *I* suggest you take a few days leave. It is obvious that you are . . . overwrought,' he added with an attempt at sympathy that sounded as sincere as a political promise.

Burroughs shrugged, feeling all in. He'd done all he could. It was up to the big guns now. He felt sure he'd be vindicated.

'Right you are, sir,' he replied dully and got out of his chair.

'Good, Burroughs,' Holman 'congratulated' him warmly. 'I am glad you're going to be sensible. MacAllister can keep an eye on things here.'

George Burroughs grunted and walked out.

When he had gone, Sir David turned to his Assistant Head of Section.

'I really believe the man is unstable. Thank goodness he is retiring this year. See to it that there are no more incidents like this again, MacAllister. It's too much.'

'Teddy' MacAllister inclined his head. He had a feeling in his bones that George was right but what could he do without jeopardising his own position? Maybe he'd have a word with his own contacts in Whitehall, but he doubted he'd get past the system protecting Holman. Burroughs was a fool to let his temper get the better of him. His language was deplorable. This thing had to be handled calmly or not at all.

Hassan Kassim arrived back in Damascus on 10 January, several days later than his original estimation. His trip had been entirely successful and detailed maps could be drawn up of the 'killing ground' he had selected, which met with general approval.

All their equipment had been gathered together by this time, with the exception of hard information on the Queen's finalised itinerary – and the vital layout of the *Britannia*.

Solenov turned up briefly, minus General Zharevsky, who had flown back to Moscow. He assured O'Neil and Kassim that they would have the itinerary in good time. O'Neil told him that he'd been on the radio again to the Brigade. They could expect delivery of the royal yacht's deck-plan and a breakdown of her crew functions in the coming week.

When Solenov inquired smoothly just how he intended to get those essential elements, O'Neil replied just as smoothly that he knew his way around these tricks. Solenov had given him an old-fashioned stare, letting it pass. Time would tell.

In fact, the official investigation later by officers from Naval Intelligence, the Home Office, Special Branch and MI6 would be unable to establish the answer to that one. Opinions were voiced but nothing hard enough to facilitate action.

O'Neil didn't even let on to his partner, Kassim, but he would always be grateful to the pretty blonde he knew in a London wine merchant's, who had been fortunate to have a conducted tour round the royal yacht during a wine-stocking exercise under their royal warrant, prior to *the* tour.

In fairness to the lady wine expert concerned, she was totally unaware of O'Neil's profession or his intentions when she agreed to meet him for dinner on 18 January in Paris, where she was over buying for her company. O'Neil had met her in October of '78 on one of her frequent trips to Europe and remembered she had spoken about her impending visit to the *Britannia.*

O'Neil had been on a buying trip, too – for arms. But the deal fell through. She thought he was in Irish linens. They got on very well together, and he was so amusing. She liked him a lot and got taken by his persuasive charm. Literally. He was awfully good in bed. So was she.

Coupled with the Naval architect plans photographed and carefully replaced in their long wooden drawer at the Naval Design Establishment, Bath, by one of the Brigade's London-based contacts, her colouring-in of the royal yacht's layout and in-board procedures was all he needed.

The one thousand pounds it had cost the Brigade funds to get their contact to perform his risky break-in was worth every penny. How the hell he got away with it, O'Neil never found out. Any security system can be surmounted – if the price is right for someone to look the other way.

The equipment list was formidable by any standards. Apart from the seemingly unnecessary amount of medical stores, it all had an obvious place in the scheme of things, even to the PAC guerillas and Brigade men as yet only guessing at their destination and objective.

Each man was supplied with either a Russian AK47, the popular and deadly Armalite 5-56 mm high velocity sniper's rifle, the Israeli Uzi or the American M60 machine-gun.

The Armalites and M60s came from a batch stolen two years earlier during a raid on the US military armoury in Ohio. The AK47 Kalashnikov assault rifles were donated by the KGB, together with three RGP7 rocket-launchers. Two American MAC-11 machine-guns completed the personal arms issue, the MACs being so deadly that they ceased to be made after several disappeared from the first batch of two hundred.

Each man was also issued with a back-pack of grenades, spare clips of ammunition for their weapons, and a standardised commando knife. Hand-guns were an optional extra but disapproved of, since speed and freedom from personal clutter was vital.

Nobody was allowed to wear his own clothes. Standard combat denims and boots were fitted for each man, devoid of any identifying or traceable labelling. The serial number of every weapon was chemically burned out. Each man would wear a woollen hood at all times during the training work-up, and for the hijack itself, so that it became an automatic part of his person.

The explosives necessary for scuttling the *Britannia*, and as a helpmate to the ship's dry dock/sea-cocks, consisted of almond coloured commercial 'plastic', its marzipan scent the chilling hallmark of its nitroglycerine base. Kneaded into dobs as per the explosive force required, it would then be umbilicalled to a detonation core of pentaerithritol-tetra-nitrate – better known as 'det-cord'. Finished off with a length of cordtex, the whole affair would be lit by a special match fitted with a bulbous red head, about the size of a pea.

It couldn't be set going with a cigarette end or a lighter. The thick fuse match ignites like the ordinary household variety but fizzes in the manner of a child's Guy Fawkes' sparkler. Fireworks – terrorist version.

Cartridge-fired grappling lines completed the boarding package. Flags of convenience and signal halyards, and a large bottle of blood-coloured dye, would come later.

They were ready for their private war with high society. Now it was 'just' a question of rigorous, urgent training – and a lot of luck.

They left the big villa for Kassim's desert base on 11 January 1979. At dawn. In a covered military three tonner.

Kassim's principal force was already waiting in the tiny Syrian village.

Nobody said much as the truck started up. The realities of it all, known and as yet unknown, sat side by side with each man.

No one saw them off, not even Major Khalid. Such gestures were not necessary anyway, but O'Neil had a brief flash of instinct that they had suddenly become pariahs for what they were about to do.

Then he dismissed that. Solenov and Khalid would be coming up to the base during the training period.

As the truck hummed along the military highway into the scrublands, O'Neil's natural optimism took over with the rising sun. He began to quietly sing a Republican song from the old days of Ireland's struggle against the British. He had a fine, light voice. Soon, the others joined in, Docherty's profound bass rumbling through the words.

Hassan Kassim stared at these Irishmen singing their battle song and smiled in a pucker of scar-tissue at Rashid Khadir. *It was going to work.* By Allah's blood and Lenin's sacred tomb, it was going to work!

Burroughs did not enjoy his few days leave, except for seeing Mr Betts again. Having instructed Chambers to keep on top of things and ring him at home if anything cropped up, he thought it would be good to have the old man up to his place for a couple of days. If the old boy felt like making the journey, in Burroughs' car of course.

When Burroughs telegrammed him, Norman Betts contacted him in similar style, having no phone. Yes, he would be delighted. There was no need to collect him. Just meet him off the Folkestone train.

As usual, the Southern Region service of British Rail did its notorious best to mess up its passengers' arangements, but had an ideal get-out because of the weather. Burroughs paced Victoria Station in a freezing cold fury for the first two hours' delay and then decided there was no point in hurting his blood pressure.

Eventually an indistinct announcement came over the tannoys about the Folkestone-Dover arrival. Burroughs was sure British Rail had some special deal going with unemployed loonies. The announcements were so indistinct and the diction so unintelligible, it was a wonder any of the public ever knew where they were going.

He walked over to one of the ticket gates and forced himself to be polite when he questioned the lad on the barrier about Betts' train. The youth looked him over with ill-disguised lack of interest – and asked him for more details.

An exasperated George Burroughs was in no mood for such stupidity.

'It's definitely one of yours,' he stated flatly.

The youth took that in slowly and thought about it.

'Yeah, it would be, I suppose,' he agreed with genuine consideration.

Burroughs had already walked away again by the time this doyen of the nationalised rail system realised the sarcastic import of the big man's remark.

In the end, the train did arrive. Burroughs was shocked at the old man's worsening appearance, even since his last sight of him just two weeks earlier. He looked thinner and very drawn. Mr Betts assured him he was feeling fine – but he would make use of this visit to pop into his specialist in Harley Street.

He stayed for three days. Burroughs recounted the latest happenings in Damascus and at Century House. Mr Betts supported his view that it deserved more serious attention than that being given to it by either Holman or Lord Pennington's people.

As Burroughs saw him off again at Victoria Station, the old man gripped his arm with friendly urgency.

'Keep well, George. Do what you can about this business but not at the expense of yourself. No one will thank you for it. If the worst happens and you are proved right, just make sure you have copies of all the paperwork on this matter – and make up a diary of everything you can remember that has happened between you and Holman over it all.'

He stared up into Burroughs' cragged face.

'God bless you, George. You know I've always thought you were the best. I should know, I taught you. Remember me.'

The train started to pull away from the platform. Norman Healey-Betts waved briefly out of the window and was gone.

Burroughs walked slowly out of the station to his car, deep in thought and not a little worried.

'*Remember me.*' It seemed such a strange thing to say. Was the old boy . . . ?

He shook his head at the thought and climbed into the Jaguar.

It was the last time Burroughs would see his old tutor. Two months later, Norman Healey-Betts, OBE, died peacefully in his sleep.

O'Neil's men settled into their new base quickly. Principally because they were given no time to do otherwise. After being introduced to all the men from the Palestine Action Commando who would be working with them, training for the operation began in deadly earnest.

O'Neil spent the first few days in harness with his men and then went back to Damascus to put through a telephone call of vital importance.

Using one of the Syrian Intelligence headquarters' international lines, which were better than the normal service in Syria, he telephoned his 'girlfriend' in London, pretending to be calling from Germany.

He was going to be in Paris on the 17th and 18th of the month. Was she around then? If so, he'd meet her.

She was delighted to hear from him but could he make it to London? O'Neil knew that was far too risky for him and made some excuse that he hadn't time on this trip. Had to stay in Paris for business reasons.

Hilary St Clere gave in without much of a fight. She was sure she would be able to get over. For business reasons, too, darling!

Having travelled back up to the desert base to let Kassim

and Docherty know a little of his plans, O'Neil left for Damascus again and a plane routing that would see him circumspectly arrive in Paris for the 17th.

Kassim hadn't liked it much. He needed the Irishman here to help with the training and keep control of his men. O'Neil was adamant. They had to have that information on the *Britannia*, and it was far too important to trust any of it to telephones or the airmail services.

He arrived in Paris late on the 17th and stayed for two nights at the Hotel Brighton in the rue de Rivoli. He picked it because the name seemed so out of place, rather like himself.

His London man turned up the same evening – with the drawings of the royal yacht. Hilary St Clere came in from Heathrow the next morning, breathless and excited to see him.

They spent a passionate night of it and Connor O'Neil used all his skills to extract the information he wanted from her on *Britannia.* The background picture she was able to paint for him brought his deck-plans alive. The *Britannia* became a living thing, no longer merely a concept at the heart of his world-rocking mission.

During a break in their love-making, O'Neil lit a cigarette while his lady friend chattered on about some ball or other she'd been to. She had already told him everything he wanted to know.

O'Neil glanced at his watch – 6 a.m. Neither of them had slept yet. He drew on his cigarette, thinking about his men so far away in the deserts of Syria. And suddenly she came into his mind.

He wondered about the slim, dark-haired girl commando – the only one in Kassim's force – and turned over again, reaching for Hilary St Clere.

Burroughs reported back to his Department the same morn-

200

ing that O'Neil was completing a final thrust into the moaning girl beneath him.

If Burroughs had known his quarry was so close at hand across the English Channel, he would probably have swum it in order to get at him.

It was a cold Friday morning. The weather had eased a little but not so you'd notice. Burroughs went in so near the very end of the week only because he knew the habits of the Department demanded a Head of Sections and AHSs fortnightly meeting with Pennington's people.

It would allow him most of the morning to gather up and photocopy the majority of the documentation he wanted at hand. Just in case.

Fortunately, Holman always took his secretary with him. One of the girls from the pool would cover his office meanwhile. Although he'd have to be 'passed up', and would be logged on signature in the Day Book (Movements), he could easily get into Holman's office on the excuse of dropping in his monthly expenses sheet.

Holman ran the place like a bloody grocer, far more worried about exceeding their piddling budget than about the job in hand. He could lift his chief's file copies for an hour or so and run them off in the Duty Room.

Getting them back again might present a problem, though. Then he remembered the repair bill on his car at the end of November. He was entitled to part-payment by the Department, since he didn't have an official vehicle like Holman or MacAllister.

He'd just have to 'forget' it on his first run upstairs.

O'Neil arrived back at the guerilla base on 21 January, glad to be under the sun's warm influence again.

The training was going well, although MacFadden had proved something of a liability on the tougher end of the physical fitness and stamina tests. Perhaps it didn't matter that much in his case. His main task would be to supervise the scuttling operation and set up the various radio frequencies they would require once on board *Britannia.*

O'Neil put his deck-plans together with the rest of the operation's paperwork and settled down to write up his notes on the background information supplied by Mrs St Clere and he grinned at the memory of her full bosomed, demanding body stretched out beneath and on top of him. He wondered what her ex-husband had been like, speculating that her sexual habits probably caused the divorce. He liked sex with the best of them but that girl would wear out a regiment.

He was sitting in the house used by Kassim, with the door open on to the baked sand. The girl commando walked by as he laboured over his notes, catching his eye. He smiled at her engagingly and received a cold stare in return. She really was rather a beauty, that one . . .

On 21 January in London, Sir David Holman received a telephone call on his scrambler phone at the town residence, where he was staying alone again for the weekend. Lady Holman had gone back to their country home to chair a local women's institute Sunday lunch. She expected to remain there for part of the coming week.

The caller was the Permanent Secretary of the Department himself. Sir David mentally stood to attention. The PS did not like Holman and was therefore brief. As brief as any political appointee can ever be, that is.

He had reviewed Holman's, ah, 'observations' at length, together with an edited version of Burroughs' report to their Minister, performed by their Minister's secretarial assistant before it got to their master.

Holman could rest assured that the report would not be going further. No further than Lord Pennington, that was.

He had advised their Minister against any 'precipitate' action at this stage, explaining to him the nature and temperament of Major Burroughs, based on Holman's own summary to himself.

Of course, their Minister had wanted reassurance that

Burroughs' somewhat forceful contentions were misconceived, if not entirely groundless, and the PS had been able to give him such assurance – again based on what Holman, as Head of Section, had been able to tell himself of, ah, Major Burroughs' behaviour patterns and general disregard for procedural norms.

The PS understood that Sir David had heard directly from their master to the effect that he felt Burroughs' report (even the edited version, that is) was overdramatic and somewhat inconclusive. His tone told Holman that the Permanent Secretary had been none too pleased at their Minister breaking Civil Service protocol by coming back to him over the PS's head. It was almost as bad as Burroughs' lack of respect for these things.

No, the PS went on, he had advised their Minister most firmly that he should leave well alone.

Whilst the Department appreciated that a proper concern for Her Majesty's and HRH Prince Philip's safety was of paramount importance, he really did not think their Minister should go worrying either the PM or the Palace with it at this time. These matters were better dealt with internally by themselves, didn't he know?

Holman agreed. The PS was pleased. Sir David would be aware, of course, that the royal tour represented many other considerations beside the obvious political desirability of maintaining good relations with the Gulf States, particularly in view of the current, er, strategic unrest in the region and the, ah, pressing energy crisis facing them all.

He would understand, too, that the expected trade orders on hand from the Gulf sheikhdoms would represent an enormous boost to the economy, and the royal visit – being something of a historical precedent – would ensure a wide-ranging series of benefits to Great Britain.

It had to be remembered as well, of course, that President Carter was entering the most crucial and difficult stage of his, ah, peace initiative between Begin and that Egyptian fellow. As allies and friends of the Americans, it was essential that we made an . . . appropriate, ah, gesture towards the pro-Western Arabs who were worried about the long-term outcome of any treaty between Mr Sadat and Mr Begin.

Therefore, the tour could not be cancelled at this late date. It would go ahead as scheduled, Holman, but with very stringent security for their royals. Apparently, the Palace was more than satisfied with the general precautions already proposed by MI5, the Home Office, MI6 and even the Cabinet Office.

Holman was both relieved and reassured personally. The PS's final remarks dampened his complacency.

'Of course, Holman, you do realise that this business with Burroughs is . . . unfortunate.'

Holman gripped the receiver more tightly as his heart sank.

'No, no. We can't have mere Principal Officers dictating policy decisions, you know, Holman. Very poor show this business getting to the Minister at all. Even poorer your not preventing the wretched fellow from getting his report so far up the line, so to speak.'

Holman tried to defend himself, but the Permanent Secretary droned on.

'Of course, not entirely your fault. Young Colehurst-Brown should have sent the thing down to me. He's new of course. Doesn't really understand how things work yet. He will . . . He will.'

Holman could hear the PS drawing breath down the phone.

'Nevertheless, rather remiss of you not to anticipate your own staff. Bad for the Department, Holman. Bad for us all. But your request for a Departmental disciplinary inquiry is overruled, I'm afraid. By me. Can't have this sort of thing aired, you know. Just see Burroughs is restrained until his retirement comes through, don't you know? I shall not expect to hear any more of this matter, unless you can bring something more, ah, positive to bear. Goodbye.'

He had gone.

Holman was left smarting from the gently-put rebuke. Damn Burroughs! Damn him!

It was perhaps fortunate for Cynthia Holman that she was away. Her husband, at his most 'difficult' when his career was further threatened, would disturb any equilibrium left in their relationship.

CHAPTER FIFTEEN

O'Neil's and Kassim's training programme went ahead in Syria, while in Century House, George Burroughs found he could do little but kick his heels – or anything else within reach.

Holman had taken obvious pleasure in informing him that their Principal Secretary had taken a dim view of Burroughs' non-procedural action in submitting a report directly to the Minister. He did not tell him that his report had been suitably doctored en route.

It certainly wouldn't happen again, Holman had assured him. From now on, he would do what was required of him by MacAllister and that was that.

Holman was further bolstered by the surprisingly inconclusive report that came in from the Head of Chancery in Damascus. It did appear to be a quite genuine car accident which had befallen Clive Danvers. The Syrians were unlikely to have sacrificed two of their own countrymen out of hand.

So Burroughs caught up on his paperwork, went home early every day – and fretted. He also spent long evenings into the night compiling a 'diary' of all the events, transmissions, task cables, etc., on his project in Syria.

Reading it through again and again, he remained convinced that he was right – but impotent. He even had Peter Chambers round for dinner one evening and it turned out to be remarkably enjoyable, especially since he'd received a telephone call from Sam Cook telling him that he had covered his transmission for him – when MacAllister had come snooping around. Nobody was any the wiser, George my old mate!

It only served to increase Burroughs' dislike of these 'career johnnies'.

Peter Chambers utilised the time in further visits to the Registry, and his diggings into the ways of the SIS convinced him, too, that George was probably right. But, like his tutor, he knew that the strictures on doing anything about it were literally insurmountable.

In the blazing heat of the Syrian desert, O'Neil and Kassim drove their combined force of twenty-two men with all the urgency of the time ticking away towards the royal couple's departure on their Gulf States tour.

The testing of their men ranged from forced route marches, obstacle courses and firing practice of interchangeable weaponry to charge-setting, hand-to-hand combat and grilling every man until he knew Her Majesty's royal yacht from stem to stern probably better than she did herself.

In the middle of one afternoon training session, when Kassim had doubled the length of the obstacle course and even found some barbed-wire and broken glass to make things more difficult, O'Neil stood watching the group go through its gruelling paces under the indifferent stare of both the stultifying sun and the village's children.

Suddenly, it was the girl's turn. He tensed as she climbed the swinging rope ladder up to the start of the pole-run, some twenty feet off the ground. No dangerous height except for Kassim's strewing of the course with old jerrycans, glass and barbed-wire.

She had got a little distance along the first pole when Kassim let go with a practice grenade. It had no lethal charge but the noise was just as effective and, at close range, blast burn was quite possible.

Armed with her rifle and a heavy back-pack, Lila Fahd lost her balance and began to fall. O'Neil moved with a speed that surprised himself.

He managed to catch her just before she hit one of the snake-coils of wire.

'You all right?' he asked, easing her to her feet.

She stared at him from within her hood, eyes angry, sweating hard.

'Do not do this!' she spat at him in bad English. 'I must be as the men!'

O'Neil shrugged and let her go.

She started to walk away, hesitated and turned.

'Thank you,' she called, before running off to join the others.

O'Neil rubbed at his chin, a quizzical smile on his sunburned face. Human after all . . .

His ruminations were interrupted by the arrival of Major Khalid and Colonel Solenov. They were both covered with dust from the long drive and it gave O'Neil some satisfaction that the camp rule decreed nothing to drink but water as part of the training schedule.

With his customary curtness, Khalid came straight to the point of their visit.

'We have the British Queen's itiner-rary,' he stumbled over the word. 'She will be flying back to Britain by RAF jet, from Oman, on Friday, 2 March, at 3.45. The Prince Philip leaves the Oman by plane for Moscow. They will not be returning on the *Britannia*.'

Privately, O'Neil was relieved.

'Nevertheless, Captain,' Solenov interjected, 'we have established that the royal yacht will pass through the Canal on her way home.'

He watched O'Neil's face for any reaction – and received only a smile.

'Good,' was all he said.

'Good?' Khalid queried coldly.

'Yes. Good, Major,' O'Neil replied, not inclined to be helpful.

'You will explain,' Khalid snapped. 'Without their presence on board, you have nothing. No bargaining point.'

'Then I suggest you read my notes again,' O'Neil snapped back. 'The *Britannia* is the bargaining point. The threat of having her scuttled bang in the middle of the Canal, right before Mr Carter's peace treaty gets itself ready to be signed, will be all we need. The fact that we'll scuttle her anyway is something the British and Egyptians won't know. Unless you're going to tell them,' he added bitingly.

Khalid seemed to be getting into the habit of flushing.

'Very well, O'Neil. Now you will tell me how you intend to time yourself to be in the Canal at the right moment?' he asked with triumphant malice.

'Read my notes,' O'Neil repeated again, growing tired of the sniping.

Solenov watched the pair of them, saying nothing.

O'Neil let go an exasperated sigh. 'I thought it had been agreed that your people and the Air Force would keep a tracking brief? You know damn well we've already timed our steaming course to put us exactly where we need to be by the time she enters the Canal through the Gulf of Aden in the south.'

Khalid treated him to a scowling nod. 'I am glad to see you have a grasp of our role in this affair. Without us you would be nothing.'

Solenov felt it was time to step in. 'So, Captain. How goes your training? I see they are working hard. You are satisfied with their progress?'

'I am at that,' O'Neil replied more cordially. 'We'll be ready to go up to Latakia by the middle of next week.'

His eyes strayed to the girl again, now engaged in hand-to-hand throws with Rashid Khadir. She beat him neatly and they ended up in a laughing heap, breaking the serious business at hand.

O'Neil felt a strange twinge of jealousy.

'Have you brought the information I wanted – and the flags?' he asked, cold again.

Solenov had caught the direction of his gaze and smiled faintly. A red-blooded man was always a better fighter.

'It is all in the jeep, comrade. The itinerary,' – he did not stumble – 'the flags, the Canal shipping-control regulations and timings.'

O'Neil nodded, angry with himself. 'Right. Is that it?'

Solenov inclined his white head and, to O'Neil's further surprise, put out his hand.

'We shall not meet again until after the operation is over, Captain. In Libya. I wish you well. I shall oversee your . . . affairs from Damascus.'

Going to ground, more likely, thought O'Neil. But he placed his own hand in the Colonel's.

'Thanks. We'll do it just fine.'

'I'm sure you will!' Solenov chuckled. 'The Comrade General asked to be remembered to you before he left for Moscow.'

That at least pleased the Irishman. He had liked General Zharevsky. He seemed a straight, if rough, old stick.

He turned to go.

'I shall be inspecting your progress at Latakia, Captain,' Khalid raised his voice to the edge of a snarl.

You can inspect your bloody navel for all I care, O'Neil thought, raising his hand briefly. He was quietly amused that the 'Comrade' Colonel had not asked to see Kassim. Nor had Kassim come over to join them. Ah well, he would tell Kassim the wherefores of it anyway.

The evening remained mild. After they had all eaten, the men settled down to clean and check their weapons before the night exercise. O'Neil took himself for a quiet stroll through the village.

As he was walking back again, he saw the girl coming across the little dusty 'square'.

'Hullo,' he said, smiling gently.

She had taken her hood off, now they were finished for a

while. Her black hair hung in a raven's wing along her neck and he noticed that her eyes were unusually light in colour, green almost.

'Would you care to walk with me?' he asked casually, expecting to be rebuffed.

'I will,' she replied simply.

The conversation had been difficult at first, shyness and language being natural barriers to be pleasurably broken down. It did not take long and they were soon chatting like old friends.

He learned that she had been married and was twenty-four. Her husband had been killed in the Entebbe Raid debacle. She had joined Kassim's unit through her friend Rashid Khadir. No, there was nothing between them.

She asked O'Neil about himself. He told her – such as he felt there was to tell. She was puzzled at him having been a Queen's soldier, as she put it, and now planning to do this thing.

He explained about his two tours of duty in Ulster; how it had changed his outlook in so many ways – and then left it at that. She felt it would take her a long time to know this tall, engaging foreigner with the devil's smile.

They parted at her quarters. O'Neil took her hand briefly. There was no resistance. Perhaps the common dangers they all faced had begun a binding process.

Docherty had seen him with her. He grunted sourly as his Captain got on to the bunk bed supplied by Khalid's people.

'We have to work with these folk, Captain. We don't have to love them, you know,' he rumbled.

O'Neil raised his eyebrows. The giant seemed to be coming out of himself since acquiring a new heir.

He said nothing though, rolling over on his side to catch some rest before the night exercise, thinking about Lila Fahd until sleep plucked her from his mind but not his heart.

The following week, the three-tonner collected the combined

force of raiders and their equipment for the long drive up the coast road to the port of Latakia.

By this time, Lila Fahd and Connor O'Neil had become lovers – in their eyes at least. He'd found himself spending more and more time with her and less with Docherty and Kassim.

Not that the training schedule allowed for much of that. O'Neil was a professional and the work came a clear first, especially being his own baby. Fathers can be very maternal at times. But the care was there between them. In their looks, fleeting touches of the hand.

Nevertheless, he was careful not to offend the Palestinians. The unit was knitting nicely, almost honed to a point that he and Kassim would find mutually acceptable.

Kassim . . . To O'Neil, he seemed to become increasingly withdrawn as the deadline for their operation approached. He could not believe that the man was afraid. Yet there was something on the guerilla leader's mind, of this he was sure.

He had tried to open him up one evening but had been met with that hawkish stare of his and an impatient tattoo of those hooks. O'Neil was not the kind to worry a thing to death, so he let it be. As long as the operation went off smoothly, that was all for the moment.

On their arrival in Latakia, the men got their first real taste of what it was all about. Tucked away at the rear of the fairly large dockyard was an old steam freighter. She looked battered and scarred from the sea, possibly even thrown back by it. But this was to be the force's home until the exact moment of the raid.

Khalid had arranged for round-the-clock army patrols to keep away any curious bystanders and the indigenous equipment of the docks and warehouses hid the vessel from anything but a waterborne view.

Still unaware of exactly what they were about, the men began the second phase of the training programme at once. By now there were no complaints and both Arab and Irish fell into their orders with a smooth, economic efficiency.

The Irishmen were still held slightly at a distance by their Palestinian comrades, but the basis of a respectful camaraderie was there. Even MacFadden had locked into the chain, a stronger physical link than when he first arrived.

Day and night, the raiders practised ship-boarding procedures, clearing the ship from end to end in imaginary 'house-to-house' fighting techniques, suffering small mishaps amongst all the jumble of iron stanchions and deck equipment, and endless little crucifixions of ego and physical hurt as they learnt from their mistakes.

By the end of another week, they were truly a force to be reckoned with. In the heat of the day or the sharp cool of the night.

O'Neil's relationship with Lila Fahd had blossomed quietly, as his friendship with Kassim seemed to go on cooling. It did not appear to affect the manner in which he was treated by Kassim's men, however.

He thought Kassim's attitude had something to do with the way he blended and softened the Hawk's harsher driving of the men with his own dry humour. Or maybe the strange little guerilla leader was feeling a threat to his position, as evidenced in the ready response O'Neil now elicited from his commandos?

Either way, the training went on and on. Remorseless, demanding, all kinds of problems, contingencies invented for these raiders who had to react, decide and act without knowing the why of their mission.

Docherty, giant amongst giants by anyone's measure, proved the tower of strength he could be when he put his mind to it. He had got over his apparent disapproval of the girl, seeing she made his idol happy.

In Docherty's world, his Captain's well-being was all.

By 12 February things were in excellent shape. O'Neil and Kassim now wielded a knife that was very sharp indeed.

Yet the drilling still went on. Each man had designated tasks, still without knowing the identity of the ship they were obviously preparing to take. From the outset, O'Neil had ensured all references to the *Britannia* were blocked out on the deck-plans, just in case someone saw them by accident. They always worked off the model made by Mac-Fadden, based on the line drawings O'Neil himself had done of their target. But he knew he could not keep its identity from coming out one way or another soon.

There were some of them who might already have guessed, of that he was certain. Nevertheless, confirmation of a suspicion is very different from the suspicion itself.

Of course, Lila Fahd knew – as did Kassim, Rashid Khadir and Docherty. O'Neil had told her during that first walk, relying on his own judgement that she would keep his confidence in the safe-keeping of her desire to know him. Had Docherty or Kassim found out that she knew, sparks would have flown and her life might have met a swift end. But it never came to that.

Standing on the freighter's rusting bridge one evening, O'Neil decided the time had come to tell them all. Why wait until they were at sea? If anyone was going to come apart at the seams or become overawed at the prospect of the prize, it would have shown during the training work-up.

Soon the men were gathered together in the cramped crew mess. The talking ceased instantly as he walked in.

'All right,' he said without sugaring the sweet, or the pill. 'You've worked hard and long. Now Kassim and I think you are ready. So I'll tell you where we're going and what the pretty prize is at the end of the day.'

The men listened to him in absolute silence – broken only by Khadir's steady translation for the Palestinians whose English was still poor.

O'Neil laid it out for them stage by stage, painting in the shocking and audacious canvas of his plan.

First, the voyage along the coast, for three to four days until they made rendezvous with the northern end of the Canal at Port Said. Then the overstay, waiting for the news that *Britannia* had entered the Canal's southern section.

They would crew the ship themselves, with MacFadden and Khadir as duty helmsmen and Kassim and himself seeing to the navigation, such as it was. Some of them would have to be allocated the role of stokers, he regretted! That got a laugh from his audience.

As to how they were going to take the royal yacht, there lay the gamble. A controlled fire would be started on deck as soon as the *Britannia* was sighted. Using the signal flags available, they would hoist the internationally-recognised distress call for assistance. Being a hospital ship in time of war as her dual function to carrying Mr and Mrs Queen about, the *Britannia* was bound to stop. In any case, the 'burning' freighter would constitute a serious hazard to shipping in the Canal, especially for *Britannia*, and she was known to have comprehensive fire-fighting equipment on board.

'We'll have no problem there, I'm thinking,' O'Neil chuckled. 'The Royal Navy are always gentlemen at sea! Right, so she's alongside or near enough for our purposes ... because we're going to hit her in the Bitter Lakes, here.'

He pointed to the map he had pinned against the grimy bulkhead.

'It's the only stretch of water in the whole Canal wide enough for ships to pass each way.'

He grinned piratically at them.

'Now, how do we do it? You'll be remembering all that medical gear we've been lugging around with us? There is a fire aboard our ship. Men have been hurt, seriously burned. We've got to get *aboard* the *Britannia*, not just wave at her. So that means displaying men in obvious need of hospital attention. And she's a floating surgery. *That* means stretcher-cases ... and away we go.'

He stared round the silent group, his eyes resting briefly on Lila Fahd's face. She smiled back at him, uncertainty faint on her mouth.

'Those of you picked to be the injured,' he went on, 'will have blankets round you, with your weapons concealed underneath. We have two of our own stretchers and they'll serve the same purpose. Lila, you and I will see to dressing-up the "wounded". It'll be the last thing they'll be expecting in the middle of Egyptian territory!'

MacFadden raised his hand. 'What about the Queen, Captain? She going to be on board?'

O'Neil shook his head, happy with his answer. 'No. She'll be flying straight home at the end of her royal toot around the Gulf by RAF VC10, and Prince Philip is going on to Moscow, of all places, to play Olympic gee-gees. That's good because we don't want half the world's security organisations down our necks in a do-or-die attempt to get them back.'

He laughed again, a harsh, tense sound on the silence.

'The yacht's a different matter, though. So is her cargo. Those they *will* bargain for – or have their pretty boat on the bottom of the Canal! In fact, we're going to scuttle her anyway, and wreck Mr Carter's peace pilgrimage to Mecca and all points west. But they'll not be knowing that, and they'll agree to anything to avoid it happening, eh?'

Some of the men were grinning broadly now.

'The next little item is her cargo, my lads. She will be carrying well in excess of a million pounds' worth of gifts from the Gulf sheikhs. On top of that, there'll be all the gold plate, personal mementos and what-have-you on the yacht as a matter of course. And we'll have the lot away.'

He stared round the group, his blue eyes hard with excitement.

'Yes, gentlemen. For those of you who haven't guessed it, Her Majesty's royal yacht *Britannia* is our target. The objective? Disruption of the Sadat–Begin peace talks and to hook the biggest fish to float in on our stretch of the river since Moses tried to claim he wasn't Jewish!'

That got him another laugh. Then someone asked about controlling the raid effectively when there would be other shipping in the Canal.

O'Neil had given this one a lot of thought. So had Kassim and Colonel Solenov. Checking of their various sources had revealed that being such an important vessel and the property of a head of state, quite apart from her size, she would be accorded a clear, unconvoyed run through the

Canal – except in the Bitter Lakes, where other shipping might be 'parked' on its way north or south.

It didn't make any difference, O'Neil declared. Once they had seized the *Britannia*, the whole world was going to know about it. Part of the object in view.

A couple more questions came up and were dealt with. O'Neil outlined the method by which they would transport the bullion and booty from ship to shore. And of the precautions they would have to take, once aboard, in order to protect their investment.

He was supremely confident that they would get the aircraft they'd need to fly them out to Libya – one which could land on the desert scrub running each side of the Canal.

He was also quite certain that neither the British or Egyptian governments would be stupid enough to try anything. Not with the royal yacht, her crew's safety and the free passage of the Canal held so tellingly to ransom.

With a twinkle shining wickedly in his blue eyes, he surveyed his force.

'That covers it from my end, my buckos. I know Kassim wants a few words but I'll say just this. We've a glittering prize in sight, both politically and financially. Just carry out your functions, keep calm, and we'll win through.'

He paused, his smile widening into a boyish grin.

'From then on in, let the bloody politicians sort it out. Her Majesty's plaything will be sitting firmly on the bottom of the Canal with its guts ripped out, and they'll need a lot more than a traffic warden to clear the tangle *we* are going to leave behind us!'

CHAPTER SIXTEEN

'I feel it would be advisable, ma'am,' the very senior gentleman from the Anti-Terrorist Squad had replied respectfully, staring directly at the embossed wallpaper above his sovereign's coiffured head.

Privately, he speculated that Her Majesty must be growing used to these sort of discussions by now. And that she must be finding it both sad, and restricting, that her personal safety really needed to be held in question.

Like all those closely concerned with the Royal Family's protection, he knew how much it distressed the Queen – and sometimes openly annoyed Prince Philip – that they were often prevented from real contact with their subjects and admirers by the strictures of mounting terrorism, which had no regard for human life or position – especially on their tours abroad.

Nevertheless, such considerations were necessary, vital even. Which was why he had found himself at this audience with the Queen in her private office at Buckingham Palace.

Personally, he was not aware of any active threat to Her Majesty's life on the coming tour, but his own highly-developed sense of danger had been sharpened by the Whitehall directive instructing him to do and say nothing that might alarm the Palace prior to the tour's commencement.

On inquiring of both Lord Pennington and Holman's immediate superior, he had been blandly informed that there was nothing at hand on their files to cause concern. This tour was dreadfully important for the country and Western strategy, didn't he know?

However, expediency demanded caution in these modern times and it was therefore advised that Her Majesty should fly home at the end of the tour rather than return at a more leisurely pace aboard the royal yacht. For Her Majesty's convenience as well as her security, of course.

With that, this distinguished gentleman had to be satisfied, although Whitehall's attitude would have appalled George Burroughs – had he been privy to these exchanges with their mutual mandarins, oriental in their apparent masked indifference to his urgent pleas.

On Monday, 12 February 1979, Her Majesty the Queen and His Royal Highness Prince Philip left London Heathrow for their four hours and twenty minutes flight to Kuwait on the glorious mach-2, arrowed beauty of Concorde.

With that private courage often unknown to the crowds who push to see them, the royal couple set off on their vitally important tour in the full knowledge that they were heading for one of the most politically unstable regions in the troubled world of today.

Although nothing of O'Neil and his comrades had been allowed to filter through to the Palace, they nevertheless faced danger every time they embarked on these long tours, throughout which they were always exposed to the gunman's sudden bullet.

As has become part of history, this first-ever visit by a woman head of state to the male-dominated Arab world was an unqualified success, Her Majesty most especially capturing the cautious hearts of these men of the desert.

The gifts they showered on her amounted to several million pounds more than O'Neil's estimation, and the royal yacht's principal strongroom was an Aladdin's Cave indeed by the end of the tour. They made the Crown Jewels look like a child's baubles.

It was privately reckoned that – apart from the Household treasures on board the *Britannia* as part of her fixtures and fittings – the Queen's gifts contained workmanship in gold, silver and precious gems unmatched by anything she had received on previous royal tours.

Since many of those tours had been to give comfort to former colonies now seeking their independence from Britain's once unquestionable wealth and mighty protection, it was hardly surprising.

Having completed a demanding but highly enjoyable itinerary, which ranged from Kuwait to Bahrain, Abu Dhabi and Saudi Arabia through to the Oman, Her Majesty flew safely home – by British Airways VC10 in actual fact, but with the Captain of the Queen's flight in attendance on the flight deck.

Prince Philip subsequently left the Oman to fly on to Moscow where, as President of the Equestrian Olympics, he was due to inspect the rings and facilities being constructed by his Russian hosts.

It added to the irony of his presence in the land of the KGB that not only were his hosts tacitly involved in the planning of an outrageous act against the British Royal Family, but that these very 1980 Olympics would become themselves upset by the Russian invasion of Afghanistan nearly a year later.

The 'Brotherhood of Man' expressed in the Olympic ideal is weakly fleshed at the best of times.

In London, George Burroughs found himself the butt of acid ridicule from his chief. The royal tour had gone ahead *and* completed its schedule – without the slightest hint of trouble.

'All that fuss from you. Embarrassment with my Minister. For what?' Holman had thrust at him, after summoning his subordinate upstairs. 'So that you could indulge your send-a-gunboat fantasies!'

Holman had plumped himself behind his desk with the air of a man who had found both God, and Burroughs, wanting.

'It is quite obvious to me, Burroughs, that these terrorists in Syria were there for nothing more sinister than the kind of internationally co-operated exchange of experience, weapons techniques and what have you which is now becoming commonplace amongst these Marxist terror groups,' he concluded, dismissing Burroughs from his wiser presence.

MacAllister had been sympathetic, but Burroughs didn't give a damn any more. Not for the AHS or for that silly little man crowing away on top of his supposed vindication two floors above the real world in Century House.

Burroughs *knew* there was still something. Now there was nothing left to do but wait for the muck to hit the fan. *Then* they'd see just where the cards fell. In his lap or Holman's . . .

The cards began to fall on 4 March 1979. *Britannia* set sail on her long steam back to the United Kingdom, secure in the knowledge that her monarch was already safely home again.

Of course the yacht was still a floating mint, but understandably her officers and crew started to unwind, released from their awesome responsibility for the royal presence and anxious for the home leave which awaited them on docking at Portsmouth.

Perhaps that word is misleading. Nobody ever *unwinds* on the royal yacht. Certainly not her complement of Royal Navy officers and men.

Commanded by a Senior Officer, *Britannia* had been laid down in 1952 and launched on 16 April 1953. She was officially commissioned into the Service on 14 January 1954.

With a gross tonnage of 5,769 tons, she runs 380 metres of truly splendid luxury, powered by a single-reduction, geared turbine, twin-shafted, that can give her a top speed of 20 knots.

Her decks are holystoned to a startling whiteness, in the traditional manner of the old men-of-war, and the crew wear rope-soled 'sneakers' to prevent damage to the spotless decking. No shouted orders are ever given aboard her when any member of the Royal Family is on board, except in the pursuit of ceremonial occasions. Otherwise, it is all communicated through a series of smart hand signals.

The discipline at such times is rigid to the point of fanaticism, and there is a story which illustrates it well. Apparently, a rating stationed at the bottom of one of the companionways, which are always manned during a royal presence, heard the footfall of a certain young lady reputed to have a 'difficult' temperament. Somewhat naturally, he turned his head to see who it was. That unfortunate man was placed on immediate captain's report, charged with looking up the young lady's skirt, and dismissed the ship back to normal Naval service.

The staterooms are something to behold. Beautifully decorated, furnished with the finest antiques, gold plate, glassware and cutlery, they are reminiscent of the finer days of France's kings and of the turn of the century when great liners still plied the oceans of the world in search of pleasure.

Equipped with the latest navigational and radar equipment, *Britannia* is installed with ultra-sophisticated communications equipment as befits her role as the seaborne home of Britain's monarch. In her other role as a hospital ship, her operating theatres and sick-bays would do credit to a major American medical institution.

Surprisingly, her armaments are negligible. She carries only the standardised armoury of any Royal Navy vessel in the way of hand-guns and rifles. Nevertheless, *Britannia* keeps her complement of two hundred and seventy officers and other ranks well and truly on their toes. Especially when Prince Philip or Prince Charles are around, sailors both.

But, for now, it was all over. The tour had been an exacting business for everyone. It was therefore understandable that the men of the *Britannia* – although seaman-like and top-notch at all times, being forever under the eyes of a critical world – were feeling relaxed and reasonably carefree as the yacht carved her graceful way for home.

O'Neil, Kassim and their deadly raiders left the port of Latakia on 12 March, bound for the Suez Canal. The men were allowed on deck only while in open sea. Otherwise, they remained below decks, checking and then re-checking their individual roles in this hijack to end hijacks.

O'Neil and Kassim were kept busy with the running of the freighter, aided by MacFadden, Khadir and the men elected to do the routine chores of any vessel at sea – including feeding them all.

Here, Lila Fahd came into her own, and not only O'Neil was glad that she was with them. He didn't get much time with her or for her. But events were clearly between them now. When all this was over, perhaps . . . ?

It was a small ship and the sea was seldom kind to her. Docherty said she rolled like an empty Guinness bottle! Several of the men were sick, although the weather was perfect and the sea never more than a running swell.

On 15 March she entered the northern end of the Suez Canal. All but the essential crew remained hidden below in the big wooden crates made up especially for this purpose. Those on deck were dressed in conventional deckhands' rigs, supported by seamen's ID papers – with O'Neil on hand to show their cargo manifesto and sailing orders to the curious.

The crates serving as their hiding-place had perfectly normal bales of cotton most of the way through, but a six-foot high section had been partitioned off in the bottom half of each crate, air-holed discreetly, and with the small trap-door covered by the manufacturer's consignment boards.

Since this was an international waterway, she was required to take on board an Egyptian pilot for the length of the Canal. He found himself at the wrong end of their guns immediately after he had boarded. With a family to think of, there was no way the man concerned was going to risk his life arguing with these hard, ruthless captors.

Through all of this O'Neil managed some brief respites with Lila Fahd. They had elected to share a crate, the bed of straw being comfort enough for their needs. In the heart of the night they found love of a sort together, their bodies a fierce harmony of deep passions held too long inside them both.

As dawn came up on the fatal day, O'Neil took her in his arms, searching her dark features intently. Maybe they could go off into the world together, when this thing was done? He thought he knew what he wanted.

She had gazed at him for a long time, clinging to the strong lines of his body. The Irishman was many things to her now but somehow . . . She could not put it into words, her language or his. But she had a premonition of doom. It all seemed dreamlike, unreal. Maybe.

'I understand you, O'Neil,' she had said gravely. He'd never been able to break her of calling him this and only this.

'We will see. Yes?'

O'Neil nodded. Yes, they would see.

On 16 March, Her Majesty's royal yacht entered the Canal at its southern end, via the Gulf of Aden. It was a lovely day. Everyone felt good. The Canal represented the start of the last leg home. Now there was only the welcome waters of the Mediterranean, and the clear run for Dover's white cliffs.

From opposite ends of the Canal they came on. O'Neil, in regular coded radio touch with Khalid's watchers; *Britannia*, sedate empress of the sea.

The two vessels steamed towards each other . . . and their appointment with an event that would shake three capitals and cost so dear.

Far away in London, Burroughs had taken the afternoon off. There were some things he'd wanted to get done, including buying a new television.

Holman was at the fortnightly Departmental meeting and

Peter Chambers continued to burrow through his 'home-work' down in the Registry, a mole of a very different kind. MacAllister was in bed, with the 'flu. He didn't know it, but it was the best place he could have been.

Lord Pennington held a small reception at his country seat to celebrate the success of the completed royal tour, and his guests found themselves with a relatively mild afternoon in which to walk round the beautifully kept gardens.

Sir David Holman was not invited.

In Washington, President Jimmy Carter battled through with the final brush-strokes to his treaty with Sadat and Begin. There were still problems – and the Israeli premier was being particularly intractable. 'Hard-assed' the Americans would have called it.

Yet the President had high hopes of a success to match the Queen's tour. As did the world.

All in all, Mother Earth did the things she always did, season by season. Men fought, died, made love, worried about their income tax or where the next meal was coming from. Women shook their heads at their menfolk, wept, gave birth, went to work and wondered about many things.

Had any of them been stopped in the middle of their affairs and told what was about to happen, they would have either shrugged in disbelief or nodded sagely at the never-ending machinations of mankind.

And had anyone known how to stop it, including George Burroughs.

CHAPTER SEVENTEEN

Her Majesty's royal yacht steamed serenely up the Suez Canal in the hard, bright sunlight. On the bridge, her Captain and the Senior Officer who commanded her talked convivially with their pilot.

The desert sand stretched away into the distance on each arid side of the Canal, and its isolation provided a whispering witness of insects and shrivelled plants to the huge vessel as she glided past on her way to catastrophe.

Her officers and men went about their business, unaware of what was in store for them all.

O'Neil's little freighter ploughed steadily downstream. He could already see the *Britannia* in his mind's tense eye.

Khalid's final contribution to the raid was supposed to be a single, coded radio sentence from one of his people, confirming the royal yacht's presence in the southern section. It turned out somewhat differently . . .

'What the hell are *you* doing here?' O'Neil snarled in amazement.

Major Ahmad Khalid looked haggard and very hungry, his uniform stained with sweat and grease from his long hiding down in the cable locker.

He eyed O'Neil defiantly.

'I wished it. I am a soldier, like you. For years I have been the – how do you say it? – "errand boy" for my superiors and our Soviet masters,' he replied coldly, his English harsh on the warm air. 'Now I *will* do something to show you what I am, O'Neil. You have always –'

'You're crazy!' O'Neil exploded. 'Stark, raving bonkers!'

Khalid shrugged, coldly indifferent, like a man who knows his own end.

'I am here now. You will find me a place in this thing. Otherwise, I will betray you all . . . when you try to board the *Britannia*,' he stated flatly.

At that moment, Hassan Kassim stepped on to the bridge, having overheard most of it. He took one unblinking stare at the Syrian – and shot him through the head.

The noise was muffled by the enclosed wheelhouse as Khalid's blood settled in a widening pool on the deck, and O'Neil dropped quickly to feel his dead pulse.

'For God's sake, Kassim!' he whispered fiercely. 'Did you have to? There'll be hell to pay when we get to Libya! He wouldn't have done it, man. He only wanted to be in on – '

Kassim interrupted him with his unblinking stare. Cold, withdrawn.

'There will be nothing to pay, Connor O'Neil. He was not part of us. Of this. He was vermin and vermin you dispose of – quickly.'

He thought for a moment.

'We can take him aboard the yacht with us. I am sure it will not be difficult to persuade Solenov that he was shot during the raid, by these British sailors.'

He laughed a shrill note of tension, a flash of his old self.

'The Russian will not want to know him, my friend! He is nothing – '

Rashid Khadir hurried on to the bridge, glanced at Khalid, recovered himself, and waved a piece of paper at them.

'She is sighted, El-Nesr. She will be upon us in fifteen minutes.'

They all stared through the grubby bridge-screen, searching the long cut of water beyond them from their position at the southern edge of the Bitter Lakes.

Sure enough, there was the *Britannia*. A squat but massive shape for their taking.

'Right!' O'Neil snapped. 'Prepare the men! Get that fire under way in ten minutes. How the hell did Khalid get aboard, for God's sake?' he asked suddenly, staring at the body and then back down the Canal.

Kassim shrugged, uncaring.

'I do not know. But it was bad that this should happen. Get him below and find someone to clear this up,' he virtually ordered O'Neil, clicking a hook at the wide pool of blood leaking from Khalid's shattered head.

'Yes, sir,' O'Neil muttered and grabbed the Syrian by his collar.

They met in the Bitter Lakes, these two ships of a shared destiny. By now, the fire on board the freighter was billowing black, oily smoke into the blue sky.

The freighter had her distress signals fluttering amid the thick smoke reaching up her foremast. She looked to be in serious trouble.

On the bridge of the *Britannia*, the officer of the watch brought up his binoculars in hasty disbelief. Oh Christ!

'Vessel on fire, sir!' he jerked out to the Captain. 'Dead ahead. I think she's out of control.'

'What!' His Captain strode across the bridge.

'She's signalling for assistance, sir,' the watch officer reported, his glasses still up to the Aldis lamp flickering from the freighter's tiny bridge.

'Who is she?' the Captain asked, suddenly cautious.

'Flying the Italian flag, sir. Can't make out her name.'

'Very well. Maintain our present heading – and watch her.' His last remark was addressed to the duty coxswain.

'Aye, aye, sir.'

The Captain grabbed the bridge phone, ordering out his fire crews, real urgency in his voice now.

The rest worked like a dream. Or at least like the nightmare it was to become.

The little Syrian freighter was almost abreast the *Britannia* now, the fire on her forward hatches blazing in a choking mixture of smoke and oil. Further smoke tumbled out from one of her holds.

Several of the 'crew' were stumbling about on deck. Two more lay in motionless injury below the bridge, obviously badly burnt, overcome by the smoke. Another was being carried towards the stern on a makeshift stretcher, his arm covered with blood.

It was chaos. It also looked totally convincing to the officers aboard the *Britannia* training their glasses on the scene. It was meant to.

The Royal Navy fire-fighting teams were already running out hoses to the port rail. Orders were for once shouted with all the voice necessary to the dangerous situation. Fires have been known to jump from ship to ship with terrible consequences. If these two touched . . .

Her Majesty's royal yacht heaved-to, anchors dropping thunderously into the murky waters of the Suez Canal.

Perhaps the events which followed will one day be openly written up in the history books. Perhaps not. For the present, they remain shrouded in the official secrecy of Whitehall, the Pentagon and Cairo's Ministry of State Security. Not to mention the vaults of the Kremlin.

Suffice to tell that, with understandable concern, the royal yacht sent over her senior surgeon and stretcher crews whilst her fire-fighters got busy playing foam on to the burning hatches.

On the freighter, the rest of the raiding party held themselves in tense readiness below deck, waiting for Kassim's order to move in.

As *Britannia*'s surgeon-commander and his stretcher crews sped across the dangerously narrow strip of water separating the two vessels, Connor O'Neil also readied himself for his personal date with destiny.

Willing hands caught the mooring ropes thrown from the yacht's motor launch. More willing hands quickly assisted its occupants aboard the burning freighter. In the confusion and ever-thickening smoke, little could be seen clearly from *Britannia*'s high bridge.

Within minutes, her medics were gently lifting the first

stretcher cases on to the dipping launch and helping the walking wounded into the rubber inflatable which had now joined her, suspecting nothing.

Speed was essential and the obvious got itself overlooked in the understandable urgency of these royal sailors' concern for their fellow men of the sea.

The surgeon commander tried to make sense of O'Neil's stuttered Italian as he pulled him towards the companionway leading down to the billowing holds.

'What the devil – !' was all he got out before O'Neil's arm locked around his throat and he was swiftly dragged below.

The first wave of raiders were helped on to the royal yacht with gentle haste, a crowd of eager assistance surrounding their arrival.

Rashid Khadir triggered off the seizure. Throwing aside his blanket, he leapt from his stretcher, submachine-gun aimed in unnerving hatred at the young officer facing him with a look of frozen shock on his tanned features.

'Back!' the Palestinian snarled, lamming the stubby barrel against his disbelieving hesitation. Blood bubbled from the officer's shattered mouth where Khadir's gun had lashed across his protest.

In seconds, six more of the raiders had thrown off their covers and were racing to their appointed tasks. The second wave of raiders, led by O'Neil and Docherty, had already made it up on to the yacht, herding officers and crew alike into tight huddles of defenceless submission.

Then that clockwork precision was marred by its first mishap.

Marine Sergeant 'Natty' Atkinson, so nicknamed because of his habit of sharp dressing when on shore leave, had of course heard the urgent orders tannoyed through the ship for fire parties and stretcher crews. He also knew his own duty. And at that moment it was to relieve his opposite number for the changing of the Watch.

He was just coming up from below when O'Neil's raiders made their astonishing bid to seize the royal yacht. As he emerged into the harsh sunlight, he stopped in amazement, not believing his eyes, and drew his regulation sidearm almost without thinking. It was the last thing he would ever do.

'Don't be a fool, man!' someone shouted from the nearest group of captives in a desperate attempt to save the sergeant's life.

His words fell beneath the snarling echo of a single burst of gunfire. With the ruthlessness so often displayed by female terrorists, Lila Fahd shot the marine dead on the spot.

It served to still any further acts of suicidal heroism. For the moment at least.

Hassan Kassim barged on to the bridge with three of his comrades, smashing past the ratings who foolishly tried to block his path.

The Captain, his Senior Officer and the other bridge personnel did not stand a chance.

'This is outrageous! I demand – ' the Senior Officer protested before he was cut off by a swinging blow from one of Kassim's cruel hooks.

It tore through his tropical uniform shirt with vicious accuracy, gouts of blood welling up in a red stain on the crisp white linen.

'*You bloody bastards!*' roared the coxswain as he rushed forward to catch his Senior Officer.

One of Kassim's men felled him in his tracks with a stunning blow from the barrel of his Uzi, slamming him to the deck. The others were shoved unceremoniously against the bridge housing, the muzzles of Kassim's guns making short work of any more resistance. Throughout the ship it was the same bitter story. Totally unprepared for the swift and practised assault, the *Britannia*'s complement proved no match for this small but heavily-armed and well-trained raiding party.

In less than ten minutes, the bridge was theirs, together with every vital station around the yacht.

Below decks, the same coldly efficient pattern had scythed through all retaliation, driving the crew along the panelled passageways in a swelling shuffle of defeat.

Yet even in this terrible event, there was an element of farce. A cook, fleeing from the huge galleys, came face to face with one of the hooded commandos. It was difficult to tell who was the more surprised in the stark comedy of clattering pots and pans as the man tried to run for it. It ended with the cook suffering a broken arm and mild concussion at the blunt end of one of his own utensils.

With the exception of the wounded Senior Officer, who was allowed brief medical attention on the bridge, the Captain and those essential to the manoeuvring of *Britannia* back into the narrow start of the southern waterway, the rest of the royal yacht's complement were herded below into the number two storage hold.

And here, the marine's murder was augmented by another tragedy as the officer of the watch tried to make a break for freedom with three of his duty ratings, despite the Admiral's forced order over the tannoys to cease all opposition.

Lieutenant Michael Campbell fell mortally wounded, slithering to a dying halt in a bloody skid of agony. Two of his ratings were also hit, although not seriously.

It all but capped effective resistance to the incomprehensible reality of their situation. Her Majesty's royal yacht *Britannia* had been truly and ignominiously hijacked.

The whole, murderous business had taken just twenty minutes.

O'Neil immediately went down with Docherty and Kassim to open up the strongrooms, after satisfying himself that the bridge had been secured before any signal could be got off warning the outside world of the *Britannia*'s shameful plight.

Already put off his stride by Major Khalid's death and now the killing of the marine sergeant and a watch officer, O'Neil did not mince his words with the Executive Commander held firmly between Docherty's massive paws.

'Tell your man to open them up, Commander,' he grated, nodding at the Chief Petty Officer in charge of strongroom security, who was held at gunpoint by Liam MacFadden.

Commander Bill Graham DSO, DSC, had been at sea all his life. It spanned a career that had seen action during the daring breakout from the Yangtse River by HMS *Amethyst*, and now this his last commission before retirement.

A widower with two grown-up sons making their own way in the Navy, the sea and the Service were his abiding love affair. He was not going to have its final moments violated by this bunch of hooded thugs.

'Go to hell,' he growled into his grey-flecked beard, and felt the giant's half-nelsons tighten on his arms.

O'Neil shrugged, a grim weariness etched in his eyes, and turned to the Chief Petty Officer.

'What is your name?' he snapped.

The Chief stared back at him coldly, saying nothing. Kassim stepped forward, a hook raised. It brushed the double row of medal ribbons on the man's chest.

'Chief Petty Officer Parker . . . to you,' he replied, his tongue reluctantly loosened by the swishing menace of those steel hooks.

'Very well, Parker,' O'Neil stated flatly. 'I want the combinations to the strongrooms. Now.'

The Chief shook his head silently, with contempt in his sea-washed blue eyes. It was enough for Hassan Kassim. He grabbed at MacFadden's Uzi before anyone could stop him and promptly shot the Chief through his right knee. The man collapsed in agony on the grilled decking, blood pumping from between his clutching fingers.

It was enough for the Executive Commander, too.

'All right, you animals!' he shouted, straining to get free of Docherty's grip. 'I know the combinations. Get some help for my Chief or I'll see you rot in hell first!'

O'Neil was already trying to stem the flow of blood, with MacFadden's help.

232

'Fetch two of those medics – and make it fast!' he lashed at Docherty.

The giant nodded, releasing the Commander, and set off with surprising speed for one of his size, his boots pounding over the grating in muffled echoes of urgency.

'What the hell's *wrong* with you?' O'Neil rounded on the silent guerilla leader. 'Hasn't there been enough needless bloodletting already for your liking, damn you!'

Kassim eyed O'Neil coldly through his hood, then directed his hawk's stare at the Commander.

'Now you will operate the combinations, Englishman,' he commanded in a fierce whisper. 'Or you will join your hero on the floor!'

The Uzi swung dangerously from the Commander to O'Neil.

'There will be all the bloodletting I consider necessary until we get what we came for, Captain,' he continued softly. 'Yours too, if that is to be the way of it.'

O'Neil said nothing and the Commander glanced at him speculatively. Commander Graham was no fool. And no coward either. Maybe, just maybe, he could use the obvious divisions between these scum to weaken their watchfulness.

' "When thieves fall out . . . ",' he quoted, musingly sarcastic, his voice loud amid the tension. 'Perhaps you'd be better off watching each other rather than me, don't you think?' he added for good measure, and moved suddenly as the two men's attention was momentarily distracted by their mutual antagonism, running for the bulkhead door leading from the strongrooms.

He did not get far. Kassim was after him in a swoop of fury before the Commander was halfway to his objective. A claw ripped through the Commander's uniform sleeve, spinning him round. The other hook clamped on his neck with terrible certainty, forcing him back towards O'Neil and the moaning Chief.

O'Neil and MacFadden were just as helpless, knowing Kassim would kill the man in the time it took them to reach him.

'You will obey me, English pig, or I will slice your throat like a knife through butter!' Kassim hissed, ramming his victim against the first strongroom's thick steel bars with a juddering crash. And let him fall. Graham's face had turned a mottled purple where Kassim's claw had started to squeeze off his life.

A vicious weal of bruising began throbbing at his throat and blood speckled his collar, the skin lacerated by that brief but terrifying encounter on the edge of death.

He could not speak as he heaved himself to his feet and staggered over to the complex of dials on the bulkhead facing the strongrooms. It took him several minutes to get the combinations sorted out. His hands were still shaking when he spun off the first of the heavy locking wheels.

The primary gates on each of the three vaults slid open on a hiss of released pressure. Then both Kassim and O'Neil were there, helping him to swing back the first of the six-inch-thick, tungsten steel inner doors ...

The sight which greeted the raiders was totally unforgettable.

Shelf upon shelf was crammed with carefully listed treasures, gathered from this tour and previous occasions. Several dinner services of solid gold, for at least twenty placings, glinted richly in the subdued lighting.

There were countless table accoutrements, beautifully worked in gold, silver and crystal. Works of fine art, each wrapped in hessian, shared the shelves with all manner of smaller *objets d'art*. There were even a number of flat boxes bearing the royal coat of arms, each one filled with bar on bar of gold bullion, worth millions. Savings for a rainy day?

The many gifts from Her Majesty's tour of eastern Arabia had still to be properly inventoried and distributed through the Royal Household's many dwellings and galleries, and they took pride of place on the rubberised, steel-lined, laser-alarmed floors.

There were jewelled cups, gold plate, a magnificent scimitar crusted with gems, silver boxes, alabaster aromatic jars, figurines in gold and silver, reams of gold-threaded cloth, furnishings, carvings. Literally piles of it.

It was the same story in the other strongrooms, although they were smaller. So much wealth it was almost obscene. Truly an Aladdin's cave of all time. O'Neil knew that Her Majesty was rumoured to be the richest woman in the world, but all this was virtually beyond his comprehension. They had expected to make a killing from the raid but this would amount to the greatest robbery-at-sea ever to grace the history books.

He was equally astonished at the relative lack of security aboard the royal yacht, considering the treasures she carried, but O'Neil had forgotten the trust which existed between this Queen and her people. It was the greatest guardian of all.

But how on earth were they going to shift this incredible motherlode of riches in the time allotted for the mission?

Time . . . it brought him out of his reverie. He turned to Kassim and the guerilla leader's eyes flashed with triumphant exultation, their recent enmities forgotten for the moment in this magnificent good fortune. Perhaps he would not have to kill the Irishman after all. There was more than enough for everyone here.

'All right. Lock it all up again,' O'Neil softly ordered the grimly silent Commander and drew Kassim to one side, out of earshot.

'We've got a lot of things still to do, Hassan. And a lot of ground to cover before we scuttle our way out of here.'

The guerilla leader nodded, clicking his hooks in a tattoo of jubilation. 'It is well said, my friend. But I think we have hit the jackpot, as you would say. No?'

O'Neil grinned at him through his hood. 'Oh yes! And this is one fruit-machine that Solenov and his little pals are not going to get a pull at! Come on, let's get to the bridge for round two.'

They left the strongroom heavily guarded by Kassim's men. The only sign of the Chief Petty Officer's wounding was a drying pool of blood seeping down the grating. He had already been removed under guard to the main operating theatre, where ironically the same surgeon commander who had suffered at O'Neil's hands.

After three quarters of an hour of being in possession of Her Majesty's royal yacht, the first radio message was patched through to Cairo in the shaky voice of the Egyptian pilot seized by the raiders.

The contents of that message brought President Sadat of Egypt out of a stormy meeting of the Arab League at the run; and the British Prime Minister from his bed in a jellied fury.

Within the hour President Carter was on the 'hot line' to No. 10 Downing Street, and the world felt the first secret rumblings of a crisis of global proportions.

Two hours later, Whitehall was alive with furious activity and Britain's Foreign Secretary was doing his best to calm a Prime Minister not renowned for his equanimity under pressure.

The opening gambits to the shattering of President Carter's Middle East peace treaty lay in terrible triumph with Connor O'Neil and his raiders as they began the long task of setting their explosive charges through the vitals of a much-loved monarch's royal yacht.

The nightmare had begun in deadly earnest.

CHAPTER EIGHTEEN

The telephone calls that took place between Britain's Prime Minister, Sadat of Egypt, Israel's Menachim Begin and President Carter would, to say the least, make interesting reading in transcript. Were they available, which they are not and never will be.

Enough to record that the calls to and from these illustrious leaders came fast and furious during the first tremulous hours of this mind-numbing crisis that could put back peace in the Middle East for another decade.

Inevitably, as in all such situations, it was not long before accusations began to fly. Menachim Begin, perhaps, displayed the greatest control, suggesting that his government mount an immediate Entebbe-type raid on the *Britannia* before the whole thing got hopelessly out of hand.

This was turned down by the British Prime Minister on the advice of his Foreign Office, who naturally did not wish any 'outsider' to rectify or expose the glaring mistakes the SIS's hierarchy had made in not taking serious note of George Burroughs' 'theories'.

President Carter's similar suggestion, during his third telephone call of the evening, that the American Seventh Fleet should be sent in, along with the US Marine Corps, got an identically negative reception from the harassed British premier.

Tightening his sweating grip on the red 'hot line' telephone in No. 10's Cabinet Room and trying to bring calm to his thinking, the Prime Minister literally shouted across the Atlantic at the equally ruffled American President.

'No, no, NO! We don't want another Vietnam on our hands. Besides, the *Britannia* and her crew are British and must be got back the *British* way!'

He listened to the President's disembodied voice reminding him that the invasion of Suez had been done the 'British way' – and they all knew what had happened to that. Were they agreed at least that this crisis *must* be kept under wraps? The consequences of the world's press getting hold of it would be unthinkable.

'Yes, yes!' the Prime Minister snapped back testily. 'Of course we are agreed on that. Sadat has already activated a complete news blackout and closed the Canal to all traffic on the excuse of this damned freighter being on fire in the Lakes.'

He glanced at his watch. Nearly 1 a.m.

237

'I've got to go, Mr President. Cabinet meeting in ten minutes. We'll come back to you with some kind of decision before 6 a.m. our time – unless your State Department can think up something realistic in the meantime.'

For a minute he listened again to Jimmy Carter's slow, insistent drawl.

'No, we haven't any details as yet,' the Prime Minister replied cautiously. 'They're bound to be the usual run of political maniacs we all have to contend with these days. I've got some fellow called Major Burroughs reporting to me from MI6 later tonight. He seems to know something about them. Goodbye.'

He replaced the receiver slowly, suddenly feeling very drained, and sat back in his chair with a heavy sigh. By God, he'd have someone's hide for this business. Holman's for a start. What on earth was the good of having a secret service if they kept their secrets from *him*?

Britain's Prime Minister squared his shoulders, thought briefly about his wife still snugly asleep in their bed, and pressed the buzzer for his Personal Private Secretary.

He was not looking forward to this particular Cabinet session one little bit.

George Burroughs was watching television when the dispatch driver rang his doorbell in Cheyne Walk. Looking at the man's face, he instinctively knew what had brought him racing through London's rainy streets with a sirening police escort.

It took him only seconds to gather his papers together and get into the car. Personally, he *was* looking forward to this particular confrontation with his chief.

Sir David bloody Holman was for the high jump with no get-out this time. And *he* was going to fire the starting pistol.

The meeting between Burroughs and his chief was brief, acrimonious and constantly interrupted by the comings and goings of high-ranking Service officers, departmental personnel and the obligatory hordes of Whitehall 'advisors' such a crisis draws in its wake. Century House was well and truly buzzing with panic, recriminations, anger and not a little despair.

'Nonsense!' Holman had snapped when Burroughs laid the blame for the whole disastrous affair squarely at his desk.

'Nonsense, is it?' Burroughs had retorted, waving his 'diary' of the events leading up to this crisis under his chief's agitated nose.

'I've taken the precaution of making up a report of everything I have tried to get you to do about my beliefs that something was on the boil out there. And I intend that the Cabinet gets it this time without any pretty deletions by you or anyone else!'

Holman fiddled with some papers on his desk.

'You may have your opportunity to do so, Burroughs,' he shot back. 'I understand the Prime Minister wanted to see you.'

He held up his hand curtly at Burroughs' sudden, triumphant snarl.

'My Minister has already advised the PM that is out of the question at the moment. You will be required here.'

He eyed his subordinate flatly.

'I expect he will abide by that . . . advice. Should you have any useful proposals to put forward on this matter, Burroughs, you will come back through me. Is that understood?

'MacAllister has flu,' he added inconsequentially.

'I don't care if MacAllister has the pox!' Burroughs flared. 'And the only thing understood between you and me is that you have fucked-up this operation from the outset, cost more lives – according to the latest reports in from Egypt – and are *still* trying to duck the responsibility you're bloody well stuck with . . . SIR!'

He wiped a large hand across his face as Holman rose angrily from behind his desk. Burroughs turned away contemptuously.

'I shall be down in the Ops Room – *if* anybody "requires" my help to sort out the mess you've got this Department into.'

With that, he slammed out of his superior's office, crashing past the Chief of the quaintly-named Imperial General Staff and his retinue. He did not bother to apologise to the startled general. As far as he was concerned, any apologies belonged exclusively to him and to those poor sods trapped on *Britannia.* Apologies from the Prime Minister downwards.

Sir David Holman, KCMG, sank back into his chair, defeat souring his complexion a deeper shade of grey. He knew there was no way out for him this time and he didn't know what to do about it. Or the stunning hijack now imploding all around him.

The Director of MI6's Middle East Desk dropped his head into his hands and cried for the first time since he was a boy.

And that was how an embarrassed CIGS and his staffers found him.

On board the *Britannia*, the raiders were in full control of the next move. Or so it seemed.

Having supervised the royal yacht's slow and careful return into the beginning of the Canal's southern waterway, they had herded the crew members involved back down to the crowded storage hold to join their guarded shipmates.

Britannia now solidly blocked the West's vital oil and trading route from the Persian Gulf, much to the delight of Kassim's Palestine Action Commandos methodically going through the sumptuous state rooms on the strict orders of their leader to list everything worth seizing, easily transportable – and not to touch anything.

Only the wounded Senior Officer, his Captain and the senior communications officer were allowed above-decks, and were held on the bridge. It was the latter who assisted

MacFadden in setting up the frequencies required for the guerilla leader's subsequent dialogue with President Sadat.

Yes, an Egyptian Air Force cargo plane would be sent in shortly. But first a makeshift runway would have to be constructed in the desert scrub alongside the Canal. He must have the raiders' assurance that they would not fire on the Army bulldozers and personnel necessary to organise the landing-strip. And no more killings.

Kassim had laughed that shrill shriek of his and leaned closer to the microphone linking him with the Egyptian President.

'That is entirely up to you, traitor to your Arab brothers,' he hissed. 'I shall expect the work to be completed by midday or I shall commence shooting the crew. One for every two hours we are delayed from leaving for Libya.'

He clicked off the set 'Receive' and laughed again with mad joy at the power he now exercised over half the Western world and this Egyptian dog. He was king of it all and everyone would know his name when he'd scuttled this Queen's precious ship and flown off with her treasures held between his steel talons!

O'Neil came into the big communications cabin as the guerilla leader got to his feet, the echo of his demented delight ringing in his ears.

He wondered if he could control this strange bird of prey until it was all over without clipping his wings permanently, as the late Major Khalid had once been moved to threaten?

In London, the monstrous hijacking continued to haunt every second of the new day.

A despondent Prime Minister reluctantly informed Buckingham Palace of what had occurred and had to endure a tongue-lashing from a certain gentleman, not known for his reticence, telling him in graphic terms to get the *Britannia* back – with her crew, treasures and reputation still intact. Or his resignation would be the least of the PM's troubles!

16

At Century House, the Foreign Office and the Ministry of Defence, plans and counter-plans rose and fell within the diplomatic stranglehold the situation had forced on its participants.

Sir David Holman was close to nervous collapse, and an exasperated Burroughs went over his head to the Foreign Secretary with his own bold idea, having forced his now thoroughly shaken chief to admit that he had been wrong. In writing.

A still dithering Cabinet grabbed at the slender straw offered them by the abrasive, bluntly-speaking officer from MI6, who appeared to be alone in having any real grip on the wretched business threatening not only the Government's continuation in office but the very cornerstone of Carter's vital peace plan for the Middle East, days away from its intended signing in Washington.

It had taken this incredible state of affairs for George Burroughs to achieve the *carte blanche* he should have been accorded weeks before, and now intended to use with a vengeance...

CHAPTER NINETEEN

'For God's sake leave it, Kassim!' O'Neil had yelled back when the urgent radio message from Cairo was translated for him in an apoplectic snarl by the guerilla leader.

Always a reluctant admirer of Sadat as a man, though an enemy of his politics, O'Neil knew they had no choice but to believe the anxious President as he told them that the promised aircraft was unavoidably delayed with fuelling problems. The President's voice, crackling with static and apologies, had sounded genuinely sincere. And that sincerity was the only positive measure the raiders could so far exact from their unseen adversary pleading for their continued 'co-operation'.

On top of the argument which had already erupted between O'Neil and Hassan Kassim over the Irishman's insistence that their hostages be fed – risky as it was to let the catering personnel out of the hold to organise it – the Egyptian President's pleas for their patience had sent the guerilla leader into a paroxysm of hook-swinging fury.

O'Neil had been powerless to stop Kassim as he strode into the crowded hold, spearheaded by six of his commandos, aggressively jittery at the sudden turn in their fortunes. The barrels of their guns cleared a swift and vicious path for their enraged leader.

Kassim stood for a long moment staring at the assembled officers and men, his chest heaving. His beak-like stare snapped this way and that as he surveyed their grim apprehension, and the steel claws that were his deadly trademark clicked with staccato menace in the deep silence and sweaty heat.

He pointed suddenly, a hook quivering with his anger.

'That one! Take him!'

O'Neil had been equally powerless to stop the execution which took place under the sun's midday glare on the royal yacht's spacious quarterdeck.

It was stage-managed by Kassim, with O'Neil and his Brigade men also held at indistinguishable gunpoint alongside *Britannia*'s Senior Officer and Captain by the grim-faced Palestinian commandos.

The young, fair-haired rating was half-dragged, half-carried into the centre of the deck, followed by Kassim's implacable stare – impervious to the lad's frantic pleas for mercy. Or anyone else's.

At least it was over quickly. A single shot from Rashid Khadir's Uzi and the seaman fell dead, the bullet passing through his heart on the express train of instant death.

The silence following the shot was more rending than

any scream; the tableau of numbed witnesses a greater condemnation than any shouts of outrage.

It was also the end of any feelings O'Neil had left for his former comrade. And nearly the end of his stomach for this thing they had embarked on together with such high hopes.

Now their aircraft was circling overhead in the blued sky, nearly two hours late and too late for the young rating whose body had been tipped into one of the lifeboats with callous indifference by Kassim's men.

Tuned-in to the aircraft's voice-band, Kassim and O'Neil listened in uneasy unity to the pilot's talk-down procedures.

The Irishman felt a flash of sympathy for the Egyptian pilot. Kassim had demanded that all the Egyptian military personnel – still waiting on the ground to assist the getaway plane's safe landing on the hastily-prepared runway – should be ordered back to the base whence they came before the plane even took off from its airfield near Cairo on its delayed mission.

Kassim was not taking any chances of his raiders being jumped as they boarded the aircraft with their booty. The pilot and his three-man crew could easily be dealt with once they had touched-down into Libya's welcoming sanctuary.

The plane droned overhead on its approach-run, its big engines beating a deep wake of sound across the absolute silence of the desert. To the watchers on *Britannia*, it all looked perfectly normal. Their release from this place at last was at hand.

Suddenly the pilot was shouting over his intercom. Something about loss of oil-pressure . . . FIRE!

Kassim raced out into the sunshine with O'Neil close behind, knowing there was more trouble in the air but unable to understand what the pilot was saying.

They stared up at the droning aircraft as it dropped rapidly across their line of vision towards the landing-strip. Far too rapidly. Black, oily smoke began to pour from one of the engine nacelles on the starboard wing. She was going to crash.

With the ponderous predictability of a falling building, the four-engined transporter – supplied by the Soviets in the days of happier relations with Egypt – headed for the earth, side-slipping wildly in her desperate attempts to hold her landing course.

'Sweet Jesu, she's going to hit!' O'Neil cried, riveted to the spot in helpless frustration as Lila Fahd gripped his clenched fist.

The plane made contact with the desert in a metal-screeching tear of ripping fabric and snapping propellers, its pancaked careering across the runway and scrub hidden in a huge spray of smoke and sand.

It reminded O'Neil of a seaplane he'd seen landing in Singapore. He thought it a queer thing to be thinking of when their escape was crashing before his eyes. But somehow he felt quite removed from it all as his hopes for the hijack curdled in his mind.

The grinding, groaning noise of the aircraft breaking up seemed to echo across the desert for a long time on the heat-stilled air. Then there was only the absolute, utter silence . . .

Connor O'Neil turned back into the ship with a deep sigh. He knew that Hassan the Hawk would already be screaming down the radio to Cairo.

The first throw in George Burroughs' gamble had paid off.

CHAPTER TWENTY

It was the end of their second day of holding Her Majesty's royal yacht and its crew to ransom.

The end of two days which had seen them turned from victors into vacillators; split from a closely-knit team of raiders with a common aim into smouldering factions of argument and near rebellion.

Britannia had pulled at her anchors and swung from being their prize to their prison.

Hassan Kassim had become almost impossible to deal with, haunting the high bridge, allowing nobody but Rashid Khadir within whispering distance of his coiled prowling.

O'Neil was sorely tempted to put him out of his madness with a bullet through his brain. Though he knew he would never get off the *Britannia* alive were he to do so. Not with Kassim's men tipping the balance in numbers and fire-power.

But the last of residual trust between them had gone, following hard on the heels of a friendship which had kindled brightly during the planning of their incredible operation – and died again amongst the hissing shock of the guerilla leader's ruthless fanaticism when opposed by the harsh realities of this nigh impossible mission.

George Burroughs could not know it yet but the second throw in his gamble with the lives of *Britannia*'s crew was paying off, too.

They were into the dead hours of the night now and O'Neil paced the decks with his lover, careful to avoid the crates of their theft piled high in neat rows to await the Egyptian President's promise of another aircraft in the morning.

Docherty loomed into view, huge in the darkness, and nodded his black curls at O'Neil.

'This thing's gone a rum turn, Captain,' he rumbled, jerking his head in the direction of the PAC guerillas manning the single searchlight sweeping the stirring waters of the Canal at frequent intervals.

All other lights had been extinguished, making it difficult to see round the yacht but equally making them no kind of target for anyone bent on thwarting their determination to quit this alien vessel.

O'Neil shook his head at his lieutenant, refusing him the comfort of a reply, and passed on by with Lila Fahd. It was a rum do all right, he thought. But what was done was done, and only God and good fortune would see them away next morning. That and constant vigilance through the remaining hours of this long night.

Up on *Britannia*'s bridge, Hassan Kassim's face was turned a greenish hue in the subdued glow of her instrumentation panels. The Senior Officer, his Captain and communications officer were still held in guarded tiredness at the port end of the big bridge, refused sleep or any kind of rest in the guerilla leader's seething impatience to be away.

The Senior Officer's wound ached in his body, the scant medical attention he had been allowed sufficient to bind the bleeding but not the pain. He had listened in stiff silence to Kassim's hissing pleasure as he informed him that the royal yacht was now comprehensively wired with enough plastic explosive to ensure her undignified scuttling when his raiders finally got free of her imperialist luxury.

There was nothing the Senior Officer could do about it at this juncture except content himself with the assurance that these terrorists would be hunted down with all the ruthlessness they had already displayed towards his crew.

Kassim suddenly ceased his endless prowling and spun on his heel, clicking a hook at Rashid Khadir. The powerfully-built second-in-command slung his Uzi over his shoulder, scratched briefly at the black bush of his beard under his hood and walked over to his leader.

'We will talk,' Kassim announced in Arabic. 'Tell our men to shoot these dogs if they have cause.'

Khadir nodded and talked briefly with the three hooded raiders doing their spell at guarding the bridge and its captives. As he instructed them softly, the royal yacht's Captain glanced wearily at his commanding officer.

The Old Man looked absolutely whacked but he seemed to be standing up to the ordeal well, despite his wound. Surely to God, Whitehall must be putting some kind of rescue into operation by now? Since the raid on the *QE2* in 1972, there were contingency plans on line, that he knew. But, like most men of practical action and command, he was loath to place his life, and those of his brother officers and men, in the hands of the Civil Servants stifling the armed services with their bureaucracy and desk-distant theorising.

When they had descended to the main deck, Kassim began outlining his own 'contingency' plans to his lieutenant. If what he said to Rashid Al-Saled Khadir disturbed the burly guerilla in any way, nothing was revealed in the deep brown eyes that could look with such gentleness on the son he worshipped, so far away in the little Syrian village they knew as home.

' . . . dispose of them all in Libya. And this O'Neil. I know already the details of the criminal elements he wishes to use in Europe for the sale of our gains.'

Kassim's shrill laugh echoed sharply on the night, tearing the silence.

'They are not of our breed, Rashid! Merely tools to be used between these . . . hands of mine! Nothing more! Go now, my friend.'

Rashid Khadir stared at his leader and then did as he was bid, guarding his own counsel in keeping with the silent night.

America's Chief Executive waited anxiously along with Britain's Prime Minister, Sadat and Begin for news of Burroughs' third and final throw of the dice so loaded against them.

It was do-or-die time and many reputations – as well as Western statecraft – stood to suffer all manner of deaths if the small, often vicious cubes of fate chose against their ardent hopes.

None of them really believed it could be done. Not even George Alfred Burroughs, huddled in his borrowed flying-suit high above the sleeping waters of the Nile . . .

Connor O'Neil peered at his watch in the starry darkness. He was alone with the night as it began to thin towards

248

dawn, and he shivered in the cold which drops at sunset in desert places. It was hardly worth his while trying to snatch some sleep now. The promised call from Sadat, telling them that their replacement aircraft was on its way, fell due in just over an hour.

He *had* to believe the Egyptian President was playing them straight. In two days, nobody had tried to pull anything on them, convincing him that the first plane's crash had been a genuine accident. Especially when he had seen with his own eyes the mangled body of the pilot being carried from the wreckage by the personnel sent in to clear it. Naval binoculars do not lie.

When the radio-call came through from President Sadat in Cairo that their relief plane was safely airborne, O'Neil was just about to light up the last of his cigarettes on the foredeck.

Rashid Khadir was with Kassim and the communications officer, their sudden jubilation augmenting the bitter defeat surging through the Admiral's wounded chest.

Lila Fahd sat in one of the luxurious cabins below-decks, oiling and working her weapons for the morning's departure. And thinking about a future with O'Neil.

Pat Docherty and his compatriots from Madigan's Brigade sought respite in all too brief sleep, resigned to the fact that the control of their destiny had passed to Kassim and his hooded guerillas.

Liam MacFadden was the exception, toiling deep in the bowels of the ship, checking out the charges that would rip the yacht into scrap.

Above him, one of Kassim's men fingered the gleaming walnut table running the length of the beautifully accoutred state dining-room, and wondered at the dignitaries from his world who had sat amongst its splendours such a little while before.

In the crammed storage hold, *Britannia*'s officers and men slept as best they could, in stifling heat. Some remained awake, their minds full of their wives, families and friends.

Commander Graham shifted on to his side and stared at the guerillas guarding their long discomfort. If only they could overpower these bastards . . .

The royal yacht waited for the dawn, and the dawn waited its turn on the bland clockface of history . . .

Suddenly, the Suez Canal exploded into life with the roar of racing engines, and the sky split itself in dazzling flares and tracers snarling over the royal yacht from somewhere out in the shattered darkness.

Connor O'Neil gave a great yell of relieved tension, slamming home the breech of his machine-pistol, and turned to face the first wave of SAS and Royal Marine Commandos swarming on to *Britannia* from the dark waters of her retribution . . .

CHAPTER TWENTY-ONE

As rescue operations go, it was costly, bloody, some would claim brilliant. And at the mercy of Lady Luck. Such occasions exact a definitive price far outside the happy endings portrayed in films.

Within seconds of being aboard, the six four-man SAS teams were 'leap-frogging' their way below, dodging from deck to deck as they sought out the terrorists and the explosive legacy they knew such men would leave behind them.

Above decks, individual fire-fights erupted along the length of the ship, spattering death and injury in all directions, ignorant of 'fair play', dealing only in who could or could not evade the neutral scoring of the bullet.

Hasty in preparation, relying heavily on experience already gained in the growing cottage industry of political hijacks and sieges damning the Seventies, the Special Air Service and Royal Marines went about their task in the name of Queen, Country, and the Public's sickness at those who seek to state their views on the claim-stake of sheer, bloody terror.

Rudely awakened in more ways than one, the terrorists found themselves caught on the hop, wasting vital minutes as they gathered weaponry and cover.

Three of them were mown down before they had fired a shot, trapped in a hail of bullets as the Marines worked their way along the decks in a grim scythe of rough justice.

Others were temporarily luckier, killing before being killed. Rashid Khadir was the last of the four guerillas on the bridge to have his life torn from his body, plummeting to the deck below in a spectacular arc of agony. It cost the lives of two Marines to achieve it.

It also cost the already wounded Senior Officer another minor injury, hit in the arm by ricochet when the Marines stormed the bridge.

As is the real way of people when they are cornered, they tended to flee downwards – not upwards in the roof-scaling chases beloved of film directors.

The bulk of Kassim's men were still below when the reclamation of the *Britannia* swung into action, and those who were not soon found themselves gravitating or being inexorably forced in that direction – rats trapped within their own sinking.

For the royal yacht that meant men and bullets flying up and down her passageways with no time on either side to respect the immovable treasures and decor of this fine vessel. The desperate rescue bid would leave many kinds of scars.

Lila Fahd was lucky. She had been on her way out of her cabin to find some more gun oil when the firing started in earnest. Somehow she was missed by the SAS teams as they moved in well-practised sweeps down through the ship.

On deck, chaos greeted her. And death. She slipped in the

blood of a dead Marine, gasping with the pain shooting through her ankle.

'For God's sake *move*!' a voice gasped in her ear and she found O'Neil gripping her elbow with a passion stronger than sexual love. The love of life – to survive.

Ahead of them, through the smoke grenades and darting figures like things from hell's own ballet, they could see Docherty's massive frame at work, felling Marines and guerillas alike with oxen swings of his rifle, long out of ammunition.

'Pat . . . PAT!' O'Neil shouted, hoarse with the smoke as the giant turned for a fraction of a second at the sound of his voice.

Then the first bullet slammed into that huge figure, spinning him round. A kind of stunned anger glazed his eyes for a moment as they met his Captain's through their hoods, then he ripped his free, the black curls spilling wildly.

'I love you, Connor O'Neil!' Docherty shouted back. 'I LOVE YOU! YOU AND OUR IRELAND! MY SON . . . !'

With that, he turned again to face the advancing Marines, giving vent to a giant's roar, and charged towards them in a final mad run of life.

Yelling his new child's chosen name, Pat Docherty came on through the cruel rain of bullets smattering his arms, chest, legs, and fell at last, dead before he hit the blood-stained deck.

Hassan El-Nesr Kassim was faring no better. Escaping the bridge seconds before the Marines came roaring to its relief, their screams designed to chill and confuse, he had used his hooks with deadly effect in his fight to stay alive.

Driven far into the bows of the upper deck, Kassim was trapped in the swinging beam of the yacht's searchlight. Snarling with all the fury of a rabid dog, he heaved himself over the bow-rail, intent on swimming for his life.

He began the long fall towards the water, arms out-stretched. And was cruelly pulled up short, banging against the merciless steel of the hull, a hook caught fast in the anchor chain's wide links.

Hassan the Hawk hung there, a struggling puppet on an iron string, and cursed it all in a high shriek of invective as the support boats began to range their fire on his dangling figure.

Connor O'Neil ran with Lila Fahd, death at their heels and the hope of life on the other side of the starboard rails. If either believed it was hopeless, they did not show it as they pulled themselves clear of their hoods, the girl's raven hair billowing out in the choking smoke.

It would have been impossible to hear what they said to each other before they jumped, oblivious to Kassim's fate. But the smile which passed between them said all that could be said in the urgency of the moment.

They jumped together, plunging into the churned-up waters of the Suez Canal as the dawn rose in ignored magnificence on the horizon of a new day . . .

CHAPTER TWENTY-TWO

TRANSCRIPT (full) of Q/A Statement by George Alfred Burroughs, Major (D) Military Intelligence 6/Foreign Office – March 20th 1979.

CIVIL SERVICE DEPARTMENT

Procedural Inquiry

(Internal/NP)

Mar 20–28th.

1979.

Disciplinary Hearings One to Eight: Military Intelligence Department 6.
Hearing Two

Subject:	"Operation Sea Crown"

Place of Hearing:	Room 104
	Burlington House
	Burlington Gardens
	London

Special Investigation Commission (CC):	Internal Administration (AG)

Commission Members:	Commander James Huntley (Chairman)	
	Deputy Director MI6	
	Sir John Raithwaite	
	Under Secretary of State	Foreign Office
	David St John-Webb	Board of Trade
		(Assessments/I)
	Sir Miles Hapworth	
	Permanent Secretary	Home Office
	Admiral Sir Keith Clive RN	Min of Defence

In Attendance:	Lord Alfred Pennington	
	Minister of State	Foreign Office
	Sir Douglas Cramer	
	Permanent Secretary	MI6 (FO)
	Sir John Wigg-Browne	Buckingham
	Comptroller's Office	Palace
	Sir Anthony Canham	Cabinet Office

Witness Statement:	Transcript (full) No. 3/AG/CC/51223D
Witness:	George Alfred Burroughs
Rank:	Major (D)
Grading:	Principal Officer
Ministry:	Foreign Office
Department:	Military Intelligence (6)

STATEMENT   Timed: 1433 hrs March 20th/79 (Reel 4/Tape 2)

(Opening remarks identified by 'Cdr H' – Huntley; 'Maj B' – Burroughs)

Cdr H – 'Good afternoon, Major Burroughs. Please sit down. No –
    there, please.

Cdr H – 'I trust you had a pleasant flight back, Major?'

STATEMENT   B

Maj B – 'Yes, sir. I arrived at RAF Lyneham at 0730 this morning.'

Cdr H – 'Good. You will appreciate that this Disciplinary Inquiry is
internal and that you yourself are not a subject of disciplinary
action. However, for the purposes of this Commission, you
will please refer to all persons concerned by their rank, grade
and department. The same will apply to your observations
regarding what we will call "foreign participants". And you will
be referred to by your substantive rank. Is that understood?'

Maj B – 'Yes, sir. I would have worn my medals if I'd known.'

Cdr H – 'That attitude will not be helpful, Major Burroughs. This is
a serious matter. Please treat it as such at all times. This
Commission is subject to Section One to Twenty-Four of the
Official Secrets Acts. A Priority One Report is being sent
to the Palace. Is that clear, Major Burroughs?'

Maj B – 'Yes, sir. Commander Huntley. I am sorry, but if this matter
had been treated with seriousness before it blew up in all our
faces then my attitude might be a little different . . . sir.'

Cdr H – 'Quite, Major Burroughs. We will come to that.'

Maj B – 'Yes, sir. Sorry . . . Commander Huntley.'

Cdr H – 'Accepted and noted. I will introduce you to the members of
this Commission from left to right. On my left: Rear Admiral
Clive for the Ministry of Defence (Navy); Sir John Raithwaite
for the Foreign Office. On my right: Sir Miles Hapworth for
the Home Office and Mr David St John-Webb for the Board of
Trade (Mercantile-Marine Investigations Branch). They will
be asking you questions, together with myself.'

Maj B – 'I understand, sir. Commander Huntley, that is.'

Cdr H – 'These other gentlemen are here as observers and they will
not be asking you any questions, unless directed by myself as
Chairman of this Commission. You will be required to answer
all questions put to you by the Commission Members. You may
ask any questions you have at the end of your Witness
Statement. Is that understood?'

Maj B – 'Yes. Thank you, Commander Huntley.'

Cdr H – 'Very well. We are sorry to have to bring you back to face this Commission so shortly after the unfortunate events of the last three days, Major Burroughs, but you will appreciate that this Commission is acting under the direct instructions of the Prime Minister and the Head of the Civil Service. It is felt desirable to keep this matter as contained as possible, with any disciplinary action handled internally.'

Maj B – 'You mean hush it up, sir. What about— ?'

Cdr H – 'I mean exactly that, Major. And you will remember that you are bound by the Official Secrets Acts.'

Maj B – 'I see, Commander. I seem to remember someone once telling me this was a democracy. It strikes me that our Civil Service is exclusively designed to protect the public from information that might alarm it. Like this Commission of yours.'

Cdr H – 'You are entitled to your opinions, Major Burroughs, but you will not express them here nor in that manner. However, we appreciate that you must be very tired and allowances are made accordingly. But you will refrain from any more comments of that nature. It is timewasting and unnecessary. This Commission has a number of other witnesses to call. You will confine yourself to answering the questions put to you. Am I making myself clear, Major?'

Maj B – 'Oh yes, Commander. I hope someone will tell the lads who were killed on BRITANNIA their sacrifices are considered timewasting and unnecessary.'

Cdr H – 'I will ignore that, Major. It is in bad taste. Before we begin the questioning, I will again remind you that the purpose of this Enquiry is to establish the facts of these events. Primarily. Nothing else need concern you.'

Maj B – 'Sir.'

Cdr H – 'Thank you. We will begin now. Please make your answers as clearly as possible for the recordings.'

STATEMENT   C

Q – 'When were you first alerted to the seizure of BRITANNIA, Major Burroughs?'

A – 'On the evening of March 16th. A dispatch car was sent round to my flat. I went straight to Century House.'

Q – 'What did you do when you arrived there? I'm sorry, Commander Huntley again.'

A – 'I went into the Duty Ops Officer first to find out what the flap was about. Holman was already in there – I mean Sir David Holman, my Head of Section, sir. He seemed in a flat spin. I was pretty rude, I suppose.'

Q – 'Quite. I think, gentlemen, we will dispense with identifying ourselves unless the questioner's identity changes. Now then, what course of action did Sir David recommend, Major?'

A – 'Recommend, sir? He didn't know his arse from his elbow. The Permanent Secretary had been on to him. Apparently, these bastards – I mean this Captain O'Neil of the Madigan's Brigade and Hassan Kassim of the Palestine Action Commando – had radioed through to President Sadat, demanding an aircraft to fly them off BRITANNIA within four hours or one member of the royal yacht's crew would be shot for every two hours delay. I understood from Sir David that President Sadat had got on to President Carter in Washington and to the PM here. It was a shambles in our Department. Everybody was flying about chasing their tails, except my AHS.'

Q – 'AHS?'

A – 'Assistant Head of Section. Major MacAllister. He was down with the 'flu.'

Q – 'What did you do then, Major Burroughs?'

A – 'I insisted that we had to mount some kind of a rescue op, sir. There was no way we could let them scuttle BRITANNIA and it was nearing the D-line for Carter's peace treaty signing.'

Q – 'Sir David's reaction?'

A – 'He was too busy thinking about seeing the PM. I was told to hold fire until he got back again. So I did.'

Q – 'I see. And what then?'

A – 'He came back at about 4 am. Apparently, half the Secret Service had been at No 10. I know the Home Secretary and the Foreign Secretary were there. And the Anti-Terrorist Squad's Commander was called in, too.'

Q – 'Go on, Major Burroughs.'

A – 'Well, Commander, nobody in the Cabinet seemed to know what to do. If they tried a move against these terrorists, anything might have happened. I mean, the BRITANNIA scuttled smack in the middle of the Canal and her crew slaughtered. You can imagine the effects on the Begin-Sadat peace treaty. It would have gone out the window. And of course, the oil and trading route through the Suez Canal would have been blocked for days.'

Q – 'Sir David told you this?'

A – 'No, sir. I told him. Look, there was a massive panic on. Sadat had already sealed off the Canal and I understand an immediate news clampdown was put into gear. It was vital to keep the thing under wraps. Once the news got out, the terrorists would have achieved one of their objectives, whatever happened afterwards. They wanted a plane, as I said, to land alongside the Canal and fly them to Libya. I suppose that lunatic was in on it and —'

Q – 'Who, Major?'

A – 'Colonel Gaddafi, sir.'

STATEMENT   D

Q – 'What transpired then, in your Department?'

A – 'Holman, Sir David was in a dither. So was the Cabinet by all accounts. I'm told Carter had been through on the hot-line offering to send in the American Seventh Fleet. Seems the PM turned that one down flat. Something about it was a British problem and a British show – after the last time we'd asked the Americans to back us over Suez. Anyway, we had all sorts of big brass from the Navy, Army and the Air Force rushing in and out. Wasn't much I could do or say. Nobody wanted to listen. So I found a spare phone and raised Number 42 Commando down at Plymouth. I'd got the germ of an idea which seemed it —'

Q – 'Raithwaite, er, Foreign Office. Surely some kind of cohesive plan, or at least suggestions, had been arrived at by this time, my dear chap? Ahm, Major.'

A – 'With respect, sir, you should know. It's all in my report. My personal diary is in front of you. At least, I asked for copies to be run off before we started in here. No, sir. Nothing had been decided and little suggested. Everyone seemed stunned or too frightened of the consequences to think in straight lines.'

Q – 'Except you. Is that it, Major? Your diary seems to be more concerned with trying to bring your Head of Section down.'

A – 'About right, Sir John. On both counts. I'd been trying to tell the man for weeks that something was on out there. You know how it is. I'm just a humble Principal Officer on operations grading. If I'd been able to get past all the crap surrounding the Minister, perhaps —'

Q – 'Quite. I think we can leave that aside, Major Burroughs. You said you had an idea?'

A – 'Yes, sir. I'd read an internal circular on the Marines' new Quick Action Group – for any trouble on the oil rigs. It had been made up of men from the Special Boat Section. So I rang the OC at Plymouth. Got him out of bed. Didn't know a damn thing about what had happened. So I told him. And what I wanted – if necessary.'

Q – 'I have read your report, Major. I understand you forced Sir David to go back to the Cabinet?'

A – 'That's right, Sir John. I told him if he didn't go, then I would – with all my proof that I'd been trying to get action going on these jokers out in Syria since late December . . . last year.'

Q – 'Jokers, Major?'

A – 'O'Neil, Docherty, this Kassim character and of course the lovely Colonel Solenov of the KGB's foreign subversion lot. We'd already had one man murdered. At least, I'm sure it was murder now. Clive Danvers. Good man. Needn't have happened if Holman had — '

Q – 'Quite, quite. You were telling us about Sir David going back to the Cabinet meeting, Major.'

A – 'Look, am I going to be shut up every time I bring up something relevant to this mess that's a bit unpleasant?'

Q – 'Huntley: No, Major, you are not. But confine yourself to the situation at hand. Personal aspersions on senior members of the Service are no part of your brief.'

A – 'Yes, Commander. But it wasn't part of my brief, as you call it, to bale everyone out of the cart they'd tumbled into, was it? All right. Yes, I forced Sir David to go back to the Cabinet with my request to be put in as Field Controller on an attempt to get the BRITANNIA back. While all this was going on, we'd had a call through from the PM's Office anyway saying that he'd informed Buck House about the hijack and Prince Philip was not exactly polite himself. So I pitched in with my idea.'

Q – 'With your permission, Commander. Thank you. Cramer, MI6. As I understand it, Holman was being totally indecisive, is that right? You came up with an operational scenario to take this Quick Action Group by Hercules from Lyneham and fly out to Cyprus as your staging post. Meanwhile, I believe you made the suggestion that President Sadat try to keep these hijackers calm with the assurance that an aircraft was on its way to them, which you suggested should be, shall we say, accidentally crash-landed on the airstrip the Egyptian army was already marking out on the southern edge of the Bitter Lakes, and thus giving us some kind of breathing-space while you got your force into RAF Famagusta. That is correct, isn't it Major?'

A – 'Yes, sir. I asked for permission to liaise with General Adin Abu-Shneif of the Egyptian Army Command. My chief came back with provisional approval – provided the Egyptians would play ball. Someone in the Cabinet – I think it was the Foreign Secretary – got on to them. It came back affirmative. Sadat agreed that it was all or nothing time.'

Q – 'Admiral Clive, Naval Operations: What happened from then on, Major Burroughs? It seems to me, Commander, that we are going to get to the facts of this business a lot quicker if the Major here is allowed to tell the story in his own way. Surely the questions can wait?'

Cdr H – 'That seems sensible, sir. I trust that is to your liking, Major?'

A – 'None of this thing is to my liking, sir. But yes, that might be better. Shall I go on? Right. We'd also heard by this time, which was around 8 am on the 17th, that these hijackers had killed, er, Lieutenant Campbell and Sergeant Atkinson, with three more wounded. Two when they hit the yacht, and then the Chief Petty Officer in charge of strongroom security. He had refused to open up the safes, so they shot him through the knee. Nice bastards. I think it should be pointed out – or at least young Chambers would think so – that this Kassim seems to have gone a bit wild once he was on board. Apparently our friend O'Neil couldn't hold him. There were only five of his Brigade in the raiding party and something like eighteen men of Kassim's. Anyway, I got myself—'

Q – 'I am sorry to interrupt, Major. Commander, may I? This Chambers. Was he one of the terrorists? I am Sir John Wigg-Browne, by the way. Comptroller's Office, Buckingham Palace.'

A – 'You're welcome, sir. Good Lord, no. Chambers is my assistant. That is, I'm training him up. Nice young lad. Lot to learn.'

Q – 'I understand. Thank you, Major. I'm sorry.'

A – 'That's all right, sir. Where was I? Yes. The Egyptians agreed that they could lay on some Komar fast-attack boats, with rocket-launchers if they were needed. The boats were to be used to take us down the Canal. They also agreed to lay on their 34th Parachute Regiment as a support force. Anyway, time was of the essence, as they say, so I told young Chambers I wanted him along and that he'd an hour to pack. I went back to my flat for some gear – my old combat outfit actually.
We were flown down to Plymouth by helicopter and I held a hasty briefing with the group 42 Commando had put together. Twenty men, to be exact. Two officers, four NCOs and the rest rankers. Four Wessex choppers took us up to Lyneham in

Wiltshire and we were airborne by 6 pm. We landed at Famagusta just after dawn on the 18th. The men ate and did a weapons check. We took only small arms, light machine-guns, that sort of thing. SLRs and the GPMG to be precise. And some Stirlings. I took my old Service revolver.

Let me see. I telephoned through for information as to whether we went on to the Canal Zone – we'd not got clearance from the Cabinet for that yet. Stage by stage, let's see what happens was their attitude. All I wanted to do was get in there and sort these hijackers out before they scuttled BRITANNIA or turned the whole ship into a slaughterhouse of our Navy lads.

I got nowhere. I waited until nearly mid-morning and then raised President Sadat. He was all for getting in fast. Apparently, he was worried sick because it had happened on his territory and he reckoned his role in the peace talks would be finished if we didn't sort out these nasties very quickly indeed.

So I tried to get Holman. Would you believe he was unavailable? As Field Controller, that left me with two choices. Go in under my own steam or try and get someone in the Cabinet to get their finger out. So I telephoned the Foreign Secretary's PPS and he got the FS on the line. He was going on about the political considerations weighed against the lives of the crew and what-have-you, so I laid it on him quite bluntly. We either went in that night and took our chances or we would have lost the initiative and there would be no way it could be kept quiet – which everyone seemed to be agreed on at least.

The FS gave me the go-ahead then, on strict instructions that I must keep London informed. We took off at 2 pm. When we landed in Egypt, I was met by General Abu-Shneif. He'd set up the lot. Paratroops, attack boats, a command vehicle.

STATEMENT F

A – 'We had an immediate planning meeting with the various commanders and got ourselves sorted out. The first aircraft sent in for the terrorist *had* been crash-landed, and it was smack across the emergency strip the Army had bulldozed out. Sadat had managed to convince the terrorists it was a genuine accident and that, if they wanted out of Egypt with their loot, they had to undertake no scuttling of the (viz) yacht and no more killing. They'd shot one of the crew, an Able Seaman Shiller, poor kid, because of the delays. The co-pilot of the Iluyshin they ditched was also killed, I heard, when she pancaked. Anyway, the terrorists had been assured of another aircraft at dawn. No chance. We decided to attack that night, just before dawn, when they'd be off-guard and tired from the tensions we had built up for them. We would split our combined force into two: Marines in the Komar boats to attack from the Canal. Egyptian Army a quarter of a mile inland opposite BRITANNIA – and myself with the command vehicle. The second aircraft for the hijackers was to be full of paratroopers, to drop on to the yacht after we'd made the first assault.

We were in position by 2 am on the 18th. Everyone was synchronised and it had been agreed that President Sadat would radio through to the terrorists that their back-up plane was on the way the exact moment I gave the order to move off. That was 3.30 am.

It was quite something. With the Egyptian Army putting down a curtain of smoke-mortars over the yacht, our Marines hared up the Canal in the Komars, coming in under BRITANNIA's port side. There was only just room to get in. The support boats gave them covering fire and my lot moved in from the desert at 3.45. I was on a Komar with young Chambers at just after four o'clock.

We took them completely by surprise but there was some hard work flushing the bastards out. I heard later that the men locked in one of the forward holds managed to overpower their guards when the shooting started and join in the fight. Your reports will give you more detail of that than I can, being in one of the boats. But my orders, for which I take full responsibility, were that no terrorists were to be left alive to talk. If this thing was to be hushed up, there was no other way.

Q – 'Sorry, Major. Commander Huntley again: Were any of the terrorists left alive to your knowledge? It is most important.'

A – 'No, sir. I was going to say about that. Apparently O'Neil's lieutenant, Docherty, was one of the last to go down. I am told he charged along the upper decks like a mad thing and it took a whole magazine before he dropped at Sergeant Maden's feet. Literally.

But I saw two things I shall never forget until the day I die. Of course, you know Hassan Kassim had these hooks. Well, he was shot up pretty badly down in the strongroom but got out on deck somehow and jumped for it, catching one of his hooks on the anchor-chain, of all things.

It was just getting light by now. The poor sod hung there for a moment before they started firing from the ship. He was shredded like paper. Then he just seemed to drop away into the water, leaving that damned hook hanging there . . .

And then there was O'Neil and the girl. Yes, a girl. It was nearly all over now. The paratroopers had dropped and were assisting with the mopping up. The hijackers were all wearing these woollen hoods but I saw these two from my boat running along the top deck for all they were worth, pulling off their hoods as they went.

They got right up to the stern and then, dammit, O'Neil kissed her – and they jumped, holding hands. O'Neil saw me, I swear it. I told Chambers to shoot the girl before the current swept her away. He refused and I stuck my revolver in his ribs. I know it sounds brutal but he had to learn what this job's about. He shot at her three times, I think, before he hit her.

Then O'Nell sort of raised his hand to me in a salute. I fired twice. A lot of blood on the water and he disappeared. Dead, I'm sure.

The rest you know, of course. All Her Majesty's treasures were recovered and the scuttling charges defused. BRITANNIA was a bit of a mess below decks. I understand they're making repairs en route for home. There's already been a lot of talk about a major refit for extra security precautions in the light of all this. We, er, lost a lot of men. So did the Egyptians. You have the figures, Commander. That's about it. Oh – there was one other thing of interest. We found Major Khalid's body in one of the guest cabins. He was the Syrian Intelligence liaison on this charmer. He had been shot through the head. We identified him from Danvers' photographs.'

STATEMENT   G

Cdr H – 'Thank you, Major. A gruelling business for you but well done indeed. You might like to know that the, er, freighter used in the hijack is now under port arrest pending diplomatic action against the Syrian Government.

You also know, of course, that it has been decided to bring your retirement forward, effective as of – let me see – this Thursday. I am sure you deserve it. I was very sorry to hear about Norman Betts, by the way. Very sad.

You realise of course that there will be no decorations for the men who took part, and no public announcements, either. Secrecy is all. For the obvious reasons. The families of those killed or wounded have already been informed that an incident occurred and that they are bound under the Official Secrets Acts, which they have now all signed.

President Carter signs his Treaty next week, so I think we can say we have saved his day.

I am sure you would like to attend the burial at sea of our dead off HMS APOLLO on the 22nd? I thought so. You will be flown out tomorrow. They're in the Med. Standing off Cyprus.

Again, well done. You will be hearing from the Palace some time today, I believe, but I'd better not say too much about that.

Gentlemen, I think we can move on to the next witness. I am sure we don't want to keep Major Burroughs.'

(Major Burroughs left the Hearing at 4 pm. He did not have any other questions for the Commission.)

Transcript ends. Timed: 4.05 pm GMT.

CHAPTER TWENTY-THREE

Burroughs stood on the bridge with the Captain as the destroyer's speed began to drop to 'slow ahead' for the burial service.

The Royal Navy chaplain had already donned his white surplice and was standing down on the after-deck normally used as a heli-pad. Two rigid lines of ratings and a Royal Marine bugler swayed with the ship's slight motion, the light breeze fluttering little sobs of life from the Ensign flying at half-mast above the stern rail.

The Commandant of the Royal Marines and the Rear Admiral representing the Ministry of Defence (N) and Her Majesty the Queen gripped their sword scabbards and descended the companionways to the waiting after-deck, followed at a respectful distance by George Burroughs.

The Admiral turned suddenly and motioned him forward.

'After you, Major,' he offered quietly. 'This is your show.'

Burroughs nodded silently, too choked up to speak. When all had taken their places, the chaplain commenced the short, simple Order of Burial at Sea that is the Navy's way with its dead.

Burroughs stared over the rail, his eyes to the horizon as the service went its sad way. Dear God, hear a simple man's prayer that all this had been worth it.

At a nod from the Lieutenant Commander in charge of the burial party, six of the ratings broke ranks smartly and lifted the first of the heavy, leaded canvas coffins from the grim row on the deck – stitched packets of grief for their families in England, so far away from these blued waters of the Mediterranean.

Burroughs shifted his gaze as the bugler sounded 'Reveille', then the 'Last Post', and saw that there were tears streaming down the Marine's ruddy cheeks.

There were only two 'coffins' left to slip down the burial ramp into the calm waters. Burroughs walked forward slowly with his wreath and placed it atop the last of the canvas shrouds. Able Seaman Paul Shiller had been just nineteen and a half years of age. He had been thrilled at being selected for a tour of duty aboard the royal yacht.

The edge had been taken off his excitement a bit because he was an orphan and had nobody close to share it with, joining the Navy straight from the Dr Barnardo's home that had been his childhood.

When Burroughs had discovered this, he requested permission to lay a wreath on his own account – for the boy. His request had been granted at once.

The service was over. Burroughs watched his wreath bobbing on the water until it was lost in the destroyer's churning wake as she turned for home . . . 22 March 1979 was a day he would always remember.

It also marked the beginning of his updated retirement.

The Admiral gripped his elbow as he passed him on his way back to the bridge. He got so little sea-time in, these days.

'Terrible business, Major. Though I think we should thank God for men like these. It would've been a bigger tragedy if the thing hadn't been stopped, don't you feel? Good of you to come,' he added.

Burroughs stared at him, noting the KCVO amongst his host of medal ribbons. In two weeks' time, he was due himself to be privately invested by Her Majesty as a Commander of the Royal Victorian Order – awarded for 'personal services' to the reigning monarch.

'I think the whole thing was a tragic, unnecessary waste of life, sir,' he replied bluntly, his voice harsh with suppressed emotion. 'And appropriately the biggest fuck-up since Suez . . . sir.'

He spun sharply on his heel without waiting for the Admiral's shocked reaction, and walked back slowly to the cabin he had been allocated for the return voyage to Cyprus. And the long flight home would begin from there.

CHAPTER TWENTY-FOUR

There was even a team from Sri Lanka.

Camera crews from every conceivable part of the globe had gathered in a raucous clamour of distant news editors' expectations, their minions rubbing lens-packed shoulders with the individual kingpins in the media/politics jamboree of the decade. All of them were searching, like chickens in a grain barn, for that one exclusive angle; the magic something that would put them ahead of the rest.

Washington was bursting at the seams in a throb of still disbelieving euphoria. They were going to sign the Peace Treaty. It was a wonder the city didn't tip over on its side.

Premier Begin and Prime Minister Sadat had already arrived, phalanxed by bevies of advisors and security men, staying apart until the last possible moment – not through enmity but caught up in a piece of stage management that would have done credit to Cecil B. de Mille. Or Moses.

President Carter busied himself with final preparations, but found time to slip into his White House study to say a quick prayer to the One without whom none of this would have been possible, if indeed God was still interested.

All the squabbles and recriminations and last-minute suspicions and open accusations (and eleventh-hour sulks) had been resolved. It was on. And whatever else he did in politics, President Jimmy Carter would rightly enter the history books as the man who made the Arab lie down with the Jew – and the Lion of War walk quietly with the Lamb of Peace.

It was a remarkable feat. If it lasted.

When all the documents had been signed before the TV eyes of the world, Anwar Sadat was seen to smile at President Carter and then lean over to Menachim Begin.

Nobody on the podium heard what it was he said, but a camera operator from an ITN News crew, positioned directly opposite Sadat as he turned to Begin, swore he picked up something about the *Britannia* on his headphones off their directional mike.

Unfortunately, they were shooting on unsynchronised stock, used for running vision separately to sound for editing purposes later. Nothing could be found on the 'wild' sound-track afterwards of what he thought he'd heard.

Despite a cynical comment in the bar that evening from his OB director that it was probably 'Wily' Sadat saying Thank God we didn't leave this to Pax Britannica – they started it all in 1948, the operator was adamant in the way that technicians often are.

It didn't matter anyway, he said, and took another pull at his scotch.

George Burroughs watched the whole thing in his apartment. Alone. On his new television set.

He didn't know what he really felt, did he? Not yet a while. He might have a jaw about it with young Chambers when he came round on Wednesday evening.

Sir David Holman was alone, too. Sitting in his town residence, with Cynthia threatening to leave him for good this time. Especially after that damnable investigation making him so impossible to live with. She had gone off to the country with monotonous regularity ever since it started.

He really couldn't see it affecting his future. It had all turned out well enough. Why, the Minister had even said . . .

Peter Chambers wasn't feeling much better. His hands still shook every time he thought about that girl in the water.

He did not even bother to watch the signing ceremony. It would focus his mind on too many things he just wanted to forget. He didn't blame George at all. He had only been trying to make him face up to his new job. But the girl's dark face when his bullets hit her.

Colonel Solenov of the KGB's Subversion Directorate went out for a meal with his mistress and refused to speculate with her why there were men stationed outside their apartment and sitting so obviously at a table across the restaurant from them.

When they got home, he made love to her with a passion that surprised her – even from this tiger of a man.

The remnants of the Palestine Action Commando sat round their base in the Syrian desert, arguing into the night about what they were going to do without El-Nesr and Rashid Khadir.

One of the youngest of their number, who had been excluded from the raid because of his youthful inexperience, stood up and declared boldly that he would lead them.

Amid general amusement, he sat down again and the mood darkened once more into a feeling of loss beyond that of mere direction, as the stars looked on from their indifferent firmament.

In South Armagh, they knew virtually nothing. Only that it had all gone disastrously wrong.

The adjutant of Madigan's Brigade had assumed temporary command until they had more detail. In over a week, all they had received so far was one international telephone call telling them that their operation had failed. His efforts to persuade the caller to tell him about the Captain, Docherty and the others was answered by the line going dead.

Although Callaghan did not know it then, it would be another week before he would begin to understand what the whole business had been about – and then not much. And what he was told made him realise that the only thing to do was keep quiet about it.

It so happened that, in the course of time, the word of their misfortune would get round the Provisionals and the Irish National Liberation Army, and Madigan's Brigade would find itself the excuse for some cruel and mindless reprisals on its behalf by their 'comrades' in arms.

CHAPTER TWENTY-FIVE

Burroughs had been officially retired for just six days. He was not enjoying it. There wasn't even Mr B to yarn with any more.

His daily routines were already becoming infiltrated with the little, time-filling ceremonies old men invent for themselves. But dammit, he was *not* old. Maybe he should get out of the country altogether and set up a small business in Spain or somewhere, trying to be nice to all those tourists . . .

He sighed and heaved himself into his dressing-gown, leaving the bed a rumpled sea. It was nearly 9 a.m. He was getting into bad habits.

The morning paper was sticking bluntly through the yawning letterbox, an accusing finger to his slackness, and he pulled it free with a touch of anger rising in his chest.

No doubt the bloody news was as depressing as ever. Still, at least Carter had got his Peace Treaty signed by Begin and Sadat. It was a start. And made some sense of the events Burroughs had so recently witnessed and could never talk about – relief in verbal masturbation.

He carried the paper through to his sitting-room on a breakfast tray of two boiled eggs, a rack of toast and a piping-hot brew of 'char' in his old enamel Army mug. Somehow it never tasted right in anything else first thing in the morning.

The newspaper was full of the historic signing ceremony that was being hailed as the first positive step towards a permanent peace in the Middle East.

Burroughs sniffed as he turned the pages and sat up sharply when his eye caught the *Daily Mail*'s AMERICA column. He felt the anger charging through his chest in a tight pain of outrage and despair.

The column related a major row which was brewing between the American public and its President. On 26 March 1979 – the day before – President Sadat of Egypt and the Prime Minister of the sovereign state of Israel had signed their unbelievable Treaty on the North Lawn of the White House.

Spectators from outside immediate government and diplomatic circles who wished to attend were charged two thousand dollars a seat by White House officials for the privilege of witnessing first-hand what some journalists had acidly described as 'the TV-networked Jimmy Carter Show'.

And the seating charge levied by his staffers had been carried out with the President's specific approval.

Burroughs threw the newspaper on to the table and sat back in his chair with the stillness of the dead, whilst the anger pounded round his system like an extra circulation.

For a man who had seen so much betrayed, it was one betrayal too many. Even this Treaty, for which such a high price had been exacted behind the scenes, had been prostituted into a commercial farce.

George Burroughs got up slowly from his chair, suddenly

feeling very old and immeasurably tired. He walked over to his bureau and went through the dark, walnut drawers until he had found the things he was looking for.

Pushing the breakfast tray out of his way, he set his service revolver down on the table and checked it was fully loaded as always. Although it was nearly forty years old, he had taken pleasure from regularly firing it off in the SIS's underground range near Tottenham Court Road station. It had helped to keep his eye in, and he enjoyed the reassuring feel of its cold, heavy presence in his hand.

It also reminded him of a time when his role was a sure and certain one, a uniform his badge of right and direction.

The gleaming row of service decorations clinked softly in greeting as he picked them up, fleetingly touching their bright reminder of his younger bravery when there had still been something clear to believe in and to fight for.

Burroughs pinned them carefully to his ancient dressing-gown, a look of wistful pride on his face, and pulled the packet of writing-paper towards him with a shuddering sigh.

The letter to his ex-wife was a brief one. There wasn't much he could say to her after all these years, except 'Sorry'. The other letter, to his former chief, Sir David Holman, KCMG, ran to eight pages of scrawled condemnation.

Satisfied and to some extent purged, he sealed them both in separate envelopes and addressed each one with care in his large, copper-plate handwriting, leaving these deep blue farewells prominently displayed on the sideboard next to the photograph of his DSO investiture.

When Sir David Holman had his delivered to him by the Special Branch two days later, at his new appointment to the backwaters of the Ministry of Agriculture, it was nearly an hour before he could stop his hands shaking.

It was done. Burroughs returned to his chair, the medals chinking on his chest like small, tolling bells, and sat for a long moment listening to the silence in his lonely flat.

He picked up the revolver, flicking off the safety-catch before placing its worn barrel against his right temple. The cold gun-metal felt strangely comforting and he smiled sadly.

The electric clock on the wall said the time was 11 a.m. He smiled to himself again. It seemed appropriate somehow. Eleven o'clock on a sombre November morning was the traditional hour the British recalled their dead of two world wars. He was only some eight months ahead of that occasion. And he wouldn't be remembered anyway.

George Alfred Burroughs, Distinguished Service Order, the Distinguished Conduct Medal, twice mentioned in Dispatches, groaned deeply . . . and pulled the trigger.

The report was deafening in the silent apartment and its grim purpose splattered a messy Union Jack of blood, bone and flesh over Burroughs' off-white, towelled dressing-gown and the medals he had earned in such poor exchange for so much pain.

In one of those cruel coincidences which sometimes bedevil life, the ambulance crew called by a horrified neighbour happened to be the same one which had collected the sad body of that little girl knocked down in Lambeth on Christmas Day the year before.

They were working a relief shift from St George's Hospital and the driver shook his head at his mate as they gently but urgently lifted the inert form into the ambulance, watched by a gathering crowd reflected in a strobe of flashing blue lights from the police cars summoned to the scene.

The driver, who was only in his twenties, laughed with a callousness born of seeing too much death. He reckoned this old boy wouldn't last long.

What a dumb way to go, wearing his medals and all . . .

CHAPTER TWENTY-SIX

EXTRACT from Party Stenographer Nadia Varashilov's Notes in Council, April 12/13, 1979.

(English translation verified by Professor Hugh Carlton, Department of Modern Languages, London University/August 8, 1979.)

Translation overlays as follows:

Supreme Soviet Presidium

In Council

Examination 341/Zhv.//79. Party Member 89111-KGB (SD) FOREIGN. Comrade Colonel Solenov – Alexis Leonid. Before Supreme Council of the Grand Presidium of the Union of Soviet Socialist Republics.

Hearing: Day Two/13 April, 79

Defender: Comrade Colonel Nevsky

Col. Nevsky – Reported Speech/Tape 3/Second Session/3 pm.

'Comrade Chairman, Comrade Colonel Solenov has listened to your comments with great respect and notes your displeasure. He asks the Council to take into account that this was a covert exercise as far as the Subversion Directorate was concerned. It was important that the Soviet Union was not seen to be directly involved in the operation's control.

'Having thoroughly investigated the viabilities towards sanctioning this operation, with Comrade General Zharevsky, his — '
(Interruption by Comrade Zharevsky – See Tape 3, edit mark 1)

'Yes, Comrade General, that is true. But Comrade Colonel Solenov begs to point out — ' (Defender spoke with Comrade Solenov for two minutes, six seconds) ' — wishes to point out that the Comrade General gave his final approval on 30 January from Moscow. Comrade Colonel Solenov proceeded as ordered. See Operational Notes, page six.

'The operation was wholly successful up to the point of boarding the royal yacht and it was taken over within five minutes of the first seizure. All agreed signals were made to Cairo, with initial terms and conditions.

'Control of the operation was lost on the second day of occupation. It had proved impossible for Comrade Colonel Solenov to intervene at this stage and maintain his covert profile. He — '
(Interruption by Comrade Chairman – See Tape 3, edit mark 2)

'That is correct, Comrade Chairman. Comrade Colonel Solenov was unable to raise Captain O'Neil by radio or to effect any supportive action without again losing his covert position. Comrade Colonel Solenov asks the Council to bear in mind that by this juncture there was considerable diplomatic radio traffic from the British and Americans. It had become obvious that the mission had failed to hold its initiative.'
(Question from Comrade Malenkikov – See Tape 3, edit mark 3)

'Yes, sir. That is why Comrade Colonel Solenov withdrew from the region. He arrived back in Moscow on 25 March.'
(Question from Comrade Chairman – See Tape 3, edit mark 4)

'No, Comrade Chairman. There was an agreed plan between the Palestine Action Commando's leader and Comrade Colonel Solenov that he would dispose of Captain O'Neil and his men once in Libya. The possessions seized in the raid were to have been apportioned between Kassim and his Commando and the Subversion Directorate's overseas fund for Region Six.'
(Interruption by Comrade Zharevsky – See Tape 3, edit mark 5)

Yes, Comrade General, it was unfortunate. However, Comrade Colonel Solenov would take leave to point out that he has already had further meetings in Regions Two, Four and Six. The scheduled subversion campaigns in those Regions will now be brought forward to compensate for the failure of this operation. The Council has the Planning Sheets and the Comrade Colonel would wish to refer you to Operations I to VI. You will see they include assistance to the Red Brigade, increased arms supplies to the Provisional IRA – who have already suggested further disruptive reprisals against monarchist prominents in Britain. The Preliminary Incursion Plans are now settled for Regions Six and Eight, namely Iran, Afghanistan and the Rhodesian imperialists.'
(Question from Comrade Chairman – See Tape 3, edit mark 6)

'Of course, Comrade Chairman. The Afghanistan//*translation not pure from Russian to English. Suggest "invasion"* – H.C.// will commence build-up on our border from 9 October. The long-term encroachment of the Persian Gulf will be propagandised as a police action to protect Soviet borders.'
(Question by Comrade Andrepov – See Tape 3, edit mark 7)

'That has been taken in consideration, Comrade Andrepov. You will know that the Politburo is leaning towards ending detente with the West as being outdated, having served its purpose in limiting the expansion of Western arms during our own increasing of Soviet ground and missile forces in East Europe. With respect, Comrade Andrepov, you yourself have stated in the Politburo that you feel any

274

damage to the Olympics propaganda exercise next year will be limited to the usual empty American protests.'
(Question by Comrade Zharevsky – See Tape 3, edit mark 8)

'He is, Comrade General. Comrade Colonel Solenov has received your sighting report from the State Security Police in the Democratic German Republic.'
(Question from Comrade Vashnevsky – See Tape 3, edit mark 9)

'No, Comrade Vashnevsky. But the Syrian Ambassador has requested further information, if we can supply it. Colonel Hafez has been told that the Soviet authorities cannot be held responsible for Major Khalid's disobeying of Syrian Military Intelligence Directorate orders. Comrade Colonel Solenov understands he was buried with the Egyptian casualties. Negotiations are already in progress to strengthen our military advisory capacity in Syria next year – in order to minimise further operational failures of this kind, particularly with regard to the Incursion Plans for Region Six.'

(Summary remarks by Comrade Chairman – See Tape 3, edit mark 9/10/ 11. Comrade Solenov was ordered to leave the Council Hall with the State Defender.)

Decision referred to Committee Three, Politburo Directorate 4 – See Tape 5, edit mark 4 to 23.

                                                SST Varashilov N.

CHAPTER TWENTY-SEVEN

The evening light was lost against the glare of the security arc lights strung along the walkways between the check-points.

The tall, well-dressed figure forced himself to walk slower as the check gate into the British Sector of West Berlin came into sight. He had got out of East Germany with remarkable ease, considering that he wore no disguise, facial or otherwise. Only his identity card and passport said he was a light engineering consultant from near Hamburg.

It had appealed to his sense of humour that he had chosen

to call himself Klaus Wilhelm Brandt, after the former Mayor of West Berlin.

He was almost at the check gate now. His back felt like a wall, too – waiting for the firing to start behind him. From the frontier checkpoint into the Democratic Republic of East Germany.

The British sergeant on the gate gave his papers a cursory glance and handed them through a small window to another soldier in the harshly lit gatehouse. The note 'Klaus Brandt' had slipped into his passport whilst on the eternal walk from East into the West had been read without any visible sign on the sergeant's face.

Five minutes later he was through and being ushered into an annexe of the gatehouse. He was given a chair and told to wait. He stared round the bare, white-painted walls, feeling sweat dampening his armpits and the nape of his neck. The door slammed to with an ominous click-click of unquestionable imprisonment. It was the middle of May 1979.

The young officer who came in twenty minutes later was as tall as his charge. He introduced himself neutrally and took out a MD-issue notebook. He stared at the visitor for a moment and then smiled in a polite, British sort of way.

The sergeant who had been on the gate came quietly into the room, closing the door carefully behind him. He noticed that the sergeant was wearing a side-arm.

He rose from the chair, taking a deep, considered breath, and began to tell the young officer who he was.

'My name is Alexis Leonid Solenov . . .'

THE AFTERMATHS

November 1979
On the day before America was suddenly plunged into the nightmare of her Embassy's seizure in Tehran, two odd incidents occurred in the little Syrian village which was still the Palestine Action Commando's home.

A parcel was delivered just at dawn to Rashid Khadir's eighteen-year-old son. It was wrapped in thick brown paper and tossed into the lad's hands by a military policeman from Intelligence Headquarters in Damascus.

The policeman said nothing to the sleepy guerilla, not even waiting to watch him unwrap the delivery.

The youth did not understand why one of the Hawk's bullet-mangled steel hooks had been sent back so many months after the failure of the *Britannia* hijack, nor how the sender had got hold of it.

Nor did he understand the anonymous, typed message telling him that the hands of the dead can sometimes strangle the lives of the living – not until the next day.

That same evening, at dusk, four Syrian Army lorries drove into the village unannounced. The guerillas were surprised to see the squat, bullish figure of a Russian general climb stiffly out of the first cab.

When the officer had finished talking with them all, there was not a man amongst the guerillas who refused to get into the back of their transport to reinstatement.

The seizure of the United States Embassy in Tehran was an act of a people who had thrown all diplomacy to the winds. And the things President Carter could do about it were limited by so many considerations, not least the lives of his citizens trapped by the student mobs.

Always doubtful himself that America could afford to be seen having anything to do with the Shah after his downfall, Carter had allowed the Rockefeller banking interests and the man many called 'Dr Death' – Henry Kissinger – to have their way.

It would soon prove an ironic prophecy when, at a staffers' briefing in the Oval Office, the President particularly asked his advisors what the hell they suggested he should do if he let the Shah into America for urgent medical treatment . . . and the Iranians took US personnel hostage against the return of their ex-ruler?

This fact was not generally known to the American public and it was ignored outside the White House by other interested parties. Except the Iranians.

On such forgetfulness, diplomacy founders and wars begin. World affairs are like a giant computer. When they break down, the machine does not stop. It goes berserk.

And an America always generous to its friends reaped a harvest of hate. It would have delighted Hassan El-Nesr Kassim.

As for the Iranians, their protestations were not all they seemed, although their religious fervour was everything old Mr Betts had predicted would precede the resurrection of Islam's power.

Whatever the basis of those protests, the Iranian people were being led by a man far from what he seemed because the figure they revered as their leader was not the Ayatollah Khomeini at all.

In 1960 an undercover double-agent operating within the Soviet-Polish spy network, and using the cover name of Colonel Goleniewski, fled to the United States, bringing much highly secret Communist film and documents with him.

Amongst that information he passed on to the CIA was the stunning claim that Khomeini was 'the most important of five top Russian agents in Iran', who reported to a senior Iraqi official, who in turn passed his reports on to the KGB through its agents in Warsaw – where Goleniewski was deputy chief and vice-director of the Polish Army's counter-intelligence network from 1953 to 1956.

Nearly twenty years later, that astonishing claim was substantiated by another event in Iran, which the world has yet to know of.

During 'Khomeini's' purge of the Iranian Army, one of the Shah's former officials tried to tell the 'court' that this Khomeini was an imposter; that he had known the real Khomeini for years and that he had one finger missing when the Shah expelled him from Iran to exile in Paris. The present ruler of Iran had all ten.

The official was shouted down by his judges; bundled from the court and summarily shot.

That event was apparently reported in detail to the White House, and it may have much to do with the visit of Russia's Brezhnev to the President of France in early 1980 that amazed other world leaders so much.

Whatever the truth of it, this Rasputin of Islam was not being honest over the Shah. He was wanted back for a show trial, certainly, but more so for the forced realisation of his vast wealth. In fact, a consortium of merchant banks in the 'infidel' West was already secretly co-operating with the Ayatollic regime to that end, assisted by this Ayatollah's own secret-police death squads.

Money will always out.

On such muddled Islamic thinking, the mullahs proposed to drag Iran anti-clockwise into the Middle Ages. Spiked on the topsy-turvy mishmash demanded by her religious leaders, she would become open house for the Marxist Fedhayeen to sweep in from Iraq, backed by the Soviet presence in war-torn Afghanistan.

But the American Eagle was already tired of it all, her talons blunted and split on the hard face of an ungrateful world. The trouble was, many other smaller birds would fall with her scattered feathers . . .

George Burroughs would have understood.

December 1979

The year was shot. Having plagued the world with a fresh outbreak of horrors, it now prepared to quit on a slightly desperate serum of goodwill towards all men. Seasonal prescription, of course.

A year of momentous events and meaningless victories, it had also been the Year of the Gun. With a gunman's mad logic.

Some good things had happened, however, to offset both the public and secret bad. Only they were difficult to recall.

The world's leaders looked forward to their annual break with all the fervour of truant schoolchildren, hoping for a quiet time of it. And were saddled with Afghanistan, to cap the business in Iran.

It was political 'business as usual' ...

The Middle East Section at MI6 had acquired a new chief – still busily occupying the staff with getting his feet firmly under the desk.

'Teddy' MacAllister found himself almost wishing for the return of its former occupant, although he would never openly admit to that.

It may have been because nothing had really changed, despite lengthy reverberations from the spring's disciplinary hearings. Or perhaps it was because he was still just the prince, passed over for the crown he had coveted for so long in a thousand cautious betrayals of his professional instincts under Holman.

Nevertheless, he could sup some winter comfort from Sir David's fate. Removed out of harm's way by a system forced to condemn his handling of the 'Britannia Affair', it had continued to protect its own.

But slow stagnation in a backwater of the Ministry of Agriculture and Fisheries was hardly the ideal way in which to edge his life towards a disgraced retirement.

Not with Lady Holman suing him for divorce *and* their

country home, including the land development aided by a grant from his new Ministry.

Pope John Paul II had achieved much on his tours of this earth's troubled places. Amongst the common folk, that is. It was still too early to judge whether the ripples of his stern but great popularity would turn the world's cesspool of political acrimony into a whirlpool of common good for Mankind.

In Ulster itself, the killings went on as before, vengeance fuelled by news gleaned of the abortive *Britannia* hijack by their 'comrades' in Madigan's Brigade and the Palestine Action Commando.

Pat Docherty's final child had turned into a lusty infant, his mother despairing of ever having enough milk to satisfy the little devil.

Her financial circumstances were eased by a joint donation from the INLA and Provisional IRA's fighting funds, given in a rare gesture of solidarity over the giant's death for the cause. She was further assisted by the monthly welfare cheque via Madigan Brigade's own scheme for its dependants, originated by O'Neil after losing three of his men during a fund-raising bank raid in 1974.

The rumour that she also received an overly-large, weekly grant from the Ministry of Health and Social Security on the instructions of a notably senior source in Whitehall, and as 'silence money' for what she knew of the 'Britannia Affair', remains unconfirmed to this day.

The giant's eldest son, illegitimate and long estranged from the rest of the family, had got his first job. Working on a farm near Newry with a strange, taciturn, limping man who often appeared to be in pain, he missed his Da terribly. Great bitterness was growing inside a frame promising the strength and size of his father's.

Back in England, the Anthony Blunt revelations had stolen most of the domestic headlines during the last months of the year, as was to be expected.

Those in the know were only surprised at the timing. Peter de Vere Chambers discovered that his own growing cynicism had made his reactions to it all that much tougher. That would have pleased his former tutor.

The sorry state of Britain's economy and the harsh remedies it had forced on the Conservative Government had seemed small beer at the time. But they would herald a long and bitter confrontation with the trade unions in 1980.

Mrs Thatcher's Cabinet, not noted for skill at public relations, would find itself with an uphill climb to convince the nation that she knew best, although the coming New Year might see the kind of peace-time leadership the country had survived on through the war years under Churchill.

Many would not agree, of course, and the Politics of Envy would persist whoever was in power. Only time would tell if the Iron Lady was right, half right or wholly wrong.

People bitched about having America's cruise missiles on British sod, forgetting that NATO and the Common Market were bedevilled and weak from internal squabbles. And that fixed American missile sites had been in the country for years.

Those same folk would have been shaken by the confidential briefing given to selected British journalists by the USAF commander prior to the new missiles' arrival.

Pointing to a tactical map of Europe, he let his finger hover over the Berlin Wall and then landed it smack in the middle of the British Isles.

'Gentlemen,' he was claimed to have said. 'Our defence of Europe starts and ends right here.'

In other words, America would let mainland Europe fall to Russia in the event of a nuclear confrontation. Her historical links with the British, from the Mayflower onwards, would determine both strategy and interests. The English-speaking alliance beloved of Churchill.

It was something else George Burroughs would have approved of, too.

So the first half-year of Britain's first woman Prime Minister was nearly complete.

Having been buffeted by the Blunt fiasco; suffered world outrage at Mountbatten's murder and Warrenpoint; mauled over her turnabout economic policies and defence proposals; savaged on all sides in the endless Rhodesia Talks (which would persist until Soames pulled off his amiable elections); and let down, even ridiculed, by her partners in the EEC, Britain's new leader could be forgiven for feeling bruised.

It was not surprising, therefore, that the Government of the day, and the Establishment which controlled it, congratulated themselves that the 'Britannia Affair' had remained a closely-guarded secret.

As cover-ups went, it was an enormity. As the unforeseen forerunner to the SAS's triumph in the siege of Princes Gate, it had served to slide-rule just how costly is the blind refusal to see what is coming.

There are some lessons the British never appear to learn, preferring to rely on the 'backs-to-the-wall' guts that turned Dunkirk into a legend and the obvious likelihood of terrorism at London's Iranian Embassy into a TV epic.

However necessary that *Britannia*'s blueprint hijack should stay secret, there were ministers of the Crown and Whitehall mandarins who would spend uncomfortable moments of their Christmas wondering how long it could stay that way. And what would happen if it didn't.

Whatever the answer to that one, the world spun on its axis towards the joys of Christmas and Anno Domini 1979 was shot. Dead.

EPILOGUE

Christmas Day 1979
On a morning marked by a bitterly cold darkness, two men restless with thoughts and conscience felt its bite as they headed for the only place that would provide them with any kind of salving. It was 7.30 a.m.

One was a lanky figure with a livid bullet scar gouged across his left cheek. He was still feeling very tired after his risky journey as he limped into London's deserted Bayswater Road, the wound in his hip aching a painful reminder of its long healing process. And of the journey still ahead of him.

The other drove slowly towards his destination, face pinched with cold despite the harsh whirr of the car's heater. For him this was a day without celebration. At least, not yet.

Hunching deeper inside his hooded dufflecoat against the freezing weather, and keeping a constant ear cocked for the Special Patrol Group units policing the city throughout this festive period in case of a repeat performance of the IRA bombings carried out the year before, the man with the limp made his careful way down the wide, frost-paved thorough-fare.

The only sound to be heard, other than his own tight breathing on the sharp black air, was an occasional cough from one of the down-and-outs sleeping off his Christmas on a Hyde Park bench across the way, oblivion his sole comfort.

The man in the car stopped just short of the gates, fingering the flowers on the seat next to him. He hated the rain just starting to slap against the windscreen, especially at this time of the morning on this special day.

But he had wanted to be here and the flowers held stiffly

between his gloved fingers as he walked along the neat paths were the only present he could bring for the tutor who had forced him to grow up amongst the swirling waters of the Suez Canal.

The man with the limp maintained a steady pace, turning into the smart, stone-tailored avenue making up the Holland Park beginning to Ladbroke Grove. The rain sweeping across his journey did not worry him. Discomfort was a way of life now.

Before long, the avenue's assurance changed as the street stretched on, and away from the wealthier environs of London's West End. Its houses grew tatty, disused, boarding covering properties no longer considered habitable by even the squatters who pestered the hard conscience of this city's housing chiefs.

The other man had reached the familiar grave. He sighed to himself and placed the flowers in the little stone vase provided by a thoughtful borough council, resting his hand briefly on the wreath faded after so many months of vigil.

Dear God, if only he could do something to make up for such an end. It shouldn't have finished this way. Not to this man. Not here.

The limping man doggedly kept going, dogged now by a non-descript mongrel as scruffy as the surroundings. Such shops as there were sold junk or catered to the ever-growing Moslem community's taste for their alien meat. It was utterly depressing.

The Westway confronted him in the dawning light, and London's underground broke out of its subterranean passages to run in sooty abandon along the rooftops and corrugated-iron hoardings, aerosoled with the graffiti of an underprivileged language more suited to New York's violent ghettos.

His unintentional companion pulled his raincoat closer about his neck and made for the sighing trees bordering the path. He sat down against a trunk, wishing the rain would stop, and shifted uncomfortably at the hard pressure of the shoulder-holster beneath his coat, thinking it a damned nuisance he had to carry the thing at all.

But they had made him operational grading now and, with the threat of more trouble via the IRA, weapons were to be worn until stand-down was issued. It would have amused his old tutor to see him toting a damned great Colt .45 around – especially with his eyesight.

The man with the limp had come at last to the old canal, filthy with idleness and arched by an iron Victorian bridge that must once have been beautiful. Tall warehouses, long abandoned to vandalism, leaned in on his difficult passing and the man grinned briefly at one aerosoled art form declaring that 'God hasn't given up the human race, brother. He's working on a better project.' It was surmounted by an evocation to 'get' the National Front.

The dirty dog slowed too, tired of its silent partner, and slunk out of his wake as the man turned under the grim shadow of the local gasworks into the Harrow Road. The creased face of Paddington's northerly boundary displayed itself in the day's unwelcome light, as unattractive as a whore when the morning curtains are drawn and she has to be paid.

He could see the graves quite clearly from the shelter of the trees. They shone with a ghostly marbled whiteness in the rain. Why was it, he wondered, that sadness always seemed to be accompanied by the wet?

He tugged out his cigarettes. The first match fizzed to nothing in the steady drizzle. He shrugged. Another reliquary to his tutor's bad habits. Smoking. And George's life had been a bit like that match. He supposed he'd have to make a move soon. Father was expecting his presence for Christmas dinner. If only . . .

The limping man's journey was nearly over and he briefly touched the high, grey walls of Kensal Green's Cemetery – prison to the dead. The huge iron-wrought gates swung open noisily at his second push and the man stopped, listening intently for any change of sound in the icy stillness.

Apparently satisfied, he limped along the neat paths glistening with the season's melting decoration and resolutely followed the signposts to the municipalised acreage housing the recently dead.

His unobserved counterpart got up and stretched, glancing at his watch. Time for one more cigarette and then he really had to be on his way.

He stared up at the sky. Patches of blue were biting through the scudding rain clouds. The promise of a fine day after all made him feel better. It might ease the ordeal facing him at home.

The man with the limp found George Burroughs' resting place without much trouble, stepping carefully round the freshly-dug holes awaiting the next crop of expected dearly departed, if the winter's cold did its work on the aged and infirm.

He paused to listen again before cautiously opening his dufflecoat and bringing out a small object, placing it gently against the grave's simple headstone.

Peter Chambers stepped on his cigarette, listening to it fizz into damp shreds under his heel. Thank God the rain was easing. It had been worth it, though. He'd never know a man like George Burroughs again. Perhaps they didn't make his sort any more. There existed neither the ideals nor the circumstances requiring such a breed these days. That's what George always used to say. He sighed. Time to go.

Suddenly he stiffened, stared in the direction of the graves, not believing his eyes. A figure was bending over George's tomb. Who else would want to be here at this ungodly hour? In this weather?

Someone else's wreath, tattered by its long remembrance through all weathers, greeted the limping man's smaller tribute. The plain band across it read with faded simplicity:

March 31st 1979. For a hard colleague and a new friend. I could never love you, but respect will keep you always remembered. Peter.

If it affected the man in any way, his face did not show it. He stood for a moment, staring down at his own wreathed message with a soft smile on his scarred features. There was a small inscription card pinned to the garland of poppies shining blood-red in the shivery rain. The ink had already begun to run tearfully down the cardboard. It said:

When men of ideals meet men of action in the uncomfortable clash of Life, only Death knows the answer to who is right under the Force of Arms.

Chambers had almost reached George Burroughs' grave when he saw the man start to turn away. His breath fought in his chest, shock and fear conspiring to stop his heartbeat. Maybe he *could* give George a real Christmas present. One to make up for all of this.

He hesitated, hearing again Burroughs yelling at him to 'shoot first professionally and regret afterwards personally, damn you!' and pulled his revolver free, squinting down the barrel with a new certainty behind his rain-spattered spectacles.

'O'Neil!' Chambers called sharply, holding the revolver straight out in front of him in a classic doublehanded grip.

The figure whirled in surprise, scar vividly purple against the white of his face and the red hair, raising a hand as if in protest, maybe pleading, as he stumbled back from the edge of a newly-dug grave.

And the shameful ghosts of their calling rose up to meet him in the cemetery's hissing rain . . .

THE END